"Mother of God!" Sam breathed. "*Look* at that thing."

A dull and deadly black, the hull annihilated light. They felt drawn into it, hypnotized by its brutal, almost criminal precision. It conjured up blades and blood, an instrument of sudden death, hanging in the damp gray air like a creature in a cocoon. A touch might wake it.

Jake swallowed and reached out with his hand . . .

THE BLACK YACHT

THE BLACK YACHT

JOHN BAXTER

A JOVE BOOK

For M.-D.M.

Grateful acknowledgment is made to
the following for permission
to reprint previously published material:
New Directions Publishing Corporation: "The Yachts"
by William Carlos Williams, *Collected Earlier Poems*.
Copyright © 1938 by New Directions Publishing Corporation.
Reprinted by permission of New Directions.

—

THE BLACK YACHT

A Jove Book/published by arrangement with the author

PRINTING HISTORY
Jove edition/December 1982

ISBN: 0-515-06159-X

PRINTED IN THE UNITED STATES OF AMERICA

The international yacht-racing community is not known for its ease of access, nor are its members inclined to speak freely before strangers. As a result, it was necessary during much of the research for *The Black Yacht* to employ techniques more common in investigative journalism than fiction. I am grateful to those people in New York and Newport, Rhode Island, kind enough to supply me with information and insight into the intrigue surrounding the America's Cup while wishing to keep their names confidential. Commodore John Stewart was most courteous and helpful in describing the 1958 *Sceptre* challenge. I also received invaluable assistance from the late Mr. Angus Primrose, tragically drowned at sea while the book was in preparation.

. . . The yachts

move, jockeying for a start, the signal is set and they
are off. Now the waves strike at them but they are too
well made, they slip through, though they take in canvas.

Arms with hands grasping seek to clutch at the prows.
Bodies thrown recklessly in the way are cut aside.
It is a sea of faces about them in agony, in despair

until the horror of the race dawns staggering the mind,
the whole sea becomes an entanglement of watery bodies
lost to the world bearing what they cannot hold. Broken,

beaten, desolate, reaching from the dead to be taken up
they cry out, failing, failing! their cries rising
in waves still as the skillful yachts pass over.

—"The Yachts"
William Carlos Williams

CHAPTER ONE

You could tell from the way she moved and from the contours of her body—a little small-breasted for American tastes, the ankles too slim, the hips too full—that the girl in the gray silk dress was foreign.

Sal Polito watched her from inside the coffee shop on the corner of 44th and Sixth Avenue as she waited to cross. He guessed she was Italian. Or maybe Brazilian. She looked good—relaxed and unsuspecting in the morning sun. Not in a hurry. A tourist for sure.

When the lights changed and she stepped into the street, Sal dropped two quarters on the counter for his coffee and slipped from the stool. He followed her up West 44th, pacing her on the opposite side of the street as she checked numbers.

She entered the shadow of the Algonquin Hotel's marquee; for a second he worried she might be a guest there. The doorman would nail him before he got across the lobby. But she went on by, and he smiled as she halted in front of 37 West 44th, a few doors east of the hotel.

It was a narrow building—six stories of gray sandstone streaked with white where rain had leached out the stone's chemicals. Some of the cornices were already rotting from the action of magnesium and acid rain, but so far the first-floor windows, intricately carved to imitate the stern-castles of eighteenth-century warships, were intact. Most tourists passing down West 44th on their way to Fifth Avenue paused to admire and grin at the windows, then walked on, uninterested in the function of the building or what went on behind the frosted glass doors.

Nor did the building offer any clues. There was no brass plate by the door, only a puzzling pair of flags hanging limply over the street: a faded Stars and Stripes, and a triangular blue pennant crossed with red, a single white star at its center.

1

The girl didn't pause to admire the windows. With the air of someone who knew where she was going, she pushed through the doors and disappeared.

Sal checked his watch: 10:17. Since he knew what the building was, though he'd never been inside, he figured she would either reemerge in ten seconds or he was in for an hour's wait. After a minute, during which she did not appear, he spat in irritation at an inoffensive fireplug, bought a copy of *Hustler* from the store next to the parking garage, leaned on an empty sunlit stretch of wall by the Royalton Hotel, and leafed through the magazine. The girls didn't particularly interest him, and although he enjoyed the magazine's cartoons—mostly concerned with defecation, disease, and violence—he hadn't bought it to read. It was a tool of trade to Sal.

The quartermaster on duty that morning straightened up as the doors of number 37 opened and squealed shut. When he saw the girl, he stiffened his seventy-seven-year-old spine a fraction more.

He examined her closely and was impressed. Wide cheekbones, a generous mouth, thick auburn hair falling in soft waves over her forehead, brown eyes . . . he stopped at the eyes, odd in that folds at their corners made them seem exotic, almost Asian. The rest he'd taken in at first glance: the tan that made her legs brown enough to need no stockings, the square platinum Cartier Santos watch, the plain gold cylinder like a pencil that hung from a thin chain around her neck, the soft shoulder bag of brown leather. He knew without doubt that she was no casual tourist, curious for a glance inside the mysterious number 37.

"Miss?"

She walked over to his lectern. Trained in a fine appreciation of wine and perfume, he recognized her scent as Calèche.

"Can you tell me who I must see to look around?"

He guessed at the accent. French, obviously. But not Parisian.

"What name, miss?"

"Valois."

"I believe we have a guest card for you, miss." He took the heavy white envelope from the slot over his desk, slid out the card, and handed both to her. He'd written it out himself just the previous evening, after the committeeman's call.

AT THE REQUEST OF
Mr. J. D. Hellman
THE NEW YORK YACHT CLUB
TENDERS TO
Mme. J. Valois

THE PRIVILEGES OF THE CLUB HOUSE
FOR THE PERIOD OF
One day.

"Merci, m'sieu."

"Je vous en prie, mademoiselle." Twenty-seven years with one of the best families in New Orleans's Garden District had given him a respectable accent. "Please make use of all the club's facilities. The bar is at the rear of the building. If you do use the bar or the buffet, just sign in the name of the member who invited you." He smiled. "Your money's no good here, I'm afraid."

"Ah, *merci.*"

As she walked away, he turned to admire her and was caught as she stopped and looked back, puzzled by the flight of wide marble steps in front of her and the side entrances to other parts of the building.

"I was about to say, miss," he improvised hurriedly, "that you should take a look at the Cup while you're here."

She frowned. "The Cup?"

"The America's Cup, miss. They're racing for it next week. That's why the club's so empty. Everyone's up in Newport. I'd take a look at it if I were you, miss. Perhaps the English boat will win this time and take it back to London."

"Then I must see it." She looked at the marble steps. "Up here?"

"Straight up, across the landing, and down the other side. You can't miss it."

Fanning herself slowly with the card, she walked up

the steps, wondering who J. D. Hellman was and how he
would feel about drinks charged to his bar bill by a
woman he had never heard of. But that, she assumed,
had been taken care of by her employer, just as he had
taken care of everything else so far.

A sealed glass case blocked her way on the landing.
She bent to examine the fully rigged ship model inside
and read the brass plate: British Second Rate, About
1850. Presented by J. P. Morgan, 1900.

The hall to her left was crowded with more trophies.
They covered the walls beyond the black wood balcony
that circled the room up to the ceiling with its centerpiece
of green and yellow leaded glass.

The trophies were mostly half-models—wooden minia-
tures of yacht hulls, sliced in half and mounted on the
wall. The floor was crowded with glass cases holding
larger models, beautifully detailed, of boats long since
burned, sunk, sold for scrap. Most were of the old J
class, monsters of teak and steel, 150 feet long, whose
7,500 feet of sail needed crews of forty. In them, Sir
Thomas Lipton and Harold Vanderbilt had made yacht
racing what it remained in the eighties: the sport of millionaires and millionaire syndicates who sailed vicariously
through professional crews—tough hired sailors and
builders who competed on their behalf for prestige,
power, and influence, the prizes of international
yachting.

The girl wandered among the glass cases, fascinated
despite herself. The names of the older boats—*Viking,
Corsair*—nakedly advertised their owner's greed to win.
But the greed in the newer boats, winners from the big
races of the fifties and sixties—*Constellation, American
Eagle, Nefertiti*—went beyond names. Sleek, sharp,
sharklike, with bows like knives, the new boats pro-
claimed one overwhelming need in their design—the
need to triumph, whatever the cost.

For more than a hundred years, the New York Yacht
Club had acted as the meeting place, the forum, the controlling power, the maker of rules and the breaker of rep-
utations among these millionaire sailors. She could
almost smell the money.

"Miss Valois?"

He'd come up behind her, hidden by the tall glass showcases. She'd been careless, wrapped up in her thoughts.

"My name's"—he smiled—"Traven." He said it awkwardly, as if it amused him. Lifting the blue manila folder in his hand, he weighed it in one leather-gloved hand and met her eye. "I think this is for you."

"Not here." Her carelessness still put her on edge. "Is there somewhere quiet?"

He glanced around with a smile at the empty room. "Quieter than this?"

As if to illustrate her fears, footsteps whispered across the marble landing outside. They waited, not breathing, until the steps disappeared.

"We could go up to the library," he conceded, "if you're worried."

"Anyone who does not worry is a fool. Why meet here? Why not a hotel, the park? It is a foolish risk."

He led the way towards the door. "I don't agree. The old man downstairs doesn't notice anything these days unless it's under his nose. Anyway, what could be more innocent than a member dropping in one August morning for a quiet drink and falling into conversation with"—he smiled at her—"a beautiful stranger?"

She watched the tight smile, the too-bright eyes, and realized he was enjoying himself. Amateurs—they thought it was all a joke. He would learn otherwise. She would make sure of that. The girl resolved that her dealings with Traven would be arranged with the highest degree of precision, at the highest cost.

"Is the library quieter?"

"I suppose so. I don't think I've ever been in there." With a lopsided grin, he pointed to a card propped against a small table by the door. "We shouldn't talk here anyway. I wouldn't want to infringe the club rules."

The card said: Members are reminded that business papers may not be displayed in this room.

She followed him up the winding staircase that spiraled around the ancient elevator, her eyes on the folder in his hand. Already the thought of what it contained made her heart beat a little faster and brought out a mist of perspiration on her upper lip.

The top-floor library was stuffy and empty. A clock ticked heavily. As they entered, a tortoiseshell cat on the rug glanced up, changed position insolently, and went back to sleep. Nothing in the room, least of all the leather-bound volumes of naval history and yachting lore that filled the glass-fronted cases, seemed to have been touched for fifty years. They were not meant for reading; to the outsider they were the accumulated wisdom of ten millionaire generations turned to vellum and calf and heavy rag paper.

Traven sat on a leather-covered bench beside a low table with a display of knots and fancy rope work sealed under its glass top. He pushed the folder towards her with one gloved hand. She took it and spilled its contents onto the glass, unconcerned that the only prints on it now would be her own. Let her pursuers find her if they could. Dozens had tried and were still trying. But even this man, with all his evident influence and money, had needed three months to discover the telex code that was the only channel of communication to her. And still he knew nothing about her, not even her real name. To him she would always be Jean Valois; the woman hunted by Interpol, London's Special Branch, the Sureté, and, for all she knew, the KGB as Marie-Ange Planchet would remain a stranger. With fools like this one, it was necessary to be careful for two.

But, sorting through the dossier, she had to acknowledge he had done his job. Photographs. Newspaper clippings. Typed schedules of times and dates. Even maps. A thorough piece of work.

Her long fingers with their clipped, unvarnished nails lifted out the photographs and laid them side by side.

"This one." She consulted her list. "Keble?"

"Charlie Keble. No problem with him, I should think."

She studied the color Polaroid print of a tall, blonde, freckled, grinning young man and privately agreed with Traven. This one had been brought up soft, like most Americans. He was a living advertisement for Coca-Cola and Mom's apple pie.

The other pictures showed a family group; the father, tall, with pale hair—bleached or gray, it was hard to tell—the wife, smaller, younger, blonde. They had their arms around a young boy. The woman was the surprise. Something about the mouth—a sensuality, even violence, one didn't expect in American women.

"Jake Forrester. Forty-eight. The woman's his wife, Elaine. Younger, of course. The boy's twelve. Peter, but they call him Petey. You might have a problem, since they travel a lot. Elaine runs a boutique in Mobile, their hometown, and Jake has a boatyard there. Very profitable too. He's near enough to a millionaire."

There was nothing remarkable in a yachtsman being wealthy, but she glanced back at his face. Her reaction surprised her.

"There is something about him. . . ." She looked up. "He was a soldier." Her tone showed she did not expect to be contradicted.

"He was in the army. Korea," Traven conceded. "But only as an intelligence officer. He never saw much combat."

"He will give me no trouble?"

"Jake? No." The idea seemed to amuse him. "People race for all sorts of reasons—the excitement, the fame, the money. With Jake, it's the boat. Nothing else. He'll sail as *crew* if he thinks a boat is hot; never mind that he's one of the top skippers in the world and a pretty fair helmsman besides. Half the time I don't think he knows other people exist. You could deck him with a brick, and he wouldn't know what hit him. Or who threw it."

She looked at the photograph again. It was true the face lacked something—an edge, anger. But something waited behind those crinkled, pale gray eyes. She would not know quite what until she saw him face to face, and with care that would never happen.

She closed the dossier and slipped it into her bag. "You have what we agreed upon?"

He took a hard pack of Marlboros from his pocket and handed it to her carefully. Obviously it no longer contained cigarettes.

"If you know the trouble I had finding those."

She glanced inside the box, and for a long moment, her eyes gleamed, looking down into the shadowed interior. Then she dropped it into the bag with the dossier.

"How can I reach you if I need to speak with you?"

"Never in person. This is our first and last meeting. You have the number I gave you. Leave a message on the answering machine for Traven." He looked at her quizzically. "You know who he was?"

She shook her head.

"A writer. Not very fond of publicity. He wrote *The Treasure of the Sierra Madre.* Even in France you must have seen that movie. Humphrey Bogart?"

She shrugged. Distantly, the elevator motor whirred. "It is better that you leave first," she said. It was a dismissal.

At the door he looked back. She was bent over the tortoiseshell cat, tickling its chin with one forefinger. Stirring and stretching, it jumped into her lap, stamped a place for itself, and settled down.

Stepping out of the elevator beside the Trophy Room, Traven headed towards the steps leading to the main entrance. Then, on a whim, he turned in the opposite direction and walked down the seven steps into the Trophy Room.

There was nothing remarkable about the Trophy Room. A heavy, red plush curtain separated it from the bar. Hideously uncomfortable chairs and benches lined the walls, on which hung old photographs of some famous boats of the old days. Most visitors passed through, ignoring the single perspex case standing on a small marble table in the middle of the room. Only if one bumped against the case and found it solid and immobile, bolted to the tabletop, which was in turn attached by a steel bar to a plate buried beneath the floor, did one realize the contents were regarded as valuable.

It is hard to see why. The silver jug inside is by any standards of taste a monstrosity—less than two feet high, it swells from a flat base into a series of bulging, heavily decorated balusters, each one wider than the one below, then narrows into an awkward neck, another bulge, and a grotesque, heavily lipped mouth. The handle, curved and recurved, is impossible to grasp with any normal hand, just as the jug would insult any liquid placed in it. The fact that it's solid silver, worth a hundred guineas when it was made in 1851, does not disguise its absolute ugliness.

But those who compete for the America's Cup care little for its aesthetic attractions. To join the names and boats engraved on its every flat surface, to know that it remains in its case at the New York Yacht Club—as it has remained there, despite challenges from all the world, since the *America* brought it back in triumph after beating all Britain's comers in the first and only race for the cup ever held outside American territorial waters— through *your* efforts—no yachtsman asks for more.

Traven placed his hand lightly on the flat top of the trophy case, over the gaping mouth of the cup, as if to warm it from some phantom heat rising out of the dark emptiness inside. Lying beside the case were a few glossy brochures. He picked one up.

DEFIANT SYNDICATE NEWS. SUPPORT THE CUP
DEFENDERS.
INSIDE:
JAKE FORRESTER, *Defiant*'s SKIPPER,
ON THE CHANCES FOR SUCCESS.

Traven smiled for a moment at Forrester's face, staring out from the printed folder, and returned the brochure neatly to the pile. Waving casually to the quartermaster by the door, he stepped out into Manhattan's coffee-time sunshine.

Sal had almost given up hope when the girl finally left the club. He was certain she must notice him as he jerked upright, rolled the magazine into a tight cylinder, and dodged across the street. She wasn't hurrying; that was great. Sal decided it was his lucky day.

Judging his pace, he intercepted her under the marquee of the Benihana Restaurant, a few doors from the Yacht Club.

It worked like a dream, as usual. He fell in beside her, casually jostled her arm, slowed, and half-turned as if to apologize. As they drew level with the restaurant entrance, his hand grabbed her upper arm, the rolled magazine jabbed her ribs, and he leaned hard on her hip.

"Inside!"

He knew that the door was open for deliveries but the restaurant itself was empty. The front staff didn't show up until noon. The doors sighed shut behind them, and they were alone in the dark, airless foyer, filled with the smell of stale booze and old fat. In the gloom he sensed rather than saw the potted plastic palms, the life-sized Japanese idol by the hatcheck booth.

"Okay, lady, Just the bag."

She didn't move. He snatched at the strap.

He liked this part best. They screamed here or tried to struggle, and he could hurt them—punch them in the belly, the tits. Some guys liked to piss on them as they lay moaning on the floor, but Sal could never manage. You can't piss with a hard-on, and he always got a bone as big as a racehorse when he did a good-looking woman.

It surprised him that this one didn't struggle. Disappointed him too. As he yanked at the bag, she let its strap slide from her shoulder. But she hung onto it with her left hand while the right fumbled with the front of her dress. He realized it was halfway open, and glimpsed a swell of breast.

"Listen, you better . .. "

She swung at him with her right hand. He braced himself for an open-handed slap, already planning how he would retaliate.

Something exploded in his head.

The needle-sharp spike pierced the temporal process above and in front of the ear, the thinnest of the twenty-two bones that make up the skull, and went deep into his brain.

Sal opened his mouth. Nothing came out. He fell to his hands and knees, the strap of the purse slipping from his fingers. Ten seconds separated him from clinical death.

Blood from the punctured blood vessels poured into the crevices of his brain, blocking some functions, disturbing others. His sight went out as if a light had been switched off. Yet his sense of smell was suddenly vivid. He smelled something—ripe bananas?

He groped for the side of his head. The fingers that

closed around the thing sticking out of his temple jerked
it half an inch inside his brain. Its point sliced through
more gray jelly, rupturing more blood vessels, and came
to rest in the dorsomedial nucleus, just in front of the
posterior hypothalamus.

It *was* Sal's lucky day. The dorsomedial nucleus controls sexual pleasure. He died ejaculating. It was the best
come of his life. And the last.

Marie-Ange waited in the stuffy darkness, listening to
the last scrabbling sounds of extinction. When they
ended, she put two fingers against the side of Sal's neck,
feeling the pulse grow heavy, slow, then die.

Circling the body, she knelt one knee in the small of its
back, took the handle of the blade in her left hand, and
pulled it free. A few cc's of blood pattered on the greasy
carpet. She wiped the blade on Sal's shirt. The weapon
was conical, six inches long, handmade from surgical
steel by a forger in Stockholm who derived his main in-
come from the manufacture of micromanipulators sharp
enough to slice a single cell. It had cost Marie-Ange a
great deal of time, energy, and money to persuade him to
make a weapon that looked enough like a piece of
jewelry to fool any policeman or customs official.

Winding the chain around the handle, she pressed the
blade back into the hilt until it clicked, then dropped everything into her bag. It would need cleaning before it
was used again.

Then she went out into the sunshine and walked un-
hurriedly towards Broadway, her mind already occupied
with the job for which Traven had hired her. If people
were to be murdered before the America's Cup was
raced, she had less than a week to make her preparations.

CHAPTER TWO

From New York City, the coast runs northeast in a saw-toothed arc, fretted with bays and inlets, creeks, sounds, beaches, points and ports. U.S. 95 struggles to follow, linking Stamford and Bridgeport, Bridgeport and New Haven, New Haven and New London, striving for a direct route to the crooked skeleton finger of Cape Cod that curls far out into the Atlantic.

It fails.

Two bays break the coast. Old river valleys, eroded deep, they have been flooded by probing fingers of salt water thirty miles inland. One, Buzzards Bay, is the bite that almost separates Cape Cod completely from the mainland. The other, a sinuous, probing explorer, has dug the guts out of Rhode Island, chewing fifty miles inland to where the urban sprawl of Providence contains it like a suture over the Providence River.

Over millennia, rivers gouged this bay deep, piling up sandbanks where the bottom was soft, turning the intractable sandstone bluffs into islands streamlined by the flow, joined to the mainland only when the tide slipped out and exposed tongues of white sand. Narragansett Bay is less geographical feature than descriptive convenience—a catchall term for the channels that wind around the islands between Providence and the sea: Conanicut, Prudence, Block, Dutch, Aquidneck. It all but maroons the people of Aquidneck, at the foot of which lies a town where a cape juts into the sea, sending a curving point west towards Conanicut to all but plug the entrance to the best deep-water anchorage on the mid-Atlantic seaboard. Part village, part resort, part fishing port, part land, part island, this town's existence justifies and encapsulates this place of shifting boundaries and bitterly fought contentions. Newport.

It all makes sense from the air. The pilot, dropping

down towards the bay, sees the protection from storms and attack that made Narragansett a great naval base and Newport a navy town. Here and there among the islands, bridges as flimsy as the trails of water spiders link mainland to island. But the old land route to Newport from the west—north up the bay, over the river at Providence, southeast to Fall River, southwest to Tiverton, across the narrow neck of Mount Hope Bay, and down the island to Newport at its tip—explains why the people became sailors almost from the moment they sank their house timbers into the salt sand.

In Newport sailing once meant survival. But it was not a survival earned easily; the tidal channels were rigged with sand traps, shoals, and wrecks that could tear out the hull of a ship in seconds. And its winds were the trickiest on the coast; air rolling in from the ocean picked up the confused messages from cool currents and warm land, from brisk offshore breezes and slow-moving whirlpools of trapped air, and lost all logic. Shifting breezes, sighing down to a feather, busting up to a gale, became standard complications in the Newporter's life.

Good sailors noticed the conditions and were impressed, even challenged. To sail Narragansett and its island became an amusement of the rich, and Newport became their resort. Cut off from the rest of the world, accessible only from the sea, it offered a haven during the unbearable months of high summer on which they could place their indelible stamp of ownership. Seizing the best cliff-top sites on the peninsula, they built their summer "cottages"—hundred-room mansions, filled with music and dancing for ten weeks of the year, empty and shuttered for the rest as the Vanderbilts, Astors, Lorillards, and Oelrichs returned to the real world. The Newporters didn't complain; realistic people, they were thankful that, for nine months of the year at least, they owned their town.

They owned it less when the navy moved in, but even then, the service kept its men to itself, and the bars and cafes did good business on Saturday nights. They were even complacent when, after twenty-one years of dormancy, the America's Cup races were revived in 1958, and Newport was chosen as their setting. It seemed a minor matter; when the giant J class raced for the Cup, only the rich and respected could compete. The Cup and the honor of its defense from foreign challenges had been just another opportunity for cheerful wrangling among the millionaires of Bellevue Avenue, like the huge formal balls and parties, the accumulations of furniture and art with which hostesses impressed one another in the great days of the 1900s.

Everyone underestimated what would happen when the Cup was opened up to the new twelve-meter yachts. A dozen men could sail them; they needed no forty-man crews. They could be built of modern materials—stainless steel, aluminum, plastic—at a cost which, if still enormous to the individual, might be met by a syndicate of eight or ten wealthy men. The New York Yacht Club tried to impose a code of gentlemanly conduct on the sport, insisting that twelves still retain the facility to cruise by including bunks, stoves, heads, and furniture in their design.

The instrument of their power, the Twelve-Meter Rule, was an intricate code of calculations that defined whether or not a boat was truly a racing twelve or just some unacceptable and lowly imitation. It was surprising how often the boat of a rude, vulgar, argumentative competitor was found to infringe some aspect of the rule and was thus removed from the race.

Newport resigned itself to a limited invasion of its privacy. The navy was moving out; pleasure-boat men might provide a partial substitute for the sailors' useful revenue. Someone suggested replacing the unwieldy old ferry from the mainland with a bridge; it was grudgingly agreed that the suggestion had some sense. Some elders of the town may have regretted the fact that the America's Cup would be sailed only every three years, and then only if foolhardy challengers from other countries were prepared to sail their boats across the Atlantic (another restriction of the rule, subtly designed to take the edge off the most feisty European crew). If any did so lament the generous schedule, they repented very quickly, when they saw how twelves affected yacht racing.

Interest in the new boat scene exploded. Suddenly no

newly rich industrialist was fit to be seen in the board-room or at the golf club unless he could boast a boat. Forming a syndicate to race a twelve was no longer a matter of coercion and persuasion. Property developers, engineering tycoons, men in electronics and the movies clamored for the pleasure of pouring millions into the design and construction of a boat that, if it was very lucky, built by a genius, and crewed by tough profession-als, just might be good enough to make the runoffs that decided which American boat would have the honor of defending the Cup.

Newport blossomed. Foreign boats, anxious to gain ex-perience with the Narragansett winds, moved in a year before the challenge, took over a boatyard, and started work. American boats, built and tested at places like City Island, within sight of Manhattan, or in the yards of New Jersey and Connecticut, arrived at Newport by the month, ready for fitting sails, stepping masts, fine tuning, and rigging. Upstairs meeting rooms in the old two-story wooden houses of the town were turned into sail lofts, dry goods stores to chandlers, fishing wharves to boatyards. Bars only busy on Saturdays in the old days found themselves inundated with the new society of the yachting world. Journalists, stress engineers, designers, and sail makers, who looked like they had never been to sea in their lives, sat noisily at tables in the back, arguing about wind flow, fabric stress, and metal fatigue. Busi-nessmen, dressed for the yachting season by Abercrom-bie and Fitch, held court for their circle of women, admirers, hangers-on. The boatmen themselves were a new breed—tough professionals who sailed all year, every year, moving from country to country as the races dictated: the Admiral's Cup around Cowes and the Isle of Wight, where *America* had won the first America's Cup race; the Fastnet, from England to Ireland and back, across some of the most treacherous waters in Eu-rope; the Pacific and Atlantic Conference races; the Syd-ney-Hobart in Australia; the Trans-Atlantic and Round the World races. They worked for the millionaires, but they were their own men—hard and tough and capable.

And in any America's Cup week throughout the 1980s, the best of them were to be found in Newport.

Jake Forrester cruised through downtown Newport and looked around in distaste. It wasn't just that he had not slept well, that the worries of skippering the defending boat against the British challenger in three days' time kept his head filled with formulas and calculations until three A.M., He'd raced in the Cup before, though always as helmsman, crewman, or tactician, never as skipper. He knew the stresses could be borne, if not enjoyed.

It was not even the inevitable tensions that Elaine would impose during the next few days. They saw one another so seldom that any opportunity was seized with alacrity, even if it was during Cup week. And being seen at the social events of the week without Elaine would start rumors of estrangement, divorce—the sort of talk that did no professional sailor any good. To sail under New York Yacht Club rules was as onerous as being in the Senate; infringements, moral or social, were noted and used by one's enemies. And nobody in the yacht world lacked enemies.

What angered Jake was Newport.

It wasn't *his* Newport anymore. The art galleries and smart restaurants that lined Thames Street had the blank impersonality of a film set. The more they aimed for authenticity with faked lumber facades and antique hanging signs, the more Newport looked like the Universal backlot. A few relics remained of the old town—the navy recruiting office, windows grimed with dust, posters fading inside. But that was soon to be closed down. And the old armory, ridiculous with its rough-hewn, gray stonework—they would have torn that down years ago if it hadn't been the largest public building in town, ideal for press conferences during Cup time.

He could date the ruin of Newport to 1969. That's when they opened the new bridge joining the islands to the mainland. The navy finished moving out around then as well, releasing large stretches of the waterfront for re-development. Tourists and businessmen poured in.

Even well into the sixties, the town was not entirely spoiled. Jake remembered great nights there when he was a crewman on Britton Chance's beautiful, doomed *Nefertiti,* perhaps the finest twelve of the decade. They'd rolled from bar to bar—Jake, Elaine, Sam Lewis, and the gang—drinking Narragansett beer, eating in clapboard restaurants where the crabs and lobsters came snapping-fresh from boats moored just across Thames Street at Bannister's Wharf, then strolling back home to the crew headquarters along brick-paved streets. When he and Elaine had made love, the old wooden house had creaked around them like a ship at sea.

Good days. Not *all* good though. He frowned, remembering that it had been on that challenge, in 1962, that he first realized the power of the NYYC to impose its will on the sport. *Nefertiti*'s helmsman, a crusty, brilliant Bostonian named Don MacNamara, had made his irritation with the administration vocally evident; the Club had ordered him from the course.

If only they would just let you *sail*. But there were always syndicate members worried about their investment, crewmen with problems, hang-ups at the yard, delays in getting vital equipment, and the inevitable regulations. Just the previous day, Aaron Hart, this year's NYYC Race Committee Chairman had . . .

The car in front pulled up sharply. Jake jammed on the brakes. Traffic was solid for the next two hundred yards, right to where Thames joined America's Cup Avenue, as some idiot had grandly rechristened the old harbor road.

A cycle cop idled his big Yamaha down the other side of Thames, U-turned, and stopped a few yards away. Jake rolled down the window.

"What's the trouble?"

The cop turned his head slowly. Jake saw himself reflected in the mirrored bronze of dark glasses. "Sanitation crew."

"Again?" Newport was a small town trying once every three years to handle the population of a city. During Cup week, the sewers regularly clogged up at least twice, flooding restaurants and bars. The power likewise failed nightly. Jake settled down to a long wait. Now that the window was down he could hear the radio from the car in front: the brassy blare of two bars from *America the Beautiful* in pat imitation of the Beach Boys segued into the announcer babbling, "Eight-o beee-utiful seventeen on this dynamite day, and you're listening to WLAC Racing Radio, the voice of the America's Cup. . . ."

It *would* be Tom Needham's station. You couldn't escape it, any more than you could escape Tom. He seemed to be everywhere; his chain of TV stations, his magazines, and his newspaper gave him the biggest opportunity for self-promotion on the East Coast, and he wasn't averse to using it. Tom was bucking for the governorship of Maryland—perhaps the White House—and the media outlets he owned were in there pitching on his behalf. So, Jake supposed, was he, since Needham was chairman of the syndicate that built *Defiant,* and the major contributor.

The radio began to get on Jake's nerves. He turned to roll up the window and found the cop staring at him.

"Say, you Jake Forrester?"

Even now, after more than twenty years as a boatman, he wasn't used to being recognized. Elaine laughed at his reticence, bullied him into giving interviews, bulldozed him so that he showed up at the right parties and made himself agreeable to the rich and influential. He would never have met Tom Needham if Elaine hadn't arranged it. "I'll make you famous if it kills me," she had said.

"That's what it says on my driver's license."

The cop hinged up the shades, revealing unexpected innocent blue eyes. "Thought it was you. How's that boat of yours, Mr. Forrester?"

He might have known a Newport cop would know sailing.

"Pretty good. Still some work to do on her."

"What about that carbon-fiber rudder? How do you rate that?"

The short answer was that Jake didn't know. Carbon fiber was one of the new miracle materials in sailing, like the continuous films Kevlar and Mylar that were used for sails. It made a light, tough material, ideal for the rudder and trim tab that steered a twelve.

"We're trying it out," he said evasively. "Hard to know until we get a real blow."

"They didn't work too well on the Fastnet in '80."

Jake didn't need to hear this. When the Fastnet fleet ran into heavy gales off Ireland, the rudders were the first equipment to fail. Thirteen men died.

"That was a hurricane. We don't figure on that sort of weather out on the Sound."

"I guess not." He looked critically at the sky. "Good sailing day, looks like."

"We'd be out, but I'm picking up my wife in Providence." He looked at his watch. "Guess I'm going to be late."

The cop slid his glasses onto his nose. "Maybe we can do something about that."

Hitting his siren, he beckoned Jake out of the jam. With the cycle wheep-wheeping in front of him, Jake sped past the lane of stalled cars, around the sanitation crew clustered over an open manhole, to the empty stretch of America's Cup Avenue. As the cop peeled off, Jake put down his foot and waved his thanks.

Another skipper would have expected that kind of treatment, even demanded it. Ted Turner, for instance, spent very little time waiting in line for anything. As Elaine never tired of pointing out, Ted was Yachtsman of the Year in 1973, when he was thirty-five, America's Cup defender four years later, and a multimillionaire three years after that. Jake was close to his forty-fifth birthday before Tom Needham tapped him to captain *Defiant*.

Perhaps he could have kicked more asses, or kissed them. But that wasn't in his nature. As a boy, Jake had sailed with his father on the choppy, shallow waters of Mobile Bay and learned the rules of boating survival. "Be precise. Be safe. The sea won't forgive you if you make a mistake." The sage words stuck long after his father went off to war in the old *Alabama* and never came back. They were almost his epitaph.

Jake knew what others said about him: "Good old Jake. A good man to have at your back. No crazy stuff with Forrester."

What was wrong with that? Wasn't it the boat that mattered? Getting it right, perfecting the machine and the crew, pursuing that elusive excellence? If not for that, why sail at all?

For an answer, he had only to think of Elaine's mocking smile.

She came through the doors of the terminal just as he

pulled up, and he was astonished all over again. There was something fresh-minted about Elaine Forrester. Every edge was crisp, every eyelash in place; the hair that streamed halfway down her back, honey blonde, would be so clean that a comb could run through it like silk. Jake already smelled the sun-warmed crispness of it.

They kissed lightly as she slid into the car. Jake said, "You look good."

She looked him over critically. "You too. Lost more weight."

"A few pounds. What was I last time?"

"God, who remembers?" She took off her sunglasses and shook out her hair. "We don't exactly spend every weekend together, love."

Jake stared at the road. No point in hacking over this old ground; once she'd gotten it out of her system, which usually took only a few minutes, they could settle down to rebuilding a relationship that in almost any other world except that of the professional sailor would have been regarded as near divorce. But lengthy separation between sailors and their wives existed long before the America's Cup, and there were traditions to maintain. One was: Never ask questions. What people did during the long voyages was their own business. Another was: Enjoy what you have.

"I meant that about you looking good," Jake said. "I won't be able to get within ten feet of you tonight at the ball."

"I'll save you a dance." She tilted the rearview mirror to look at her face. Jake bit back his protest. It was the kind of habit that broke every rule of safety—but that was true of almost everything Elaine did.

"I guess I don't look too bad at that," she said.

At thirty-six, Elaine looked half her age. She could still get away with clothes so simple that a teenager might have chosen them: a denim jacket from Yves St. Laurent, leather trousers from Skin in London, and a crisp white silk shirt from Bergdorf Goodman.

She tilted the mirror back in place. Jake readjusted it gratefully.

"I didn't expect to see you up here," she said. "You

usually send one of the gofers. How come you aren't sailing?"

"Sam's got some idea about the trim tab. He hauled her out to tinker with it. Gives us a chance to clean down the hull as well."

Fidgeting with twelves before a race was a constitutional affliction with helmsman like Sam Lewis. The trim tab, a secondary rudder just behind the bladelike keel, used for minute adjustments during a race, had to move as precisely as a surgical instrument. Sam was never quite satisfied with *Defiant*'s; in the middle of the night he would have a new idea about it and would be down at the yard by dawn to try out the scheme.

"My lucky day," Elaine said. But she was smiling.

"How's Petey?" he asked as they turned out of the parking lot.

"Oh, you know. Difficult. Twelve is supposed to be a difficult age. He probably read that someplace and decided he wasn't trying hard enough."

"I'll talk to him when all this is over."

"Jean will straighten him out. She's good with kids." Jean was Jake's mother. With Jake and Elaine traveling so much, her home in Mobile had become Petey's as well.

"That reminds me. I called you on Tuesday. Jean said she hadn't seen you all week."

"Marianne couldn't get to New York for the shows. I did them instead."

Elaine managed a boutique with an old school friend. Hardly more than a hole in the wall in a big mall outside Mobile, it managed to lose a spectacular amount of money. Elysée—usually mispronounced Elsie by the customers—existed, Jake had decided long ago, mainly as an excuse for Elaine and Marianne to make frequent buying trips to Paris, Rome, London, and New York. Not that he complained. Twelve-meter racing, even with a boat owned and supported by someone else, was a pastime expensive enough to make Elysée look trivial.

Jake turned automatically onto Route 138. The two bridges over Narragansett Bay should be almost empty this time of the morning.

"I booked you into the Treadway. I didn't think you'd want to be up at the house." The *Defiant* team, like all crews, hired a house for the months before the race.

"Thanks. All that locker-room atmosphere gets me down." She laid her hand on his knee. "Do you get to visit now and then?"

"I'll check the diary."

They climbed the long arc of Newport Bridge. From the top Jake could see the whole blue sweep of the bay, with Long Island Sound in the distance. A breeze buffeted the car. Far below them, a twelve glided towards the ocean, mainsail and foresail taut as drumheads, the sharp edge of the pale gray hull carving the water with scarcely a ripple. He recognized *Suomi,* the Finnish boat, knocked out in the eliminations by Baron Bich's *France IV.* But Paavo Taakinnen and his crew would be out for a run around the Cup course being surveyed for the first race between *Defiant* and the British challenger, Tony Stephens's *Victorious.*

Elaine read his mind. "Don't worry. You can be out tomorrow. The rest will do you good."

"Uh huh." He frowned at the sky, streaked with high cirrus. Long plumes of vapor trailed below and behind the cloud; ice showers dropped down into the slow winds beneath. There would be a good breeze out to sea. He wondered why Stephens had chosen to take a lay day and not sail; every instant of practice was vital if you didn't know the waters of the Sound. But he was glad the British boat was not an extra day up on *Defiant.*

Whoever built the Treadway Inn knew his business. It took up the best slice of the waterfront vacated by the navy when it moved out. The sliding windows of Elaine's room opened on a broad sweep of grass. The harbor lay beyond. Made for fishing boats, it was clogged, thousands of tiny craft taking up space barely big enough for hundreds. Further out were the big yachts, most of them newly arrived for the America's Cup Ball that night.

Elaine took one look at the view and pulled the curtains firmly closed.

"Don't like it?"

"I just don't want to be part of it. Half those boats probably have their binoculars on these windows day and night. Especially night." She sat down heavily on the bed. "Help me with these boots, darling."

The long suede boots clung to her calves. Jake had to yank them off. Hooking her thumbs into the waistband of her pants, Elaine eased them off with a sigh of relief. "These looked wonderful in London. I forgot it never gets hot over there."

Under the pants she wore briefs of coffee-colored lace, hardly covering her blonde pubic hair. She followed Jake's admiring glance.

"Janet Reger. From London too. We sell them in the shop now."

"I'll take a dozen."

"You'd be surprised how many customers are men." She smiled. "For their wives. They go out of their way to mention that."

She unbuttoned her blouse as she talked. Her breasts were still as high as a teenager's, with the swelling, almost protuberant nipples that never failed to arouse him. They were so sensitive that a few moments of careful licking and teasing made them swell with blood; a few moments more and she would be moaning with pleasure and tearing at his clothes.

Jake cleared his suddenly thickened throat. The sound was almost deafening in the still, stuffy room.

Opening her suitcase, Elaine lifted a shimmering formal dress of green silk and held it against herself. "For tonight. Like it?"

"For tonight, sure. Not for now."

She widened her eyes. "I thought you had to get back to the boat." But she came eagerly to his arms.

With Elaine, it was always like taking a new woman. After their long separation, she was as hungry as he was. Almost before he had stripped off his clothes, she was on top of him, thighs straddling his chest, nibbling, fondling. Her breasts drooped above him, the perfect nipples looking sharp enough to pierce his skin. He nipped them with his fingertips and felt the rising, moaning response in her.

"Oh, you mustn't. You mustn't. . . . You know what that does to me. . . ."

He took one between his lips, touched it with his tongue, and sucked until he knew it must hurt her.

"Now! Come on, come on . . ." Her face blind with desire, spots of high color glowing on her cheeks, she grabbed his penis and lifted one knee to spread herself. He slipped inside her effortlessly and was swallowed in swimming wetness.

He grabbed her wrists, forcing them behind her back so that her whole weight was supported on his grinding hips. He seemed to be probing deeper into her than he ever had into any woman. As Elaine threw her head back in ecstasy, he knew he had touched her tenderest, sweetest part.

"I'm coming." There was wonder in her voice. An instant later her whole body bucked and jerked over him. Her head thrashed. Then she settled forward on his chest, covering his face in her hair.

"Nice?"

She was breathless with delight. "Nice? My God . . . nice . . ."

She rolled on her side, wriggling against him so that he had to make room for her on the bed. As she snuggled closer, he realized what she wanted and let her slide under him. Again her warm wetness engulfed him. He took her wrists in his hands again, forced her hands above her head on the pillow. Her long, long legs were wrapped around his hips, her breasts thrust against his chest. They wrestled together, each movement forcing their bodies into closer and closer contact, until Jake felt swallowed up by her.

"Darling, I'm coming again!"

The same thrashing, moaning torment of pleasure, the same soft relaxation. After a long, drowsy minute, she opened her eyes. "Now you."

"We've only just started."

"I don't care. I want you to come inside me." She sounded angry.

Her tongue licked into his ear, her nails probed the creases of his body while she writhed under him in a slow, intricate dance of pleasure that excited every inch of his skin; her lips whispered in detailed obscenity just what she expected to feel any . . . moment . . . now. . . .

He spurted helplessly inside her. The muscles of

her vagina milked him delicately until it seemed his orgasm must last forever.

He rolled off her body, drained, and lay watching the rippling patterns of light on the ceiling. Elaine, beside him, breathed in shallow, tense gasps, like someone who had run a mile.

"Are you all right?"

She didn't answer. There had been something desperate about her lovemaking, as if with it she staved off a fear that pursued her. It had not calmed her as it had him; she seemed even more charged with energy, more vividly alive. He wanted to say "I love you" and opened his lips to do so.

Then the phone rang.

He let it burr for a few seconds, then sighed and reached for it. "Feel like a boat trip?" Sam Lewis asked.

He sat up. "What about the trim tab?"

"Cruddy crane's busted. I can't get her out of the water."

"Are you working on it?"

"Well, right now I'm frigging around on the phone with my skipper. But it looks like all day to me."

Jake checked his watch. Almost noon. "I'll be right there." He hung up and reached for his trousers, avoiding Elaine's eyes.

"It could have been worse, I suppose," she said at last. "At least I got half an hour."

"It'll be all over in a week."

"The Cup or our marriage?"

Stuffing his shirt inside his belt, he reached for his Decksiders. "The ball doesn't start till nine. I'll be back by six. We can have a drink."

She stirred lasciviously on the bed, delicately parting her thighs and trailing her fingers over her nipples. "Or something."

"Elaine . . ."

"Go on," she smiled. "Get down to your damned boat. I'll see what I can pick up in the bar."

The image of her body stayed with Jake halfway down the hall. But by the time he reached the lobby, he was thinking about *Defiant*.

"Pardon me? Mr. Forrester?"

The desk clerk held out a house phone. Jake grabbed it, expecting Elaine.

"Mr. Forrester? It's Charlie Keble."

Keble crewed on *Defiant*. Foredeck man. A young marine engineering student chosen by Sam—Jake hardly knew him.

"Charlie, I'm in sort of a hurry."

"Oh, sorry. I thought, since we had a lay day . . ."

"Not any more. The crane isn't working at the yard. We're taking the boat out. Are you at the house?"

"Yeah."

"Then round up the guys. Tell them to get down to Deepwater, will you?"

"Okay." He sounded depressed.

"I can take a minute, I guess. What's on your mind?"

"Uh, well, I really wanted to see you in person."

"You will—in half an hour."

"No, I meant alone."

"What about, Charlie?" Jake detected something more than diffidence in the boy's voice. He sounded scared.

"I'd rather tell you that when we talk."

"If that's how you want to handle it, sure. How about we get together this evening? After we dock." So much for hopes of spending more time with Elaine. But Keble was obviously badly shaken.

"That's great, Mr. Forrester." He sounded relieved.

"Okay. Get the guys moving, huh?"

In the house at Hazard's Beach that the syndicate had hired as its headquarters, Keble put down the phone and went to the big cabinet set under the windows that looked out over the ocean. On its top, the gilt figure of an eagle with outspread wings stood between two tiny china owls. A card tilted against them said: If You Want to Soar with the Eagles by Day, Don't Imitate the Owls at Night.

He opened the cabinet, half-filled a shot glass with Chivas Regal, and drained it at a gulp. He knew that they were going to kill him; they had made that clear. He still had the note in his pocket: "I know you won't disappoint us." Unsigned, innocuous in its wording, deadly in its implication. Nobody could think it threatening, yet

Keble saw the threat, and it terrified him. He should never have suggested, even *thought* of asking for more money. The idea of going to the police should never have entered his mind. The moment he had mentioned it, instantly regretting it the next second, he had seen that look in their eyes and known the inevitable punishment. Of course they knew he wouldn't disappoint them; they were going to make sure he never had the chance.

CHAPTER THREE

Halfway down the side street that led to Deepwater Marine, Jake ran into the crowd. It swarmed over the car; a girl with long blonde hair rapped on the window, pressing the current issue of *Yachts and Yachting* magazine against the glass. His own face looked back at him from the cover: America's Cup Issue. Forrester, Lewis, and Needham on *Defiant* and the Pursuit of Excellence.

She mimed scribbling. Jake wound down the window, took the pen, and wrote his name across the cover.

"Wow, thanks." Jake looked up into her adoring, heart-shaped face. She could not be more than eighteen. It seemed a century since he had been so intense about anything except boats and sailing. "I think *Defiant* is just the most beautiful boat. Just . . . wow. Ya' know, like, beautiful."

Jake smiled back at her and wound up the window. He was whistling the first few bars of "We've Only Just Begun" as he parked near the big prefabricated workshop.

All around him the yard hummed and bustled. The *Defiant* syndicate had made a deal with Win Golitzen, who owned the Deepwater yard, to devote it entirely to their challenge for the year preceding the race. It was costing Tom Needham and his three fellow backers better than ten thousand dollars a week for the use of Deepwater's two yacht berths and the heavy lifting equipment with which they were fitted, as well as the services of Deepwater's technicians and office staff, and God knows how much more for the items Needham had insisted be added to Deepwater's facilities. The workshop had been carted up from someplace in New Jersey and assembled on specially poured concrete foundations. Inside was an assembly of technical equipment that would make the builders of City Island squint in envy. Over in the office, a $6,500 IBM computer terminal handled Sam's calculations, ingesting the numbers that would, in time, turn into strategy for sailing *Defiant* at peak efficiency. The terminal was linked on a time-sharing basis with the main computer of Tom Needham's Mediametric Corporation; through it, they could tap into·data banks all over America.

"It's a lot of money," Jake had told Needham when he first outlined his strategy to win the Cup. The media man had just smiled the slightly impish grin that was his trade-mark and shaken his head.

"You know what it costs to produce one hour of filmed drama? More than one hundred thousand dollars. Just to put the news on for one day costs thirty thousand dollars."

"That's still a long way from three million dollars."

"It's worth it. Jake, I *want* this one. Give me a win. I don't care how you do it or what it costs. The syndicate can come up with the money. Spend it. I don't want to hear later that any expense was spared. If we lose, then we lose to the better boat, not because we wouldn't spend a few thousand for something we might never need."

Jake took him at his word. *Defiant* was the best. He had made sure of that. He was there when Sam Lewis made the original drawings. He followed the testing of the hull model in Olin Stephens's tank in Hoboken. He watched the casting of the keel that would keep her wedged in the water against the enormous sideways pres-sure of her eight stories of sails. He superintended the welding and polishing of her stainless steel hull, the deck-ing-in, mast-stepping, the choosing and cutting of the sails, and their recutting and re-recutting in search of an absolutely perfect shape.

Jake helped Sam and Christie Pfaff, the deck boss, choose the ten crewmen and supervise their training. He jogged with them, exercised with them, dieted and gave up drinking with them, lectured and drilled and indoctri-nated them until they responded to orders almost before they were yelled. In a sport where wins were often mea-sured in seconds, races went to the quickest; a boat was only as good as its crew, and Jake knew he had the best in the world.

And the best boat.

He walked towards the dock, his chest tightening like a man going to his lover.

Defiant rode calmly in her slot, bare-masted, proud, white and beautiful. Seventy feet from prow to stern, forty-four feet at the waterline, a shell of resin, magnesium, and stainless steel balanced over twenty tons of lead, she was the ultimate expression of man's need to sail free of any link with the land. No engine marred her perfect balance, no propeller protruded through her hull; she would trail no stinking haze of fumes as she carved through the water. She was a creature of the winds, and they could make her fly or break her contemptuously into a dismasted wreck.

Though a twelve is twice the length and weight of the biggest tractor/trailer on the road, at her best speed, she moves barely faster than a man can run. Surface-skimming catamarans have been known to hit more than thirty knots, but a twelve, needing the stability of a heavy keel and the flexibility of big sails to catch the tricky winds of a Newport autumn, cannot compete with the lightweight multihulls. Average speeds in America's Cup races seldom climb above eight knots, and those must be achieved in breezes that would not blow a child off its feet.

The twelve's hull is little more than a foundation for its tower of sails. Sail makers are the superintellects of the boat world, vague, untidy men happier with a pocket calculator than a sailor's knife, largely unaware of the sea even when they sail on it. For them the only reality is the relative efficiency of a sail that must be full for reaching and running, flat for working to windward, not so thick that it impedes the boat nor so thin that the fabric tears at its anchor points. The deck of a racing twelve is spotted with their compass roses painted on the deck to check direction at a glance, their scales and measuring lines glued down along sheet leads; the sheets themselves are ringed with colored tape every few feet so that the sail man can judge to an inch the tension on the sail.

Crewmen learn that most of their time will be spent squatting at the double-handed "coffee grinder" winches, adjusting the sail tension from minute to minute as the wind dictates. For months before a race, a motor tender will follow the boat, watching the angle of the sail, the movement of water around the hull, the balance of the boat, and then radioing back the sail man's orders by CB radio. Then, just when perfection seems to be achieved, a disheveled designer will announce a "little idea" that involves recutting the mainsail and shifting the ballast. And everything starts all over again.

There is no logic to all this; to an outsider, the obsessive pursuit of excellence is always incomprehensible. Jake had long since given up trying to explain why racing twelve-meter yachts gave him the only true fulfillment in his life. Sometimes he sensed that the evanescence of it all had a lot to do with its attraction. A twelve was like a butterfly, hatched in ugliness, destined to fly for only a few days before the need to create more butterflies destroyed its beauty and lightness. Twelves were little different. Too flimsy to survive the giant rollers of the deep ocean, too spartan for pleasure cruising, they had only one destiny—to race other boats, built to the same rigid and demanding rules, in the chancy autumn winds off Rhode Island.

The race over, the boats become so much scrap. Technology, science, the new skills, novel materials, radical techniques that go under the catchall term *state of the art*, all push ahead the possibilities of the twelve, and the boats themselves are left behind. Between *Columbia*'s win in 1958 and *Defiant*'s defense twenty-five years later, the average winner's speed had increased by more than one knot. Just five hundredths of a knot can mean a lead of two minutes over the America's Cup course; a boat even one year old was already hopelessly out of the running. But that extra speed doesn't come cheap. Some genius with a flair for numbers had worked out the cost of those extra vital seconds and determined that for every five hundredths of a knot added to the speed of the twelve, some syndicate had spent a million dollars.

Left behind by the years, the best twelves can be sold off to other Cup contenders as trial horses, or they can be painfully converted for pleasure cruising, their bare interiors fitted up with bunks and kitchens, their hulls pierced to fit an engine. They were sad, desolate boats,

failures in a race for which there could be only one winner and one chance to win.

Jake Forrester's chance was racing towards him. In
only three days, *Defiant*'s motorboat tender would tow
him out into the Sound, trailed by another boat hauling
Tony Stephens's *Victorious,* the British challenger. Then
there would be only the wind, the water, the measured
triangular course—and the men.

Stepping off the dock, Jake slipped down into the deep
well of *Defiant*'s cockpit. This was his country. During
the race he and Sam and perhaps one other man—tactician, sailing master, owner—would share it, making up
the afterguard, the brains of the boat. Jake would handle
the left hand of the two three-foot aluminum wheels,
controlling the main rudder; Sam, the second wheel that
moved the tiny trim tab behind the fin, making minute
adjustments to the changing moods of wind and water.
Around them were grouped the instruments that showed
wind and water speed, temperature and barometric pressure, and the computer that integrated them into a picture of *Defiant*'s rush through the water.

Ahead of the cockpit, in the big open well of the main
deck, in an area swept by the big boom of the mainsail,
the other ten men of the crew would manhandle sails and
operate the big six-speed winches. At his orders they
would unbag the spare sails and link them to the rigging,
change position to balance the boat, struggle with the
oddities of the wind to get that last possible fraction of a
knot out of her.

But it was Jake's boat. As skipper, his was the responsibility, and the triumph. Skippers had been dispossessed
of their boats often enough by irate syndicates; the most
recent British challenger, *Lionheart,* had changed captains halfway through the series, and even Ted Turner
had been fired in his time. Jake wondered what would
happen if Needham ever tried that. He suspected that
blood might flow. In a year of practice, he had come to
know *Defiant* better than Elaine or his son and to love it
almost as much as he loved them. Perhaps more, he
sometimes thought. He was solicitous, jealous, obsessed.

Pulling the yellow plastic cover from the port wheel, he
moved the cold metal through a few inches of arc. Below

him, in the muddy green water of the bay, the rudder twitched an inch, like a sleeping shark flicking its tail, and he sensed all that power gathered under him like a living thing.

Heavy footsteps approached from the dock. Sam Lewis was storming towards him, his face thunderous.

"Isn't that frigging crew here yet? I called 'em twenty minutes ago!"

"I just talked to Charlie. They'll be here. I guess most of them were sleeping in. We sailed their tails off yesterday."

"That's what their tails are for."

"What about you? Get any sleep yourself?"

Lewis glared over their heads at the gantry hovering above the boat and the giant block and tackle that should have hauled *Defiant* out of the water. "I've been up since four with that fucker."

Jake knew Sam well enough to guess a bottle of Jack Daniels had kept him company. They went back a long way. To Korea, where, as two fresh lieutenants, they shared a drainage ditch at Inchon while Chinese mortar shells drummed around them. In the lulls they discovered a mutual interest in sailing. By the end of the war, they were planning the marina they would open with their combined savings.

It didn't quite work out that way. Jake opened the marina in his hometown; Sam backed off into designing, a field where his drinking and his volcanic marriages didn't interfere with making a living. Inside five years, Lewis boats were winning races, and after ten almost everyone rated him among the top five designers in the country, a skilled tactician but a hard man to work with. Somehow, he and Jake never fell out. Their friendship survived Sam's hard drinking, his three disastrous marriages, his bouts of murderous rage. Jake was even used to his smelly cigars, permanent stubble, and pungent vocabulary.

Sam spat out a fragment of cigar leaf. "What about sails? Four ounce or five?"

Jake looked at the streaks of cloud, the loose movement of the water. The winds around Newport in the fall were chancy, and the fragile twelves needed careful handling. A sudden gust could carry away a $10,000 main-sail, snap a $50,000 mast like glass tubing. If the sails were too light, they ended up in rags; too heavy and they dragged the boat back.

"Four. And the spinnaker."

"Feeling brave, huh?"

"We've got to get used to the thing."

"You're the boss. But if she goes . . ."

Jake nodded. When their sail makers, Hoods, had offered them a radically new lightweight balloon spinnaker made from a continuous-film plastic first used in the space program and just released for private use, Jake had balked at the price and was only persuaded to use it after a call to Tom Needham, who had authorized the expenditure of $25,000 without complaint. That sum joined the others in Jake's brain; he woke some mornings with a sour taste in his mouth and the numbers tumbling in his skull.

Two Ford Estates drove through the main gate, Ford/Defiant America's Cup Defense painted down their sides. These were sponsor's gifts, like almost everything the crew drank, ate, wore, or used. When the America's Cup became big business, manufacturers clamored to get a slice of the glamor. Now few challenges or defenses could keep going without the hidden sponsorship of companies that made everything from sails to yachting clothes to breakfast cereal and beer.

The crew piled out, looking rumpled and irritated as they straggled down the dock. Charlie Keble, the last in line, seemed ill; he walked in a daze, almost staggering. Jake opened his mouth to call him over; then Sam bawled, "Cummon, you guys, you sailboating or what?" They doubled past Jake and jumped down onto the deck, Christie Pfaff in the midst of them, yelling orders, yanking the covers off the big sail winches. Jake dropped into the cockpit. There'd be time to talk with Keble after the run. And right now they were losing valuable time.

In the scramble to get *Defiant* ready for sea and link her bow bitts to the towing cable of the tender that would take them out to the course, neither Jake nor any of the crew noticed the Laser with its single passenger slide out

of a patch of shade at the far side of the dock and glide
down the bay.

As *Defiant* glided out into the bay on its long trip into the
Sound, Elaine Forrester drowsed on the bed in the
Treadway Inn. She hadn't dressed after Jake left; sex
calmed her as much as Valium, and right now she needed
to be calm.

Someone in the next room was watching TV. A soap
opera. She tried to make out the dialogue and identify
the show, but the walls muffled it to a blurred murmur.
Not that it mattered—they were all the same. The ease
with which some of her old college girlfriends drifted into
a life of chores, children, and soaps had initially amused,
then chilled her. She had been in retreat from that life
for the last ten years.

She looked down critically at her nude body. Not bad
for thirty-six. No stretch marks. No fat. Good muscles.
There had been no second and third children to push her
out of shape, no husband coming home every evening for
two hours of whining and double martinis. She exercised
twice a week, ate lightly but well, kept herself thinking
young, gave in occasionally to the pressure of some at-
tractive man and enjoyed a brief affair, all the more deli-
cious for knowing it would end.

Which was how it all began . . .

She stopped trailing her fingers lightly over the skin of
her stomach. Anyone watching her would have seen her
face stiffen, grow tense and frightened. She shivered, got
up from the bed, and put on a wrapper.

The phone rang explosively in the silence. She
snatched it up.

"Elaine?"

She recognized the voice instantly. "I was just going
out."

"Ducking me, darling?"

"Don't be ridiculous. Do you imagine I'm going to
hang around a motel room all afternoon? I thought I'd
take a swim."

"Not too far, Elaine. We've got things to talk about.
I'm looking forward to seeing you tonight."

"There's nothing to talk about. Everything's settled. Don't you see that?" Her voice was desperate but defiant.

"Perhaps, perhaps. That's what we have to talk about. I think you owe me that much—for old times' sake."

Elaine smiled wryly. "You must be . . ."

Someone knocked on the door. She put her hand over the phone. "Yes?"

"Maid."

"Come back later, please."

The footsteps shuffled away down the hall. She lifted her hand.

"Who's there? Is someone with you? Are you taping this, you bitch?"

"What if I was?"

There was a long pause. Recognizing her advantage, she pressed it with a kind of desperation. "We can talk tonight if you like, but you won't change my mind. And in case you're planning anything tricky, just remember, it's out of my hands *and* yours now. You can't touch me."

"If you say so, my poppet."

"I *do* say so, my poppet. No tricks." She allowed herself a small smile of triumph. "Or momma spank. Momma spank *hard*."

At the same moment, in New York, the sharp snap of an auctioneer's hammer rapped, the sound reaching only as far as the front row of the audience before the deep pile carpet and damasked walls of Sotheby Parke-Bernet's Madison Avenue showroom swallowed it up. The only audible sound in the room was a rustle as one hundred catalogs turned to the next page.

"Lot 87, ladies and gentleman." The auctioneer looked around the room as the red velvet dais behind him turned, taking the last painting out of sight and bringing into view the heavily gilded frame of another—a seventeenth-century warship in full sail on a rough sea.

"The Caravelle Adolphus Frederick in the Skagerrak by Jan van Eysenck. I must begin at ten thousand dollars."

Beside Tony Stephens, Saul Steiner flinched.

"Bear up, Saul," he said out of the corner of his mouth. "It's in a good cause." He raised his catalog and waved it. The bidding started to rise in thousand-dollar leaps.

Tony felt nostalgic for the untidiness of Sotheby's London headquarters, where porters in dowdy green dusters held up the item with a bored indifference, unchanged whether it was a Picasso worth millions or a chamber pot valued at two pounds. It was too much like a church here—the reverent hush, the laundered air. But perhaps that made sense. Money *was* the only thing worth reverence these days. What else would have made him lose a priceless day of practice on *Victorious,* even leave Newport for New York, a city he despised.

As the bidding reached fifteen thousand, Steiner nudged him. Tony, risking a quick glance over his shoulder, saw the familiar shape of O'Neal in the doorway, spiky hair almost brushing the lintel.

"Seventeen," the auctioneer said. "I have seventeen thousand in the back of the room." He looked at Tony expectantly.

"Eighteen."

A minute later, it was knocked down to him for $29,000. For a painting, not bad. For bait, vastly overpriced. He let five more lots go through before closing his catalog and getting up. He and Saul kept their faces expressionless as they made for the door. Luckily, O'Neal saw them first. His wide-shouldered shape suddenly blocked their way.

"Stephens? Was that *you* who bought the Eysenck?"

"Mr. O'Neal!" Tony took the gnarled hand. Whatever Karl O'Neal knew about shipping, which was almost everything, he had learned the hard way, as stevedore, deckhand, mate, and captain. His hand was like a curriculum vitae. Every callous told a story; twenty years of boardroom battles had not softened one of them.

"What the hell are you doing here during race week?"

"We had a lay day. The boat's in good shape, so I decided to treat myself to this sale. A sort of sentimental journey, really. This picture was in my family when I was a boy."

"Hell of a lot for a keepsake." Tony sensed O'Neal's

irritation. He wasn't used to being beaten anywhere, either in business or on the sales floor.

Tony ignored the remark. "And of course I had to see Saul. You know Saul Steiner, don't you? Runs the New York office of our firm?"

"Yeah. Sure." His big hand engulfed Saul's. "Seems I heard something about you talking to my people on this North Sea thing."

"Well, trying to, Mr. O'Neal. Nobody wants to make a move without your okay."

O'Neal grinned. "Glad to hear it. They don't leave much for me to do these days."

"That wasn't my impression."

Tony said, "Maybe we could talk about it while I'm here."

"Maybe, maybe." He looked over their heads. "But right now I'm buyin' pictures."

"After the sale?" Saul persisted.

"Could be." O'Neal looked at Stephens. "You staying in town tonight?"

"No. Cup Ball tonight. As challenging captain, I'm supposed to make a speech." He held out his hand. "Nice seeing you, Mr. O'Neal. I hope next time we've both got more opportunity to talk."

As they waited for the elevator, Steiner said, "Do you really have to go back tonight? Sounded to me as if he was offering us a meeting."

"Never. That old crook saw right through us."

"Didn't look that way to me."

"Then apparently they don't teach you everything at Harvard Business School."

The elevator doors opened. Tony got in. "Saul, I want you to pick up that picture, take it down to O'Neal's office, and present it to him with my compliments. He'll have to talk to you, if only to be polite. Ring me in Newport."

The doors closed. Steiner stood staring at the lighted call button, wondering if $29,000 could conceivably be charged as a business expense. Not that there was much point in worrying about a tax break if you were fighting for your life as Tony Stephens was.

Downstairs, Tony slid into a cab, looked at his watch, grimaced and shoved two twenty-dollar bills at the driver. "Two more if you get me to La Guardia for the three o'clock plane." The car burnt rubber as it pulled out into the traffic. —

CHAPTER FOUR

The wave came across the Sound like a live thing.

At one moment white-flecked green water stretched to the crisp horizon. The next moment, the fat curling lip of a single swell was rolling towards *Defiant*, swallowing smaller waves as it came.

Twelve-meter sailors prayed for chances like this. Powered by wind alone, the twelve's adhesion with the water kept it glued firmly to the surface. Lifted out on the crest of a wave, however, the boat, only a third of its hull in water, could surf like a catamaran.

Jake didn't need to check the chattering readout from the cockpit computer to see a chance was being offered to him. They were almost up to the buoy that marked the end of the course's first leg. He could see the six-foot orange cylinder bobbing beyond the bow.

If *Defiant* could round the buoy before the wave crossed their course, they might surf on it for a quarter of a mile at eight or ten knots. He'd seen Jock Sturrock in Australia's *Gretel* do it in the 1962 races, snatching a ride on a cresting swell and riding it for two hundred yards past an astonished Bus Mosbacher in *Weatherly* to win by forty-seven seconds in a new course record. It *could* be done, but it was dangerous.

Jake looked up at the curving expanse of *Defiant*'s mainsail, towering eighty feet over his head, listened to the hum of air racing across the drum-tight fabric, judged the bowing of the mast, reviewed the position of the crew in the well—four men at the big Lewmar winches, three more forward, ready to handle sails, the rest flattened to the deck to reduce drag—and made his decision.

"Ready about!" A quick glance over his shoulder told him the wave was maybe fifty yards behind them. Ahead, the buoy loomed, then disappeared from the corner of his eye as *Defiant*'s bow blotted it out. Could he make it?

Rushing in behind the boat, its force could lift it into perfect position to surf, but if it hit them broadside as they rounded the mark, the same power could flip *Defiant* like a butterfly in a gale.

But he was committed now. And with the commitment came a fierce confidence. "Spinnaker ready."

They could ride the wave with regular sails. But this was a chance to test *Defiant* to her limit. The ballooning spinnaker bulging out over the bow would tow the boat into the unknown.

Months of drilling paid off in the next seconds. The crew responded like sprinters to his order; two foredeck men leaped forward, dragging the spinnaker pole. Two more linked it to the fat roll of red fabric stowed beside the mast. When the sail went up, that flimsy length of toughened alloy would hold open the lower corners of the triangular sail, allowing it to catch the maximum amount of wind.

In the cockpit beside him, Sam braced himself and shifted his cigar. "Here goes nuthin'."

The oncoming wave was a living presence over Jake's shoulder. He could feel those tons of water, gathering to strike at *Defiant*. Then, suddenly, the orange shape of the buoy, a fat orange cylinder anchored by cable to the sea bed, was racing past. He spun the wheel. For a moment the starboard edge of the deck dipped as the boat heeled. Green water foamed a few feet from the cockpit.

Then they were around.

"Get her up!" Sam bawled.

Christie Pfaff slapped the back of the man holding the end of the spinnaker pole. He let go. Like a butterfly erupting from its chrysalis, the glistening gossamer of the crimson sail unwrinkled in the sun, catching the breeze with a soft thunderclap, bulging so that the wrinkles were smoothed away and the fabric sprang taut as young skin.

Defiant surged under them. An instant later, the bow dipped slightly as the wave gathered under the stern.

"Hang on," Jake called.

The stern rose. Jake felt the rudder kick in his hands and swung the wheel through the three points that he instinctively knew would place *Defiant* deep into the crest.

Then she was up! Half out of the water, keel still buried deep but the whole dripping length of the bow out in air and gleaming sun, she rode the wave like a surfer. Sam stared at the water speed indicator in fascination as the vanes whirled in the automatic log trailing behind the boat. Six knots, 6.5, 7, 7.5, 8 . . .

"Jesus, Jake, just look . . ."

Then everything went wrong at once.

Later, Jake could never separate the three incidents. They came in what seemed the same millisecond, as inseparable as the notes of a musical chord.

First, something struck the mast. He heard a muffled metallic *thung*.

Then the spinnaker exploded. A fat tomato of sail turned to tatters in an instant, shreds of fabric flapping from an inverted V of wire. *Defiant* sagged, dropping back into the chop as the wave ran ahead.

And suddenly the crew was yelling, scrambling up the tilted deck to lie flat and point back in their wake. A sodden shape swirled once in the green-white foam and dipped under a wave.

Christie scrambled along the lower edge of the deck and slid into the cockpit. "Keble's overboard."

Jake had already killed *Defiant*'s momentum by turning her into the wind. The crew needed no orders. They trimmed the boat for a tack that would take them back over the wake in the shortest possible time. Their motorboat tender had turned too, cutting through the foam of *Defiant*'s trail towards the orange splash of the life jacket.

"What the fuck happened?" Sam snarled.

Pfaff ran his hand through his hair. "No idea. When the 'chute went up, I looked around for a second. Next thing, I see Charlie standing up. Then he went over backwards."

"Something hit him? Spinnaker pole?" A spinnaker pole attached by only one end to the huge sail could be deadly, scything down half a dozen crewmen in its wild swing.

"No way. It was linked." Christie nodded towards the ruined spinnaker. "Still is."

Jake watched the tender reach Keble and haul him

aboard. They had been lucky—lucky that the tender was not waiting for them at the finish line but trailing the boat to check trim; lucky too that on practice trips the crew wore life jackets. During actual races they were left behind to save weight.

The tender caught them up and pulled alongside. Jake left Sam at the wheel and hung over the side, looking down into the motorboat. "That was a dumb thing to do, Charlie. If it happened on a race . . ."

He stopped as he saw the anxious faces of the three-man tender crew kneeling over the still body of Keble. Sightless eyes stared at him, hair plastered over the forehead; his open mouth gaped. Tendrils of blood veined the water running from his soaked clothing across the white fiberglass of the deck.

In Baltimore, at the headquarters of Mediametric Corporation, Tom Needham was at work. *Hard* at work. He was watching TV.

Not everyone would have seen it as such, but Needham had discovered long ago, in his earliest days running the tiny ABC affiliate in West Virginia—his father's idea of starting at the bottom in the family communications business—that a long, careful look at the options in any situation was the essential basis for any decision.

That it paid off was evident in the growth of the chain under Tom Needham III: from twelve radio stations and six TV stations to a nationwide cable TV chain, a network of radio outlets, a publishing house, magazines, newspapers. Needham had no real need to keep watching; he had trained staff to do that for him. But he liked to keep his eyes in practice.

Six twenty-four-inch TV monitors filled one end of the darkened room, a semicircle of unwinking eyes suspended in lightless space.

The same smiling blonde appeared on all of them. Long shot. Close-up. Profile. Half-profile left. Half-profile right. The last, in the center, showed a single ultra-close-up that rendered her mascaraed eyelashes as wires coated in soot; her creamy skin, a cratered landscape of yellow clay.

The intercom bleeped in the darkness. He picked it up. "I said no calls. Don't you listen out there?"

"I'm sorry, Mr. Needham. It's Mr. Forrester. Very urgent."

Needham stood up. "Okay. I'm finished here. I'll take it back in the office."

As their boss came out of the screening room, Nelson Birdwell, public relations director, and Merv Auerbach, head of personnel, straightened up from where they were leaning against the wall. Their murmured conversation stopped abruptly.

Needham said, "I don't know, Merv. She doesn't *read* current affairs to me. Does she read current affairs to you, Nels?"

Birdwell looked hunted. He disliked being caught between his boss and a colleague.

Auerback said, "She's done a lot of different stuff. Broadway. Some movie work. A spell on *As the World Turns*. We're lucky to have a shot at her. Her husband's a VP with Harborplace, so she wants to move to Baltimore."

Needham smiled. "Merv, you're putting me off. God forbid I should encourage anyone connected with *that* place." The eighteen-million-dollar conversion of Baltimore's old inner harbor into an arc of ultramodern shopping malls, restaurants, and waterside walkways where costumed performers presented clumsy recreations of sailors' hornpipes and reels was a sore point with Needham. The station had run a series of blistering editorials on the subject, perhaps because most of the land had belonged at one time to the Needham family.

"But it isn't *that* I worry about. There's something familiar about this girl. Didn't she do some commercials?"

"I guess so. Years back though."

"Not *that* long ago." He turned towards his office. "Walk me back to the office. Maybe it'll come to me."

The two executives trailed their boss. Auerbach thought sourly that the scene almost classically summed up life inside this corporation. Up front, the genial, smiling, slight figure of Thomas Needham III, lick of hair falling boyishly over his forehead, suits always impeccably tailored, shoes glistening, and manner just as carefully prepared; always the right phrase, the apt joke, the name remembered, the wife of a guest complimented on her dress, the children asked after. All without the card file of the professional politician or the ingratiating manner of the political hopeful. He was *made* for the White House, and he'd soon be on his way. Word was that the mayor's spot would be his in six months. After that, governor. Everyone knew it paid to be on Needham's team. If you could stand it.

Needham turned at the door of his office. "Cheese. Some kind of cheese spread. Kraft, I think."

"Nobody remembers old commercials."

"If *I* remember, then so will the sponsor. They'll dig out those old spots and swamp the state with them. I'm not selling their stuff unless they pay prime-time rates. Better keep looking for a new anchorwoman, Merv. I expect to see some new faces when I get back from Newport."

In his office Needham dropped into his chair and picked up the phone. "Jake. How's it going?"

He listened for half a minute, looking out his window at the billboard on top of the building opposite. *Tune To The America's Cup Station.* No need even to give the call letters; already, most people must imagine that the Cup was organized and run exclusively by the Needham network.

"Well, there's not much we can do about it now," he said at last. "I'll come down early and drop by the hospital."

Cradling the phone, he went to the window and looked down into the well of the city. Cars crept by in choking fumes. He found himself almost hungering for the cold, clean air of Newport.

Inch by inch, *Defiant*'s mast was lifted from the deck. It swayed over the heads of Jake and the workshop foreman as the yard crew, working with an improvised block and tackle, swung it towards the gang waiting to manhandle it into the shop.

"Better check everything, Bill. I want to know if the sail blowing up had anything to do with the winches or the tackle. Maybe we've just got a sprung wire."

One strand unwinding from a worn cable could rip a sail to shreds, even slash through flesh. But Jake didn't seriously believe a cable was responsible for what happened out on the Sound.

"You want me to save the sail?"

"What's left of it." A Kevlar sail once worth $25,000 was now so much scrap, but the shredded remains might tell them something.

The foreman headed towards the shop. Jake stayed on the dock, looking down at the abandoned, dismasted *Defiant*. She looked like a derelict, all defiance gone. Slipping into the cockpit, he ran his hand over the dark smears on the coaming where some of Keble's blood still remained. It had dried hard.

One of the yard gang came out of the shop. "Mr. Forrester? You got a minute?"

He went inside, under the harsh yellow work lights, and saw the whole crew gathered around one section of the mast. He was peering in surprise at their discovery when he heard the unmistakable roar of Sam Lewis's car outside. Sam was climbing out of the battered red Camaro. He looked bleak.

"How is he?"

Sam silently handed him a sheet of paper—a xeroxed admission sheet from the Naval Regional Medical Center. "I figured you wouldn't believe it unless I showed you in black and white."

Jake took the paper and nodded over his shoulder. "Take a look at the mast if you want to see something really weird."

He read the hospital report with growing disbelief and went back inside. Sam looked up from the gleaming inch-long gouge on the metal of the mast. "So now we know. An exploded 'chute, a lump blown out of a magensium mast, and a crewman with a bullet in his brain. Some shithead took a shot at us."

"That's crazy."

"Not really. Fishing boats carry .30-30s sometimes. For sharks. It could have been some nut with a telescopic sight."

Jake replayed in his mind the last moment before the sail blew. He'd been rounding the buoy, his mind on the boat alone. But for an instant he'd looked up to check the progress of the wave behind them, and his eyes had automatically swept the horizon.

It was a clear, cloudless day. Visibility was good, more than five miles. Well beyond any rifle shot.

Except for *Defiant*'s tender, there hadn't been another boat in sight.

For twenty minutes after *Defiant* and the tender headed back towards Newport, Marie-Ange remained behind the buoy, clinging to the anchor cable.

She wore a full-length wet suit and a mask. Even if someone did spot her, she would be unidentifiable.

From time to time, she hauled herself out of the water onto the slick neoprene surface of the buoy and searched the horizon. Nothing. When she was sure nobody had been sent out to look for her, she took a bearing from the big scuba diver's compass on her wrist, kicked away from the buoy, and swam in a steady crawl due west.

After two hundred strokes, she trod water and took another bearing, then slipped the mask over her face and dived.

Visibility was good in the top fifteen feet of the water, sunlight slanting down through the green. She saw the Laser at once, hovering just two yards beneath the surface, hull uppermost, the mast and rigging dangling below like the tendrils of a gigantic jellyfish. Most fiberglass boats have good buoyancy; even when swamped, they'll float, though very low in the water. Air-filled buoyancy chambers inside the hull keep them riding high enough to sail in, but if those chambers are punctured and filled with water, the boat will be dragged beneath the surface by the weight of its metal mast.

Marie-Ange swam down and surfaced under the up-turned boat, where a shallow pocket of air remained trapped. Almost level with her face were the two tiny tanks of compressed CO_2, linked by copper tubing to the punctured air chambers. She turned the wheel on the end of each tank; gas hissed into the flooded tanks; water gushed out through the one-way valves she had fitted to the carefully drilled holes. The boat began to rise above her, bobbing back to the surface like a fishing float.

When the hiss of gas replaced the gush of water from the tanks, she closed off the valves on the gas tanks, ducked from under the boat, and surfaced in the sunlight. Anyone seeing her now would take her for yet another amateur sailor who had toppled her boat; the Laser was popular as a learner's boat because of its virtual unsinkability.

Slithering up onto the hull, she reached under the water, grabbed the underwater edge of the hull, and threw herself backwards. Fighting the weight of the mast and rigging, the boat reluctantly turned on its side. She grabbed and heaved again, and the Laser was back on an even keel, mast glistening and dripping in the sun. Climbing in, she pulled off her rubber helmet and shook out her hair. Then she unzipped the front of her wet suit.

An awkward-looking short-barreled gun lay between her small breasts—a Smith and Wesson .38 remounted on a .44 frame. It had given her a maximum hitting power for what she had known would be a difficult shot. It had finally taken three shots, one of which missed altogether as the buoy on which she rested the pistol jerked in an unexpected swell. But the second shot was fired as *Defiant* rounded the buoy, canting its deck towards her and opening up the whole central well to her view, with the crew laid out like ducks in a shooting gallery. It had struck the mast and fragmented, sending a scrap of the bullet through the spinnaker. Keble half-stood and looked around; had he heard the shots? If so, it was the last thing he ever did hear, because she had actually seen the spurt of blood as the third bullet took him under the ear.

The gun had done a good job, but she spared no sentiment on it as she disassembled it into a dozen pieces, dropping them one by one into the green water.

The double polyethylene bag fastened inside the hull with waterproof tape had behaved equally efficiently; the clothes inside were bone dry. She skinned off the wet suit, toweled her naked body dry with the terrycloth shirt and shorts, put them on, and used the bag to bail out the pool of water lying in the bottom of the boat.

There was a southeast breeze, usual for Newport at this time of year. Dropping the centerboard, she ran up the tiny sail, turned the tiller, and headed towards the distant smear of Newport.

Jake had driven back towards the team headquarters in confusion. He hadn't rung Elaine; he'd found it hard enough to talk to the crew and the police. Thank God Sam headed them off with some double-talk about a fragment of metal flying off the spinnaker pole. Nobody would be fooled for very long, but Tom Needham was coming up early, and he could deal with it. It was the kind of thing he handled effortlessly.

Who would want to shoot at them? Surely nobody could want to win the America's Cup *that* much? It was a game—a pastime for the rich, in which millionaires competed for an ugly, old-fashioned silver trophy they couldn't keep and didn't want. People like Jake and Sam were hired mercenaries, pawns in the game. They could be fired and disciplined, offered inducements and tempted by the power of the big syndicates, but they were never injured, never killed. That wasn't . . . gentlemanly. And yet . . .

Jake had stopped at a light on Bellevue Avenue. For the first time, he took in his surroundings: the wide, tree-lined streets, the mansions with their trimmed lawns. Just visible over the trees, between him and the ocean, stood the bulk of The Breakers, where tonight's ball would be held for racers and backers, the high point of Newport's social season.

There was nothing sentimental about those houses that lined Bellevue Avenue all the way along Cliff Walk; they'd been built by men who wanted to make money more than they wanted to be loved or respected. Corsairs and pirates, ruthless and grasping—no different from the men who backed big-time yacht racing. What if one of the gentlemen had opted out of the gentlemen's agreement? All that money and power, harnessed to Jake's benefit, could open any door, smooth any path. But it could just as easily close doors and end lives.

And if the rules were suspended? Then he was vulnerable to anyone who could be bought. At that moment a sniper might have the cross hairs of a telescopic sight trained on the back of his skull.

His jack-rabbit start as the light changed left two smoking streaks of rubber across the intersection. He was still jumpy as he parked the car in front of the house at Hazard's Beach. His was the only car in the lot; everyone else must be either at the yard or with Sam at the medical center, waiting for news. He poured himself a stiff high-ball, ignoring the injunction on top of the cabinet, and sat down facing the sea. It was late afternoon; belatedly, he remembered his date to see Elaine before the ball. He would have to call—but not just yet. He took a stiff belt of the whiskey and tried to concentrate.

Someone *had* shot at them. It was no use taking refuge in theories about loose bits of metal and unlinked spin-naker poles. The evidence was overwhelming that *Defiant* had been the target of a sniper. And, Jake guessed, a sniper who fired more than once; no bullet could have struck both the mast and Charlie.

Who had he been shooting at? Not at Jake. Standing in the cockpit, glued to the big wheel, he had made an easy target. No, it did not take a genius to put together Keble's nervous phone call of that morning, his need to talk with Jake, and his subsequent shooting. Charlie had known he was marked. Perhaps if he had taken the time to talk to him that morning . . . Jake put the thought out of his mind. In any event, it was too late now. The damage was done.

But by whom? And how? Jake had no answers. Only a gnawing sense that this was no isolated incident.

A phone shrilled downstairs. When nobody answered, Jake picked up the extension.

"Is everyone crazy?" It was Elaine. She sounded angry. "I've been ringing all over for you, Jake. The yard. The Deepwater office. Nobody knows where you are: Nobody knows where *anyone* is."

Jake ran his hand through his hair. "We had an accident. Out on the Sound. Charlie Keble was hurt. The rest of the guys are at the medical center with him. I suppose the office didn't want to say too much in case you were press."

Elaine's next question came after such a long pause that Jake thought they had been cut off. "What happened?" She sounded stiff—in other circumstances he would have said frightened.

"Well . . . someone took a shot at us, looks like. We don't know how. Maybe with some sort of high-velocity rifle from the shore, though God knows how they could manage that. Maybe from a fishing boat . . . we just don't know."

"How . . . how is Charlie?"

"Head wound. That's all I could get out of them." He frowned. "Did you *know* Charlie? For some reason I thought you'd never met him."

Her response was furious. "Do I have to *know* someone to be sorry he's shot? It could have been Sam or Christie or any of you; it could . . . oh, for Christ's sake." She was sobbing as the phone slammed down.

Jake stared at the phone for a second, rattled the instrument to get a line, and dialed the Treadway. They rang Elaine's room twice but nobody answered.

CHAPTER FIVE

In 1892 the Lorillards' summer cottage on Cliff Walk burned to the ground in a blaze that lit up most of the island. Cornelius Vanderbilt bought the ruin, and in less than three years, his Paris-trained architect Richard Morris Hunt rebuilt The Breakers as the grandest mansion on Bellevue Avenue, a monument in fireproof steel and Indiana limestone to the glory of the Vanderbilts.

Jealous of his competitors among the millionaires of Newport, he brought in furniture makers and decorators from Italy and France, locked them in the house, and kept them there for the months needed to create a degree of luxury impressive even to the Astors and the Oelrichs. For one brief decade, The Breakers inhabited the pinnacle of ostentatious luxury, and inhabited it alone.

Like all the so-called cottages, Vanderbilt's showplace outlasted the society that built it and the fortune it celebrated. By 1940 it was a shuttered relic. In 1948 it passed to the Newport Preservation Society, which restored it lovingly to its original opulence. Now, by day, The Breakers belonged to the tourists. Blue-rinsed matrons led them in discreet parties across the Carrara marble floors, encouraging them to admire the bronze chandeliers, the Boulle cabinets, and the Louis XIV furniture. In one of the sixty bedrooms in the house, the guide paused respectfully to indicate the custom-made beds, the heavy linen bedding, the private bathrooms with three taps above each bath—fresh hot water, fresh cold water, and salt.

But every third year the rich reclaimed The Breakers. The chairs and tables of the Preservation Society were cleared from the main foyer, the racks of postcards and brochures stored away. The seven-ton wrought-iron gates of the thirty-foot-high main entrance creaked open. Lawns were trimmed; new gravel spread on the drive.

Down in Newport, dukes, princesses, and the occasional king came ashore at Bannister's Wharf from the big yachts moored out in the bay, the women lifting their hems away from the tar on the wooden dock. Men with snow tans and men with boardroom pallors leaned together and talked quietly about money as their Rolls Royces and Mercedes Benzes carried them smoothly through town, up Mill and Pelham, to turn into Bellevue and head for the lights filling the velvet sky.

The three-story Romanesque frontage was floodlit. Passing under the arches and colonnades, they strolled inside, where the fountain bubbled under the huge double marble staircase and an orchestra played discreetly in one of the dozen anterooms. They wandered on the mock-Roman mosaic patio under the painted awning of blue and gold and looked out towards the ocean. Lawns as smooth as green baize swept to Cliff Walk, and the sea beyond shimmered like hammered emerald.

It was nice to be back, they thought.

Jake turned through the gates and cruised slowly along the path, looking for a parking spot between the Continentals and Lancias and Mercedeses. Out of the corner of his eye, he shot a glance at Elaine, sitting pale and silent beside him.

"See anyplace we can squeeze in?"

She shook her head. When he had arrived at the hotel, she had been dressed and ready to leave. Since then, she had said less than a dozen words to Jake. It was like the aftermath of a ferocious domestic argument without the argument. When he had rung the hospital and repeated to her the nurse's news that Keble's condition was stable but unchanged, she had just turned away.

He finally found a spot under a big chestnut tree, too small for the big cars but just about right for his hired Plymouth. He nosed in and turned off the engine.

"Well, are we going to this party, or do we sit here and talk this out?"

For her answer, Elaine slid out of the car, yanking her

wrap from the back seat. Reluctantly, Jake climbed out too.

"Elaine . . ."

Heavy tires crunched on the gravel. A huge maroon car rolled past them. Jake saw red and white Maryland tags and the familiar plate—TOM III. Too late for talk now.

Tom climbed out of the back seat of the burgundy Rolls Royce Phantom VI; to Jake it looked as roomy as a railway compartment. Already Needham was traveling in presidential style.

"Elaine! Jake! What a superb reception committee." He kissed Elaine's cheek, looked from her stiff face to Jake. "Uh, did I interrupt something?"

"I don't think either of us are in the mood for this thing."

"The guests of honor? You could hardly *not* show up, Jake. Anything I can do? Elaine, would you like to rest a while in the car? There's quite a good bar in the back of the seat."

Elaine pulled the wrap around her bare shoulders. "I'm fine. Jake exaggerates, as usual." She linked her arm in Needham's. "You know how to show a lady a good time, Tom. I feel like dancing, all of a sudden."

Needham looked over his shoulder with a smile of amused resignation as Elaine steered him towards the house and the pool of glaring light around the entrance. Jake knew with a sinking feeling in his stomach that this indicated the presence of TV cameras. He was in no mood to give interviews tonight.

Someone honked at him. Realizing he was standing in the middle of the drive, he stepped aside and let the new arrival go by, obscurely pleased that his car would not now be the least opulent in the lot. The brown Pinto with one plate hanging by a single bolt and a deep scratch down the passenger side made his look almost acceptable.

The girl who climbed out didn't bother to lock the door. Only half-concentrating, Jake watched her stop a few yards from him, looking, as he was, at the main entrance with the same diffidence.

She was short; probably only a kid. The light from the

lamp, half-hidden in the big chestnut, threw a fretted screen of illumination over both of them. Of her, it revealed only glittering highlights in black and blue. As his eyes grew accustomed to the strange pattern of light, he saw that the blue was a skintight evening dress in a waxy wet-look fabric that clung to a body as smoothly streamlined as a seal's. Her tiny breasts hardly interrupted the line from scooped neck to hem.

The black was her hair. It streamed down her back like a tide of molasses, so featureless he decided it was still wet from shower or swim until she turned her head suddenly in his direction and it swung lazily, a mane of jet.

"Are you going in?" she asked.

"I'm thinking about it."

"Are you by yourself?"

"It seems like it. Actually, my wife has gone on ahead with a friend."

"I don't much care to go through that crowd by myself. No particular reason, but I'd be more comfortable with an escort."

"You wouldn't be crashing, by any chance?"

She held her hand out towards him, palm up, showing her wrist; an invitation card was clipped inside a bracelet. He realized she carried no handbag.

"Sorry. I'll be glad to . . ." He took her hand and turned it to the light to read the name on the card: Miss K. Ryker. Close up, her face had a beguiling animal liveliness; she looked at least half fox cub. Or, with that hair, otter, mink, seal. "*K*—Karen? Kathleen?"

"Kimberley. Kim."

"I'm Jake Forrester."

She stared up at him. "God, so you are. I've never seen you in anything but pea jacket, Decksiders, and slacks. Look"—she shook off his hand—"I'm way out of my league. I thought you were just some crewman in a rented dinner jacket. I'm sorry, Mr. Forrester."

Jake grabbed her hand again, slipped it inside the loop of his arm. "I *am* just some crewman in a rented dinner jacket. And that's Jake, Kim."

They strolled towards the entrance. Jake waved to a few acquaintances following the same path. Nobody came over to talk; he wondered what they were saying behind his back.

"I know why *I'm* here," he said, "but what does the America's Cup Ball offer a girl like you?"

"Ask my father." She sounded sour. Jake ran through the list of people associated with the Cup and finally came up with a Ryker among the skippers of American boats who had competed unsuccessfully with *Defiant* for the right to defend against *Victorious*.

"He owns . . . what is it? *Expeditious?*"

"Sometimes I wonder if it doesn't own him. That boat costs more than a penthouse apartment on Central Park West."

"He sailed well," Jake lied. Kim looked up at him. Her gaze was disarmingly direct and challenging. "All right," he amended, "he made some mistakes. We all do."

"He can't afford to. Oh, he deserves his hobby, I know that. I love to sail. But when it becomes a business, not a sport, all the fun goes out of it. I don't think he's enjoyed one minute of this Cup. It's all show, all advertising. He even came along early to the ball to catch people before the crowds arrived."

"If that's why we met, I'm glad he did." They were on the fringe of the TV lights now. The antenna of an ENG outfit was perched on the roof of an OB van parked by the kitchen entrance. Tom Needham waited calmly on the edge of a small group of people watched over by an assistant director with a clipboard and ear-mike, while a stocky gray-haired man in a blue NYYC blazer interviewed Armand de Jussac, the French skipper of *France IV,* in front of the cameras.

Kim followed his gaze. "I guess we aren't going to make it."

"I guess not." The assumption that he would not dare to refuse an interview with Billy Weems, ABC's biggest sports commentator, irritated Jake, but it was based on fact. Some degree of public exposure came with the territory; it was the part of being a Cup skipper Jake disliked most.

Kim walked towards the door, skirting the knot of celebrities, then looked back. "Maybe we'll get to have a dance?"

"I'm not much of a dancer."

"It's never too late to learn."

"Thanks for the offer. I'll keep it in mind."

"I wasn't really offering. But do keep it in mind." She disappeared beyond the glaring lights.

The TV assistant spotted him as he joined Needham and scribbled his name on the clipboard. "Billy'll be through in a minute. Would you like to stand here, please, Mr. Forrester?"

"Who was *that?*" Needham said at his elbow. "Don't tell me you're into nymphets now."

"She's Ryker's daughter," Jake said, momentarily sorry he had let her go in alone. He looked towards the crowd milling by the door, but there was no sign of the electric-blue dress. "Where is Elaine, anyway?"

"Taakinnen took her in. Have you two had a spat or something? She's in a poisonous mood."

"There's *something* on her mind. God knows what. She seemed very upset about Charlie." The incidents of the afternoon suddenly returned to his mind in all their vividness. "Did you see him? How is he?"

Needham glanced around. "Not really the time or place, Jake."

Jake felt his temper slipping. Weems was beaming at the camera, showing off his carefully tended tan. He fancied himself a yachtsman and ran a huge yawl, to which he threatened to retreat every time the network refused a salary hike. It was an open secret that Weems himself could not negotiate the mile-wide entrance to Newport Harbor without radar, a sailing master, and a six-man crew.

"I don't think I can take this clown tonight. Let's go in."

Needham frowned. "He isn't my favorite person either, Jake, but we need him. The sponsors don't give us all that help because of our big blue eyes. They want exposure.

"Not with Charlie lying down there in hospital. For

Christ's sake, Tom, there has to be *something* we won't
do for money.''

Needham was silent for a moment. Then he said,
"You're right, of course. I shouldn't have pressed the
point. Jake, I apologize. Wait here a moment."

Jake watched him chat quietly with the director, smile,
squeeze his arm. What was he offering him? Probably an
exclusive after the first race on Friday. He came back.
"All fixed."

Crowds milled inside the double doors. There was no
sign of Elaine, nor—Jake was embarrassed to notice that
he was looking—of Kim Ryker either. They were suddenly the center of a gabbling, beaming, handshaking
crowd; flashes exploded in their faces as guests who had
smuggled in cameras grabbed their own private memen-
tos. Jake grabbed Needham's sleeve and leaned close to
his ear.

"We have to talk about this afternoon," he bawled, his
voice lost in the babble. Needham nodded and guided
him inch by inch towards the uniformed marshal standing
against the wall of the foyer.

"Mr. Forrester and I need to have a short private conference. Is there someplace we can go?"

"Sure, Mr. Needham." He indicated a small mahogany
door with a wrought-iron grille. "Private elevator. Leads
up to the mezzanine. Nobody up there yet. You'll be
okay."

"Thanks." They squeezed into the tiny cubicle, designed for some forgotten and infirm Vanderbilt too
weary from high living to ascend the marble staircases.
Even this elevator was a microcosm of the millionaire
life: rosewood paneling, a folding seat upholstered in rich
hide, porcelain-topped buttons to call for help if it was
needed. It seemed to ascend without motion, and when
they stepped out onto the mezzanine that ran all around
the main ballroom, it was as if they remained in the
world of eighty years ago. Below them light from the
crystal chandeliers flamed on diamonds and decorations,
stiff white shirtfronts, and golden breasts. Teddy Roose-
velt was president; one almost expected to see the toothy
grin, the bushy moustache, the glinting pince-nez.

"Did you go to the hospital?" Jake asked.

"He died while I was there, Jake."

Jake felt numb.

"There wasn't much they could do. Massive trauma; the bullet hit the mastoid bones. Fragments right through the brain. He never woke up."

"What happens now?"

"I talked to the police. They'll keep it as quiet as they can. A murder in Cup week, with all these tourists around, makes the place look bad. But we can expect some problems when they hold the inquest. I'll look after his family. Did you ever meet any relatives?"

"I hardly knew him. And what about afterwards? Aren't you curious about what really happened?"

"Yes. Curious, but not obsessively. They'll probably decide it was a random shot from some fishing boat."

"There *weren't* any fishing boats, Tom!"

"I didn't say I believe it—just that it will probably be their decision. Police don't have a lot of imagination."

"What's your theory?"

"I don't have one. If you want, I can come up with half a dozen possible culprits. But what's the point, Jake? It's done. Charlie's dead."

Jake remembered Keble's desperate phone call; his own failure to see the urgency and make time for him. "I won't leave it there," he said savagely.

Needham stared at him for twenty seconds—so long that Jake wondered if he was being challenged by the silence to do just as he threatened. Then Tom said, "All right. Let's review the possibilities." He looked down into the crowd. "We're ideally situated to do that, in fact. Most of the suspects are down there tonight."

Jake looked over the milling mass of guests: millionaires, distinguished yachtsmen, sailors like himself, diplomats, wives, mistresses, and daughters. Which of them had decided to breach the gentlemen's agreement?

The chatter below rose a few decibels. People gathered around a new party pushing in from the main doors. Jake thought he glimpsed Elaine's green silk dress among the crowd, then lost it. He was more interested in the tall, lanky man with a disordered mop of hair at the center of the new group. Tony Stephens, captain of the British challenger, *Victorious*.

"There's a suspect for you," Needham said quietly.

"Tony? You're kidding!" Stephens was an old friend. They'd partied together at Cowes, crewed together on pleasure trips, been friendly rivals on the Admiral's Cup and the Fastnet. Tony was Petey's godfather.

"Who has a better motive? He's your only opponent."

"It was Charlie Keble who got shot, not me."

"So he hired an incompetent hit man. It happens."

Jake forced himself to see Tony Stephens as something other than an old friend, a fellow yachtsman. Could Charlie's death be the result of a random shot? It would make sense of some things; for instance, the second—and third—shots he suspected had scarred the mast and blown the spinnaker. And Tony had been absent from Newport all day—less than three days before the crucial first race with *Defiant*.

Grudgingly Jake acknowledged, "I suppose it's possible. But why? Does he want to win that badly?"

"It isn't just the race—it's the spinoffs. How successful would your marina be if you weren't the top twelve-meter skipper in the country? Don't you think it helps me to be head of the *Defiant* syndicate? In the stock market and the boardroom, these things *matter*, Jake."

And at Democratic National Headquarters, Jake added privately. Out loud, he said, "But Tony's rich. He doesn't need money."

"Don't be so sure. He's on the board of something called Anglo-Scottish Shipbuilders. They're looking for contracts to build service ships for the North Sea oil fields. All his capital's sunk in that, plus a bit more besides. He's been working on Karl O'Neal to come in with him. If he needs to squeeze money from that old shark, you can be sure he's already tried all the softer options."

Jake shook his head. This picture of Stephens hardly agreed with what he knew of the man—friendly, easygoing, even soft in some ways. He remembered birthdays, sent amusing postcards in the long periods when they didn't meet, acted in every way as a true friend. "I don't believe it. Not Tony."

"Neither do I, to tell the truth. I'm just trying to open your eyes to the possibilities." Needham's eyes swept the crowd again. "What about your girlfriend's father?" He made a sorrowful *tch* sound. "Where did he get that dinner jacket? J.C. Penney?"

Jake saw Kim Ryker before her father. She stood, almost obscured by him, as he harangued Aaron Hart, the race committee chairman. For a moment, he tried to make out more of her than the fragment of blue dress, then turned his eyes reluctantly to the short, swarthy, sweaty man to whom Hart was doing his best to be polite. His thin, pale face, however, was set in an expression that Jake knew well—it was the polite, almost amused contempt of the old boat world face to face with the new.

"*Expeditious* went out in the first round."

"Indeed. Then Ryker's got nothing to gain from shooting at us."

"Maybe not. But think about this. What happens if *Defiant* drops out before the defense—because the boat's damaged or you're hurt?"

"Someone else takes over, I guess. Sam. Or you."

"Not necessarily. There aren't any precedents. The committee might decide to hold a rerun among the other competitors. *Expeditious* could have a second chance. Maybe that's what Ryker is talking to Aaron about right now—checking out the possibilities."

Ryker suddenly half-turned to grab a glass of champagne from the tray of a passing waiter. Jake saw Kim, looking bored, even angry. Consciously, he looked away, aware that the girl was beginning to exert an almost magnetic effect on him.

"What about motive? What's the dirt on him?"

Needham looked pained. "Don't blame me if I keep tabs on my opposition. This isn't just a sport to me, Jake. A lot's riding on this tie."

"Sorry. But there *is* dirt, I assume?"

"Everyone's in *some* kind of trouble. Ryker runs an electronics company in Los Angeles. Microchips. That's like a gold rush. The word is, he's overextended; pretty desperate for cash."

Jake tried to penetrate the gleaming face for some sign of the underlying character but failed. He looked like every other businessman he'd met: too glib, too eager, a good man to pass the time of day with at a party or share

a couple of drinks with in the first-class lounge of a New
York to Los Angeles flight, but nothing more than that.
These men were as uniform as Detroit cars.

"All right. I'll buy Ryker. What do we do next? Call
the cops?"

Needham held up his hand as if to restrain him.
"Whoa! I didn't say he did it—I just put him up as a
possibility. We haven't even got to *my* personal favorite
yet." Leaning over the balustrade, he looked down and
drew Jake to the edge. "Right under us."

Though the rest of the floor was crowded and people
were already wandering up onto the mezzanine, the little
group below them had carved out a private piece of territory that gave ample space to the single man who stood
inside the carefully casual ring of seven helpers. Jake did
not even need to see his face; the formulation was familiar from countless receptions and televised press
conferences.

So was Takeo Fujita. Almost as if he knew he was
being watched, he lifted his head, and Jake saw the familiar bristly white hair, the square skull, the ridges
above the eyes that gave him a permanent angry stare.
He wore a superbly tailored dinner jacket that did not
hide a brutally efficient body—a wrestler's shoulders, a
strangler's wrists and hands.

If you bought a TV, a radio, an electronic game, a
digital watch, a pocket calculator, a videodisc, a record
album or tape, a sonar outfit for your boat, or a computer to run your bank, you had probably made Takeo
Fujita a little richer. Tora, his conglomerate, dominated
the electronics market worldwide.

And Fujita was likely to be in any newspaper you
opened; *People* was tired of recording his activities, and
Time's personalities page treated his multitude of purchases and endowments as a joke. Fujita seemed to be
everywhere; at one of his many houses—Maui, Boca
Raton, Sloane Square, Gramercy Park, his penthouse on
the Tora Building high above Tokyo. He bought things—
a bank or a Braque, the oldest Bentley still running or
the newest communications satellite channel. Lately,
he'd bought boats. Twelves, mostly. In one, *Tora Queen,*
he had won the newly inaugurated Atlantic Race for the

fastest trip from New York to London, coasting into the Solent half a day ahead of his nearest rival.

Jake could entertain the prospect of Fujita plotting against *Defiant*'s defense; it would fit in with the Japanese entrepreneur's known business methods, largely based on conspiracy, double-dealing, and the principle of divide and rule. Nobody knew quite what Fujita owned or where his interest would come to rest next.

"I don't necessarily agree with you, Tom, but for the sake of argument, why should *he* of all people try to put us out of the race?"

"Simple enough. *Defiant* loses, *Victorious* gets the Cup. And however highly you think of Tony Stephens, we both agree he isn't the best skipper in the world. Fujita could easily beat him. . . ."

"So he gets the Cup in three years' time."

"It's possible."

Jake looked down at the mass of people crowded on the dance floor. Fujita's group had disappeared in the crush. Suddenly Jake had no more patience for the deviousness Tom had outlined. He needed to think things out.

"I have to get out of here."

"Aren't you supposed to reply to Stephens's speech?"

"You do it. That's your line of country."

"If you insist." He patted Jake's arm like an elderly uncle. "Everything will look better in the morning."

"It had better."

Downstairs, Jake found Elaine at the center of an attentive group and led her away. "We're going home."

"We only just arrived." He'd expected her to protest, but except for this mild resistance, she let herself be steered into the foyer. They separated there, Elaine to get her wrap, Jake to fidget, unable to fight down an unclassifiable feeling of alarm.

"Jake! Not leaving already?"

Tony Stephens was loping towards him. The tall Englishman looked more like a shirt ad than ever. As he held out his hand, Jake wondered, as he always did when seeing Tony, how one man could always look so goddam neat.

"Sorry, Tony. Something I have to look after."

"Can't it wait until tomorrow?" He looked around. "This is supposed to be neutral ground. The only good thing about the ball is the chance it gives old friends to chat. I came back from New York especially."

From the corner of his eye, Jake saw Elaine slip out of the cloakroom. She held up one white-gloved hand with the car keys dangling from her forefinger and slipped through the front door.

"Tony, I'd like to but . . ."

"Let's have a drink at least." He stopped a waiter and took two glasses.

Jake glanced at the door. Elaine had gone. The same whisper of alarm tugged at his consciousness, but he took the glass.

"The best boat," Stephens said.

"The best boat."

They drank, and Tony looked around. "Where's Elaine? I saw her in here a moment ago."

"She's waiting for me in the car. Tony, I don't know how to apologize. We've run into something. . . . After the race, I'll be glad to tell you everything, but right now . . ."

"Anything I can do?"

"No. We'll sort it out." He looked around for somewhere to put his glass. Finally, he thrust it into the hand of a passing guest, who stared at it with distaste.

The need to get out of the building had taken on a new urgency. He could not isolate a reason. But his sixth sense nudged him as it did when a boat he was skippering carried too much sail or visibility in a fog cut his safety margin in half. Something, someplace, had begun to go terribly wrong.

In the parking lot, Elaine Forrester slid into the front seat of the rented Plymouth and fumbled for the ignition. It was dark. The big chestnut shaded the car from the yellow lamps lining the hedge.

"You all right, Jake?" Stephens frowned at his expression.

The key rattled against the stubby head of the cigarette lighter. She felt along the dashboard with her left hand, found the keyhole, and guided her other hand to it.

"Elaine?" Jake turned to the main door, half-expecting to see her standing there.

The key slid in. She felt the steering lock click open. The wheel became loose in her hand. She turned the ignition, one foot reaching for the gas pedal.

Without knowing why, Jake walked towards the door. Within two paces he was running. Guests recoiled as he shouldered past them.

He could feel it—something terrible. Something dark and deadly.

From under the hood of the car came no engine sound. Just a faint crackle, like an electric spark.

The bundle of gelignite wired to the firewall blew off Elaine Forrester's legs just below the knees and threw the rest of her body against the roof of the car. She was in shock as she rebounded from the ceiling to lie draped across the front seat, nose broken and teeth knocked out by the impact.

She had time to sense the pain and reach one hand towards her ruined face before fragments of red-hot metal from the heater fan dropped into a pool of gasoline trickling from the severed gas line. The engine cavity ignited with a whoomph, blowing open the hood. Three seconds later fire reached the main gas tank. . . .

The blast crashed against the facade of The Breakers like a trailer slamming into a brick wall.

In the center of the huge front door, a round hatch flew open, like a mouth gaping in terror. A mob of guests washed out of the house onto the drive.

From the parking lot, a pillar of flame-shot smoke climbed into the sky, glaring orange on the stone of the building and the dazed faces of the crowd.

Jake sprinted towards the flames. The car was a crumpled shape, fire pouring from its windows. The chestnut tree had been stripped of leaves by the blast. They rained down on him, crisped and blackened, mixed with cinders and twisting scraps of molten plastic.

He stopped, paralyzed, at the edge of the heat, and felt arms around him, holding him back. He struggled without knowing what he would do if they let him go. Nobody could survive that furnace.

The car next door—Tom Needham's Rolls—was smoldering, paintwork blistering and bubbling. Its windows had been blown in. Burning debris littered the huge back seat. A quarter of a million dollars of automobile began to go up in flames.

Chauffeurs scrambled out of the kitchens, struggling to reach their cars before the fire spread along the already burning hedge. Two of them gunned their engines and crashed through the hedge out onto the lawn.

"Jake? Jake Forrester?" Someone shoved a microphone in his face. He recognized the smart tan, the round complacent face. Weems.

"Just a few words, Jake." He dragged his cameraman towards him. The man automatically framed a two-shot.

Weems said quickly into the lens, "This is for news. Intro later." He turned to Jake. "Any clues, Jake, as to what might have happened here? Can you tell is if anyone was in . . ."

Jake swung from his belt. The punch took Weems on the point of the jaw. His teeth clunked together like a rabbit trap. The famous gray eyes glazed. He sagged into the arms of the man behind him.

For a moment there was only the hum of the quartz lights. Then they died, with a crackle like eggshells. Jake was alone in the dark.

CHAPTER SIX

There's peace in something as simple as shaving, a calm and order that seem eternal. In the eight months since Elaine's death, Jake had learned all there was to know about the few refuges in which peace could be found, and he inhabited them with determination.

He watched the long blade of the old cutthroat razor scrape down the face in the mirror as if the features belonged to someone else. His father, perhaps. The razor had been his. Jake had inherited it on his twenty-first birthday, had never used it but kept it honed. After Elaine's death, he took it out of the old leather case with the red plush lining, laid it on the shelf in the bathroom, and every morning thereafter carefully shaved with it— shaved himself until the skin was chafed and red from scraping.

He splashed water on his face, staring at the reflection in the mirror as if this morning the ritual might reveal something new and unexpected—another Jake Forrester. But he recognized the face well enough. It was too familiar to deserve even a smile, an old friend with whom he had shared too much to pretend.

Jake looked down at his hand, at the gleaming, open blade. Carefully he laid it on the shelf, stepped back from the basin, and dried his face and hands. Turning his back on his reflection like a murderer turning from his victim, he went downstairs to breakfast.

"Eggs?" Jean Forrester asked from the stove, not looking around. He knew she watched his reflection in the black plastic door of the microwave oven.

"Sure. Thanks." He sat down opposite his son. "Hi."

Petey looked up from the comic pages of the paper. "Hi, dad."

He went back to *Doonesbury* with exaggerated calm. Jake drank his juice, imagining Jean's sermon to her grandson when Jake returned home to Mobile the October before: *If I hear you saying one thing to upset your father, I'll send you back to the academy so quick your head'll spin.*

Anything was preferable to the discipline of military school, so around his father Petey maintained a monosyllabic politeness just short of formality. Any reference to events more than a week in the past was rigorously censored from the conversation.

Jean put down a hot plate with two fried eggs, three slices of bacon, a buttered English muffin, and a pile of grits with a pat of butter melting on top—the kind of breakfast she'd served when he came home from college. Food for a growing boy. Already he was putting on weight.

He forked up a mouthful of grits, the meal's familiarity yet another refuge. While he ate, his mind drifted. When he looked at the plate again, it was empty, but except for a full belly and grease on his lips, he had no memory of having eaten. He reached for his coffee.

"What are you doing today, Petey? Want to go downtown and shop some?"

"Sure, Dad. That'd be great."

Jean said, "I thought it was today you and Tommy Comoli were going to the movies."

"Oh. Right." Petey's face betrayed his conflicting emotions. He'd been briefed to agree with everything his father suggested. Now here was alternative programming. He looked at Jean in mute appeal.

Jake said, "We'll go shopping another day. Go to the movie."

"Dad, I'd really like . . ."

"Go to the goddam movie!"

Jake heard the crack of breaking china. Something jabbed his hand. Coffee made a spreading brown stain on the tablecloth, mixed with red where blood trickled from a gash in the base of his thumb. The cup handle still dangled from his forefinger.

"Go on, Petey." Jean leaned over the table and started wiping up. Wadding his napkin against the oozing hand, Jake stared at the table in silence until the front door closed.

"You taking the pills?"

Jake went to the sink and held his hand under the cold water. "Not any more."

"Might be a good idea if you started again."

"It'd be a lousy idea, Jean." On Valium the world receded. Everything became a refuge—and if everything was a refuge, then there was no escape from the worst moments except in more pills. Without pills, the worst of the days were made bearable by the knowledge that in shaving, eating, watching TV, he could momentarily immerse himself in the blankness of ritual.

"Better than taking it out on Petey. He doesn't know what to do to please you."

Jake inspected the cut. "Any bandages in the house?"

She turned over his hand. "Just about stopped bleeding. A Band-Aid should be enough." She competently taped the cut. Jake flexed his hand, almost relishing the pain. It parted the skin that separated him from the world. A little life slipped in.

"Why don't you go down to the bay? Carl's rung up a dozen times in the last month." Since Elaine's death, Jake had left the running of his boat business to Carl Bangsund, his foreman. As the months passed, the desire to get involved in the boat world became less and less pressing. These days, he barely thought about it.

Through the window he could see the old side yard of the house, with sumac and elder drooping after last night's rain. Between the trees Mobile Bay shone like polished tin.

A calendar hung beside the window. He glanced idly at the picture of a twelve reaching against a stiff breeze, tearing through the familiar choppy waters of some offshore sound. With a little effort, Jake could put himself on that deck, wrestling with the wheel, spray on his face, the shell of the boat thrumming as it crashed the waves. . . .

His thoughts were interrupted by two things. One was the name under the picture of the company that issued the calendar. Forrester Marine. The other was the month on the topmost leaf.

He stopped himself from asking: Is it really April?

Jean saw him looking at the calendar. "Nice picture."

"Who chose it?"

"Carl, I guess."

Eight months. Grief wasn't supposed to last this long. He'd recovered from his father's death in a day or two. No emotions marked him particularly deeply; there was always work in which to lose himself, always another boat, another race.

Perhaps that was the problem. In the notoriety of those last few days, Jake had found himself isolated; he was the man whose wife was blown to bits, whose crewman was shot; the man who knocked Billy Weems cold in a famous incident that the network, after at least five seconds of soul-searching, ran on the evening news. Weems became a national joke, the man of action laid out by an uppercut that, without the usual added sound effects of the crime shows, looked like a love tap; "One Punch Weems" made it to *National Lampoon*.

Without sailing, Jake had time to think and to remember. Wondering if the horror was still there, he recalled the worst moment of all, the identification of Elaine's body in the Providence morgue, testing the pain like an athlete leaning weight on an old injury. He closed his eyes involuntarily as the scene leaped back into his mind with the old clarity—the mangled, seared remains, scraps of green silk still glued by blood to the few areas of skin not broiled black like overcooked pork. . . .

He'd barely been able to turn away before throwing up all over the feet of the policeman. The cop never complained; like all the authorities, he had been understanding. Or perhaps he only remembered it that way, fuzzed by tranquilizers and shock. All their understanding had not stopped them from asking a lot of questions. You don't stand close to a double murder without being suspected. After a while, though, the questions stopped, and when, around Christmas, he rang the Providence police, at Jean's urging, to find out if there were any leads, it took the officer in charge a few seconds even to remember the case. Rhode Island had other murders to worry about; those of Elaine Forrester and Charlie Keble found their way into the bulging file labeled Unsolved.

Jake didn't mind them staying there. Whether or not any court would convict him, Jake knew he was responsible—morally, if not physically—for Elaine's death. If he hadn't let her go to the car first, the bomb meant for him might never have touched her.

"You want more coffee?"

"I suppose so." Jake sat at the table again. "Better put it in a tin mug."

She placed the cup in front of him. "If you can joke, you can't be too bad. Want to check on the mail while you're feeling so chipper?"

She dropped four letters by his plate. One of them was long, white, and official. Jake had not read a letter for months; all the mail was redirected to the boatyard. This would have followed the rest if Jake hadn't noticed the embossed crest on the top of the envelope. County Board of Supervisors, Middesex County, Virginia. He ripped it open.

Consequent on the rezoning of the property in this county the land known as Mooring 187 is now to be considered. . . .

He had to work through the legal language twice before its sense reached him. As it did, he felt anger eating into his calm. They were selling his land. His, and Elaine's. *Their* place.

Years before Jake got into the twelve-meter world, he and Elaine had bought a piece of land on the Rappahannock River in Virginia. Jake built a boathouse and a tiny dock, big enough to moor his old boat, *Snow Goose*. The Rappahannock mooring had been their hideaway, a weekend retreat where they could sail or sleep or enjoy themselves without having to think about the marina or Elaine's shop.

After he became involved with Tom Needham and *Defiant*, Jake had less and less time to go there. But it remained at the back of his mind, a refuge and a resource.

He handed Jean the letter. "According to this, they're rezoning our mooring. Someone wants to buy me out."

Jean wiped her hands and read it. "All double-dutch to me. I don't guess you have to sell if you don't want to."

"I sure as hell don't want to." He took the letter back. "It says they've written before. Did you see the letters?"

"I sent everything down to the yard, like you told me."

The letter mentioned decisions taken in January and February. He looked at the calendar, flexing his hand, fingering the cut on the base of thumb that had started to throb with a pain that was not entirely unpleasant.

Jean left the table and started piling plates and cups into the dishwasher, keeping her back carefully turned towards Jake. After a minute she heard the front door slam. Through the window she watched him, hands stuffed in the pockets of an old canvas jacket, walking down the street towards the distant gleam of the bay. Smiling, she poured herself a third cup of coffee and allowed herself the luxury of two spoonfuls of cream.

The yard was busy. Jake counted four big boats moored along the high pier and two more on cradles ready to be hauled into the boathouse for major overhaul. There was a crowd in the equipment shop too. He wandered down the dock, glancing into the boats as he passed. Their decks were littered with tackle, their brightwork smudged with salt and grease. It was years since he'd mixed it in this kind of tough, hard boating, where you matched your skill and strength against the only competitor that really mattered—the sea.

"Jake? That you?"

Carl Bangsund climbed up the ladder from a little yawl in the process of being remasted. Carl had been his foreman ever since he opened the yard; his leathery face and watery gray eyes made him a walking advertisement for the sailing life. It seemed more his business than Jake's, though nothing Carl said or did implied that he regarded himself as more than employee. Years before, Jake wrote into his will a clause giving Carl management of the company in the event of his death but never told him about it. Some things were all the better for being unsaid.

"I needed to see some letters."

"There's a good pile up in the office. Nice to have you back, Jake." Carl was beaming.

Without knowing whether he was back or not, Jake followed Bangsund to the office.

There was an unnatural neatness about everything there: the dusted desk, its empty trays neatly squared; the desk calendar turned to today's date, just as if he had turned it himself; and the stacked letters in the center, two heaps six inches high.

An impulse to close the door, turn his back, return to the house almost overwhelmed Jake. His hand on the doorknob was suddenly greasy with sweat. He felt his unwanted breakfast rising in his chest.

"Looks like quite a bundle."

His first step into the room was agonizing, the second bearable. The room had no memories of Elaine, no ghosts to accuse him. He peeled off his jacket and tossed it over the visitors' chair.

"Think you could find me a cup of coffee, Carl?"

"Coming right up."

When he returned, Jake had already opened four letters and was reading a fifth. He hardly noticed the cup placed at his elbow. When he did look up to taste it, it was tepid, and his watch told him, incredibly, that it was three hours since he had sat down.

A lot of the mail was junk. He soon filled the wastebasket with circulars, complimentary copies of new magazines, requests to write for or speak to someone or other.

The magazines he knew, like *Yachts and Yachting*, he put to one side, though some masochistic streak made him slide the September issue out of its brown paper wrapper and stare at the cover picture of *Defiant* balanced on the crest of a wave, surfing home in the last race of the tie, *Victorious* almost invisible on the horizon behind her.

He turned to the lead article:

OWNER NEEDHAM SKIPPERS BAD-LUCK BOAT TO VICTORY.

In the photograph under the headline, Tom Needham and Sam Lewis split a bottle of Bollinger in *Defiant*'s cockpit, the jammed crowds on Bannister's Wharf hysterical behind them.

Writing the copy, Sally Goldstone, the magazine's editor, had been as kind as possible in a world where no premium was placed on kindness.

Tragedy overshadowed the runoffs in this year's America's Cup tie, but it was a gesture in the great traditions of racing when *Defiant* syndicate head Thomas Needham III took over the running of his boat and guided her to victory in one of the most dramatic ties in the history of the America's Cup. "Jake Forrester is too old a friend," Needham told this reporter, "for me to let all his work go for nothing. He supervised every aspect of the boat, chose and trained the crew, tuned *Defiant* to racing pitch. This is his win, not mine." This week, NYYC officials were silent on their attitude towards Forrester's controversial assault on ABC sports director and this year's Murrow Award Winner, William A. (Billy) Weems . . ."

The article reminded Jake that a number of letters with the NYYC emblem remained to be opened. He sorted them into date order and read through, from "The Committee therefore formally invites you to appear and give an explanation . . ." to the final "In view of your failure to respond to our invitations and communications, we have no alternative but to suspend you forthwith. . . ."

Jake knew an appearance, an apology would have placated them, but three months ago the energy had not existed to offer that, and now it was too late. But he was surprised at his own indifference to the suspension. The letters from the Middlesex supervisors worried him far more.

He read and reread them, trying to extract some sense from the formal language. Something about the whole correspondence *smelled* wrong. But that might be more paranoia, more guilt.

Shoving the letters into his pocket, he sorted hurriedly through the rest. Most were business—bank statements, reminders of meetings now long past. One registered envelope contained a safe-deposit key from the bank downtown and a covering letter explaining that locks were being changed, asking him to return his old key in the postpaid envelope. He was trying to wrestle his old key from the ring on his key wallet when someone knocked on the door leading from his room into the noisy business office. Tilly Tandy, who kept the books, looked around the door.

"Mind if I ask you a few things, Mr. Forrester?"

"No. Come on in, Tilly." Jake gave up trying to force the old key off the ring and slipped on the new one, leaving the other still in place.

It took half an hour to clear up Tilly's problems. Afterwards, he needed air. He left the office and walked down the dock.

A stiff breeze blew off the land. It buffeted his jacket and rattled the rigging against the metal masts of the boats docked below him. A steady chop marched across the bay, chipping the gray water with white.

He came to the end. A sailing dinghy rocked at its mooring, paint job crisp and new, the canvas cover still drawn over its well. One of the old car tires used as fenders had worked loose, and a black smear already marked the new paint. Climbing down, Jake wrenched the fender back in place.

For the first time in eight months, he felt a deck under his feet. The boat quivered with an urgent life of its own. On impulse, Jake popped the fasteners on the cover, rolled it back, and slipped into the well. The trapped tang of resin, oil, and canvas billowed up. Almost without willing it, he unfurled the tight white mainsail from the boom and hauled it up the mast.

An hour later, Carl Bangsund stood on the end of the dock, watching Jake maneuver the dinghy back alongside. When it came within a few feet of the ladder, Bangsund climbed down and caught the mooring rope. Jake clambered out. His face was red with windburn, his windbreaker soaked.

"Wondered where she'd got to. Thought maybe Petey took her out."

Jake glanced back at the dinghy. "This Petey's boat?"

"Uh huh. He got her kind of banged up in that squall late in the summer. We cleaned her up for him."

Forcing himself not to ask: What squall? Jake secured the sail and dragged the cover back into place. There would be time to ask Petey about recent history when they had established a relationship again.

"Miz' Forrester rang. Said you got a visitor."

For an instant, Jake experienced the pang of remembering Elaine; Jean was the only Mrs. Forrester now.

"Better get up there, I guess."

"You look froze. Should I get you some clothes from the shop?"

Jake flexed his arms. After only an hour of sailing, he was stiff. The muscles just weren't there anymore.

"I guess I'll jog a bit. I need loosening up."

He trotted down the dock. By the time he reached land, he was running.

Jean looked out the window.

"Here he comes. Running! You should have seen him the last three months. Couldn't get a walk out of him with a pointed stick."

The door slammed. Jake stumbled, panting, into the kitchen and slumped into a chair.

"You bucking for a heart attack or something?"

Jake blinked away the sweat and for the first time took in the stocky figure sitting over a can of beer at the kitchen table.

"Sam!"

"I been meaning to look in," he said. "Just happened to be down here this week, so I rang Jean. She said you were sitting up and taking nourishment, so I got over here to see how the old boy was doing."

"Old boy?" Jake faked a punch. He was too weak to reach across the table. "Jean, has he drunk all of those?"

She put a can of Coors on the table. Jake tore off the tab and drank half of it in a swallow. His heart was pounding. His hands hurt from the ropes of the dinghy, and sweat soaked everything he wore.

"You really look great," Sam said sarcastically. "Glad I got here in time. You won't last until nightfall."

"I just took Petey's dinghy out on the bay. An hour wrecked me. I need to get back in shape."

"Come up and stay with me. I've got a place at Virginia Beach. Just outside town. Slipway, workshop, lots of bedrooms. Couple of weeks there'll do you good."

Jean said, "It wouldn't hurt you to get away, Jake. Maybe I could get the house clean again."

Jake felt in the back pocket of his trousers for a letter he'd taken from the pile in his office. It was crumpled and waterstained.

"I got this at the yard. It's about the shack down on the river."

"What about it?" Sam said.

"They're going to rezone the land. They want to buy me out."

"Not much you can do about it, buddy. The government's got us all where the sun don't shine."

"I'm not going to give the place up just like that. I think I'll go up there and crack a few heads."

Jean said, "There's plenty to do here, if you're looking for work."

Jake could almost see her mind working. To spend a week or two with Sam was fine, but *Snow Goose* and the Rappahannock were reminders of Elaine. Oddly, Jake felt that was hardly true. The mooring had always meant more to him than to Elaine. And an hour out on the bay had put him back in touch with the world that the mooring represented—one where things he did mattered only to him, where responsibility receded and left only the problems of personal survival.

"Where are the deeds to that place anyway?"

Jean said, "I guess in the bank." She sounded grudging.

Sam seemed to catch her mood. "Jake, forget about it. I'm driving back up to Virginia Beach today. It's my birthday on Sunday. We can tie one on, maybe get a few of the guys to come down."

Jake considered. Virginia Beach wasn't far from Norfolk. He could rent a car and drive up in a few hours to the Rappahannock.

"When are you leaving?"

"Any time. Right now, if you like."

Jake stood up. "Okay. You convinced me. I'll just go pack a bag."

Jake put a change of clothing, heavy boots, and a toothbrush into a carryall. In the bathroom his hand hovered over the old straight razor. Then he went to the cupboard, rummaged for a battery-operated electric razor, and dropped it in with the clothes. The need for ritual seemed past.

Sam was waiting for him at the bottom of the stairs. Jake went into the kitchen.

"Look after Petey for me, Jean."

"And you look after yourself." She wiped her hands, took one of his between them. "You sure you're up to this?"

"Only one way to find out."

"Yes. I suppose. Back on Monday?"

"Back on Monday. Or I'll call."

"See you do."

Sam and Jake went outside into the bluster of the early afternoon. For the first time, Jake noticed the car standing opposite the house. A sand-colored Mercedes.

"This isn't *your* car?"

"Sure. Why the hell not?"

Sam's bankruptcy was legendary. What he didn't spend on horses and poker, he drank or gave away. For as long as Jake had known him, Sam's cars betrayed his chaotic financial situation.

"Business must be good," Jake said, sliding into the front seat, feeling solid hide under him.

"Hotter than a firecracker. They line to wipe my ass. Building *Defiant* didn't hurt my reputation one little bit."

The car accelerated smoothly away from the house and headed downtown.

"So . . . what's new?"

"In the business? Same old stuff. The Japs are very big. Fujita's been cleaning up with this *Tora Queen* of his. Fastnet. Pacific Conference. Hot boat."

"What do you hear from Tom Needham?"

"Tom's around." Sam sounded guarded. "Very high profile just now. Mayor of Baltimore soon, they say."

"That won't satisfy Tom, will it?"

"I hear he's got the governorship sewn up. The party's right behind him. Makes a change to have a clean-cut candidate after all that stuff about congressmen screwing on the Capitol steps."

"Anything new about Charlie and Elaine?"

"Not that I've heard." He looked out the window. "Say, how about a hamburger?"

"Dammit, Sam, I need to know! They haven't told me anything."

"Okay, okay. The cops talked to me a few times; to all the crew. Needham too, I guess. Interviewed everyone who was anywhere near the place. Autopsies—well, I guess you know all that. All they came up with was what we all knew a minute afterwards. Charlie was shot in the head with a .38. Elaine died of multiple injuries when someone wired gelignite to the firewall of the car. They guess both were shots at you—someone with a grudge. They talked to just about everyone you ever fired. Result—zilch. So they figure, some crazy."

"I don't buy that."

"Let's hear a better theory."

"Maybe after the weekend. I need time to think." He noticed for the first time they were downtown. "Pull in over there, Sam. I want to pick up those deeds from the bank."

Sam snapped his head around to look at him. "For Chrissake, Jake, can't you drop it? Who cares what happens to a cruddy mooring up some creek? Live a little."

"I'm planning to. I'll get drunk on your birthday, but I want those deeds."

Reluctantly, Sam pulled into the bank parking lot.

There was no problem getting into his safe-deposit box. He gave the key to the girl behind the desk, submitted to having his signature checked and his appearance verified from the photographs on file, then went into the cubicle where the box was waiting.

He opened it. And paused, staring.

It was filled with money. Bundles of new tens and twenties, still with paper bands securing them. Piles of old hundreds, tied with rubber bands. A thick sheaf of heavy papers he recognized as gold certificates.

Other currencies he didn't recognize. The top bundle

of bills was still in its plastic wrapper, fresh from the bank. Ripping it open, he took out a blue-green bill—an English five-pound note. There were a hundred in the pack. Underneath, he found Swiss francs, deutsche marks—thousands of dollars' worth.

Obviously he'd been given the wrong box. Then he remembered the signature check, the ease with which the key turned in the lock. Something caught his eye, stuffed down the side of the money. He fished for it. It was a deed to premises at 907 Paperwood Mall, known as and trading under the name Elysée. It was made out in the name of, and signed confidently by, Elaine Fox Forrester.

CHAPTER SEVEN

From the window of the Holiday Inn at Virginia Beach, Jake had a good view of the bay and the sunrise that turned water and land a vivid orange. But his mind was not on either, nor had it been concerned with more than a single subject since he opened the safe-deposit box back in Mobile.

Sam put his silence down to depression. By the time they had reached Virginia Beach, after sixteen hours of driving during which they barely exchanged half a dozen sentences, he had reluctantly dropped Jake off at the motel. Jake could feel Sam's disapproval. Even now, he was probably talking to Jean, warning her that the trip away from home had been as disastrous an experiment as she had feared.

Ringing Jean to explain things came some way down Jake's list. At the top was another call, which he was trying to make through an unhelpful switchboard.

Finally the voice leaped into his ear, surprisingly close-sounding despite its alien accent.

"Anglo-Scottish Shipbuilders."

"Mr. Stephens, please."

Tony Stephens looked up in irritation from the unrolled drawing on his desk as his intercom burred. He snatched up the receiver.

"What?"

"Sorry sir. It's trans-Atlantic. A Mr. Forrester."

He lifted his hand instinctively from the end of the tightly curled drawing. It snapped back like a spring released, rolled off the end of the desk, and fell to the floor.

"*Jake* Forrester?"

"Yes, Mr. Stephens. Shall I say you aren't available?"

"Wait a moment." He put down the phone and went

to the window, staring across the wide gray stream of the Thames at the dome of St. Paul's until his pulse slowed. Drawing a deep breath, he went back to the desk.

"Put him on."

"Tony?"

"Jake, I couldn't believe it. How are you?"

"On the mend. I just got around to opening some letters. Thanks for yours. I would have written but . . . well, you know."

"I wish there had been something more concrete to offer. I don't have to tell you that if there *is* anything at all I can do, Jake, you just have to ask."

"There might be."

In the motel bedroom, Jake picked up the plastic wrapper from the English notes and smoothed out the gummed-on label.

"Just ask," Stephens said.

"You want to take this down, Tony?" Jake read out the numbers on the label. "Seven-eight-three-oh-oh-nine. Midland Bank, Liverpool Street. It's the handling code for some currency. Five thousand in fives. I want to know who might have drawn them. They probably have records for such large amounts."

Stephens said, "I don't know, Jake. They're not too happy about giving out that kind of information."

"Well, anything you can do."

"Do you mind my asking what this is about?"

"Oh, just a problem I'm trying to work out. Probably isn't as complicated as I think it is."

"Well, I'll try. Where can I reach you?"

"I won't be near a phone for the next few days. Ring Jean in Mobile if you come up with anything—I think you have the number. You likely to get over to the States any time soon?"

Stephens switched ears. His hand felt sweaty on the plastic of the phone. "Not really, Jake. We've got a lot on. Trying to do a deal with the Swedes and the Norwegians to supply them with tenders for the North Sea. I seem to spend most of my time escorting gangs of industrial journalists around the oil fields. But they're taking millions out of the North Sea every day; a chance to cash in on it is too good to miss."

"Well, maybe I'll make it to England. I could use a holiday. Tony, I'll get back to you in a few days if you haven't called Jean."

After the call, Stephens looked at the figures he'd written on his pad. His secretary looked around the door. "We've got acceptances from *Asahi Shimbun*, *The Sydney Morning Herald*, and the *Washington Post*."

"How many does that make?"

"Nine, maybe ten."

"All right. I'll tell them up at Aberdeen to lay on the press kits and the transport. You'd better alert Clive to have the helicopter ready. After lunch will do."

When the office was empty again, Stephens went into the outer room. The telex terminal stood in the corner. Awkwardly he started punching out codes that by now he knew by heart.

Late in the morning, Jake hired a four-wheel drive Jeep in Norfolk and took Route 17 north. At Saluda he left the main road, threading the heavy vehicle across country on a route he could drive in his sleep.

This was flat, wooded country, old alluvial flats, scattered with a few small farms. Nothing much had changed here for a century. The Civil War was an incident. The industrial revolution washed over the land and left behind electricity, a few gas stations, a drive-in movie or two, and TV. Sometimes, stopping off on a forest track to stretch his legs on the long drive, Jake had found the ruins of mansions lost in the silent stands of oak and beech and elm, piers of crumbling red brickwork climbing into the green gloom. Once the land around them had been cleared, cultivated; in less than a century, the forest reclaimed everything.

Outside Urbanna he turned off again, bumping down a rutted road past the ruins of a restaurant, a sagging white clapboard building on the edge of a river reach, with corroded lobster pots and heaps of whitened oyster shells piled around the peeling walls. The road ran on, and suddenly he was running along a bluff above the Rappahannock River.

Like the forest, the river never changed. The whole

inexorable force of nature was summed up in the wide, slow movement of water towards the ocean. The ripped red clay cliffs on its banks betrayed the primeval strength contained in those billions of tons of water. It tore through the flat forested land and sucked out everything too weak to hold on, spewing the remains out into the Chesapeake through a mouth that had grown to a five-mile-wide monster.

Boats gingerly sailed the Ráppahannock, keeping to the shores where friction slowed the current, taking refuge in the silent reaches—curving bays and inlets off the main stream that offered peace and privacy. Jake had navigated the big river so much that it no longer held any terrors for him, but for the amateur its shifting channels and erratic tidal flow could be fatal. A smart sailor risked the Rappahannock only by day, or if forced to sail by night, stuck to the well-lighted commercial channel used by the fishing boats. Anything else was near enough to suicide.

Jake pulled up as the track along the river dipped suddenly. Tree branches half-choked the road, and underbrush had begun to sprout in the hump between the tire ruts. He crawled down in first gear, tearing scraps of purple wisteria from the trees as he passed. They trailed behind him on the red rutted road.

After a hundred yards, the track widened into a clearing. He stopped the Jeep and climbed out.

He never knew who had cleared the strip of forest along this little backwater, but it must have happened long before he was born. When he bought the land, old weathered logs of oak and beech still lay around in the undergrowth. He salvaged them and built a tiny wharf. The piles were gray and leaning now, but they still kept the crooked footway a few feet above the still waters of the reach.

A boat was moored to the dock—an old thirty-three-foot sloop, single-masted, clinker built, wide-hulled, steady, comfortable. Despite the cracked gray paint job, it was still possible to make out the name across the stern: *Snow Goose.*

Around the bend of the backwater, a quarter of a mile away, the Rappahannock tore its way to the Chesapeake, but there was no sign of that turmoil here. Trees leaned out over the gray-green water, coating it with a carpet of dead leaves, and silent cyclones of midges whirled in the soft, moist air.

Jake walked down the jetty, arms full of paper bags, slipped the padlock on the companionway hatch, and wriggled down the ladder into the stale-smelling cabin. It was like coming home. He looked around in satisfaction at the spartan simplicity of the boat: two narrow bunks, a tiny propane-gas stove, a few books. The newest things were electronic—a Tora eleven-inch portable TV and a UHF/VHF Sony receiver/transmitter wedged on a shelf above the bunk. The dial lit up instantly when he flipped the switch; Jake paid the private security firm that kept an eye on these isolated docks and boats to come in once a month to replace batteries and check that *Snow Goose* was ready for sea. Obviously they were doing it still, even though he'd not had the boat out for at least twenty months.

Jake stacked the groceries around the cramped galley, opened a can of Coors, and sat down on the bunk. He'd rigged the TV at the lower end of the bed, the screen visible between his feet, and he turned it on. Reruns of *Pink Panther* cartoons; it was too early for *Wide World of Sports*. Turning down the sound, he opened a bag of taco chips and drank some more beer.

He had been worried that returning to the *Snow Goose* would revive old memories of Elaine and the times they'd spent here. But any thought of Elaine brought to mind instantly the money in the safe-deposit box. All the obvious answers made no sense at all; Elaine the secret (and successful) gambler? Absurd. Some unexpected inheritance? But she had no close relatives, and even the distant ones were characterized by their singular lack of a fortune. He speculated that she might have sold Elysée for some fabulous profit—but the deed was still in the box, unassigned. Perhaps . . .

Something banged against the side of the boat. A moment later a hand rattled the latch on the companionway. "Anyone home?"

Jake pushed back the hatch and climbed out. A man in a blue suit watched him from the dock; another loitered by the Jeep. Jake got the impression he'd just taken a long and careful look at the contents of the cab. Despite his clothes, Blue Suit looked like a strong-arm man. His companion—from the moment Jake glimpsed his profile, with its long-nose, he could never think of him as anything but Beaky.

"You the owner here?" Blue Suit asked.

Jake nodded, still watching Beaky as he cruised around the Jeep, hands in pockets.

"Saw you coming down here. Thought we might have a talk."

"What about?"

"I guess you heard this area's been rezoned for development."

"They sent me some letters. I thought I'd go down to the county seat next week and talk with them. Doesn't make a lot of sense to me. This has always been classified as nature reserve and private use."

"Last county supervisors' meeting posted it light industrial."

"So?"

"Our clients are prepared to offer a good price for your lease."

"Is that a fact?"

"What have you got here? Two acres?"

"Three."

"We might go as high as . . . eighteen hundred dollars?"

"That for everything?"

"Land and dock. You can keep the boat."

"Thanks," Jake said wryly. "But I'm not interested."

"Eighteen's a good price."

"I'm sure it is."

"We might go a little higher. You wouldn't like to think about it?"

"No. But *you* sure as hell should. What kind of development do your clients have in mind?"

Blue Suit seemed to pluck a phrase out of the air. "Oh . . . light manufacturing."

"What will they use for labor? Most of the work here's seasonal. Tourism. Hotels. You won't find too many folks willing to work in a factory. And what about transport? Nearest interstate's thirty miles away."

"We could use the river."

"Main channel's on the far side. You might dredge a new one, but this river has a shifting bottom. It'd cost millions. Then there's power, water . . . I guess I should take advantage of you, but, to be honest, I'm not sure I could depend on getting my money."

Blue Suit didn't seem either surprised or disappointed. "Final decision?"

"Yeah."

"Well, nice talking to ya." They walked back past the Jeep and up the path. Jake realized he hadn't seen their car. It must be parked back at the top path.

Jake went back into the cabin and lay down on the bunk. Whatever Blue Suit and Beaky wanted, it was not to redevelop the reach. They had looked more like heavies in a TV crime series than realtors. Their offer might make more sense when he'd talked to the county supervisors.

Turning down the sound on the TV, he switched the radio on, casting about among the spatter of traffic for a familiar voice. But pleasure boats dominated radio space on weekends. He let their rambling small talk simmer in the background like Muzak.

He was thinking of other Saturdays.

Elaine and he would have been down here before dawn, Elaine packing the galley with beer and sandwich makings, Jake shaking out the sails and getting *Snow Goose* ready for sea. By eight they were on the river, arguing about where to go that weekend—south to the quiet bays of the Carolinas, or north into the Chesapeake, where there would be parties, races, and the chance to watch the twelves glide insolently among the pleasure boats. Good days, all of them gone. . . . He opened another beer and turned up the TV sound as *Wide World of Sports* began.

Billy Weems opened the show with a piece on the just ended South Pacific Race, won by Takeo Fujita's *Tora Queen*. A quick shot of the big boat crashing through a light sea, spray flying from its bow, with Diamond Head in the background, was not too brief to disguise how well the boat handled, nor the speed with which the crew moved.

Jake looked away as Weems's genial face filled the screen. It brought back memories of other things. The morgue at Providence. A bundle under a white sheet. Torn flesh, a twist of blonde hair . . .

He had left his pills in the car. Walking to the Jeep where he'd parked it by the edge of the forest, he dug them out of the bottom of the carryall.

His system responded slowly to the drug. Four pills were a typical dose. This time he swallowed three, washing them down with another can of beer. There was tennis on the set when he came back. Nastase and Borg. He turned down the sound, lay down, and closed his eyes.

A noise woke him up, a hollow rattle he took for applause at the tennis match. Then he remembered that the sound was turned down. Focusing on the screen, he saw a cloaked figure stalking a wide-eyed blonde across a shadowed cellar. Black and white. An old movie. He recognized Bela Lugosi, looked at his watch. 2:17.

He must have slept for twelve hours.

The noise came again. A rattle like gravel on the plywood deck. Rain.

The cabin smelt like a kennel. Lurching down to the ladder, he pushed back the hatch and stuck his head out into the gusty darkness. Cold rain and a stiff breeze battered his face. He breathed deeply until his head began to clear.

He felt hollow, sick. The pills did that. In the galley he dug out bread, ham, cheese and built himself a large sandwich, smearing on the mustard. There was one can of beer left, but he poured a glass of milk instead.

The radio blatted.

Halfway through a mouthful of sandwich, he turned and looked at it. He'd forgotten it was on.

"You seeing us yet, dammit?" The voice was terse and angry.

"Not much of an echo. Rain's screwing up reception.'

"Well *un*screw it. I'm not going to hang around out here all night waiting for you to get off the dime. And use call signs."

"Right. Sorry . . . uh, Nighthawk. We're retuning. Hold on a minute."

Jake sympathized with anyone navigating on a night like this. It didn't sound like a big boat either. Probably some playboy in a cabin cruiser fumbling his way to an anchorage.

He put down the sandwich.

Then why the secrecy? And who was guiding him?

He checked the frequency. This time of night, radio carried. He might be hearing something from as far south as Charleston.

"Nighthawk, this is Bobolink. We've got you now. Steer oh-three-seven magnetic. I say again, zero-three-seven. Watch for two lights, one above the other, to starboard. High tide is in seventeen minutes. I repeat, one seven."

Jake knew the tide tables for this coast better than any place on earth. High tide for tonight came at 2:30 A.M.

These people weren't down in North Carolina but between him and the mouth of the Rappahannock, twenty miles southeast, waiting for the top of the tide, when the flood of water from the Chesapeake briefly reversed the river's flow and allowed a boat upstream.

A boat that did not want to be seen.

He picked up his sandwich again.

This was none of his business.

A lot of dope came ashore along the East Coast, shipped up from Colombia or Panama, transferred to small boats, brought in at night. He hadn't heard of that going on too much on the Chesapeake, but that might mean only that they were more efficient than their competitors.

Anyone who got in their way was just plain crazy.

On the TV Bela Lugosi chased the girl down a flight of stone steps and cornered her against the wall. Jake put down the glass of milk on the edge of the sink.

Maybe just a quick look . . . They could be only a mile or two away; maybe even just outside the entrance to the reach.

His waterproof clothing was jammed right up in the forepeak, buried under a mound of gear. He hauled it out and struggled into the brittle orange jacket and trousers. His flashlight was dead; the caretaker's maintenance didn't extend to small items like that. Bashing the case against the edge of the bunk, he shot out the old cells, corroded by acid, and pushed in four new ones. To his surprise, the light flashed the first time.

He climbed on deck, flinching from the hard-driven rain.

The dinghy tied to *Snow Goose*'s stern had been used even less than the boat. Water pooled in the bottom. The rowlocks creaked as he jammed in the oars. Casting off, he pulled a few yards into the reach.

It took long minutes for his eyes to adjust to the dark. Then he checked his bearing with a quick flash at the compass and, balancing the tiny instrument on the seat that divided the dinghy, pulled towards the river, rain spitting in his face.

He reached it almost before he expected. The wind had a bite, and he felt the dinghy fall away in the face of the breeze. The water around him was suddenly alive.

Forrester, you're crazy, he thought.

He would have turned and rowed back to *Snow Goose* at that moment if the wind hadn't died to a light breeze. For a moment he glimpsed the dark shape of the bluff on the far side of the river. It didn't look too far away.

He took a deep breath and pulled on the oars. The little dinghy surged out into the river.

Normally, he would have been swept down towards the mouth. But it was slack water, and a steady four- or five-knot breeze blew upstream. The incoming tide and the breeze held back the mass of river water; for ten or fifteen minutes he could row on the Rappahannock as if it were a lake.

Keeping the breeze on his right cheek, he pulled towards the only place for which Nighthawk could be headed—the main west-east channel by the river's southern shore.

After fifty strokes his forearms began to hurt. The ache spread to his shoulders, trickled in stabs of pain down the muscles of his back. The rough seat rubbed his ass; he could feel the rawness of incipient blisters. He didn't dare think what all this was doing to his hands.

Forrester, you're not only crazy, you're criminally insane.

He counted two hundred strokes and fell forward over the oars, gasping for breath. All he could hear was the rasping of his own lungs, the slap of water against the dinghy, the sigh of the wind, and the rattle of rain against his clothes. He might never even hear the smuggler.

If it *was* a smuggler and not just some millionaire with a fifty-foot cruiser groping his way up to the Tides Inn for a late supper.

The dinghy heeled as a gust of wind roared up the river. Water slopped over the gunwhale, and his feet were instantly soaked. The compass slid off the seat and landed with an ominous *plop*. Groping for it, Jake felt three inches of water slopping in the bottom of the boat—more than could be explained by rain or the odd wave. The dinghy was leaking.

If there had been anything in the boat to hit, he would have hit it. But he was alone, unarmed, and on the edge of real disaster.

Old instincts cut through the haze of beer and pills and fatigue. In the army they taught you to think on your feet if you wanted to stay alive. Jake suddenly realized that he *wanted* to stay alive. He filed away this interesting revelation and concentrated on simple survival.

Switching the flashlight beam to full, he scanned the water. Planks, clumps of vegetation, even runaway boats often came downstream. One of them might keep him afloat if the dinghy sank.

The light caught something on the edge of the beam. A shape . . .

The boat came out of the darkness like a ghost.

He'd been listening for engines, the gurgle of a V-12 idling at half-throttle.

This boat was under sail. A genoa and main, half-reefed but with enough area to reach against the steady breeze. She was a twelve.

She slid past less that fifty feet away. In the few seconds it was in sight, Jake raked it with the beam of the flashlight.

Two white faces in the cockpit stared at him as he pinned them like startled deer in the beam. Then the wash from the boat hit him, and the dinghy bobbed wildly. He saw an oar slipping overboard, dropped the flashlight to grab it. The beam swung up, a pencil of light filled with the flicker of rain.

It saved his life.

Because there was another boat out there, keeping station on the first slightly behind and to starboard. And it bore down on him now with an unstoppable force that made his courage shrivel. It was a boat the like of which he'd never seen in his life, an *impossible* boat, as savagely efficient, as unstoppable as a great shark.

It was almost on top of him before he unfroze his body, took one step towards the end of the dinghy, and drew a single deep breath into his lungs.

The dinghy lifted under him in the bow wave. A knifelike bow sliced into the gunwhale, and he was suddenly in cold water, slipping down into roaring darkness.

The man Jake knew as Blue Suit used the barrel of the shotgun to slide back *Snow Goose's* hatch. He wrinkled his nose at the stuffy air, then lowered his head to peer in.

"Ain't here. But the lights are on."

"Get on with it then," Beaky said. "I'll watch the road."

"Yeah, yeah." He wriggled down the steps. The radio hissed suddenly. "Bobolink, Bobolink. Come in, Bobolink."

"Receiving you, Nighthawk."

"Intruders. I repeat, intruders."

"Nothing on our screens, Nighthawk." The voice sounded worried.

Blue Suit yelled "Hey!"

The other man looked down from the hatch.

"Boss's on the radio here."

He looked suspiciously at the radio. "You been frigging with that thing?"

"I've only been here a minute, for Chrissake."

"It was tuned like that when you came in?"

"I told you."

He looked worried. "Get the hell on with it then."

Dragging the bedding from the bunk, he tossed papers on top of it, unscrewed the cap from a can of Crisco, and soaked the heap with oil. He dropped a match on top, and, as it caught, swept the books from the shelf above the bunk.

Stepping back, he watched with satisfaction as the flames licked at the paper. The lighted face of the radio set caught his eye. Tearing it from the shelf, he dropped it into the flames and backed away towards the hatch.

Jake came to the surface coughing and choking. He must have swallowed a quart of river water. The rank tealike taste of rotted vegetation filled his mouth.

Whatever ran him down had disappeared. There was no moon, no stars. He couldn't feel any current in the water, but the tide would turn soon, and that would be the end of him. No man could fight the Rappahannock.

But he could die trying.

Treading water, Jake struggled out of his clothes and kicked off his shoes. Lighter in the water now, he swam a few yards, scanning the darkness for some kind of light. Nothing. He jumped chest high out of the water, four times in succession, trying to orient himself so that he covered the whole 360 degrees.

On the third jump, he saw the glow.

A boat? A house? Or the lights of the nearest town reflected off the cloud base? To swim towards it might take him out into the center of the river, only to exhaust himself struggling against the current. But he didn't have a lot of choice. He struck out.

After three minutes he knew he was headed for land; the light silhouetted a line of trees. Almost immediately, he realized the light came from his own reach. Even filtered through the forest, it was strong enough to glitter, red and shifting, on the water. He rounded the end of the reach and trod water fifty feet from shore.

Someone climbed out of *Snow Goose* and ran down the jetty. Behind him, flames licked from the hatch. The coaming caught and then the sails. They curled and flared like dried leaves.

He recognized the men who had called on him earlier in the day—Blue Suit and Beaky. One of them was smiling as the boat burned. The other stood by his Jeep; as Jake trod water, he tossed something into the front seat.

The cab burst into flame. They backed towards the jetty and watched the fire catch.

Every rational impulse told Jake to retreat back into the darkness, to hide and wait. He could not identify the force that drove him towards the fire, that dictated the silent breaststroke with which he swam to the shallows. His hands found warm mud. He slithered ashore.

Blue Suit was slightly closer, five or six paces nearer the water. He cradled a pump-action shotgun in his arms. Jake scrambled across the fifteen feet that separated them, grabbed a bony ankle, and heaved. With a yelp, the man crashed, face down, the gun flying from his hand. As he tried to rise, Jake kicked him in the side of the head. His toe crunched painfully against the man's skull; he'd forgotten that his shoes now floated somewhere downstream. But Blue Suit fell back, eyes glazing.

Beaky had half-turned when Jake reached him. He managed one startled look before a fist with all the weight of Jake's fury took him in the face. He went down soundlessly, nose squashed to a bloody mess.

Snatching up the shotgun, Jake hobbled towards the jetty. But *Snow Goose* was finished. Deck and mast were completely alight. She would burn to the waterline now.

The heat boiled steam from his underclothes. Shading his face, he watched the words Snow Goose blister and fume on the planking.

He had half-turned when she blew up. A wave of flame washed over him as the propane tanks inside the cabin blasted the burning shell apart. Something smashed into his right side with stunning force, and he sprawled semi-conscious in the mud under a crushing weight.

The man with the smashed nose struggled to his feet, watched in a daze as blood dribbled off his chin and onto the remains of his shirt, and groped for a handkerchief, which he pressed with a sob against his face. He stumbled towards the heap of debris at the water's edge under which Jake Forrester lay, stirring feebly.

Scrabbling up the Winchester from where it had fallen, he jacked a shell into the breech and moved in a circle, lining up a shot at Jake's exposed left side.

The other man crawled to his knees. "Gimme that gun."

"I'm gonna kill this bastard."

"And have everyone know it was murder? You crazy? Leave him burn. This place is gonna crawl with people. You can see the fire for miles."

The man with the broken nose lowered the gun. Then, in a spasm of fury, he ran at the unconscious Jake and kicked him three times in the ribs. He would have kept kicking if the other had not dragged him off. They stumbled away from the mooring, leaving it to the flickering sparks that circled like fireflies in the soft night.

CHAPTER EIGHT

The thing lay unmoving under the water, dead as a stone on the white tiles.

Sometimes refraction patterns in the pale green water made the body ripple and elongate, but the head remained motionless, crimson and black, horned, blind-eyed, the face staring up through twenty feet of water at the sky.

The men in black suits stood in a line along the edge of the pool, hands clasped in front of them like mourners, heads bowed.

After half an hour, only the junior employees remained. Senior men had drifted to the railing around the roof. They chatted quietly, looking down into the sea of yellow smog that hid the ground.

At 10:48 a technician who had remained to watch stepped back from the edge of the pool and coughed deferentially. "Excuse me . . ."

The executives returned quickly to the poolside.

The thing rose slowly, its head turning, questing, growing more distinct with each foot. Then it seemed to explode from the pool, the black, opaque eyes bulging, as big as oranges, water gushing from the meshed hole where the mouth should have been.

"Help him out of it," Kuniyoshi said.

Takeo Fujita hauled himself onto the tiles, water streaming from his torso, and stood with head bowed while two lab assistants hurriedly unlaced the straps that held the mask and lifted it away.

A line of puckered flesh ran around his face in front of the hairline and ears, under the chin. The skin in front of it was slightly flushed. It made his own face as much a mask as the object they had just removed.

Like most Japanese, his body was hairless. His genitals bulged in a bathing suit of green nylon. A servant slipped a robe over his shoulders and toweled him briskly under it.

"How long was I down? Thirty minutes?"

Kuniyoshi said, "Almost exactly."

"There's a slight smell in the mask."

Kuniyoshi was head of research. He looked over his shoulder at one of the group of assistants.

"We set the filters to work on pure water, sir." The young man took off his glasses and fidgeted with them. "The water in the pool is contaminated. Hydrocarbons, esters, chlorine, some acids dissolved from the air. The mask keeps back any molecule smaller or larger than oxygen, but we would need to retune it to exclude everything."

Fujita grunted. "You have one under destruction test?"

Kuniyoshi said, "For a month. Except to change the filters, it has operated perfectly."

Fujita smiled for the first time. "Exceptional." He glanced at the research team. "You have done very well."

They bowed in unison. In a lifetime working for Fujita and Tora, they would be lucky to get more than one such compliment.

Fujita glanced towards the glass wall separating the roof pool from the rest of the building. A crowd of girls in identical green one-piece costumes and beige caps milled, giggling like schoolgirls as they waited to take their midmorning break. Everyone at Tora exercised. The company provided facilities for swimming, volleyball, and callisthenics right in the building, and the day began for everyone with ten minutes of physical training.

Fujita headed for his private elevator, trailed by Toshira Ozu, his personal assistant. When the elevator door closed, one of the company managers signaled and the glass wall slid back. Lithe and indistinguishable as seals, the girls poured out to plunge into the water.

A few of the executives paused to admire the splashing, kicking crowd in the pool. Most hurried back to their offices; every moment spent away from one's department increased the risk of a junior employee or a colleague gaining some advantage.

In his private suite twelve floors below the roof, Fujita changed into a dark blue business suit laid out for him. He called to Ozu from the dressing room. "Who designed that thing?"

"Kuniyoshi-*san* led the team. . . ."

"I know who's head of research. Who *designed* it?"

"I believe . . . Akutagawa."

"The boy with the glasses?" He remembered how Kuniyoshi had turned to him for details about the mask; everyone there had grasped the implication. No man in the executive group should be fool enough to come to a meeting unprepared or to actually ask a subordinate to provide the information he should have had at his fingertips. "Tell me about him."

"He's twenty-seven." Anticipating the question, Ozu had called up Akutagawa's details on the computer. "A Tora man since high school. His father was with us for eighteen years, a sweeper in the Nagoya Plastics Division."

Fujita knotted his Sulka cravat and checked the effect in the mirror. Even though most of his time on the bottom of the pool was spent fast asleep, he was still tired.

He came out into his office and sat at the desk. "Akutagawa's a good man. I'm giving him the research department."

Ozu showed no surprise. "And Kuniyoshi?"

"Retire him. See that he's looked after. Give him a bonus. For the mask, if you like. Akutagawa won't mind waiting for his reward. It might even make him more ambitious."

Ozu didn't argue. Even Morita at Sony had less power than Fujita over his corporation; ruthlessly, to the frustration of his subordinates, Fujita retained total control over the company he had founded, dispensing decisions with all the dogmatism of a medieval *shōgun*.

"They have all arrived," Ozu said. "Will you go down now?"

"In a moment." He flexed his shoulders inside the jacket. "I need some new suits."

"Madam has arranged that. An appointment has been made for next Thursday, if that is convenient."

Fujita put his hand on his stomach. It must show more

than he realized. Women always saw these things before men did. His wife would have a quiet word with the man from Poole's of Cork Street, and any thickening of the waist would be subtly and discreetly compensated for. At a thousand dollars a suit, plus the return air fare for fitter and cutter, one expected no less.

Abruptly, Fujita realized he was killing time, delaying the inevitable. The next hour was not likely to be among the most pleasant of his year.

"What's happening down there?"

"With your permission . . ." Ozu pushed the button that slid back the cover plate set into the desk. A TV screen underneath showed the main board room ten floors below. The elaborate gold Tora chrysanthemum emblem behind the president's chair held a battery of cameras and recorders.

Fujita watched his area chiefs coldly as they played with the new products laid out around the room. A new gadget brought out the child in everyone. These men had charge of multimillion-dollar Tora corporations in a dozen countries, yet there was Patel, who controlled Great Britain, standing side by side with Larry Kuo, the Manchurian in charge of Western Europe, as they used the new wristwatch monitoring unit to compare heart-beats and blood pressures. Gul Yara, his flat Mongolian face gleaming with sweat, bent over a scale model of *Sasori*, arguing some point of styling with Jimmy Karalua, the Papuan who ran Singapore and Malaysia.

Others stood around the room, talking quietly—an anthology of racial types in every skin color, except white. Fujita knew the value of an outsider's ambition. All his enterprises were in the hands of men from some racial minority. Men without countries, totally isolated in the countries to which they were posted, they owed allegience only to Tora.

He rolled the ball control for the TV zoom, and the camera moved jerkily to focus on two men standing by the big windows that looked out on downtown Tokyo.

Sandhu, the plump old white-haired Sikh who had run the Australian branch for twenty years, was almost due for retirement. He'd survived every palace revolution inside Tora; his quick-wittedness and ability to gauge the balance of power was almost miraculous. Never a candidate for any position of influence, he sat the fence with supreme confidence.

In that case, Fujita wondered, why was he in deep conversation with Hamilton?

Hamilton, the ultimate mongrel, had been born in Puerto Rico to a family that could trace itself back to a dozen races. Intermarriage, slavery, migration, and rape had made the Hamiltons a miscellany of races: Spanish, Portuguese, Western European, Chinese, Indian, Japanese—every generation added something to the pot, stirred it, freshened the brew.

The latest Hamilton was fifty but essentially ageless; he would look the same in thirty years—tall, gray-haired, with the long face of a cardinal, the eyes of a torturer, and skin the color of a gold *louis d'or* worn satiny with use. When Fujita put him in charge of the United States operation, he had, he now realized, made his biggest mistake.

Hamilton was one of those businessmen who believe in the visible, the profitable, the rich. Perhaps one of the pirate forebears who had raped some Hamilton girl in Port-au-Prince two centuries before had passed onto this distant grandson the love of plunder and the joy of acquisition. If he had had his way, Hamilton would have turned the corporate finances into gold bars and kept them behind glass in the Tora headquarters in New York.

Nobody could fault his efforts on the company's behalf. Turnover on Tora electronics quadrupled after he was placed in charge; he licensed cunningly, stole crucial information from competitors with a larcenous ease totally in keeping with his piratical background, saw holes in the market where none had been noticed before. But his vision was that of a buccaneer; he could see no further than the point of a cutlass or the sights of a pistol, nor could the colleagues with whom he surrounded himself. *Colleagues?* Fujita raised an eyebrow. They were more like a pirate mob—gunmen, bodyguards, spies, ex-convicts, martial arts freaks who could crack a skull with one blow. And had done so more than once.

When, in the past, Fujita moved to change the direc-

tion of Tora, to diversify into new products or pinch off
old ones whose optimum worth had been reached, it was
Hamilton who protested the change, who produced
alarmingly well-researched details of potential losses in
revenue. Often he carried some of his fellow directors
along with him. What he might do when he heard the
news Fujita would be announcing today was problematic,
but there was no doubt at all that he would be utterly
opposed.

Fujita sighed and cut off the screen. "Let's get it over
with."

The big boardroom fell silent as Fujita and Ozu entered.
One by one the men found seats at the table. There were
no greetings, no handshakes. So-called board meetings
were ritual gatherings. Business came afterwards, in conferences with sales directors, merchandising men, designers, and engineers.

"You have seen the new products," Fujita said without
preamble. "Some are important. Others, like the wristwatch, have more use in keeping our name before the
public. Toys, if you like." Kuo, who was still wearing one
of the watches, removed it surreptitiously.

"Other items are still in the development stage. We
expect to perfect them within a few months. Our research department has had considerable success with a
biomedical monitoring system. With it, we can eavesdrop
on the unconscious mind and even, to some extent, control its function. Another new development is an underwater mask. It filters oxygen from water. Conventional
scuba equipment will be obsolete overnight."

A murmur of interest ran around the table. Medical
hardware and scuba gear were carriage-trade items, the
profit margins astronomical.

"Questions?"

Hamilton said, "We're picking up rumors that something like our digital recording system is going on the
market from an outfit called Ryker Electronics. Could be
a patent infringement."

Hamilton's spies had been at work.

Ozu said, "This is a minor matter, surely. It can be
dealt with by our legal department."

Fujita looked down the table at Hamilton's somber, unblinking eyes. Better to meet the matter head-on than to let Hamilton snipe at him for the rest of the meeting. "We've licensed Ryker to use the digital process for two years."

Sandhu raised his eyebrows. "It's one of our best sellers. Why give it away to a competitor?"

"It sells well now; it won't continue to do so, in our opinion. And this situation is exceptional. Ryker's firm is heavily mortgaged. We now own most of his notes. When the time comes, he will be closed down. All franchises then revert to us."

"Seems like we're handing him a rock to beat our brains out," Hamilton said.

"The possibility is remote. In any event, it was necessary. Ryker is performing certain valuable services for us."

"We must owe him one hell of a favor," Karalua said. Already Hamilton had an ally.

"Without him, we could not have considered entering the America's Cup in two years' time. Ryker has contacts inside the yachting establishment, and other . . . assets. He is also in desperate need of money. We could not hope to find so useful a collaborator."

"Ah, yes. The America's Cup," Hamilton said. "I've been adding up our costs." He laid a calculator the shape and size of an address book on the table and tapped a key.

"Account seven seven nought three." The flat, mechanical voice of the vocoder seemed hard enough to scratch the silvered surface of the boardroom table. "Warehousing and storage—dollars twelve thousand, four hundred and two; cents eighteen. Transport and maintenance—dollars nine thousand eleven; cents none. Staff and overheads—dollars ninety-seven thousand, three hundred and forty; cents sixty-six."

"Total?"

"Dollars one hundred and eighteen thousand, seven hundred and fifty-three; cents eighty-four."

Hamilton leaned back. "And that's just for one month. A lot of money to win a boat race."

Fujita glanced sideways at Ozu. The assistant's face

was carefully expressionless, even blank, but he sensed his horror at what was happening. Fujita-*san* was *never* contradicted. To do so violated every rule of Japanese business practice. Even at the private criticism sessions most corporations held from time to time, only the mildest of doubts were voiced. If, in the celebratory drinking party that followed, rage and frustration finally exploded into speech, note was taken and adjustments quietly made. To tell the truth in drink was one thing; to express a criticism cold sober was unthinkable.

But Fujita had spent enough time in the West to adapt his ideas. Infighting like that between him and Hamilton took place every day in the boardrooms of Manhattan and Los Angeles. Subordinates routinely did as Hamilton had done, gathering their own intelligence, spying on colleagues and superiors. Aware that this was a crucial test of strength, Fujita attacked.

"Our America's Cup project has so far cost more than ten million dollars." He looked around the table, amused at the stunned looks on their faces. Even Hamilton was silent. "We expect to spend another two million on preparations. These figures you mention . . ." He brushed them away with the swipe of his hand, as if the calculator had littered the surface with numerals like confetti.

Sandhu cleared his throat. "Speaking purely for myself, I must confess to a certain confusion about this project. We have all rejoiced with the chairman in his many successes as a yachtsman. In Australia there have even been certain commercial advantages—as you know, Australia has challenged for the America's Cup on eight occasions, and they respect a competitive sailor as they do any serious sportsman." He shook his head. "But . . . twelve million?"

Fujita said, "Winning the America's Cup is no longer a question of sport. The costs I mentioned will be met out of our budget for research and development. There are ample funds because all work on electronics and related areas has been halted."

Most of the men at the table looked dazed. Finally Patel said, "But . . . what will we sell? Tora is an electronics company."

"It was. But all our market analyses suggest that business will decline sharply over the next decade. By the mid-1990s Tora will control less than nine percent of the international electronics market. Our home video and audio equipment, our digital recording process, our cameras, even new developments like the scuba mask face the same problem as all consumer durables: They are simply *too* durable. A microchip is almost indestructible. Plastic has become unbreakable; circuitry is printed— there are no wires to come loose, no fuses to blow, no valves to be replaced. We have worked too well. There is no profit in something that the buyer purchases once in a lifetime, which never wears out. To survive, we must turn to new markets."

"We'll have to sell a lot of boats to make back twelve million," Hamilton said.

Fujita ignored the remark. "It is not necessary to say, I think, that *Sasori* and our America's Cup project are merely the first steps in a reorganization of Tora. *Sasori* is an experimental machine; we have learned much from her, and we will learn more. The boat is unique. For three years our engineers and chemists worked on her. The design incorporates every significant development in yacht construction, hydrodynamics, navigation, and synthetic resin technology of the last ten years. Her hull . . ."

Hamilton raised his eyes to the ceiling. Some of the other board members were taking their tone from him; Fujita saw looks of resignation, even hostility.

". . . but I see I am boring Mr. Hamilton. Let us then move on to the next step after *Sasori*—her big brother. Perhaps then I will recapture the attention of our colleague from New York."

The windows around the room faded slowly to black as an electric current altered the molecular structure of the surface layer, polarizing it against the light. From the center of the conference table, a sheet of glass rose to a height of two feet and lit up instantly as a pencil-thin beam of green light speared from the center of the Tora seal to splash a picture across the screen. Those who recognized a laser beam flinched away instinctively. Hamilton was motionless.

"Three-D motion picture holography," Fujita said.

"We had hoped to have it ready for marketing in about a year. A trivial thing beside what it will show you. Pay attention, gentleman, to the future of Tora: *Izanagi*."

For ten seconds the men at the table stared in astonishment at the screen, where the eerie three-dimensional image of a huge ship floated on a gray sea. From its deck three silver towers climbed a hundred feet in the air. As they watched, the towers unfurled into complex vertical vanes that turned like sunflowers under a single silent direction.

"*Izanagi* is the most sophisticated vessel ever built; consider America's space shuttle, and imagine that degree of technical skill applied to the problem of international ocean transport. Then you may have some idea of her potential. She offers the promise of cheap, efficient transport to every corner of the world served by a harbor. We are negotiating with NASA to put a multichannel communications satellite in orbit exclusively to provide guidance for *Izanagi* and the boats that follow her. In ten years she will have wiped every other form of transport from the seas of the world."

Hamilton remained silent in the hubbub of question and argument. The noise obscured a faint buzz produced by each touch of his fingers on the calculator as he operated the hidden camera inside.

Fujita stood up. "*Izanagi* represents the future, gentlemen. You'll be given summaries detailing its potential. If you wish, visits can be arranged to the ship itself. I know you will come to share my confidence in its promise." He left the room with Ozu at his heels.

Had he convinced them? They were at least intrigued, impressed despite themselves. Even Hamilton would balk at opposing the full weight of the board, though no doubt he would continue to do everything possible by covert means to undermine the plan; to a pirate, the only function of a ship was as transport from one victim to the next.

But now, more than ever, a win in the America's Cup became crucial. It would establish Tora's credibility in this new area, create public interest in the new technology of *Izanagi* and public confidence as well. Nothing could be allowed to interfere with that. *Nothing.*

When Ozu looked into the dressing room, Fujita was peeling off his clothes. Not only his shirt but the lining of his suit was soaked in sweat.

"Will you see Akutagawa now?"

"Not now!"

Standing just behind his employer, Ozu watched him watching himself in the mirror. The naked body was as rigid as an overinflated rubber toy. The skin seemed to bulge over the chest. A vein pulsed in his neck.

Picking up the desk phone, Ozu said a few words into it. A minute later, someone scratched at the door. A slim Japanese girl in a Tora uniform of green nylon slipped into the room. Her face seemed artificial, so careful was its composure—a bronze mask. Her hands were thin and delicate, with long nails on all but the second finger of the right hand. Over the cuticle where the nail should have been was only flesh, smooth and unscarred.

She bowed and went through to the bedroom. Ozu had a glimpse of the wide bronze-colored bed with its seamless rubber covering and the smooth, naked back of the girl as she slipped off her coat and began her preparations.

CHAPTER NINE

Sam Lewis opened the door and stared. "Jake? Jesus!"

The reaction was no surprise. Jake still remembered his own startled look in the mirror at the precinct house. Mud-caked, red-eyed, bandages wrapped around his head, right arm and shoulder crimson with second-degree burns—he was no picture postcard.

Sam started to lead him into the house. Jake shook off the hand. "I'm okay."

"You sure as hell don't look it, pal."

The big pine-floored living room didn't lack for comfortable chairs. Jake collapsed in the nearest.

"Coffee? Drink?"

"Coffee sounds fine."

"You got it." He went into the kitchen.

"Lucky I remembered your number," Jake called after him. "I'd still be there, otherwise."

"Why the hell didn't you wait? I said I'd come and collect you."

"Sam, it isn't as bad as it looks. The head's just a scratch. The burns will heal up in a week. I'm no invalid. The sooner we all stop thinking like that, the sooner I can get after those bastards."

"Cops got any ideas?"

"No. I looked through some mug shots. They all look the same to me. And they never gave me any kind of name, not even phoney ones."

"I don't get it. Why the fuck would anyone do a crazy thing like burning you out?"

"I've got some ideas."

"Like?"

"Their offer to buy the mooring sounded genuine. I think that if I'd taken their eighteen hundred bucks and gotten the hell out of there, they'd have been satisfied. And someone went to the trouble of getting that part of the river rezoned, just so they could buy it up. They couldn't build on it; that cover story about wanting to set up a factory was ridiculous. So they wanted it to guarantee privacy—to make sure nobody saw . . ."

"Saw what?"

Sam came in from the kitchen with a mug of coffee and a potbellied bottle of Hennessy brandy. A generous slug went into the coffee. Jake's hands shook as he swallowed two mouthfuls. Two more spilled down his shirt front.

"Christ knows, Sam. I hardly know if I even believe it myself now."

Sam gently took the mug from his hand. "You need a rest, pal. I've got plenty of rooms. Grab some z's. We'll talk about it then."

He was put to bed in a vast bedroom empty except for a king-size water bed that gurgled alarmingly as he collapsed on it, and went off instantly to sleep.

When he came downstairs again, it was late afternoon. Boats crowded the bay in front of the big house. A Hobie-cat, grasshopper green, heeled up on one float, pilot hanging out at right angles to balance the weight. Crazy Sunday sailors.

Sam had not exaggerated the size of his new house. Under the accumulation of boating junk, piled magazines, and still-crated utensils, it was luxurious. Sam had gotten rich this last year.

Sounds of movement came up through the hatch open in the middle of the big living room floor. Jake went down the staircase. Sam looked up from his drawing board, casually pulling a sheet of paper over the sketch on which he'd been working.

"What the hell are you doing out of bed?"

"I'm mending. I told you I would."

"Yeah," Sam said grudgingly. "I guess you don't look as grungy as you did this morning."

"You try waking up with two hundred pounds of lumber on your back."

"Lucky they didn't wait around to finish you off."

"Yes."

Jake wandered around the studio; any boat designer would give his arm for a layout like this.

Under the clutter was a good deal of hard boatmaking

gear, most of it well used. Sam hadn't been wasting his time. Photos and sketches of his other boats covered the walls. He recognized one of the sketches—*Defiant*, spinnaker ballooning, prow out of the water as she surfed a rolling breaker.

"Some ride," Jake said, remembering the perfect moment before the shot that killed Charlie Keble.

"Where is she?"

"*Defiant*? Sold to the Australians. Workhorse. Guess she's Down Under someplace."

"So Tom doesn't have a boat."

"Not right now."

Jake lifted the sheet of paper Sam had pulled across the sketch on the drawing board. Underneath was a design for a twelve—narrower than *Defiant*, slim, sharp-bowed, with a more obviously raked mast, and a second cockpit, smaller, behind the main one.

There was a name lettered along the top of the sketch. *Andromeda*. Client—Thomas Needham III.

"What's this going to cost him?"

"Two five. Maybe more."

Two million, five hundred thousand dollars. The whole *Defiant* challenge had not cost that much.

"What's this behind the cockpit?"

"Computer, man. New thing. Don't have the electronics in the cockpit anymore. They go back there, with someone who knows what he's doing. There's a lot of new stuff on the market since last time. And we can take satellite weather information up to five minutes before the race too."

"Useful." Even as he said it, Jake didn't believe it. Sailing was done by men, not machines. The sea could spring a trap too quickly for any machine to spot. Depending on electronics in a twelve-meter race was like hunting tigers by radar.

"It's a beautiful boat, Sam."

"Yeah. Well, maybe we'll both sail in her." He looked away as he said it.

"You know they barred me."

"I heard about it. I'm not saying you should have turned up and eaten a little crow—you know me better than that. I'm only saying it might have helped."

"I sort of hoped Tom would go to bat for me."

"He did. We all did. But Weems has a lot of friends. And you know how they are about bad publicity. They like quiet people who stay out of the headlines. It's a shitty situation. We'll get it changed. Give it a little time."

Jake pulled another sheet of paper from the shelf over the drawing board and pinned it down. "You know all the boats. What's this one?"

Awkwardly he sketched in the lines of the twelve he'd glimpsed in the flashlight. Sam looked over his shoulder.

"You sure about that counter? The chisel shape?"

"Uh huh." Every line of the boat was imprinted on his brain.

"They weren't doing that before '78. It looks like one of those Australian boats. *Kurrewa*." He scratched his ear. "Or *Expeditious*."

Expeditious. Ryker's boat. He remembered Kim Ryker at the America's Cup Ball; her father was a Californian, in electronics; overextended . . . desperate for cash, Tom Needham had said. Desperate enough to involve himself with strong-arm men and midnight journeys on the Rappahannock?

"Okay. Try this one." On another sheet he haltingly drew a new shape. Knifelike bows, with a high forepeak. An almost impossibly slim hull. Raked mast. And, fanning out behind the cockpit, a wide, flat counter like the flared tail of a racing car. The boat that ran him down and almost drowned him.

"What the fuck is *that*?"

"You tell me."

"Not any twelve *I* know. It wouldn't fit the rule. Not with that waterline. Anyway, where do you put the gear? It looks like a canoe."

He took the charcoal, frowning. "Though I guess, if you had something new in the way of winches . . ." He sketched, scribbled, scrubbed out. One hand reached for his pocket calculator.

Jake grabbed his wrist. "Before you get too involved, one more thing." He scraped the charcoal broadside through hull and sails, leaving only the area around the cockpit untouched. "Around here"—he stabbed at the cockpit—"all I saw was lights. Green and red telltales. It looked like the cabin of a 747. They haven't just got one little back seat for the electronics. The whole thing's wired.

"But the rest," he went on, "is black. The whole damn thing. Hull, sails, deck. Dead black."

Sam stared at him, surprised at the vehemence in his voice.

"Okay, okay," he said, placatingly. "Black. Right. I suppose it could be. The rules say white, but maybe that was undercoat."

"It wasn't any damned *undercoat*, Sam. That thing was meant to be black." He would never forget that moment of terror as the night suddenly seemed to beget this great silent monster, the angel of death made manifest, a creation that went beyond normal reality into the realms of nightmare.

Sam was staring at him. Jake realized he was not making a lot of sense. He would never be sensible about that apparition until he faced it head-on.

"I'm going back there."

"Back where?"

"The river. The reach. Those boats had to be going to a mooring upstream. They'll still be there."

"Is that such a good idea, Jake?"

"You don't have to come. This is my problem."

"What's got into you? Of course I'll come. Ever hear of me missing out on a fight?"

"There mightn't be a fight."

Sam looked down at the rough sketch of the black boat. "Something tells me these guys mean business. I think we'd better take a gun."

Kimberly Ryker cruised the Pinto on the last curves of the river road.

She'd been coming to her father's lodge on the Rappahannock ever since she was a child; one reason for enrolling at Briar Rose College had been to be within three hours of the old wooden house jutting out over the silent backwater. The big living room with its windows looking out over the reach, the quiet woods that crowded down to the back of the house were her private symbols of peace.

Not many relics remained of Kim's childhood. When she was nine, her parents had separated, her father going to California to start the electronics business that increasingly occupied his life. Dorothy Ryker stayed with her daughter in New York, using the Virginia house as they had always used it, for summers and weekends. After her mother's death, Kim persuaded her father not to sell the lodge. He grudgingly agreed to keep it on, half-believing her improvised suggestion that it would be ideal to entertain clients on his visits to the East Coast, but in two years of college, Kim had visited it dozens of times, always to find it shuttered and empty.

When she got sick of studying, she often drove down for the weekend to watch TV, read, straighten herself out. A couple of times she brought a friend. Pat Zetland, the associate professor of art with whom she had been sleeping most of her sophomore year, got to like the house so much she suspected he kept the relationship going just to have access to it.

Pat had angled for an invitation there over this Easter vacation, but Kim had avoided offering. Lately, school seemed to permeate most of her life; she needed time to think about what she would do with the rest of her life, and with whom she would do it.

For almost ten years, her emotional life had revolved around an increasingly distracted father, affectionate when he was around—which was seldom—but completely out of touch when his business demanded his presence in California. Lately, that had been most of the time. The college shrink had once asked her if she loved her father. Kim didn't have to think about her reply; it came automatically: "I probably would if I knew him."

His involvement with the twelve-meter world had not improved their relationship. Kim hoped that sailing together might give them the chance to become closer while sharing a sport both of them loved. She soon gave up trying to compete with the boats; twelve racing had more in common with the electronics business and the stock exchange than with the boating she learned as a child, dinghy sailing on the reach below their lodge.

Those twelve-meter sailors she met didn't impress Kim. The syndicate money men, despite their baked-in Bermuda tans and custom-styled blazers, couldn't shake the dust of offices from their shoulders. As for the professional sailors, they ranged from beery jocks who waited barely five minutes before making a pass to abstracted specialists hooked on yoga, macrobiotic foods, TM, and vitamins.

Kim remembered only one twelve-meter man with any real warmth—a tall, gray-haired skipper with whom she had exchanged barely a dozen sentences on the night of the America's Cup Ball. She had read about Jake's tragedy with horror and wasn't surprised when he sank from sight; too many people paraded their griefs. "Look," they shouted, "I'm suffering. Isn't it *interesting?*" She understood why a man would take his pain away to heal in peace; she had done the same thing all her life.

Glancing out the window, Kim recognized some familiar landmarks—an old dead oak hanging over the water, tangled with wisteria. Another season would see it uprooted and sunk to the bottom, its jagged limbs furnishing yet more snags to threaten unwary pleasure boats. Most maps marked these upper reaches as unnavigable; the Sunday sailors kept well away.

The oak was still there, but other things were missing: a rock shaped like a huge toad that used to hulk at a sharp corner; a row of beech saplings like a paling fence on one of the last straightaways before she reached the house. The road seemed to have been widened, and the soft verges were gouged with the ruts of heavy trucks.

The road swung left in what she remembered as the last turn before she saw the house. Braking suddenly, she stared.

Her first thought was that the house had been torn down. Then she realized it was still there but dwarfed by a clutch of new buildings that surrounded it.

On the lower level of the reach, where there had been a meandering path leading to the dock from which they sailed their little fourteen-foot racer and the speedboat, two large boathouses prefabricated from aluminum squatted on a glaring new concrete foundation that dipped a few yards from their doors to shelve into the water of the reach. Heavy lifting gear stood to one side, and a pair of wheeled cradles like those used to haul big boats out of the water sat like roosting metal seabirds beneath it.

The house did not seem changed, except that most of the forest had been cleared around it, creating paths leading around the top of the reach to another new building; long, low, utilitarian. She guessed it was a dormitory—the place was crowded with men, all in green T-shirts and white pants, all small—all Japanese.

There was also a gate, high and solid, blocking the road.

She drove cautiously up to it. Two men came out of the small hut beside the gate. They wore yellow windbreakers with a stylized chrysanthemum on the left side. She knew the emblem. Tora.

Kim rolled down the window. "What's going on? Is my father in there? I'm Kim Ryker."

"It is quite all right, Miss Ryker. If you wait a moment, the gate will be opened."

She drove through and parked on the new concrete apron. As she got out, another Japanese, wearing a white houseboy's jacket—it was a relief to see no Tora emblem on *that*—came smiling down the steps.

"Shall I take in your bags, miss?"

Kim handed him the keys. "Is my father here?"

"I believe so, miss."

Kim turned towards the boathouses. What operation could possibly need so much space? The equipment would rouse envy even in the boat builders of City Island, where the rival workshops scrabbled for a few extra yards of elbow room.

She walked down the slope towards the buildings. They looked raw, unfinished, ready to be struck at any time like a film set. The first door was open. She peered in. *Expeditious,* her father's boat, hung on a cradle, the deck out of sight over her head as the deep keel and fin of the boat was revealed. She rubbed her hand over the white hull. It came away slightly soiled with the algae, oil, and dirt that any boat collected after only a few hours in the water. Twelves had to be cleaned down and polished by hand every second day to be kept in racing condition; obviously *Expeditious* had been in the water recently.

And that was puzzling. Last time she had heard of *Expeditious*, it was up for sale in a yacht broker's at Norfolk. Her father always claimed he could no longer afford to sail her.

The doors of the second building were shut. She yanked on the latch, but they wouldn't move. Locked from inside. She had turned to go when she heard the oiled rumbling of a door rolling on its track. Someone was coming out.

She meant to slip past him as the door opened, or at least sneak a look, but the man who eased his thin body through the opening left no room for either.

Kim stared at him, all ideas of discovering the contents of the boathouse driven from her mind.

It was as if a gigantic snake had reared up on its coils to tower over her. Six feet of ash-gray flesh was stretched over a seven-foot frame. His ragged T-shirt showed ribs like the joints of a centipede. Stained jeans ended halfway down skeleton calves. Dirty sneakers had split across the broad bony insteps of huge feet.

There was a special horror in his face—flat, with high cheekbones and deep-set black eyes above a thick-lipped watermelon mouth, it belonged on a *Kabuki* devil mask.

Kim moistened her lips. "What's in there?"

"Private." His husky voice almost gargled its vowels. A cleft palate?

"Vincent Ryker's my father."

"Nothing there." Reaching behind him, he drew together the two sliding doors. They moved like paper screens, though both must weigh hundreds of pounds. The demonstration of strength was effortless and threatening.

"I'll tell my father . . ." Conscious she was making a fool of herself, she backed away and hurried to the house.

The furnishings had improved. Instead of rejects from their California house, eeked out with local garage sale finds, there were new chrome and leather chairs, a bonsai azalea with vivid pink blossoms, wall coverings that looked like beige silk.

She heard her father talking. The den next to the kitchen had a new door covered in black leather. It was ajar.

Vincent Ryker switched the phone from his right ear to his left. His hand played with the gold cuff links in the shape of tiny navigation buoys that he'd just removed from his shirt. For some reason, he'd felt the need to roll up his sleeves to handle this call.

"There's no trouble. I told you. Forget it. The police chief's an old friend of mine."

He listened, stretching his right forearm out over the desk, clenching the fist, watching the muscle rise under the thick black hair.

"The radio doesn't mean a thing. So he had it tuned to our frequency—so what?"

Kim closed the door, surprised by the tone in her father's voice. Behind the truculence, he was scared.

Her bedroom looked much the same, except for a new bedspread—a real Shaker quilt. She went through the dressing room and bathroom that connected her room with her father's. Someone moved in the bedroom. She peeked in.

A naked girl moved across the new dark brown carpet and knelt gracefully in front of a cabinet of black lacquer that replaced her mother's old dressing table.

The room looked bare. Most of the old furniture was gone, making way for an enormous bed covered in pale yellow fabric with a sheen like rubber. The place reminded Kim of a laboratory. She went back into the bathroom and washed up. When she emerged, her father stood in the living room, looking out over the activity below.

"Hello, kitten." He hugged her gently. "What the hell are you doing here?"

"Easter break, remember? I usually come down to the lodge."

"Do you?" He looked sheepish. "I should know that kind of stuff, shouldn't I."

"It might prevent embarrassing moments. Like this one." She waved her hand at the new buildings, the slipway. "What *is* all this? I didn't even recognize the place when I came in. They practically made me produce a pass!"

"Yeah. Guess I should've told you, but . . . well, you know. You make decisions, and people take them out of your hands."

"Have you sold the place?"

"Hell, no. We still own it. And Tora put up the money for the buildings. They just want a base over here for some stuff they're doing. I offered them this place; next minute, the construction gangs are moving in." He looked into her face. "I guess you don't like it, huh?"

"Do you need to *ask*? It's gross! You've just ruined . . ." She stopped herself, realizing she was close to tears, closer to an argument. "Look, I'll push off, dad. Maybe go up to New York and stay with some people."

"Stay just one night, huh? There's someone I'd like you to meet. But if you want to leave tomorrow, that's fine. I've got some people coming down in the evening anyway. Why don't you take a trip? Bermuda or something? Take your friends with you."

"Small matter of money, in case you've forgotten the stuff."

He smiled. "Money's no problem. Go where you want, spend what you like." He grabbed her arm. "Come and look at this."

In the dressing room, he opened one of the fitted wardrobes, shoved back the clothes to expose a small safe in the wall—another new addition. Kim glanced towards the bedroom door. Closed.

"The combination's the same as my birthday—twelve, eleven, thirty-six." He swung it open. One shelf was covered with piles of currency; if they were all hundreds like those on top, the safe must contain a quarter of a million.

"Help yourself, honey."

Kim grinned and shook her head in astonishment. "Hold on, hold on. Let me get used to the idea. Where did all this come from?"

"Business is good." He swung the door closed. Just before he did, Kim noticed the flat black boxes stacked on a lower shelf. What were they? Gold bars? "Remember the combination. In case . . ."

"In case of what?"

"Well, you never know." He looked worried. Then his face cleared. "You gonna stay?"

Kim thought about her father's expression, the tone of discomfort, even menace that hung over the house, the strange, grotesque man at the boathouse. Leaving now would be an easy out. "Sure. I'll stay around if you want me to."

He put his arm around her. "Great! And wait till you taste the food this new cook turns out!"

The food *was* good; Kim had more trouble with the guest her father had wanted her to meet. Even fully clothed, the girl from her father's bedroom was readily identifiable. Her name was Keiko Sakahura.

"Keiko's our liaison with Tora. You said you wanted to meet my daughter, Keiko. Well, here she is."

"I'm pleased to meet you, Kimberly." Taking her hand, Kim noticed the second finger of her right hand had no nail—only smooth flesh. There was none of the scar tissue of a nail torn out; this had been done surgically. Kim wondered why she didn't cover the area with an artificial nail. The disfigurement added even more to Kim's disquiet.

Keiko dressed in Western style, simply but expensively. Kim recognized the beige pants and white jacket as Thierry Mugler, and not some Seventh Avenue copy; the real thing, straight from Paris. Her bracelets were gold. Paid for by her father? Kim felt her stomach clench. She ought to be used to her father's mistresses by now, but each one grated. As he held back Keiko's chair, Kim tried to remember if he had ever done that for her mother.

"I saw a real horror down by the boathouse," she said sharply. He looked like a snake. I didn't know Japanese grew so tall."

Keiko smiled. "You must have met Jubei. He is not exactly Japanese. His father was an American GI. A black soldier of the occupation."

"Is he 'liaison' too?"

Her father glanced at her sharply. Keiko seemed not to

know anything was meant by the question. "He does whatever he is told to do."

The houseboy who took Kim's bags earlier in the day came in, wheeling a trolley that contained bowls of sauce and a large plate of shrimp, intricately arranged with the precision of a jigsaw puzzle.

"These are great, kitten," her father said. "You'll love them. The sauce's got ginger in it and some kind of mustard."

The servant put shrimp on each plate. Keiko picked one up and began peeling it delicately, piling the pale pink shells on the side of the plate. For the first time in her life, Kim realized how much shrimp resembled insects. It was like watching someone prepare to eat a cockroach.

"Jubei has had an unhappy life," she said. "As a mixed-blood, he was *burakumin*—like the Indian untouchables. His mother sent him to live with relatives by the Inland Sea. He scraped seaweed for them many years as a child. Have you ever tasted seaweed, Kimberly?"

Using her full name turned the conversation into a lecture. It was like grade school again. "No."

"Some of it is excellent. But Jubei did not enjoy farming seaweed. When he was sixteen, he stole all the money of his relatives and ran away to Kyoto. He became a *yakusa*. A gangster. The man for whom he worked let Jubei keep order among his prostitutes. He was very good at it. Jubei is most cruel."

Kim sensed the note of warning again. Directed at her father perhaps?

"But now he works for Mr. Fujita. Like you."

"Oh, yes." Keiko smiled and popped one of the shrimp into her mouth. "We *all* work for Fujita-*san*."

Kim shot a look at her father. He was pale.

Kim woke up late in the night, listening. The noise she heard had no name. It was neither human nor mechanical—a cry like something being torn apart.

She got out of bed and went into the bathroom. The dressing-room door was half open. Beyond, the closed door of her father's bedroom. A line of yellow light showed underneath.

The noise came again. Goose flesh sprang out on her arms as the light under the door turned from yellow to an acid green that flickered and dimmed.

Backing away, she went back into her bedroom, firmly closed the door, and leaned against it, trembling.

Her father came in late for breakfast. He looked dark-eyed and exhausted.

Only two places were set at the dining table.

"Where's Keiko?"

"She left early this morning. Sweetheart, I told you I had some people coming down today . . ."

"I'm ready to go." She paused. "Only there's something wrong with the car. I'll have to see if I can fix it."

The Pinto in fact was running as well (or as badly) as it ever did, but Kim was becoming curious. What was Keiko doing here? She was obviously more than her father's lover. What was in the locked boatshed? And who was he so anxious she shouldn't meet? With a little careful disconnection of wires, it should be possible to delay her departure until after the arrival of these mysterious guests.

After breakfast, Kim took a shower and put on cutoff shorts and a T-shirt. She knew they made her look good. Her body had the smooth streamlining of a seal, echoed by the long, straight black hair falling halfway down her back. Her tiny pointed breasts, olive skin, and narrow waist went well with her physical suppleness and agility. Her workouts on the parallel bars in the gym drew crowds of admirers, not all of them male.

As she came out onto the concrete, her father was walking towards the boatshed with two men. Too tall for Japanese—she tried to remember where she'd seen them before. Then the gangling shape of one of them jogged her memory; Weisell used to be her father's driver when he lived on the East Coast. The other one must be Levitt; they seemed to work as a team. They stopped and turned by the first shed, and she recognized Levitt. She assumed the other was Weisell, though a huge surgical dressing planted in the middle of his face made it impossible to be sure. Obviously Weisell had run into a door—

or someone who hit just as hard. She wasn't sorry. They had always seemed to her a loathsome and sinister pair.

Lifting the hood of the Pinto, Kim yanked loose two spark plug leads and reconnected them in the wrong positions. More and more, she was anxious to see what her father was up to.

CHAPTER TEN

Jake watched the Virginia forests race by outside the car. They had been driving for two hours, and it was close to twilight. A white clapboard church floated by, its cracked bell tolling flatly through the heavy evening air.

"Almost there," Sam said.

"Another half an hour to the river. Still think I'm crazy?"

"I can think of better ways to spend Sunday, yeah. These guys aren't some Little League ball team; there's a lot of money in this. People won't kill for ideas too much, but they sure as hell will for cold cash."

"Tom Needham said the same thing."

"He oughta know."

"Sam, there's no reason in the world why *you* have to put your head on the block just because someone busted up my mooring. Just leave me at the bridge; I'll handle it from there on in."

"Shut up, will ya? You know how to use that baby in the glove compartment?"

Jake took out the .380 automatic and pulled out the clip.

"Soft-nosed," Sam said. "Put a hole the size of a tea-cup in anybody who has a go at us."

"Sam, do me a favor: Don't shoot at them before they shoot at us."

"Me?" Sam looked wide-eyed. "Quietest guy you could hope to meet. Never plug anyone without at least a two-second warning."

They drove for another twenty minutes through the thickening dusk. Jake recognized the landscape and watched the road rise before them with a sudden lurch in his stomach. Then they were on a long concrete bridge spanning the river. Sam drove to the center and pulled over.

"This it?"

"Yes." They got out of the car.

Dusk turned the river into a gray-backed animal, its surface marbled like the hide of a gigantic reptile. Below them, where it gathered to slide through the gaps in the bridge, eddies splashed the hide like scar tissue and tiny vortices resembled old bullet wounds. Both of them sensed the unstoppable force dormant in that vast weight of water.

"Looks mean."

Jake nodded.

"These guys navigated this at night without markers?"

"Yes."

"I sure admire their balls. Where's your place?"

Jake pointed upstream. "Fifteen miles."

Sam squatted to check the trailer hitch that joined his car to the small speedboat and slid back behind the wheel.

"Guess we'd better get to it then."

In twilight the ruins of Jake's mooring looked more desolate than when he had woken among them the day before.

Snow Goose's gutted hull floated, half waterlogged, near the remains of the jetty. Everything above the waterline was gone, scattered in splinters around the clearing. High tide had doused the charred timbers, but a burned smell and a haze of gray smoke remained in the still air. It would linger for days until the wind changed and flushed out the reach.

"Didn't leave much, did they?" Sam said.

Jake didn't reply. If his attackers had set out to cut him off from his old life, they could hardly have done a better job. When *Snow Goose* had burned, half his memories had burned with her. It was brutal therapy, but effective. He looked back on the eight wasted months since Elaine's death with embarrassment. They made him all the more determined to solve the mystery of the black boat.

It was dark by the time they backed the trailer into the water and floated off the boat. Jake gunned the outboard. It caught first try. Sam jumped in, the automatic tucked in the back of his trousers—out of the way, but out of sight as well.

"Where the hell are we going anyway, you crazy bastard?"

"They have to be upstream."

"That covers a lot of water."

"Don't worry. We don't have to look into every reach."

You could no more maintain a twelve in any convenient creek than service a Formula 1 Maserati in a home garage. The big keel demanded deep water and a firm bottom, good wharves, workshops, winches or a crane for the constant work of antifouling, polishing, and grooming. Then there were crews and mechanics—twenty men or more who had to be housed and fed.

Only a few places on the Rappahannock offered that kind of potential, and most were already staked out by hotels or big landowners. The two or three that weren't lay higher up the river, in the bays and reaches of the eastern shore.

Jake took his seat in the bow, zipped up his windbreaker, and pulled his cap down over his eyes. It would be cold out on the river, pushing upstream. The opposite bank was fading into a dull smudge, like a weak photograph exposed to the sun. Already it was hard to make out details.

"Stick to the bank, Sam."

"You're the boss."

The little boat curved out of the reach and onto the river. Immediately the choppy surface threw up spray that soaked their clothes. Sam curved back further into the bank, following its line except where ominous vortices pointed to snags just below the surface.

After ten minutes a shimmer of light reached out of the bay ahead of them, glimmering on the water. Sam turned towards it.

"Don't bother. Tides Inn."

They cruised by the big hotel from a hundred yards out, skirting the pool of light. Couples who might have stepped out of a TV commercial strolled in evening dress along the big wharf, where a dozen cabin cruisers lined up like piglets around a sow. Music drifted across the water.

"Looks nice," Sam said. "Don't suppose we could stop for a steak and a couple of drinks?"

"Later."

Resignedly, Sam swung the tiller, and they were back on the river.

It was pitch dark. No traffic disturbed the silent desert of water around them. Jake visualized the big twelves he'd seen the previous night, imagined them heading upstream, desperate to reach a mooring before the current reversed itself and the power of their sails could no longer draw them through the water. They could not be far away.

He crawled back to where Sam sat by the motor. "Go slow along here. As close to the bank as you can."

"You onto something?"

"Don't know. Just keep cruising. And give me the flashlight."

He went back to the bow, fanning the flashlight beam across the surface of the water. He almost missed the first sign. Something bumped the side of the boat. Waving for Sam to stop the motor, he played the light over the water until he spotted it. A piece of raw yellow lumber. He fished it out.

"So?" Sam said.

"Someone's building around here." He dipped his finger in the water, tasting the brackish under-flavor. "Lime."

"From cement?"

"Probably."

"Might be a holiday shack."

"Not up here." Jake stared into the darkness. He knew this part of the river. The banks were steep, heavily wooded, hard to build on. Rotted trees and mud banks clogged the narrow reaches.

"Pull in."

They drifted to the shore on quarter power. Jake slid out in the shallows, floundered through the soft mud, and looped the painter over a low branch. Mosquitoes rose with a soft hum and descended greedily on his hands and face. Behind him, Sam swore comprehensively.

The bank was steep, choked with wisteria. It took ten minutes to tear through the underbrush and reach the top.

And suddenly the woods disappeared. The ground was bare clay, sheered off by a bulldozer blade. Jake sat on his heels and waited for his eyes to adjust to the dark.

Somewhere to the right he heard a faint metallic ticking.

Sam leaned close to his ear. "What the hell?"

Jake sniffed. Carbon monoxide.

"Car engines cooling."

He scrambled towards the sound and nearly bumped his head on the first car. There were four of them. Big limousines, engines contracting in the evening cool. He risked a flash at the number plates. Orange and blue New York tags. Some rich gentlemen were a long way from home.

Now a glow was obvious from the opposite side of the cleared area. A path led down through the forest to a reach they had not been able to see from the river.

Sam stopped in front of him. "Bingo."

A boatyard.

Long concrete dock, with a cradle hoist to lift boats out of the water. A pair of prefabricated boathouses. Further up the reach, a big bungalow that had obviously been there long before the rest. And beyond it, on the other side of the water, a low building that had to be sleeping quarters and workshops.

No people were in sight, though the lights in all the buildings were on. The door to one of the boathouses was open a foot, letting a long slice of bright light out onto the dark slipway.

"You wanna try it?" Sam asked.

"I guess so." He tried to hide his growing sense of danger.

Sam checked the pistol and put it back in the waistband at the back of his trousers.

"You planning to shoot somebody?"

"Only if they shoot first. Come on, hot shot." He scrambled ahead down the narrow path. They sprinted across fifty feet of concrete and slipped through the open door.

Sam glanced at the cradled twelve. "*Expeditious*. That's her. What about next door?" They pushed open the doors and went in. "Mother of God!" Sam breathed. "*Look* at that thing."

A dull and deadly black, the hull annihilated light. They felt drawn into it, hypnotized by its brutal, almost criminal precision. It conjured up blades and blood, an instrument of sudden death, hanging in the damp gray air like a creature in a cocoon. A touch might wake it.

Jake swallowed, and reached out with his hand. The gesture restored sanity. "It's some kind of plastic. Feels like that Teflon coating they use on nonstick frying pans." "You can't have a plastic hull. It would crack."

"They're building Lear jets out of it now, pal. Stressed carbon fiber baked into a polyester base. It's so hard you need a diamond drill to work it."

They walked around to the stern. The hull over their heads was spotted with silver discs the size of quarters, set into the dull black plastic. Sensors. Jake remembered the wide fanned-out counter, the cockpit flickering with telltales. The stern must be crammed with electronics.

Sam backed off, trying to see over the high stern into the interior of the boat.

"Hey. It's got a name. *Sasori*."

The silver letters ran in a shallow curve across the stern, with their Japanese equivalent underneath.

"Japanese," Sam said. "Guess we don't have to look too far to figure out who owns this baby. Fujita and Ryker. Weird." He stared at the name. "*Sasori*. What the hell's that mean anyway?"

"Scorpion," someone said behind them.

They both turned. The man was no more than ten feet away—gangling, gray-faced, a scarecrow with a cobra smile. Jake waited for his forked tongue to flick out.

"Scorpion?" Sam said easily. "That right? Well, that's some boat. Not that I'm any judge of these things. You in charge here?"

Jubei nodded.

"Our boat broke down. Fuel line. You got a phone here we can use?"

He put his hands on his hips. Jake sensed he would go for his gun any moment now. He looked around for something that might give them an edge if there was trouble. A few feet to his right festoons of chains hung down from a winch used to haul equipment out of the boat. If he could get to them . . .

"I know we're trespassing," Sam went on, "but hell, what could we do? Stuck out on the river. No motor. No food." He looked suddenly towards Jake. "And my pal here's hurt too. Jake, show him that arm."

For an instant the hooded eyes of the tall man wavered. Sam's right hand reached under his jacket, groping for the pistol butt.

Jubei moved like a snake. One hand whipped out to dash the gun from Sam's fingers before it was halfway leveled.

Sam charged him.

His shoulder hit the big Japanese hard. But not hard enough.

He never had a chance.

Jubei had mastered *tae kwon dō* to fifth *dan* level. Sidestepping, he took Sam's shoulder on his hip and, as he blundered past, hooked his left forearm around his throat.

The right hand drew back like a piston, palm at right angles to the bony wrist. He drove the heel of his hand into the back of Sam's head.

A *tae kwon dō* blow, traveling at sixty feet a second, delivers seven hundred pounds of force, enough to split eight layers of tile.

Sam's eyes bulged as if a hammer had smashed him on the skull. He gagged, gaped, and sagged limply. The Japanese held him for a moment, savoring the weight of the unconscious body.

"Put him down."

He turned slowly. Kim Ryker stood in the doorway of the boathouse. She was pale.

Jubei had his orders. No harm to anyone unless it became necessary. Ryker and this girl were friends of Fujita-*san*. He was to be friendly to them. For now. Later, he wanted the girl. But for now . . .

He grinned. "Fujita-*san* say no people . . ."

He realized the girl wasn't looking at him, but over his

shoulder. He let Sam's body slip to the ground and half-turned.

The length of chain in Jake's hands crashed into his chest and wrapped itself around his body. Jake waited until it locked, then yanked hard. Jubei spun around and fell to his knees, clutching his chest, momentarily breathless.

Shortening his grip, Jake pivoted on his heel and swung the four-foot length like a baseball bat. The last three inches, traveling at sixty miles an hour, slashed across Jubei's forehead. His eyes rolled to the whites, and he sprawled flat on the concrete.

Jake bent over Sam. He was gray-faced, his breathing a hoarse flutter. Kim squatted beside him.

"I need a boat." There was no way he could manhandle the unconscious Sam across that brush and down to the river.

"There's an outboard."

"Where?"

"Slipway. Let me untie it before you come down." She looked at Sam. "Is he dead?"

"Not yet. Who the hell are these people? What's going on here?"

She started to reply, then both of them froze as a group of men walked by the boathouse. Jake listened to their murmuring voices fading, relieved that none of them had spared a glance at the half-open boathouse door.

"My father's taking them back to their cars. He won't be back for ten minutes. I'll get the outboard."

While he waited, Jake gingerly felt the back of Sam's head. The skin felt swollen and bruised under the hair, but there was no obvious sign of skull fracture and no blood from the ears. Jake knew what a *tae kwon dō* blow could do; the thug must have pulled his punch.

Kim stood in the doorway. "Now! You've only got a moment."

She helped him drag the unconscious Sam across the slipway to the old motorboat bobbing on the dark water. They slid him into the bottom, and Jake grabbed the rope to start the motor.

"Come with us!" he said suddenly.

She looked over her shoulder. "I can't. My father . . ."

"Then get away when you can. I'm in Virginia Beach. At Sam's house. Or the hospital."

"I'll try. Now I have to go." She disappeared into the darkness towards the old house.

It took three attempts to start the old outboard, each more noisy than the last. When it finally caught, Jake was certain he'd woken up the whole reach. He steered towards the entrance of the narrow cove, remembering what had happened last time he sailed the Rappahannock in a small boat at night. Sam lay in the bottom of the boat. He was still breathing, but that was about all.

Jake felt a pang of guilt that the person whose safety was most on his mind was neither himself nor Sam, but Kim Ryker. Seeing her framed in the doorway, as he could see her at any instant just by closing his eyes, had thrown him into an emotional turmoil that, minutes later, still made his heart thud and his pulse race. Smashing down Jubei as she watched had been one of the most profoundly satisfying moments of his entire life.

CHAPTER ELEVEN

From a thousand feet, the Pacific had no detail; a blank white glare blazed back from the surface.

Ryker mopped his forehead with a soaking hand-kerchief. Why wasn't the damned chopper air-con-ditioned? You would think they could manage that. Everything else—the flight from Hawaii, the rendezvous with the tanker, the switch to this smaller helicopter—had run as smoothly as a military operation.

"Try one of these, Mr. Ryker."

Fujita's man leaned forward and lifted the lid from a round wooden box on the table between them. Rolled red hand towels were curled inside like fat slugs. He took one, hot with steam, and rinsed his face and hands, breathing in camphor and sandalwood. For the first time in an hour, his head cleared.

"Wow. That's great."

The little man let him fidget with the crumpled towel for a few seconds before indicating the wastebasket beside his chair. Its shiny floor swallowed the towel with a flicker of movement. It might never have existed.

That was the Fujita operation in a nutshell. Maybe there was a button that would tip *him* through the floor. His hands tightened a fraction on the arms of his chair.

"We are very close now."

"Yeah?" He looked out the window at endless ocean. "I can't see anything."

The man took off his watch and held it out.

"Please try it on. You will be interested, I think."

Ryker took off his own watch. The new one had a seg-mented metal band that fitted firmly around his wrist, like a bracelet. For the first time, he noticed the red fig-ures lined up under the conventional time-keeping face. They flickered as he watched.

"The figure on the left is Greenwich Mean Time. The

rest can be set to any available data source. At the moment they are tuned to our air-speed indicator. You will see that the figure to the right shows eighteen miles to our destination. They can also be set to monitor body functions: blood pressure, heartbeat, skin reactions."

Ryker felt his pulse rate rise; the dial instantly reflected it. At the same time, another display relentlessly counted down the miles to their destination.

"One of our development projects required high-level telemetry of bodily functions." He smiled. "This is a novelty, a spinoff."

"You . . . uh, planning to put these on the market?" He was already figuring the possibilities for merchandising. Heart attack victims, people with high blood pressure, just plain hypochondriacs would love them.

The man smiled. "I am sorry. I have no information."

The cabin tilted. An island swung past the window, a crescent of black volcanic rock coated with vegetation like green frosting.

They coasted over a bay, the shadow of the helicopter sliding across the white sand bottom, echoing the movement of three sharks that restlessly roamed the pale green water of the lagoon. Under the sand Ryker glimpsed familiar oblong shapes, blurred by time and rust.

"Was there fighting here?"

"The Americans occupied the Midsummer group briefly, as a radio base. Since 1948, they have been a British protectorate."

Ryker watched the familiar shape of sunken LST's slide astern. The Japanese might have lost the war, but they sure as hell won the peace.

He didn't see the circular concrete landing platform until they were settling towards it. Built into the scalloped edge where jungle met beach, it looked like one more patch of white coral sand.

A wave of damp heat enveloped him as soon as he stepped out. Before he reached the shade of the trees, he was drenched in sweat. A golf buggy driven by another Japanese bumped out of the jungle and curved to a stop on the concrete. As he got in, the helicopter door closed, the rotors started to turn.

"What's their hurry? How the hell am I going to get back?"

The driver grinned and ignored him.

They wove through the jungle on a path as smooth as the best fairway at Pebble Beach. A few yards on each side, the jungle rioted, lianas twisting to the sun, clinging to the trunks of trees already bent under the weight of a thousand parasites. A blue and silver butterfly with wings like swatches of velvet flew into the path ahead of the buggy, veered from its bow wave, and blundered off down the corridors of sunlit green.

Following it with his eyes, Ryker caught his first glimpse of the house, an impression of metal and glass as disconcerting as a glass eye in a flower arrangement.

The buggy pulled up on a patio of gray flagstones. Ryker got out, and the driver was moving again before he could turn around. A curved glass wall slid back, and he felt a whisper of icy air. He stepped inside.

Takeo Fujita came through the *shoji* screen on the other side of the room and held out his hand.

"Mr. Ryker. Did you have a pleasant trip?"

He wore Japanese dress. Black silk kimono, blue obi, *geti* on his feet.

Ryker wiped his hand and shook Fujita's dry palm. "Your people did a fine job."

Fujita sat in one of the three green vinyl armchairs in the room.

"I would hope so. That is what they are paid for. Would you like a drink?"

"Well . . . yeah. Sure. Thanks. I sweated quarts just coming up from the beach."

A girl in the green nylon wrapper that was the uniform of most Tora employees came through the screen with a tray and one glass, beaded with cold. For an instant, he thought she was Keiko.

"A bourbon highball. Jack Daniels. I believe that's correct?"

Ryker sipped it. "Fine. You're not joining me?"

"I do not use alcohol."

Ryker put down his glass guiltily and looked out the window at the curve of the bay. "Uh, beautiful place."

"It's one of many Tora owns. Occasionally we use it

for meetings. The first trials of *Sasori* took place out there."

Ryker visualized the black boat slicing through that green water. Like the sharks he glimpsed as they flew in.

"It paid off. The committee was impressed."

"So you said on the phone. You do not anticipate difficulties?"

"They took some measurements. We may have to let them look her over again."

"She conforms to your rule. There is no doubt of that."

"Well, you know these old establishment organizations. Lots of ridiculous rules. Like this thing about your challenge having to come through a club, not an individual."

"The Imperial Japanese Yacht Club can trace its ancestry back to 1217, Mr. Ryker. We were winning great sea battles when Newport still belonged to the Algonquin indians. I am not worried about the New York Yacht Club. The incident that took place as *Sasori* was being brought to your mooring concerns me far more."

Ryker drank more of the bourbon. "Just an accident. Pure chance. We had no idea Forrester lived down there. My men went along to buy him out like all the other small holders."

"Did they burn other boats? Were other individuals beaten?"

"We didn't have to—the rest saw sense. Look, Mr. Fujita, you have to decide. Do you want this shot at the Cup or not? If you do, maybe we have to break some heads. What about that thug of yours, Jubei? When Forrester and his pal sneaked into the compound a few nights back, he nearly killed Sam Lewis, according to my daughter. Smashed him in the head with some sort of karate punch. Sam Lewis, one of the country's top designers! I don't call *that* a smart diplomatic move—but I see why you let him do it. This isn't a game; we're fighting to take something away from these people that they don't want to give up."

Fujita ignored Ryker's points, whether out of disdain or agreement he couldn't tell. "What is Lewis's condition?"

"Not too serious. Concussion. He's out of danger now."

"Will there be investigations?"

"I'm handling that. The boats are gone by now. So are your men. A couple of my guys are there to keep an eye on things. Any sign of trouble and they'll get lost."

"Forrester does not sound like the kind of man to give up after having been attacked. The day after your men left him for dead he was investigating our base. It seems to me he will do the same again."

"Let him investigate. There won't be anything to find, nobody to talk to." Ryker had finished his drink. He put down the glass. Anxious to change the subject, he said, "Mr. Fujita, while I'm here, there's a couple of things I'd like to talk to you about. On the way over, I saw some interesting new Tora items that I'd be pleased to distribute in the States. On the same deal as we have on the digital system."

"I'm glad some of our humble efforts meet with your approval, Mr. Ryker. What did you have in mind?"

"Well, that wristwatch with the sensors—interesting item. I think I could do something with that."

"Yes. Perhaps you could. You might also be interested, then, in examining our three-D motion picture holography; the development staff now have it ready for mass merchandising. Also a new type of underwater breathing mask that will replace the so-called aqualung."

Ryker licked his lips. "You're suggesting I might be able to buy licenses for these?"

"It is possible."

"Well, hell, I'm certainly interested."

"One thing concerns me. Three people still exist who witnessed these . . . difficulties. Your two men and your daughter."

"They're safe. They won't talk. But if you're worried, I can send Weisell and Levitt out of state."

"And the girl?"

There was a long silence in the room. Outside, an insect as large as a toy helicopter blundered into the glass and fell scrabbling to the stone flags.

"She's my daughter, for Chrissake!"

"No harm will come to her."

The insect on the patio rattled dispiritedly against the metal track of the sliding wall. A man in a green coverall appeared from around the corner, brushed the creature into a flip-top dustpan, and was gone.

"Mr. Ryker, I assure you. By now you must be aware that our aims are your aims. We do not misuse our associates. It is not the Tora way."

He reached out and touched a button on the desk. A panel slid back from a TV monitor. The screen showed a room that, at first, Ryker took for his own bedroom back in Virginia. The lacquer chest. The wide, gleaming bed.

"As you see, we have prepared quarters for you. You are welcome as long as you care to stay. And Miss Sakahura will be arriving in less than twenty-four hours. She has important work in Hawaii, but she asked particularly that she be allowed to spend a little time here with you."

Ryker turned away from the screen with an effort. He thought about Fujita's offer. It meant millions.

"I can't just leave my business like that. My staff will be expecting me back."

"Your quarters have telephone, telex, and secretarial facilities; I naturally also need to remain in touch with my business while I am on the island. You will have complete privacy. Now . . . Miss Ryker?"

Ryker moistened his lips.

"What do you need to know?"

Later that night, Keiko Sakahura knelt by the low red lacquer table. After ten minutes of meditation she began the preparations for the ritual of the Nineteenth Way.

She was naked. The soft light from a tiny oil burner sheened her smooth skin like bronze. Her pointed nipples were the color of corroded silver.

She opened the first of the four black lacquer boxes. It was filled with a dull yellow dust. Gold, milled to the fineness of talcum powder.

With a tiny plastic scoop, she measured out enough to fill the bottom of the cup in front of her, tapping the scoop delicately against the edge to dislodge the last few grains.

The second lacquer box contained a glass laboratory flask with a sealed stopper. Keeping her head turned away, she removed the seal and dripped three drops of the clear glycerinelike fluid into the gold. Her nose wrinkled as a whiff of the chemicals reached her mucous membranes. She almost sneezed as she placed it carefully back in the box.

Too thick to soak in, the three drops of fluid lay on top of the powder, clear pearls magnifying the granular gold so that she seemed briefly to be looking through a microscope at the tiny grains. She reversed the scoop, using the handle to mix powder and liquid into a paste the consistency and color of *gai lat*, the sharp mustard of eastern China.

Outside, over the lagoon, the moon was rising in the swollen, lopsided configuration of the third quarter. Keiko could almost feel the tidal tug of its force.

From the bed behind her, she heard a low, muffled grunt and looked over her shoulder.

Vincent Ryker lay spread-eagled and naked on the gold vinyl bedspread, ankles and wrists ringed by straps attached to the metal bed-frame. A rubber band circled his face above the chin; a thick bite of the same material kept his teeth parted.

He grunted again, twitching his head to the left.

Keiko sat on the edge of the bed, trailing her fingers along his arm until she found the spot that itched. She scratched it carefully with her long unlacquered nails. Ryker closed his eyes gratefully, opened them again, raised his eyebrows.

"Very soon," she said. "Just a moment for the solution to settle. Are you ready?"

He nodded. She could see he was trying not to look eager, but no man who had experienced the Nineteenth Way could do that. Once tasted, it became an addiction.

She trailed her fingers down his chest, combing through the thick black hair, and flattened her hand on the area of bare skin just below his navel. His genital area was as hairless as hers; it would never be otherwise, as long as they lived. Surgical electrolysis had sealed off the follicles below the epidermal layer. Her hand stroked and teased him into erection while her mind counted off the seconds until the solution would be fully matured. After 160 seconds, she stopped abruptly, went to the table, and returned with the tiny cup in one hand and the third lacquer box in the other.

The third box held three objects.

The first was a gold capsule ringed with white metal, half an inch long.

Keiko slid her left hand under Ryker's hips. With the other she reached between his legs, the capsule between thumb and the finger that, alone among her fingers, lacked the long pointed nail, and pushed the capsule into his anus. His sphincter tightened around her finger, then loosened as she guided the capsule into the rectum until it lay close against the prostate gland.

The second object in the box was a tiny brush, its bristles softer and finer than human hair. Keiko dipped it into the solution of gold and carefully began painting the head of Ryker's penis. The solution flowed thickly, like nail polish, and it took more than a minute to cover the whole of the circumcised glans. With the rest of the paste, she painted a wide line down the underside, along the bulging tube of the urethra.

Then she took the third object out of its narrow glass tube.

It might have been an old-fashioned eight-inch hat-pin except for the way it quivered as Keiko drew it carefully from the tube. The micro engineers at Tora Electronics had developed the acupuncture needle to a fineness undreamed of by the Chinese.

In coating his penis, Keiko had been careful to leave untouched the tiny area around the opening to the urethra. Ryker flinched as the needle slipped between the tiny lips, but her careful hands stroked him until he was again calm. The needle disappeared inch by inch, following the ducts and passages that it had been designed to probe. She stopped only when her fingers felt the tiny gold stud that marked its end.

It was delicate work, hard on the body and nerves. Sweat gave her skin a glow that made her more than ever like a figure of metal. Wiping her hands on her thighs, she ran through the nine mental exercises that would prepare her for the next stage of the Way.

She returned to the table, and the fourth box. Ten gold caps slipped over her fingers. As her fingertips came in contact with the tiny electrodes inside, she felt the nerves of her hands jump and twitch. A tiny spark of blue static electricity leaped from one nail to another as the separate parts of the mechanism adjusted themselves to her body aura.

They spat again, briefly, savagely, as she lifted out the last object in the box. When it too was in place, she turned to the naked man on the bed.

His whole body was greasy with sweat. As she crawled up the bed towards him, lifting herself over the flesh and gold machine she had created between his thighs, she could feel the charge surge between them.

The hairs on Ryker's chest stirred as if an amber rod had been passed over them. She straddled him, showing the glistening open fold of her sex, the slim tautness of her perfect body—a body that had only one function. To give him pleasure.

She bent forward. Her lips brushed the tiny gold stud, suspended like a teardrop at the end of his erect penis.

She opened her mouth.

And it was gold. A smooth, fleshless cavity of yellow metal.

The prosthesis of surgically pure gold covered her teeth and palate and pressed the tongue to the floor of the mouth. In the sockets from which her wisdom teeth had been extracted, power cells energized the metal with a charge opposite to that of the battery lodged against Ryker's prostate.

Her open lips enclosed the crusted gold head of his penis.

A surge of electricity jolted through his already distended, supersensitized genitals, flooding down the metal catheter and arcing through the prostate. Power recoiled through the system, surged back along the circuit into the golden cavern of her mouth, and was returned once more.

Something neither organic nor electrical, a seething plasma of cells, fizzing with power, exploded from his body, to vaporize on the shining surfaces inside her mouth.

A groan of intolerable pleasure escaped around the gag. His body arched.

The power recoiled again. Another ejaculation. Two seconds later, a third. And a fourth. And a fifth.

By now the seminal fluid was exhausted. But the nerves, locked into the circuit between the twin terminals, spasmed helplessly.

Keiko raised her eyes, looking along the arching, twisting body, its muscles twitching uncontrollably like the bone-breaking fit of the epileptic grand mal. In ten seconds the cardiovascular system would begin phasing in sympathy. He would begin to die.

She opened her lips and drew away, watching with clinical interest as the body on the bed twitched and quivered, sliding on the sweat-greased vinyl.

In ten minutes she would begin again.

CHAPTER TWELVE

The second of the two big trucks with the green and white paintwork crawled up the narrow track and disappeared in the trees. Kim watched them go from the edge of the slipway beside the now empty boathouses.

The trucks had turned up that morning, unannounced. She caught a glimpse of the interiors and the huge cradles that filled them; then the Fujita crewmen doubled down the slope from the dormitories and slid back the boathouse doors. Within an hour both boats were loaded. The crews piled in beside them, the back doors swung up and locked shut.

Later, she wandered up to the dormitories and looked down the rows of narrow beds, the bedding folded neatly at the foot of each. No pinups on the walls. No notices. Not even a matchstick or candy wrapper to show that more than sixty men had lived here.

She shivered and went back to the main house. There was nowhere else to go.

Since her father had left, Weisell and Levitt had taken over the big living room. They had also opened up the bar and the deep-freeze. Levitt scooped taco chips into a pot of guacamole, sucking the green paste from his fingers. Weisell's nose was still stuffed with blood-soaked tape. Periodically he reached into one nostril, twitched the end of the wadding, and winced.

"Any calls?"

Neither of them answered.

"I thought maybe my father called."

Levitt shook his head. "Won't be back for a couple of days."

"Where's he gone?"

"Business trip," Levitt said.

"Yeah," Weisell chimed in. "God od a bidness trib."

"Don't worry. We'll look after you."

Weisell grinned. "Yeah. Bod ob us."

Kim went into the bedroom, closed the door, and pushed the stud that locked it. Her knees were trembling as she sat down on the bed.

She sensed the danger she was in. Her father had always underestimated the opposition to his schemes—he would be a more successful businessman otherwise. His projects always hovered on the edge of disaster through undercapitalization, poor research, indifferent market analysis. He would not have become involved with Fujita if he'd taken the trouble to look even one or two steps beyond the quick profits to be made from the deal. Now he was trapped; Fujita owned him. And that made Kim vulnerable too.

She didn't hate her father. The situation was too familiar for emotion. It came with the territory. Ryker himself seemed to know that. He always provided an escape hatch, sometimes not realizing he was doing so. It was his way of saving his loved ones from himself. He was like the suicide who fails to take a sufficiently large overdose, or who does so just ten minutes before a friend promised to call.

Where was it in this situation? She remembered him giving her the combination of his safe and went confidently into the dressing room. Weisell and Levitt would not try anything in here; she could still hear the TV yammering in the other room. She had plenty of time to make plans.

The safe opened easily. Most of the money still seemed to be there. She took a thousand dollars and her passport. The pile of flat black boxes remained on the lower shelf. She took one and slipped out the videotape cassette it contained. There was no label on it; just the Tora emblem impressed into the plastic in yellow. They all seemed to be the same. On impulse, she took one; if they were important enough to be locked in the safe, they might be a useful bargaining counter if she ran into trouble.

Back in the bedroom, Kim changed into a T-shirt and a long skirt, a woolen turtleneck, and high boots. Emptying her handbag onto the bed, she removed credit cards, driver's license, identification, stuffed the rest in the bag, and put it in her dressing table. The less signs she showed of her intention to get the hell out of the place, the better. She shoved everything else inside her waistband.

She opened the door and walked almost eagerly towards the TV set and the two shapes slumped in front of it.

"I'm going down to the store. Anything I can . . ."

Her voice stuck in her throat. Panic washed over her like sickness. The faces of the two men were plum-colored. Their eyes stared at the chattering, brightly colored images of Bugs Bunny and Wile E. Coyote on the screen, but they saw nothing. They were dead. Peering around the side of the chair, Kim saw the livid marks of fingers on Weisell's throat. He had been strangled with one giant hand.

She backed away, trembling.

From behind, another arm took her around the neck. Her heart stopped.

The grip tightened. She smelled sweat, sweetish bad breath. Then there was no breath; no air to scream.

She twisted spasmodically, trying to break the hold. All the time, some fraction of her brain remained in control, desperately calculating her chances, and remembering . . .

Remembering a length of metal chain crashing into Jubei's ribs a few nights before, his obvious pain, his collapse. The ribs must be bruised, perhaps even cracked.

Which side? Which side? Her head was whirling; spots jiggled before her eyes; her ears roared.

Desperately, she drove her left elbow backwards. At the same moment, she jackknifed her body, thrusting her hips back into what she hoped was his stomach.

He grunted in pain, and momentarily his grip slackened. Her feet touched the floor. Twisting away, she scrambled across the room, crashed through the door, and fled across the concrete to the Pinto.

The engine refused to catch. Looking up desperately, she saw Jubei's shape silhouetted in the open doorway. He was hunched, clutching his side, but those long legs ate up the six steps leading to the house in one stride. Then he was coming at her across the concrete. She saw his face, more skull-like than ever, pale with pain, but grinning still.

She prayed as she turned the key one more time. "Jesus, Mary, and Joseph, *please* . . ." It caught. The car rocketed forward, swerving past his clutching hands and on into the dark.

Jubei stood, indecisive, watching the taillights fade along the river road. By the time he took the car key from Weisell's body and started after her, she would have ten minutes' start. Fujita-*san* would be angry if she got away but angrier if he knew he had tried to take the girl for himself. His orders had been very clear; keep her in the house and wait for the father's return.

Nor had he been ordered to kill the two men. But they wanted the girl too and . . . Jubei did not remember much of the rest. When the haze had passed from his mind, they were both dead. His slow brain grasped the fact that he had performed very badly in this. Perhaps so badly that Fujita-*san* would make good his threat, issued when Jubei dealt too roughly with the man Lewis, to finish with him forever.

He looked around at the darkness like an animal smelling out its habitat. There was nothing here he knew; the rotting smells of the reach, the heavy perfume from night-blooming orchids rooted in the dark mud of the bank, the drone of insects over the shallows all confused and frightened him. He lusted for Japan with an animal hunger. He wanted crowds, the clang of the *pachinko* parlors, the rank smell of a woman, sweaty and fat.

The light speared out of the darkness at the edge of the forest, blinding him. His weak eyes peered towards its source, at the same time as he lurched forward automatically towards the person holding it.

"Stop there." At the same instant that Jubei heard the voice, a bullet pinged off the concrete. He looked down at the white chip an inch from his right foot.

He halted. "In case you think that was accidental . . ." Another shot. The white mark this time was equidistant from his other foot.

"Perhaps we could go in the house. I don't want to hurt you. Go on, please. I'll follow."

Jubei climbed the steps into the living room. When he

was well inside, the man with the gun followed him. Jubei recognized him as soon as he entered the light.

"Yes. We've met." Still holding the gun on Jubei, he glanced around the room, pausing at the two bodies in front of the TV set. "I see you've been busy. Rather careless to leave them sitting there. What if I was the police?"

Jubei retreated towards the door to Ryker's office. From there, he might get away through a window. The newcomer smiled, waving his gun in a gesture of disapproval.

"That would be very silly. What could you do loose out there in the woods? The police would catch you as soon as the sun came up. This is the South. They use dogs down here. I don't suppose they'd take more than an hour to hunt you down." He smiled. "On the other hand, that might be better than having Fujita after you. All this mess . . ." He waved his gun towards the two corpses. "*And* letting the girl escape . . . he won't be pleased, will he?

"On the other hand," he went on, "I think we can be useful to one another. My car is parked up on the top of the hill where we stopped the night I came down here with my friends. We could be away from here in a few minutes. I have a house where you can hide." He reached inside his coat with his left hand and took out a wad of bills. "And there's enough here to get you back to Japan. Or any other place you care to go."

He waved the bills and knew from Jubei's narrow eyes that he had him hooked. "All I require in return is a little assistance."

CHAPTER THIRTEEN

Jake came down the steps of Norfolk General and looked wearily at the morning. A coal train out of West Virginia rumbled across the railway bridge at the far side of the huge parking lot; its squeal and rattle conveyed something of his exhaustion.

Last night, his hired Oldsmobile had been one of a hundred cars in the lot. Now it stood almost alone.

The only other car nearby was a battered brown Pinto, and that was parked behind him, almost nose to tail. It looked abandoned, though it hadn't been there when he had parked. The hood was sprung, the left-hand fender and headlight caved in. Scraps of newly splintered wood were jammed into the crumpled metal.

He peered through the unwashed window, tried the door. It opened. Something stirred under a blanket on the back seat A small face appeared, drawn, white with fatigue; the eyes, blue pits.

Kim Ryker. He opened the door and got in.

"Hi." Her voice was a croak, slurred.

"Hi yourself. What are you doing here?"

"Want to talk to you. Police said you were at the hospital."

"Why didn't you come in?"

She shivered. "Someone's trying to kill me."

He patted her shoulder. His arm and back ached where the burned skin had begun to tighten. His joints were as stiff as if he had slept on concrete. But she looked worse.

"Anyone in particular?"

"The man you saw the other night. Jubei. He works for Fu . . . Fujita." She closed her eyes, wearily opened them again. "Can we go someplace? Please?"

He looked at the dashboard of the Pinto. "Does this thing run?"

"I put it through a fence. Something's wrong with the steering."

"Better take mine then."

She climbed out. "There's some things on the front seat."

He gathered up a passport, a bundle of bank notes, a small wallet, and a black cardboard box. She was already curled on the passenger's side of his car, clutching her arms around her sides. He put on the heater.

"How's your friend?" she asked.

"Not too bad. Severe concussion. It's a wonder that ape didn't fracture his skull."

The image of Jubei leaped into Kim's mind. She felt those arms tightening around her and instinctively moved closer to Jake. He heard her teeth start to chatter, and dragged a blanket out of the back seat to drape over her. She began to doze, though how much was exhaustion and how much shock, he couldn't tell. Her lips looked blue. He drove home as fast as he dared, not anxious to be stopped by a cop and asked to explain the exhausted girl in his car. Every few moments he shot a glance at her, surprised at the rush of affection for the small, curled figure. It was years since anyone had placed themselves so completely and trustingly in his hands.

At the house he carried her upstairs and put her into the big bed in Sam's guest room. The kitchen at least had some tea; he made a pot and carried it back up to her, holding her head while she sipped.

"Better?"

"Hmmmm." She was already slipping back into sleep.

Jake knew nothing about medicine, but he'd seen shock and exposure often enough at sea. Hot, sweet tea with rum worked as well as anything. That, and rest.

He looked around the room. Not too long ago, Sam had put him to bed in the same way. Leaving, he noticed a pile of boating magazines in the corner. On top, a *Sea* with his own face, smiling, confident. It seemed twenty years since he had felt that good.

Closing the door silently, he went back downstairs and collapsed into one of the big armchairs, resting his feet on the coffee table. He had to fight back his own fatigue, the feeling that his eye sockets were lined with hot sand. He needed to think. . . .

He woke up with a crick in his neck and a dry feeling at the back of his throat that told him he'd been snoring. When he had sat down, the sunlight had slanted across the living room floor two yards away. Now it fell on the far wall. He checked his watch. 4:00 P.M.

There was coffee in the Coffeemaster. He poured a cup and went back into the living room.

Kim's possessions were still piled where he had put them, on the coffee table. He glanced through her passport, feeling like an intruder.

Kimberley Linda Ryker. Born 1964. Nineteen. What was *he* doing at nineteen? Working behind the soda fountain in Amerson's Luncheonette, driving a clapped-out 1937 Hudson, necking on the dunes on weekends with Susie Lee Kaminsky who, if you didn't look too closely, was almost the spitting image of Judy Garland in *Meet Me in St. Louis.*

He snapped the passport shut and picked up the box. A VHS video cassette. It slipped out into his hand. Except for the Tora emblem, it was unmarked. He weighed it in his hand. Viewing it would mean taking one more step into the chaos that had already killed Elaine and Keble and that threatened his own life. Why not drop it right now?

The reason was obvious. He could not do so and live with himself. The attack on them at Ryker's boathouse had committed him. He found Sam's videoplayer and shoved in the tape.

The screen went shiny black, then bloomed with the green Tora chrysanthemum. Then he was looking at the ocean on a sparkling clear day. *Good sailing weather,* he thought automatically.

Something black glided into the picture, so dark that the sunlight seemed momentarily dimmed. *Sasori.* The camera panned with it.

It looked more sinister in bright daylight than under the glaring fluorescents of Ryker's boathouse. There it had been impotent, out of its element, caged. Now he saw the boat in all its arrogance.

He fiddled with the sound control and got only tape

hiss. This wasn't a promotional film. Whoever put the tape together meant it as raw information. He could imagine the men who owned those New York cars watching the screen while Ryker lectured them with facts and figures. Jake settled down to learn.

Red figures flickered along the top of the screen. A digital readout. The figures must relate to the boat's performance at that moment.

One number, the first in the display, fascinated him: 9.4 . . . 9.3 . . . 9.4 . . . 9.5 as the boat caught a swell.

It obviously represented the boat's speed in knots.

But nine knots for a twelve was phenomenal! The America's Cup record was 8.01 knots, set in 1937 by *Ranger*, a huge J-class sloop with a pyramid of sails that needed twenty men to sail her. Even in the best conditions, modern twelves seldom reached six knots.

If this tape was true, *Sasori* could outrun any twelve-meter afloat by almost four miles an hour.

He was still digesting this when the image on the screen changed abruptly. Computer animation froze the boat, turned the photograph to a graphic and revolved it through 180 degrees. Now he looked down into the deck area. Red lines indicated the intricate winching system that controlled the sails. Sam had guessed right in most cases. The cross-linking of this system would have American boatmen tearing down their twelves and firing off orders to the precision equipment manufacturers.

A zoom in on the mast. Hollow, rounded in front, with a knifelike trailing edge. More red figures showed the stresses endured by the mast under sailing conditions. They would have crumpled *Defiant*'s mast like a straw.

There was more. Flow patterns over the hull—*Sasori*'s hydrodynamics were impeccable. Sail efficiency—Jake could not guess from what material the black sails were made, but it was strong, thin, light, yet not so fragile that the points where it met metal cables needed heavy reinforcement. The perfect sail material. Beside it, Dacron polyester and Mylar were like linoleum. Telemetry—the tape revealed little about *Sasori*'s electronics, but it was obvious from the way she handled and the speed with which sails were changed to suit wind conditions that the

computer buried deep in her hull could outsmart anything the Western world cared to put up against it.

When the tape ended, Jake ran it through again. He
dug out Sam's calculator and rechecked the figures, ran-
sacking his rusty memory for formulas on stress patterns
and wind dynamics.

It was night before he finished. The reams of scratch
paper that surrounded him just confirmed the evidence of
the tape.

Sasori was as close to unbeatable as any boat could
get.

Sliding the tape back into the box, he replaced it
among Kim's belongings.

When he opened the door of the bedroom, the movement dislodged the contents of an overloaded hook. A
pile of clothes slumped to the floor. The bundle in the
bed stirred. One sleepy eye opened.

"How are you feeling?"

She didn't answer, just stretched luxuriously under the
bedclothes. Jake glanced away, embarrassed by a rush of
desire.

"Anything you need?"

"Maybe a glass of water?"

He filled a glass in the bathroom. She drank it without
pausing for breath.

"Wow. Great. I'm parched. How long have I been
asleep?"

"All day." He looked at his watch. "It's past eight."
Holding up the glass, he said, "More?"

"Please."

As he filled it again, Jake looked at his reflection in the
mirror. Not much seemed to remain of the old Jake who
watched himself and thought about suicide.

She drank the second glass as quickly as the first. He
sat on the edge of the bed.

"I just watched the tape."

"Tape?"

"The one you brought with you. About *Sasori*."

"Is that what it was? I just saw a bunch of them in the
safe and decided to bring one along."

"Was there anything else there? Plans? Specs?"

"No. I didn't have too much time to look. I can't remember . . . did I tell you what happened there last night?"

"You said you drove your car through a fence. And somebody tried to kill you."

"Jubei." She shivered. "You don't suppose he'd know I was here, do you?"

"We weren't followed from the hospital. And nobody's been around, as far as I can see." He thought about the length of chain thudding into the man's side. "I think I can hold him off if he does turn up."

She smiled. "Yeah, that's right. I forgot about the other night." Squirming down under the blankets, she stretched again, her small body outlined once more under the blanket.

Jake stood up. "Hungry?"

"Mmmmm. Starving."

"I found you some clothes." One of Sam's girlfriends had left shirts and shorts in the bottom of a closet. "When you get dressed, come and help."

As he went down the stairs, he felt an unexpected cheerfulness. He was actually whistling as he opened the refrigerator and pushed aside the bottles of ginger ale and daiquiri mix to reach the eggs.

"Pepper, please."

Jake passed Kim the pepper mill. She ground a few turns into the pan and stirred the eggs some more. The action did wonderful things to the curve of her neat buttocks against the outsize T-shirt.

"Where do you think your father's gone? Is he meeting Fujita?"

"I guess. He never told me what he was up to."

"What about the men who came there the other night. Did he tell you who they were?"

"Only that they were important. He was sweating a lot." She tipped the eggs onto the plate. "You don't think they'll do anything to him, do you?"

"No," Jake lied. "I'll go set the table."

When Kim came into the dining room, Jake had just put down the phone.

"I'm going to New York tomorrow." Piedmont and

Eastern both had early flights. He could be there by lunchtime. Obviously, from the tags he'd seen on those cars, the real action in this matter had shifted to New York.

"Just so we aren't going tonight." He looked down at her clothes. "I need to find something to wear."

"I said *I* was going, Kim. No reason for you to get involved in this."

She put her fork down hard on the table. "I'm involved already, remember? Jubei killed two men last night. He tried to kill me. He smashed Sam Lewis in the head. God knows what he plans to do with my father. Right now, you're the only friend I have. And you're not going anyplace without me." She frowned at the food around the table. "Did I forget the ketchup?"

CHAPTER FOURTEEN

"How long ya leavin' it, mister?"

"Day or two." Jake nodded towards the other side of 44th Street, where the doorman was helping Kim with their luggage. "We're at the Algonquin."

The checker at the parking garage ripped off the stub of the ticket. "Don't forget ya gotta get it validated."

The man gunned the car up the ramp with a roar that vibrated through the avenues of concrete. Jake turned to leave.

His eye was caught by one of the row of cars parked in the reserved space on the ground floor. He walked down the line, noting the numbers. He was frowning as he headed towards the gray stone building with the flags hanging limply over its entrance.

"Mister Forrester." The quartermaster looked startled as Jake pushed through the main doors of the club. "Glad to see you again, sir."

"Glad to be back, Miller. How's that daughter of yours? Still in law?"

"Indeed she is. Made judge last year."

"Comes from that good Alabama breeding."

"Very likely, sir. Are you . . . er, meeting someone, Mr. Forrester?"

"Nobody in particular. Just wondered if any old friends might be in town. Any objection if I look around?"

Miller looked embarrassed. "Well, Mr. Forrester, I'm not sure . . . that's to say, I believe your membership is no longer in force." He fidgeted with the guest cards in the slot over his lectern, as if hoping to find one there with Jake's name on it. "I'm sorry, sir. The committee made it quite clear to me that only members in good standing should be admitted." He looked at Jake uncomfortably. "It's the rules. I'm truly sorry."

Jake controlled his anger.

"Is it okay if I send up a message?"

"Of course." Anxious to retrieve the situation, he gave
him a card and the pen from his own pocket. Jake scribbled a few words, folded the card, and waved for a page.

"Give this to Tom Needham."

Miller and the page exchanged a glance. Miller licked
his lips.

"I'm not sure if Mr. Needham's in the club right now."

"His car's in the parking lot opposite. I also notice the
cars of the commodore, Gerry Cornelius, and a few other
boating gentlemen. Try the Afterguard Room."

Three minutes later Tom Needham came down the
staricase, smiling, hand outstretched.

"Jake! Didn't know you were in town. Great to see
you."

"I only arrived ten minutes ago. Miller here won't let
me in."

"That's absurd. Miller, Mr. Forrester's my guest. I'll
sign him in if necessary."

The quartermaster looked relieved. "Quite all right,
Mr. Needham."

"Come and have a drink."

The bar was stuffy and deserted behind the red plush
curtains. Jake ordered a beer and drank half of it at a
swallow. His anger was subsiding.

"We all wondered what happened to you, Jake. I
wrote. A lot of people wrote. Not everyone feels the
same way as the committee."

"Ancient history." He laid the video cassette on the
bar. "I came up to give them this. But I guess it comes as
no surprise to you."

"If it's the *Sasori* promo tape, then no. Most of us at
the club have known about the Japanese challenge for
some time. How do you mean, 'No surprise to *me*'?"

"I saw the cars the committee drove down to Ryker's
mooring when they looked over *Sasori*. A few of them
are parked across the street, in the club's reserved space.
I remembered the numbers. Were you there? I didn't
notice TOM III.

"Aaron Hart drove me down. His chauffeur has better

nerves than mine. Those country roads are ridiculous."
He smiled. "So is this whole melodrama."

"Ryker's men burned *Snow Goose* and my mooring.
One of Fujita's thugs smashed Sam Lewis in the head
and put him in the hospital. Neither of *us* are laughing.
Neither are the men who burned me out—the same man
who slugged Sam killed both of them yesterday."

Needham stared at Jake. "Are you *serious*? Ryker told
us that Sam was injured while trespassing . . ." He saw
Jake's anger and held up his hand to stave if off. "His
phrase, not mine. Of course I got onto the Norfolk Hospital straight away. Sam seems to be okay, thank God.
But arson? And murder?"

"I don't remember you being too surprised after
Charlie Keble's murder. You had half a dozen suspects
picked out. Ryker and Fujita were among them. What
changed your mind?"

"Jake, we don't *know* who killed Charlie and Elaine.
Maybe we'll never know. Both of them had motives, I
grant you; if they had wanted to win the last Cup that
much, they might, I say *might*, have hired someone to
shoot Charlie and wire your car. Not that the police ever
found a scrap of evidence to involve either Ryker or Fujita. And frankly, Jake, having gotten to know Takeo
Fujita in the last months, I personally don't believe he
could be involved in any such scheme. Ryker, perhaps,
but not Fujita."

Jake watched the process of whitewashing Fujita with
something like awe. It was no less appalling for its familiarity; throughout history, the rich and the powerful
closed ranks whenever one of their own was threatened.
In this very building, more than a hundred years ago,
Morgans connived with Rockefellers and Rockefellers
with Astors to excuse their manipulation of the stock
market and disguise their exploitation of the nation's re-
sources. Now Takeo Fujita was part of the club; one of
the gentlemen and thus entitled to the benefits of the
gentlemen's agreement.

And Vincent Ryker? He sweated too much, wore ill-
cut suits, did stupid things like setting his goons on to
inconvenient adversaries. No gentlemen, he was tailor-

made for the role of fall guy. Jake began to suspect that, if he ever had a chance to talk to Ryker, he'd learn the real key to this puzzle.

"The club really wants Fujita to challenge, doesn't it?"

Needham looked embarrassed. "Every challenge is entitled to consideration."

"Tom, it's a setup! You know that as well as I do. Half the time the club *invites* challenges, especially if the British don't look like they'll be able to get the money together to field a boat. They practically rolled out the red carpet for Sir Frank Packer and his boats in the sixties. They needed the Australians. Now they need Fujita—right?"

"It's simplistic, but . . . all right, I suppose they do. Fujita has plans that will galvanize the whole boat scene. You can't imagine the work that's gone into *Sasori*. That hull: It's ground graphite and epoxy resin bonded to carbon-fiber strands. Thinner than cardboard and stronger than steel. That continuous film in the sails? A thousand dollars a square *foot*. All the metal components are titanium honeycomb. And the electronics . . . Jake, this boat will push the state of the art ahead ten years in one leap."

"And make lots of people rich."

"Have you got something against being rich? Don't think you'll be left out, Jake. Right now, you've got a lead on your competitors in the boat building and servicing field of at least a year. You could deal with Fujita like Ryker did; buy licenses to manufacture and distribute this technology. His people are ready to talk; I've been approached myself. So have a lot of people in the business."

"Then why the hell are you building *Andromeda*? I thought you wanted to hold the Cup."

"I do and I think I will. *Sasori's* an incredible creation, but you know about new technology—it takes a while to get the bugs out. She's fast, but she's fragile. I think we can beat her. I sure as hell want to try. But . . ." He shrugged.

"Boating is one thing and business another?"

"If you like. Look, Jake, let me lay it on the line for you. You're an old friend. I respect you. But you're making waves, and a lot of people are unhappy about that. We didn't want the Japanese challenge to become public knowledge just yet. It would have been far better to announce when *Andromeda* is launched at Christmastime. You've forced our hands . . ."

"Ryker and his goons did the forcing, Tom."

"All right. I agree Ryker brought a lot of this about. It's done. We'll live with it. But back off, Jake. That's my advice, and I want you to take it. A lot of people are already very upset; you've caused a great deal of trouble. Understandably, but that's beside the point. It's time to drop the whole thing. Speaking for myself, I don't have the time to waste on this. There's *Andromeda* to be finished, for one thing. Olin Stephens has been working on her ever since Sam delivered the preliminary plans. Jake, she's a great boat. You know what a genius Sam is. You'll love her."

"It sounds like you're offering me a job."

"Of course. It wouldn't be the same without you on the team."

"What sort of job?"

"Well, I haven't thought it out. Caller, I guess. We need someone with your feel for tactics."

"Who'll skipper?"

"We haven't really chosen . . ."

"*Who?*"

"Well, *I* did pretty well last time, Jake."

Jake put down his glass. "Thanks for the drink."

"Don't decide right away. Think about it."

"I don't have to, Tom. This whole thing stinks. You may have forgotten about Elaine and Charlie. I haven't. Do what the hell you like—you and the rest of your gentlemen sailors. I'm going into business for myself."

The headquarters of *Yachts and Yachting*, the boat world's most popular magazine, took up an entire floor twenty-seven stories above Park Avenue. Looking around the lush foyer with its framed oil paintings of America's Cup winners, Jake tried to square it with the old office, crammed into one corner of an East Side print shop, blocked off from the machinery by matchboard partitions.

But that was before the boating boom, when the only advertisers were backyard builders offering their home-designed products to a few thousand specialists. He had glanced through the current issue while he waited in the reception area. For every page of editorial, there were ten of ads: electronics for navigation and communication, announcements of boating events like the New York National Boat Show ("See and board 500 boats—over 100 sailboats, plus luxury yachts, powerboats, inflatables . . ."), prestige advertisements for Volvo marine engines, Texaco gas, Chivas Regal whiskey. Business was good.

The receptionist, pretty in a boyish way, watched disapprovingly from under her bangs as Jake paced the carpet, slapping the Fujita cassette against his thigh.

Sally Goldstone burst out of the offices like a squall. "Jake Forrester! Jesus, it's good to see you." Linking her arm through his, she hauled him through a vast room filled with people typing, drawing, and laying out pages, and into an opulent office with a corner view of Manhattan and a tiny balcony.

"How the hell are you, Jake? I heard all sorts of crazy things. You were a drunk. Died. Gone to South America."

"All true." He sat down opposite her. "How are things with you, Sal?"

She spread her arms to take in the office. "You have to ask? *Sylvia!*"

A pretty girl looked through the door. Boyish again. He began to remember things about Sally Goldstone.

"No calls, sweetheart."

The girl beamed meltingly.

"Not bad," Jake said when the door closed.

"She's a sweet little thing. One of the perks of this job is the pussy."

"The magazine business must be doing well."

"It's okay in the summer, but postal rates . . . . *meshugge!* No, here's where we pull in the real money."

She skimmed an ad layout across the desk. The blonde wore only bikini briefs and a straining T-shirt. On it was printed: It Takes a Twelve to Satisfy Me.

"It's shit, but they lap it up. T-shirts, posters, badges,

bumper stickers. We do a kit as well—build a Laser in your garage. It's big business. You should be in on it, pal." Her square, mannish face broke into a grin. "Sure, why not? They still remember you from last year. We can build it up. Maybe a lecture tour of boat clubs. That's a big thing now. Get a grand, fifteen hundred at a time. Third to us and you're still rolling in it."

Jake put up his hand to stem the flow. "Sal, I don't want to go into the promotion business. I brought you something."

She picked up the videotape, noticed the Tora emblem on the pack. "This anything to do with the Fujita thing?"

"It's the film they made for the Cup committee."

"I'll take a look at it, Jake, but I'd guess there won't be much in it that isn't in here."

She dumped a book bound in black vinyl in front of him. Ring-bound inside were photographs, specifications, pages of data on *Sasori*.

"Next week all the boat writers get flown to Newport for the grand unveiling. Should be quite a bash. And the agencies are suddenly spreading around *lots* of Tora advertising. Not nickel and dime half-pages either. Color. Ten-page inserts. If they want to make friends in the magazine business, that's how to do it."

"Do you know about Tom Needham's boat?"

"*Andromeda*? Yeah, I hear things. You involved in that?"

"He offered."

"You turned him down?"

"He can't win."

"The boat isn't *built* yet, for God's sake."

"Whatever it's like, it can't win." He got up and went to the window. "Sal, I've seen this thing. There's nothing to touch it."

She nodded. "I saw Fujita in the Fastnet last year. Those crews! I don't know what he does to them, but they work like machines. And they're very tricky too. They don't exactly break the rules, but some of them get awful bent. Like it was life or death."

"That's why *Andromeda* doesn't have a chance. Everyone has too much riding on this to let Fujita lose."

"So you're going to sit this one out, huh? Well, that

makes sense. What about being our Newport correspondent? We'll pay top dollar."

Ryker, Needham, now Sally Goldstone, all trying to buy him. Until that instant he'd had no serious plans, but suddenly he realized only one course was open to him.

"I'm not sitting it out. I'm going to enter a boat myself."

He regretted the statement almost as soon as he'd made it. Where would he get a boat from? All his life he'd been a paid professional, sailing other men's boats, relying on the big syndicates for the crucial financial backing without which a twelve could not sail. Seeing the complex Fujita had built on Ryker's land had dramatized to Jake once again just how much this was a sport of monied men, in which the sailors took orders and, if they had criticisms, voiced them only to one another.

Yet—did it *have* to be this way? The Australian newspaper millionaire Frank Packer had mounted his first challenges alone (though it was said around the business that his motives for doing so were, in his phrase, "alcoholic delusions of grandeur"); the British traditionally worked hand-to-mouth in their challenges, actually appealing for public funds and holding charity auctions to get the necessary nut together. Jake had contacts; he had the boatyard; he had the skill and the reputation.

What he did not have was a boat.

Could he build one? He rejected the idea immediately; even if he were to start now on the designs, any boat of his would lag behind the competition by at least six months.

An old boat, then. But what twelve meter was not already consigned to the scrap heap by the inexorable march of new technology? They were all out of date— even *Defiant*.

But he'd find one. He was committed to doing so—not on paper, but inside, where these commitments mattered.

Sally watched him with level eyes across the desk, almost as if she sensed the tension within him.

"You? Where's the money coming from?"

"I'll find it."

"What about the NYYC?"

"They're backing Tom's boat."

"Then you haven't a prayer, bubbie. If they're against you, you aren't even in the race. Haven't you noticed how they always find some little point where your boat doesn't fit the rule? Remember Halvorsen? They fixed him without even getting out of breath."

"Halvorsen?"

Lars Halvorsen had been one of the sixties' great boat designers, a pioneer of all-metal construction when twelves still had wooden hulls, a genius of hydrodynamics, and a first-class pain in the ass to the boating establishment.

Sally said, "I'll get together some material for you. Like the man says, those who don't learn the lessons of history are doomed to repeat them. Where are you staying?"

"Algonquin."

She made a note and held out her hand. Jake shook it. The palm was as rough as a lumberjack's. "And think about that correspondent's job. Not that I have any use for 'em myself, but I hate to see a good man wasted."

CHAPTER FIFTEEN

Fifth Avenue was jammed with lunchtime traffic. Jake took a cross street to Lexington and cruised towards 39th.

He'd been a week in New York—one of the most frustrating of his life. The day after his talks with Needham and Sally Goldstone, he'd sat down in the hotel and written out a list of priorities.

Elaine and Charlie—Link with Fujita?
Talk to Ryker
Race Challenge

After the last, he inserted a question mark, then angrily crossed it out; what had begun in Sally Goldstone's office as a gesture of bravura now seemed more and more possible. It would mean selling the yard, mortgaging the house—and using the money in Elaine's safe-deposit box.

That remained the most puzzling aspect of the whole mystery. Jake realized he had lived in a mental isolation cell of his own construction for the last two years. Shut off with only *Defiant* on his mind, he had not noticed the thousand hints that would have given him the clues he needed now to solve the puzzle.

Neither the shots aimed at *Defiant* nor the bomb in the car were meant for him; Keble and Elaine had not died as his proxies. They were targeted by a professional assassin who did his job with such precision that nobody suspected they were anything but the random gestures of a madman. If Jake had not found the money, he might have gone on believing the same.

As the killer's employer hoped.

Somewhere, probably within the circle of privileged and powerful men and women who ran the boat world, that person must be getting scared. Each moment Jake Forrester stayed in New York, probing and asking questions, was another threat to his safety.

Jake decided to start applying pressure.

Ryker was the obvious weak point—no one is more ready to betray his master than a discredited servant. Jake rang his California office a dozen times. He was never in. Perhaps, like Weisell and Levitt, he was dead. Or, more likely, Fujita had taken him out of circulation, hoping his absence would outlast Jake's interest.

But Jake was determined. He could wait out Fujita. And there were plenty more weak points on which he could bear down.

Elaine's murder, for instance.

He went to the New York police, asked if they could give him a report on the progress of the case. They were helpful, getting the details telexed down from Providence. He took the copies to an attorney recommended by the police captain in charge of the case and retained him to consider the possibility of a suit against "person or persons unknown" for the murder of his wife and resultant loss of earnings and conjugal rights. Such suits were known, if not exactly common; the attorney happily took his retainer and started the paperwork. Running into Gerry Cornelius of the NYYC in the Algonquin bar that evening, Jake casually dropped news of this latest development. The sun-tanned face froze in an expression of gentlemanly distaste. Before midnight, news of this latest breach of good taste would be all over New York's yachting community.

Jake could almost feel the pressure building up; soon, something would crack.

Traffic on 39th was moving smoothly. He cut across to Sixth, then turned into 44th. Kim was waiting at the hotel, ready for the lunch they'd promised each other. They might eat at the Sky Club on top of the Pan Am Building at the end of 44th. She had a child's enjoyment of things like that. His disappointment in his investigations was balanced by the fun they had together. Elaine had known everything and everyone, had been everyplace—Kim was fresh and new, an opening into worlds Jake had forgotten existed.

Their relationship remained in the limbo between like and love, intimacy and sex. They shared a bedroom but not a bed; Jake wondered what might have happened had the hotel not automatically allocated them a suite with two queen-size beds and a drawing room—the accommodation he and Elaine had always taken when they stayed at the hotel, which remained on record in the Algonquin's discreet card file.

He wanted to say so much to Kim—to reassure and explain. But at each opportunity he confronted a division in his emotions he could not resolve; no matter how hard he tried, the tangled threads of feeling refused to unravel themselves. Elaine haunted him still.

People took them for father and daughter—occasionally he found himself behaving towards her as if she was Petey. Kim took his hand if she was tired or frightened, and there was a confident, trusting look in her face whenever, as often happened, their eyes met over a meal or in sharing a joke.

Yet he wasn't blind to Kim's pert body or bold, flirting eyes; she wouldn't allow him to be. Coming into the hotel room the day after they arrived, he found her on the phone, ordering lunch from room service, her back to him. He caught a glimpse of her flawless bare back, slim legs, the tight band and curved net of black briefs taut over neat buttocks, and retreated, swallowing, into the hall. They never mentioned the incident, and later he almost convinced himself he'd imagined the brief flash of her eyes over her bare shoulder and the look of complicity there.

He was suddenly eager to be with her; the crowded streets along which he crawled seemed part of a conspiracy to keep him from her. He grinned, realizing the effect his investigations had begun to have on his thinking process; there were enemies everywhere. The sudden opening of a parking place almost directly in front of him as a huge chauffeured limousine pulled out from the curb made the thought even more ridiculous. He dived into the space.

It was good not to be driving any more. He sat in the car for a moment, thinking only about Kim, about lunch—and, perhaps, after lunch. . . .

Something pattered on the roof. For the first time he noticed that the building frontage a few yards across the sidewalk was webbed with scaffolding and draped in brown burlap. Steam cleaning was in progress. Drops of dirty water plopped into the dust on his windshield and dribbled down. The car would need a wash, but it was worth it for the space.

He reached for the curbside door handle. Pedestrians were skirting the wet area of sidewalk, walking along the outside edge, their coats brushing the car window. He would have a problem getting out. When a tall man stopped right beside the car door, blocking it totally, Jake wound down the window halfway and called, "Hey, pal?"

The man turned, crouched to stare in the window. Jake saw a round, open, amiable face under a soft felt hat.

"Would you mind . . ." he began.

There was a sound like the roar of steam and a grinding howl of ripped metal. The car shuddered and bounced. Jake turned his head to stare at the rod of rusted metal that had speared through the car six inches from his shoulder. A twenty-foot tube of steel scaffolding weighing two hundred pounds had fallen twenty-three stories from the building roof, pierced the car above the front seat, sliced through metal, insulation, upholstery, carpet, and floor to bury itself eight inches in the asphalt of 44th Street.

Jake gaped at the three-inch tube slanting past his ear. The man on the sidewalk leaned forward, half-squatting to look into the car. "Jesus, take a look at . . ."

Jake heard a thump. A look of pained surprise passed over the man's features. A stream of blood exploded from his open mouth, drenching the half-open window. He drooped, lolled, but didn't fall—his body was pinned to the sidewalk by another length of pipe that pierced his back between the shoulder blades.

Jake's pale reflection stared back at him in the bloody glass. A mounting confusion of shouts, screams, and pounding feet welled up around him.

The next moment, he was deafened by a sustained roar like some insane, intolerable drumming. Scaffolding

pipes showered on top of the car, bounding and pin-
wheeling as they rained down on the street and the line
of parked cars. A severed steam hose coiled down out of
the sky, to lie twisting and writhing on the sidewalk,
gushing a widening plume of steam that soon filled the
street from side to side with mist.

Screaming pedestrians stampeded through the confusion, crashing into one another, clambering over the
parked cars in their madness to escape from the rain of
death.

High above the street, on top of the building, Jubei
hung over the stone lip of the facade, staring down like a
gargoyle from some medieval cathedral. The screams and
shouts carried up to him out of the chaos; as the steam
eddied, he saw bodies littered on the sidewalk and
spreading pools of blood. The shaft of scaffolding that
pierced Forrester's car was still visible; so was the corpse
that leaned against the car door. Jubei smiled his death's-
head grin at a task effectively performed and, as police
sirens started to keen in nearby streets, padded away
across the buckled tar paper of the roof towards the service elevator. Before they connected the carefully sawn
supports on the scaffolding storage hopper with a successful murder, he would have long since disappeared
into the vast city whose streets and avenues stretched in
every direction from his rooftop aerie.

Heaving on the car door, Jake forced it open a foot
against the sagging weight of the corpse and squeezed
out. As he did so, he saw the dead man's open coat and
the thick wallet in its inside pocket. Almost without
thinking, he took the billfold, shoved it into his pocket,
and replaced it in the dead man's coat with his own.
After a disaster like this, the police would not be looking
too carefully at identification. As far as they were concerned, it was Jason "Jake" Forrester who died here on
the sidewalk of West 44th Street, pinned like a butterfly
on a specimen tray. Whoever planned this trap would
believe the same thing.

Torn loose by the tumbling scaffolding, the brown burlap screen billowed down to envelop the sidewalk. Jake
slipped under it and groped through its dusty folds until
his hands found stone. An office doorway gaped a few

feet away. He slipped in and hurried down the empty corridor, looking for a way through the block to 43rd.

Kim stood by the window, staring obliquely down the street towards the confusion. Below, on the sidewalk, feet pounded in a steadily increasing clatter, but whether running towards the event or away from it, she couldn't tell.

When the phone rang, she left the window impatiently to pick it up.

"Kim?"

"Hey, where *are* you? There's some sort of accident up the street. You should see . . ."

"I know. I was in it. Listen, grab everything valuable and get out of there."

Her stomach turned over. Her card house of composure, so carefully constructed in the last week, tumbled. She started to tremble.

"You mean *now*?"

"*Right* now. Just bring valuables. Credit cards. Money. My passport's in the lid of the brown leather case. No clothes—just what you're wearing."

Kim looked down at her nude body; the noise had begun up the street just as she stepped out of the shower. Somehow, the oddity of her fleeing from the Algonquin stark naked overwhelmed her fright. The next time she spoke, her voice was steady. "How about clothes for you?"

"I'll be okay. Go across the street to the Royalton. The coffee shop's in back. I'll wait for you there." He hung up.

Kim used up thirty seconds standing silently in the middle of the room, planning. From her own clothes, she took a pair of long black boots, a cotton skirt, a blouse, and a leather jacket. Into her largest handbag she shoveled the contents of her other purse and Jake's valuables as well. Since there was still room, she stuffed in socks, underpants, and a cashmere sweater that could be wadded into a small bundle. The bag bulged, but not enough to arouse suspicion.

The aged elevator seemed to take longer than usual.

When it finally delivered her to the lobby, she waited a second before stepping out. Above all, she had to appear calm, unobtrusive. . . .

The lobby was empty; guests and staff crowded by the door, staring up the street. She walked towards them.

"Miss? Miss!"

The desk clerk could only mean her. She put her head down and made for the door and the sunlit street.

"Miss?" Someone took her arm. Surely they wouldn't try anything here, in public?

"This just came for Mr. Forrester. Will you be seeing him?"

She looked at the old bellhop and the heavy brown envelope and grinned with relief. "Probably. I'll take it."

She reached for the flap of her purse, remembered its incriminating contents. "I'll catch you after lunch."

Nobody noticed the girl who hurried across the street and entered the Royalton. Up by the intersection of 44th and Fifth, the ambulance sirens howled with increasing hysteria.

She found Jake at the back of the Royalton's faded and run-down coffee shop. The coffee in front of him was untouched; he was going through a billfold, making tidy heaps of its contents—business and credit cards, a check book, a healthy wad of bills.

The late Jay Sloane Eastman, Jake decided, was a solid citizen. Gold American Express Card. Also Diner's Club, MasterCard, and a dozen others. Six hundred dollars in cash.

Kim stared at him. "You were *in* that mess?"

"It was planned for me. A pile of scaffolding fell off a building, but they missed me." He held up Eastman's driver's license. "This poor guy wasn't so lucky."

"How come you've got his billfold?"

"I took his and left my own on the body. It might put them off for a few hours."

The old panic threatened to return. She took his coffee and sipped with trembling hand. It helped a little. "What now?"

"Get out of town."

"Back to Virginia?"

Jake shook his head. "They'll expect that."

"Then where?"

"Let's think while we're moving. If we've got a lead, we'd better use it."

There was as little problem finding a cab as there had been locating a free public phone; everyone was clustering around the accident.

"La Guardia," Jake told the driver as they slipped into the battered yellow cab.

"Gonna take a while, mister. Some sorta wreck up on Fifth."

"That's okay."

The driver turned on a pop radio station and slouched down in his seat as the insistent voice of Marvin Gaye filled the cab like brown velvet.

Kim dropped the brown envelope in Jake's lap. "This came for you at the hotel. I thought it'd look better if I took it."

Jake saw the *Yachts and Yachting* emblem on the corner and tore it open. Inside was a sheaf of Xeroxed pages from back issues of the magazine. Sally Goldstone had made good on her promise to send him all the material on Lars Halvorsen and his disastrous attempts to beat the iron rules of the NYYC.

The first clipping was twelve years old. "Debut For Halvorsen's Ultimate Twelve." Xerox never did justice to photographs. Of the smudged likeness under the headline, Jake could just about make out a mop of white hair and a Vandyke beard. But the text was no problem.

"Lars Halvorsen's much heralded *Calinda* makes its first public appearance on June 7 at the pretrial regatta of the NYYC off Newport, RI, and the boat community awaits vindication or final disproof of Halvorsen's recently much trumpeted claims to have created 'the ultimate twelve.'"

Jake shuffled through the rest. He'd been crewing on the *Kialoa* that year, most of the time shuttling between Brazil and the Azores to shake down a new suit of sails that never quite worked no matter how often they were recut. He remembered only some of the scandal, but the clippings reminded him.

Calinda never took the water. Disallowed by the NYYC as not conforming to the rule, it was refused entry

in the America's Cup runoffs. Halvorsen, not known for
his even temper, had hauled the boat out of the water,
slung it on a truck, and disappeared.

The other pages were just rehashes of the story in later
reports on all-metal construction and hassles with the
NYYC. Much that Halvorsen claimed for his boat was
vindicated when new builders exploited his pioneering
work in hydrodynamics and the use of all-metal hulls;
welded aluminum remained the standard form of construction for twelve-meter yachts. As for his statement
that, in styling and maneuverability *Calinda* represented
a quantum leap in boating technology, it was often re-
ferred to but never tested—after his rejection by the
club's rules committee, Halvorsen and *Calinda*
disappeared without trace.

Or perhaps not *quite* without trace.

The last page of the dossier was not from the editorial
pages; it reproduced a letter from a reader and a
smudged photograph. Putting into Kirkwall in the
Orkney Islands north of Scotland, the writer had been
surprised to find an American among those who came
down to look over his boat. The man's questions betrayed a notable knowledge of the twelve-meter scene.
Something about him reminded the man of Lars
Halvorsen, and he sent along a rather poor snapshot in
the hope that someone could identify him.

Jake put the early picture and a snapshot side by side
and showed them to Kim. "Does that look like the same
man to you?"

"I don't know. Could be. Who is he?"

"Lars Halvorsen. He used to be a hell of a boat
builder."

If it was Lars Halvorsen, and if he knew where *Calinda*
was—or had built others like her—Jake might yet get his
boat and a chance to fight *Sasori*. It was worth a gamble.

"Ever been to Scotland?"

Kim raised her eyebrows. "I've never even been to England. Why?"

The cab was out of the city now, climbing the access
ramp towards the Triborough Bridge. Below them was
the South Bronx. Jake glimpsed tar-paper roofs, an as-

phalt yard where black kids played basketball, and beyond, block after block of burned-out ruins. It would be a pleasure to get away from the violence.

He leaned towards the driver. "Make it Kennedy, not La Guardia, will you?"

Without turning round the man waved his hand.

CHAPTER SIXTEEN

The weekly steamer that meandered through the Orkneys dropped them on the stone quay at the cliff base and backed gingerly away.

The steps were like the cogs of a fine-toothed wheel embedded in the hillside. Set close together, with rises of two or three inches, they were made for men carrying heavy loads up from the little cove; men who must feel for each new level with their toes before lurching forward.

Centuries of wear had hollowed out the center of each step. A streamlet trickled down the furrow, and pads of green moss covered the rest of the stone. It had been years since anyone but the occasional visitor had used this staircase.

"You all right?" Jake asked over his shoulder.

Kim plodded a few yards behind him, almost lost in a borrowed oilskin five sizes too large. His own was just as roomy and smelled strongly of kerosene.

"How many more of these?"

He glanced ahead, where the staircase curved over the slope.

"Not many," he lied.

Past Kim, he could see the little steamer battling back to Kirkwall, sixty miles away. It wouldn't come again for seven days, unless summoned. They were as isolated on this tiny island as astronauts on the moon.

In another ten minutes, the steps turned into a flagged path, spotted with lichen and overgrown at the edges with tough grass.

Breathing heavily, Jake waited for Kim to catch up.

There was no sign of human life. Just a few stubby sheep and the occasional hovering gull riding the standing wave thrown up by the cliff.

Kim staggered the last few steps and put her arm

around his waist. She was panting with the effort. He let her lean on him, enjoying a pressure that was both comforting and exciting.

"I used to think the parallel bars were hard work," she said at last.

"You're out of shape."

"I didn't notice *you* taking the last few hundred steps at double-time."

They grinned at one another. At that moment, he wanted very much to take her in his arms and kiss her. But sudden memories of Elaine, of Charlie Keble, of the pinioned man in Manhattan flooded in on him. His smile faded, and at the same moment Kim's face became forlorn. He knew why, instantly—she'd thought he had taken the comment as a gibe about his age—but he knew no way to reassure her.

"We'd better start looking for the house," he said shortly. He started along the crooked stone path, Kim lagging behind. The wind rattled their wet-weather gear, a strange, desolate sound, like the beating of leathery wings.

His feet slipped on the stone, then slipped again. The ground was shelving; they had walked right across the island.

He had his first real look at the North Sea.

Nothing existed between them and the Arctic to break the fury of these waves. The gray, whitecapped swells rolled down from the ice cap with inexorable power—thirty-foot mountains of water sliding out of the gray haze, spending some of their force on the Orkneys before driving on, past Ireland, past France, to die at last on the equator.

And this was spring, almost summer. The winter gales must be titanic. He'd seen films, and the men in Kirkwall had described them in clipped detail. Spume from the crashing breakers whipped four hundred feet up the cliff to pour over the lip of the island and sweep across the place where they stood. Orkney farmers grazed their sheep here in the summer but took them back to mainland farms in the fall. Only rocks and lichens could survive this place in winter. Rocks, lichens, and a special kind of man.

For the first week of their search, Kim and Jake had drawn a series of blanks. No American lived in the Orkneys, though there were plenty of English composers communing with the infinite and writers trying to wring something publishable out of the bleak windswept island landscape and the potent local whiskey.

Finally, someone in the museum in Kirkwall recalled a strange American who had spent weeks poring over their stock of boating material; plans of Viking longboats unearthed from the graves of the Norse chieftains who had occupied these islands and a large part of Britain in the centuries before Christianity domesticated both the country and then its invaders.

Jake had moved north, away from the big islands towards the scatter of bleak, steep-sided rocks where few people lived—islands inhabited by gulls and sheep. As he did so, more stories turned up about the strange bearded man and his tiny impish wife who shared a house on the most desolate and remote of these rocks; a house he'd built himself from local rock and slate, buttressed with logs hauled in from Scotland.

Now he stood on the cliff above the gray swell and wondered if it had all been for nothing.

He almost missed the house. It was wedged onto a ledge below the cliff edge. A few yards from the front windows, the granite face dropped sheer to the sea.

Whoever built it was not looking for visitors. The black slate roof, heavy corner timbers, and dark stone walls blended into the cliff almost perfectly. They walked along the edge, looking down on the roof, searching for a way down to the house.

Kim, a few yards ahead of Jake, reached the edge and stared down.

"I don't believe this."

He joined her. Gooseflesh ran along his arms like cold hands.

They were looking at a narrow harbor, hardly more than a cleft, with cliffs climbing on each side. Wedged into it was a tiny beach, like a trace of white in a prospector's pan, and a stone pier. A large ship's lifeboat bobbed on the sheltered side of the stone jetty.

Another boat was entering the cove, nosing towards

the pier. A man jumped out and threaded the bow rope through an iron ring set in the stone. The rest of the crew, about fifteen men, swarmed out, holding the boat steady against the swell while others dropped fenders over the side and moored it firmly.

They were Vikings.

The boat was open, clinker built from long rows of wooden planks. The oars that drove it stood upright in the center like a spine. Its curved, high-mounted prow was carved with the snarling head of a dragon.

All the crew wore metal helmets and long tunics down to their knees. A few carried axes and swords.

The men milled around on the jetty for a few minutes, then piled into the lifeboat. It slid out of the cove and bucked against the few swells that found their way around to this sheltered side of the island.

Kim and Jake watched it disappear around the edge of the cliff. By the time they looked back to the cove, a single figure was halfway up the narrow flight of steps that led to the house. A tall, slow-moving man.

He wore a brown homespun robe that fell below his knees, and his legs were wrapped in lengths of the same cloth, tied on with leather thongs. His helmet fitted like a dome over his head, with a guard running down over his nose. The axe he carried was single bladed, hardly more than a hatchet, but its thin handle was two feet long.

His face could have been carved with it, roughly hacked from a block of mahogany. Hollows for the eyes, a gouge or two for the cheeks, a slash for the mouth. What hair the helmet revealed was as white as shavings.

He chonked the axe into the doorpost. It bit at least an inch deep and stuck, amid dozens of similar scars.

Jake and Kim stared down at him from the hillside.

"Something I can do for you folks?" he said in the pure accents of Boston. "I'm Lars Halvorsen."

Salt-crusted driftwood logs made the flames in the big open fire ripple blue-green. Kim sat on the hearth rug, leaning back against an armchair, arms folded, head bowed towards the heat. She was fast asleep.

"Refill?" Halvorsen nodded at the mug in Jake's hand.

"Sure."

"*Thrall*!"

Halvorsen's bellow jerked Kim awake, but she settled back quickly into her doze.

Karen Halvorsen came out of the kitchen wiping her hands on her apron. A small, neat woman, younger than her husband, she gave off an air of amused competence.

"Thrall yourself. I suppose you want more booze."

She took their mugs, half-filled them from a bottle of Lamb's Navy Rum, and topped them with water. The poker jammed deep under the logs of the fire was almost white hot. The liquid hissed and boiled as soon as she thrust it in.

Jake took his mug back with respect. The fumes alone were almost pure alcohol.

"Won't you join us, Mrs. Halvorsen?"

"And listen to all that Viking rubbish again? No fear. Anyhow, there's Beethoven on the BBC tonight. I'll take my tea into the kitchen."

Halvorsen toasted her departing back. "Women. Pregnant in the summer, barefoot in the winter."

Jake raised his mug in reply. He was starting to get the old man's measure.

"That's a beautiful boat down there."

"The finest I ever built. Got the plans from the archives, had her done by the best yard in Norway. Solid oak; handmade iron nails. Cross the Atlantic in a boat like that. You know it was an ancestor of mine, Bjarni Harolfsson, who first sighted North America? In 985. Years before that clown Leif Ericsson. Always my ambition to repeat the trip."

"You think it's possible? An open boat?"

Halvorsen slammed down his drink. The grog sprayed everywhere.

"Why not? You saw those boys of mine—fishermen, navy men who love the old boats. We've sailed thousands of miles in her. *It can be done*." His mug pounded out the words. "They've got the navigation instruments down in the museum in Kirkwall. The old charts . . ."

He stopped and stared at the mug in his hand. He seemed not remember where he was or what he was saying. Jake had looked up Halvorsen's biography when they had passed through London. He was almost ninety.

"They'll never let you," he said carefully.

Halvorsen glared at him under those white eyebrows. For a moment he wasn't an old man anymore, but the ghost of Bjarni Harolfsson—navigator, explorer, Viking. Then the fire faded like coals buried in ash.

"No, they won't. Bastards. They let us sail about in sheltered waters and put on fancy dress for their festivals. But the moment they get a whisper I'm thinking of putting out to sea, the Coast Guard practically launches the lifeboat." He raised his mug. "The hell with them!"

"Hell and damnation." Jake drank a healthy swallow.

Halvorsen licked a few drops from his moustache.

"About *Calinda* . . ." Jake began.

"Gone. Sold for taxes. Years ago. No idea where she is. Might be at the bottom for all I know. Why do you want her anyway?"

"To race at Newport."

"Why would you do a damn fool thing like that? They threw her out once. They'll do it again."

"The rule's changed a lot since then. I think I can get by. And the Japanese are entering a boat that I don't think anything but *Calinda* can beat. We need an aluminum hull."

"Lots of aluminum hulls around these days. That British boat—*Lionheart*. Nice piece of work."

"She lost. Too heavy."

"Well, do you wonder? Look how they make those rust-buckets. Just weld on the plates anyhow and plaster the hull with filler. Some of 'em have a *ton* of filler. The best aluminum man in the world built *Calinda*. A goddam artist. Fitted those plates sweet as you please and hand-ground the welds. You know how much filler there was on *Calinda*?" He looked into his mug and upturned it to show it was dry. "None. Not an ounce."

A log shifted in the fire. He stared at the flames.

"Jesus, she was a sweet boat. Bright as a knife. Then they made me *paint* her, stick a lot of fake furniture inside. Paneling! I still might have done it, but we couldn't get the right sails. And I ran out of money. The backers cut off my credit. That did it."

"They dropped all those regulations about the boat having to be fitted for cruising. We don't have to carry all that junk anymore. And these new film sails should suit her fine. The Japanese are using them."

"What so special about this damn Jap boat anyway?" Jake told him. Halvorsen frowned. "They gonna allow that? Plastic hull?"

"Looks like."

Halvorsen shook his head. "The whole business's going to pieces. Dacron. Computers. Plastics. Who needs them? The real sailors used oak and canvas and sailed by the stars. Real boats . . ." His voice trailed off.

"Mr. Halvorsen, if you could give me at least an indication of where *Calinda* went, I'd be grateful. I want that boat."

Halvorsen's watery eyes tried to focus on Jake, but they failed. The mumble of his voice turned to a snore, and his head fell on his chest.

Karen Halvorsen came in from the kitchen, took the empty mug from his fingers, and knelt to unwind the bands around his legs.

"He'll be all right, Mr. Forrester. He sleeps in the chair a lot these days. I think he prefers it to bed. You had better look after the little girl."

Kim was curled in front of the dying fire. Jake lifted her easily and carried her into the bedroom. Her arms reached around his neck, and she snuggled against him.

There was only one bed, low and wide and piled with furs. A tiny window showed a sky pitted with stars. Half-drunk, Jake dumped Kim on the bed and, stumbling, fell across her body. She pulled him down.

"Kim . . ."

"No. Come on. I want to."

It was almost a year since he made love to a woman, and her mouth, hot and wet on his, aroused him to a passion of which he had imagined himself incapable. Something tore as he wrestled the sweater over her head. When the waistband of her skirt resisted, he hooked his hand inside, feeling his fingertips catch the elastic of her briefs, and dragged them down her hips. A button rattled off the wooden wall somewhere in the darkness beyond the light cast by the single oil lamp.

She was tiny, beige against the deep brown fur, her breasts hard and pointed, her body agile, athletic, slippery as an otter's. The leather boots that came halfway to her calves only made her appear more nude; an image of adolescent fantasy from the pages of a glossy magazine.

Ridiculous, a voice said at the back of his mind. Unnatural. You're old enough to be her father.

He made one last attempt to block the feelings that were rushing over him. "I'll crush you."

Her response was fierce. "Yes." She flipped open the buckle on his belt, unzipped his trousers and reached with both hands to grasp him, guide him, draw him inside her, the booted heels clasped around his waist, leather creaking as she tightened her thighs. He watched her lip curl back from tiny white bared teeth as, inch by inch, she swallowed him into her belly.

Later, he did try to crush her. She demanded it, squeezing down under him, her face against his chest, her thighs parted urgently under his hips.

"I don't want to hurt you." He gathered up a handful of her hair and smelled it: salt and sage.

"You can't hurt me. Feel." Her body stiffened. Every muscle ridged against him, every bone of her pelvis and rib cage. Inexorably, she lifted his weight, inch by inch, off the bed.

"Can't I?" With every ounce of his strength, he ground down on her arched body, so that he feared the pressure would crack her bones like porcelain. But she fought him until, with a tiny squeal of pleasure, another orgasm racked her and her fists pounded drumlike on his shoulders.

"You *see*." Her grin was foxy, greedy. "Can't do it. But I love you to try."

Jake rolled off her and slumped on the fur, sprawled in a daze of contentment. The whisper of Ridiculous had never returned. He knew he could go on making love with this child for the rest of the night—no, goddammit, for the rest of his *life*.

She nestled against him, her small hand passing over his chest, reaching below the waist to fondle and tease.

"Jake tired? Jake want to have a little sleep?" She yelped in delight as he grabbed her shoulders and turned her bodily like a doll, thrusting her facedown into the bed so that the bedspread abruptly choked off her giggle—a giggle that at the last moment turned to a sob of pleasure as he entered her from behind.

A wind from the north rattled the windows; in the glass chimney, the flame of the lamp wavered, unnoticed, as the wind was unheard.

When Jake woke, watery sun shone through the window. Kim stood at the end of the bed, munching a piece of toast.

"I let you sleep. Thought you could use the rest."

He swiped at her. She danced away from his grasp. "No you don't. I spent an hour sewing my skirt back together." She lifted her skirt up one smooth thigh. He glimpsed a lick of black hair. "Couldn't do anything about the pants, I'm afraid."

Jake rolled over. "Let me get used to this gradually. I'm out of practice."

"Not after last night. You graduated with honors. Phi Beta Kappa material. Want some coffee?"

"God, yes! Is Halvorsen up yet?"

She bit off another corner of toast. "Up and sailed. I heard him go. He had his crew up here at dawn."

"Sailed?"

"He's gone to Norway. For some festival."

Wrapping the fur bedspread around him, Jake went to the window. The long ship had already cleared the cove. As he watched, oars dipped and the dragon prow turned for the sea. Jake's hopes of a line on *Calinda* went with it.

He turned away, and for the first time noticed the untidy heap on top of the huge rough-hewn trunk that was the room's only furnishing other than the bed.

"Left something for you."

Dust was caked thick on the roll of papers. He untied the string and flattened them. A wooden model of a boat hull rolled out.

Calinda.

Designs and drawings, stresses and specifications. Details of tank tests. And letters as well, the most recent dated five years ago.

Halvorsen had added a letter of his own, scrawled on the back of an invoice from a Kirkwall chandler for rope and nails.

"I don't know why in hell you want a broken-down boat made by a broken-down old man, but I wish you well in the searching. This will tell you as much about *Calinda* as I know myself. My regards to Vinland, and salute the ghost of Bjarni Harolfsson for me."

The long ship was out to sea now, bucking the low gray Arctic swell. A quarter mile behind her trailed a gray rescue boat flying a British Navy red ensign. Jake watched until both disappeared into the overcast.

CHAPTER SEVENTEEN

The first journalist off the helicopter was the man from *The Sydney Morning Herald*. Pausing halfway down the steps, he sniffed and swallowed, hard.

"Cripes! What's *that*?"

Coming up behind him with the rest of the party, Tony Stephens took a deep breath and exhaled with a satisfaction he didn't necessarily feel.

"You should know that smell, Mr. Thompson. Salt air. Fish. Sewers. Oil. About the same as you find in the western Australian iron mines today, or Rum Jungle and Catherine a few years ago when they were digging up all that uranium. It's the smell of a boom town. A town that's growing up too fast. It's the smell of *money*."

Some of the other journalists, including the man from *Asahi Shimbun*, took it all down. That should head off headlines like *Aberdeen—North Sea Slum*.

He steered them across to the terminal building, noticeably larger than when he was here two months before. Half a mile away, at the end of the main runway, gulls screeched and wheeled where the bulldozers were working on the extensions. Beyond, he could see the domes of the new refinery.

Four jet-powered Westland twelve-seat helicopters stood by the Shell hangar. As Tony went by, one of them turned over its turbines, and the vents coughed black smoke. Half a dozen men in business suits and hard hats doubled out of the terminal and headed towards the hangar.

A tall man with a thick roll of papers under his arm tagged after them. And a girl. Stephens glanced at the couple and stopped, amazed.

"Jake?"

He grabbed the man's arm, wrenched him around and stared into his face. He was trembling.

"Tony! You gave me a shock."

"Christ, man, I thought you were dead." He shook his head, as if to clear it. "It's in all the papers. Tom Needham rang to tell me."

The murder attempt with the scaffolding seemed years in the past. Jake realized for the first time since he left Halvorsen's house that they were returning to the real, dangerous world. What precious lead he had on his pursuers had just evaporated.

"It was a misunderstanding. Somehow my identification got mixed up with another man's. I would have let everyone know, but we've been"—tell Stephens about Halvorsen? Something warned him against it—"out of touch," he ended vaguely.

"We have to talk, Jake. I just can't believe this." He glanced over his shoulder at the group of journalists filing into the terminal building. "I have to show these press people over one of our boats. We won't be back until tomorrow at the earliest. Can you wait?"

Jake nodded towards the men he had been following. "These Shell people have offered us a lift to London."

"How long will you be in London?"

"I haven't thought."

Stephens fished a key wallet from his pocket and wrenched off two of them. "These open the company apartment. 706 Bayswater Road. There's a doorman downstairs. You should be safe."

Jake frowned. "Safe from what?"

"We have a lot to talk about, Jake. Stay in London till I get back. Promise me that."

"Sure. Tony, what's all this about?" His mind jumped back to the last time he'd talked to Stephens. It had been to ask him about the English money in Elaine's safe-deposit box. "Has it got something to do with that money? What did you find out?"

Stephens ran his hand through his hair, an oddly boyish gesture that made him look distracted, almost helpless. For the first time, Jake noticed the rings around Stephens's eyes, the pallor of his face. The man was nervous, scared.

"Jake . . . oh, hell, *I* gave Elaine that money. I'd almost decided to tell you when I heard about . . .

"*You*? Why would you give Elaine five thousand pounds?"

"It's a long story. I'll tell you in London."

Jake grabbed his shoulder. "Tony, I want to know *now*!"

"I didn't have any choice." He wrenched himself from Jake's grip and turned towards the terminal. "We'll talk in London."

Jake moved to go after him, but a crowd of men suddenly came between them. They wore heavy parkas and duffel coats and carried battered suitcases, as world-worn as their hard, unforgiving faces. A new shift of oil men had arrived from the south. Sourly, they looked around the bleak airfield with its cawing gulls, mentally readjusting themselves after two weeks at home to the prospect of fourteen days of twelve-hour shifts in the gales and storms and sixty-foot waves of the North Sea.

One of the Shell men walked over from the big Westland helicopter. "Ready any time you are."

Jake nodded and reluctantly headed towards the group. In the helicopter Kim went immediately to sleep; she was exhausted after the voyage by tossing motor launch from Halvorsen's island to Kirkwall, then the aged Fokker Friendship flight to Aberdeen. Jake felt tired too, but his mind refused to relax.

Tony Stephens had paid Elaine almost ten thousand dollars? And he'd had no choice?

He searched his memory for any comment Elaine might have made about Tony, any meeting about which he might not have known. It's true they were friends, but an ocean and a way of life separated them. Then Jake remembered the London buying trips, the long periods when she just faded out of his life as he became immersed in a new boat.

The money might have been a loan to help Elaine in her business. But Tony had said he'd had no choice.

Jake could think of only one set of circumstances under which a man might pay someone large amounts of cash in secret and have no choice. Blackmail.

A heavy swell slammed into the *North Sea Diamond* and

the ship lurched, sending half of Stephens's listeners staggering against the walls of the bridge. Green water flushed over the windows.

He tapped the glass. "Toughened. I'm glad it's a little rough. It gives you a chance to see the boat under working conditions. Right now we're heading for the Ekofisk field at"—he glanced at the TV monitor set at an angle into the navigator's desk—"sixteen knots. For these seas, that's remarkable. Most navy ships couldn't manage that, but of course they aren't built with oil field rescue in mind. Our fleet will take advantage of the latest technology in engine design, safety equipment, computer navigation. Even in a full gale with visibility at zero, we could find a boat in trouble or a capsized rig by satellite alone. Any questions?"

The Australian said, "That hotel rig that turned over a few years ago. What could you have done in that case? The whole thing just turned turtle."

"Actually, that's an excellent example of just where our system excels over most others. The *Christina Mortenhoe* broke away from one of her floating supports, and the building tipped in a few seconds. Eighty men were drowned. A number of them were still alive for hours after the accident, but no means existed to extract them. Each of our ships carries a submersible with a wide range of attributes; it can rescue men trapped in a sub on the sea bottom or perform quite intricate construction work at shallow depths. If you'd like to follow me . . ."

It took five minutes to negotiate the narrow companionways from the bridge to the submersible bay. After cannoning off the walls a dozen times, Tony's shoulders ached, but no worse than his head.

Meeting Jake at the airport had been one of the worst shocks of his life. Yet somewhere, deep inside, he was grateful; not many men get a second chance to shift an unbearable load of guilt.

The news of Jake's death had been a blessed relief, but almost immediately after he felt disgusted, ashamed. This time he wouldn't make the same mistake. He'd tell Jake everything, and to hell with the shadowy nemesis who had manipulated his life for the last two years.

The big hangar was cold. At the bottom of the sloping

floor the sea pounded against large double doors. The overhead light gleamed on twin metal rails set into the floor.

The deep-sea rescue sub hulked, potbellied and ugly, its yellow hull dripping with condensation.

"This is *Orion*. We can't demonstrate in this weather, of course, but I assure you it can be launched in heavy seas—heavier than these. But at half a million U.S. dollars each, we don't take any risks. What we've done, in effect, is to wrap a sub hull around a decompression chamber. It's fitted with the equivalent of an intensive care unit in a major hospital. We can deal with a rescued crew on the sea bottom or bring them straight up. . . ."

The *Diamond* shuddered as it struck a particularly large wave. Even Stephens's stomach turned over.

"But we can go into all this when we're out of this blow. I'll show you your cabins."

Some time later, Stephens woke with a sick lurch in his stomach. The boat seemed steadier, but it might just be a lull in the storm. He checked his watch. 4:17. The ship was asleep, but there was a feeling . . .

Something clanged in the corridor outside. He looked out, screwing his eyes against the white light of the wall fixtures. The door to the sub bay was unclipped. It swung and banged with the boat's motion.

Padding down the rubber-floored corridor, he looked into the bay. There was someone staring up at the submersible.

"I couldn't sleep."

Bloody woman. "I'm not surprised. Would you like a Dramamine?"

"It's just nerves. The best thing is work. I thought I would have another look at"—she smiled—"the monster."

"Yes. Of course." He couldn't remember which paper she represented, but French money was as good as any.

"Could I look inside?"

Bloody *bloody* woman. "It isn't terribly clean. You might get grease on your clothes."

"I have others."

"Well, then . . . ." He clambered up the slippery sides of the submersible and undogged the hatch. Reaching inside, he switched on the light. "I can't leave it on for very long. The batteries aren't fully charged."

She peered over his shoulder. "It is so small."

"It can take four in a pinch. Those are bunks back there." He squeezed backwards through the hatch. "Watch how I do it and follow me. It's easier."

He wriggled down into the control space, backing past the banks of instruments into the wider sleeping area, and waited for the girl's legs to appear through the hatch. They didn't.

Then the submarine quivered.

For a moment the motion felt just like those that preceded a launch.

Which was ridiculous, of course.

The big doors would have to be opened first, and the four hydraulic clamps locking the submersible to its rails released one by one.

But it shuddered again. And at the same moment he smelled the sharp salt of the ocean. The air was cold and wet.

Marie-Ange stepped back as the heavy machine glided down the silicon-coated rails and arced into the wake. There was enough light in the sky to show it wallowing heavily, dwarfed by the swells that crashed together behind the boat. Then a wave broke over it.

Stephens had clambered back into the control area. If he could just reach the main hatch, there were life jackets there. . . .

Icy water gushed through the open hatch. His mouth opened to shout, and the second wave filled it with salt water. The next moment *Orion* tilted and sank towards the black ooze five hundred feet below.

Marie-Ange left the hangar, closing the door behind her. With luck, Stephens would not be missed until dawn, and in the confusion she could easily escape when they docked. Some time before then, she would have to dispose of the stiletto clipped into her boot—the weapon she'd originally chosen to do this job. It might embarrass her if they found it during a search, though she doubted they would suspect a journalist with her impeccable (if forged) credentials. The sub was a happy chance; the sort of perfect killing method one found once in every ten contracts. She was congratulating herself on the quick thinking that allowed her to take advantage of it as she climbed into her bunk and drifted off to sleep.

CHAPTER EIGHTEEN

Summer rain sifted down over London like wet, gray sand. The carefully tended woodland of Hyde Park opposite looked soaked and untidy. So did the amateur art dealers who used the park railings as a semiofficial gallery. They had started arriving at dawn, and now the whole street was filled with them. Calendar landscapes and pink nudes swam vaguely behind the sheets of polyethylene that kept off the rain. Two London bobbies in glistening black rain capes strolled up and down the block, staring without comment or reaction at the pictures.

Jake hunched deeper into his borrowed robe and went back into the big drawing room. Kim, in a blue caftan discovered unexpectedly in the same wardrobe, looked up from *The Times* that had been pushed through their letter-box at 7:00 that morning.

"More coffee?"

Jake held up his cup. "Haven't finished this yet. What do you want to do today?"

"Don't know. Not much of a day for sight-seeing. We could read. Or watch TV." She smiled. "Or something."

"Let's try TV for a start. I'd like to catch the news." He was reaching for the control of the big twenty-seven-inch Sony when the phone rang. They stared at it for five seconds as its harsh *brang* filled the apartment.

Jake picked it up. Only Tony knew they were here.

"Doorman, sir. Two gentlemen on their way up."

"What gentlemen?" He should have told him not to let anyone in at all. Before he could get an answer someone knocked softly on the door. Jake hooked the safety chain and opened it three inches.

They looked unexceptional. One middle-aged, balding, his few strands of hair slicked to his scalp by the rain that also spotted his Burberry coat. The man behind him was younger, wearing a turtleneck sweater under his wind-breaker. He looked amused. Jake disliked him instantly.

"Mr. Stephens, is it?"

"No. Who are you?"

"I understood this was Mr. Anthony Stephens's apart-ment." The older man looked more puzzled than irritated.

"He's out of town. He lent the place to us for a few days."

"Did he? Well, in that case, perhaps it's yourself we should be talking to. I'm a police officer. The name's Mayo. That's Sergeant Dewhurst behind me there. Now if you'd be kind enough to release the chain . . ."

"Do you have a badge?"

"As a matter of fact, sir, I don't. In this country we carry what's known as a warrant card. Which of course you are welcome to see."

He held up an identification card covered in scratched celluloid. Reluctantly Jake slipped the chain.

Mayo took in Jake, Kim, and the apartment in one all-inclusive glance.

"We just got up, Inspector. It's been a busy few days for us."

"So I understand, Mr. Forrester." He smiled. "Mr. Jake Forrester, isn't it?"

"A moment ago you asked me if I was Tony Stephens."

"Did I? Very silly of me."

He nodded at the sergeant, who went to the window and raised his hand. The two policemen opposite crossed the street towards the house.

"No, I know very well who you are, Mr. Forrester. Though I must say I'm surprised to find you here. Friend of Mr. Stephens, you say?"

Someone knocked at the door. Dewhurst opened it. The two constables came in, bringing with them the smell of rain. Fanning out, they began a thorough search of the apartment.

"In the States you need a search warrant for this."

Mayo handed Jake a folded paper. It was a warrant to search the premises at 706 Bayswater Road, Second Floor, applied for and granted at Marylebone Magis-trate's Court the day before.

Forrester handed it back.

From the bedroom came the sound of doors being opened and drawers pulled out. One of the constables came out with a shallow moss-green cardboard box. A Harrods shirt box, with the shop's gold script trademark across the top.

"Found this in the wardrobe, sir."

Mayo emptied the contents onto the French-polished drawing room table. Glossy eight-by-ten black-and-white photographs and tiny colored Polaroids. A small morocco-bound book, like an address book. Some tape cassettes and one TV cassette.

Mayo took two pairs of white cotton gloves from his pocket and handed one set to Dewhurst. They sorted carefully through everything.

"Happy snaps," Dewhurst said, laying out the pictures in neat rows. Jake watched over his shoulder.

There was none of the posed stiffness of professional pornography. The men and women in the pictures looked either frenzied or pathetically uncomfortable. Flash gave all the prints the glaring clarity of forensic shots taken at the scene of a crime.

They showed one of two men tied or strapped to a bed while two women beat them with a long cane or a riding crop. In most of the shots, the people wore black sleeping masks; where they didn't, the features had been heavily blotted out with a felt pen.

Even the participants could not have found the pictures flattering. Weals stood out vividly on the buttocks and thighs of the men. The larger of the two girls, heavy-breasted and dark-skinned—probably Pakistani or West Indian from her long black hair—revealed a map of white stretch marks on her thighs. The flash showed up the blonde girl's worst qualities, making her look gaunt and bony. The men, with their erections and sagging muscles, just looked ridiculous.

Mayo and Dewhurst sorted through them like dealers examining etchings. Occasionally they slid a picture out of the heap and laid it to one side. Mayo riffled through the little book, grunted at one entry, and showed it to Dewhurst. The sergeant raised his eyebrows.

"Takes all kinds, sir."

Mayo held up the TV cassette and looked at Jake. "I imagine there's a machine to play this somewhere?"

Jake nodded towards the VHS player on the coffee table under the big Sony. Mayo took the cassette from its case and slid it in carefully.

The tape was as amateur as the photographs, but movement gave it a special intimacy. Nobody wore masks. One quickly forgot the crepe flesh of the Indian girl and the knobbly knees of her friend.

They used a different location. Jake recognized the bathroom where he had shaved that morning. A loop of rope hung from the chrome rail of the shower cubicle.

For almost a minute, the camera stared unwaveringly at the empty shower as shadows shifted on the tiled walls. Jake could imagine the person behind the camera adjusting the five-hundred-watt photofloods on their rickety stands.

Then the blonde girl led in a man. Not one of those in the photographs. This one was fat, with valences of flesh sagging over undersized genitals.

A black hood covered his head, and his hands were apparently tied behind him, because the girl, grinning, had to maneuver him until he was directly under the noose, then help him awkwardly onto a footstool.

Jake felt ill. But he could not stop watching. He felt Kim's hand creep into his.

The blonde put the noose around the fat man's throat, working it over the hood, under the double chins. Yanking the shower rail, she smiled and said something to whoever was operating the camera. Even without sound, Jake could understand the question: Will it hold?

She disappeared. For another minute the fat man teetered, naked and ridiculous, on the stool, swaying to keep his balance.

When the girl reappeared, she carried a length of clear plastic tubing and a rubber bulb. Inching around the naked man, she climbed into the shower behind him. A few seconds later the man flinched, then bent his knees and squatted slightly.

"Knightsbridge Martini," Dewhurst said. "Pure grain alcohol in the lower intestine. Very . . . sharpening, I'm told, if done properly."

It worked on the fat man. His penis stirred and

swelled. The Indian girl slid into the picture and squatted in front of him, licking and stroking. When he was fully erect she looked over her shoulder at the camera and mouthed, Now?

Turning back, she stood and put her arms around the man's waist. Slowly, she began to kneel, kissing his stomach, settling her mouth 'over him so that her long black hair was like a skirt falling across his groin and thighs.

Then she dragged him sideways and the footstool toppled onto its side.

Jake heard Kim gasp. Her nails dug into his palm.

The man must have orgasmed as soon as the noose tightened around his throat. The Indian girl knew her job, keeping her arms wrapped around the twitching legs as his torso jerked. Jake could imagine the roaring of blood in his ears, the intolerable pressure under the black cloth as his tongue began to swell, his eyes to bulge . . .

"For Christ's sake, *now*!" he heard himself saying.

A white hand reached around the hood, scrabbled for the knot on the rail and yanked it. The man collapsed to the floor like a sack.

He lay for a moment like a heap at the bottom of the picture. The blonde girl crouched over him and loosened the hood. She said something to the unseen operator of the camera, but this time she was not smiling.

Two more people came into the picture.

The first hung back, keeping away from the glare of the spotlight where it splashed the tiled wall. Even when the light did touch it, the figure looked insubstantial, ghostly.

Then someone bumped the lamp, and it fell full on her.

Black leather clung to her from head to foot. High heels, gleaming like coal. Long legs, a slim waist, and hard mounds of breasts were all covered in clinging black.

The face was featureless under a tight leather hood that revealed only bright gleaming eyes. A zipper closed the mouth tight with a skull's grin.

She bent over the unconscious man, squatting beside the Indian girl.

Another man came into the picture. He had been featured in the photographs they saw earlier. He was naked, but Jake recognized Tony Stephens.

CHAPTER NINETEEN

Mayo's office at New Scotland Yard was both modern and drab, as impersonal as the cluttered interior of a refrigerator.

"Warburton," he said, staring at the photograph of the dead man. "Solid chap. Insurance underwriter. Married. Two children." He looked at Jake. "Ever meet him, sir?"

"I don't know many of Tony's friends. We only see one another a few times a year."

"When was the last time?"

"Before Aberdeen? About a year ago."

"Would that have been the night of your wife's death?"

Jake looked away. "Yes. As it happens."

"And you didn't see him again until the day he was killed."

"Killed? *Tony?*" Jake felt sick.

"Yes, I'm afraid so. Early today. On his way out to an oil rig on this boat of his. Seems a submarine or some such went overboard with Mr. Stephens inside."

It took a moment for Jake's head to clear.

"Could it have been an accident?"

"Unlikely."

"Suicide?"

"We considered that. But a cumbersome and expensive way to do away with one's self, wouldn't you agree? Not that he didn't have good reason to contemplate suicide. We've been looking quite closely into Mr. Stephens's activities for some time."

"Is that why the search warrant was made out yesterday?"

"Very observant of you, sir. Yes, we found Mr. Warburton dead in the street eighteen months ago. At the time it was put down to a mugging that got out of hand, but at the autopsy we found semen in the urinary tract.

And his shirttail was tucked inside his underpants rather than outside. Sort of little mistake someone might make dressing a naked body. Mr. Stephens was known to be an associate of Warburton. We decided to keep an eye on him."

"It didn't seem to do much good, did it?" Jake asked bitterly. "Not if he's dead."

Mayo showed no offense. "I daresay you're right there, sir. A black mark against us, no doubt about that. Look, Mr. Forrester, I see you're upset. What say I send down to the first-aid room for a little brandy? We keep a few bottles down there—just for medicinal purposes, you understand."

He reached for the phone. Jake looked up and stared at him. Could this really be a detective inspector in one of the most respected police forces in the world? Perhaps all those bad thrillers he'd seen on late-night TV, with pompous detectives prowling around country houses in search of the man who murdered the squire, actually reflected the British police as they really were.

But he was doubtful.

"Mr. Mayo, I may be only a simple American businessman, but I wasn't exactly born yesterday. Just what *is* going on here?"

"I don't follow you, sir," Mayo said politely.

"This charade of the plodding policeman. Brandy for medicinal purposes. You've just had a murder dumped on your desk—the murder of a prominent businessman, what's more, with an international reputation. In the States, I'd already have made a deposition and had my attorney in here to make sure I didn't say anything stupid. You would have men out checking the airports and docks for suspects. Instead, we sit here talking like something out of Agatha Christie."

"No reason to get heated," Mayo said mildly. "These things take time. We'll handle it in our own way, Mr. Forrester."

Jake had a shaft of blinding intuition.

"Let me run something past you, Mr. Mayo. Just for your reaction. Here's what I think. I think you knew this was going to happen. You're not surprised about Tony's murder. And maybe you even know who did it."

Mayo played with the pencils on his desk, lining them

up side by side in order from smallest to largest. All of them, Jake noticed, were pointing at him. Finally he looked up.

"Perhaps you'll let me, as you put it, run something past you, sir. Do you have any reason to believe that a relationship of any kind existed between Mr. Stephens and your wife?"

Jake balanced his loyalties—on the one side, a dead friend; on the other a dead wife. Neither would suffer for what he was likely to say now.

"Not believe, Mr. Mayo. Say suspect." He explained about the money in Elaine's safe-deposit box and Tony's cryptic remark about having no choice but to pay her.

As he listened, Mayo rearranged the pencils into a spoked wheel, the points all meeting at the center. He looked up as Jake finished.

"What exactly is it you suspect?"

Jake took a deep breath. "Tony and Elaine may have had an affair, but that's hardly something she could blackmail him over. But I think she *was* blackmailing him—after seeing those pictures and the tape, I would guess it had something to do with his sexual . . . activities. Perhaps she found out about this man . . . what's his name? Warburton." It would fit; the notes were on top of the safe-deposit box—one of the most recent things to be put in there. And Warburton died about six months before Elaine was murdered.

Mayo nodded. Now the pencils formed two squares sharing a common side. He seemed to find something in this arrangement that pleased him, because he looked up, and for the first time since they had met, Jake thought he saw a different man; someone sharp and tough, not given to wasting anyone's time, especially his own.

"Mr. Forrester, I wonder if you'd wait in the outer office for a few minutes. There's a call I have to make."

Jake waited in the tiny anteroom, watched by an incurious Sergeant Dewhurst, who picked out a report two-fingered on a battered green Underwood, looking up towards him after every few words.

Eventually Mayo's door opened again. Jake went in and sat down.

"I couldn't tell you much until I'd cleared it with my

superior. He wasn't very happy, but I told him that in my view you were not the kind of man who took no for an answer."

"You're a good judge of character."

"So I'm told. That being the case, I don't have to tell you that anything you hear from me must be kept confidential."

"And *I* don't have to tell *you* that my conscience is flexible about things that involve my own safety and those of the people close to me."

Mayo nodded, as if what Jake had just said confirmed his worst fears. "We will just have to rely on your judgment, it seems. I hope it stands the strain. Well, where to begin? For a start, you're quite right; we expected an attempt on Mr. Stephens's life."

"Which was why you had a search warrant already sworn out the day before he was killed?"

"We felt it might be necessary to get into the flat in Bayswater Road fairly quickly, since that seemed to be the most likely place for the attempt to be made. We even thought"—he looked up and smiled thinly—"that you might be waiting there for just such a reason, even though we were pretty certain we knew the real assassin."

"Why didn't you watch him on the trip to Scotland?"

"Our suspect was still in France the day before the murder. We assumed she would . . ."

"*She?*"

Mayo sighed. "Mr. Forrester, in a moment I'll take you down to Anti-Terrorism. They've been working with this much more closely than I have. In fact, you've become involved in a rather complicated project that's been going on for more than a year, with the cooperation of the police in America, France, Germany, and Britain. Didn't you wonder why the American police weren't more diligent in their enquiries? We heard on the grapevine that a group of star sapphires went off the market a few weeks ago . . ."

"Sapphires? I don't understand."

"Star sapphires are the preferred method of payment for this lady's services. It might interest you to know that two similar packets of gems were noted to be out of circulation just before the murder of your late wife and Mr.

Keble." Mayo got up. "Now I think we might go and have a chat with Superintendent Peverell."

Peverell looked too young and too elegant to be a cop. Jake might have taken him for a banker or some ambitious young insurance official but for the marble hardness of his black eyes and the glimpse of a soft leather shoulder holster under the jacket of his three-piece gray suit.

He looked up hopefully as Mayo and Jake came in. "Anything new?"

Mayo shook his head. "I brought Mr. Forrester down. Thought you could fill him in on everything."

"I don't know if Interpol will clear him for *everything*."

Mayo glanced at the ceiling. "It's okay upstairs."

"Ah." Peverell looked at Jake with new respect. "Take a seat, Mr. Forrester. What would you like to know?"

"Perhaps if we started at the beginning," Mayo broke in.

"That could take a week."

"Highlights, then."

"Could I just ask one thing," Jake said. "What does this woman look like?"

Peverell swiveled his chair, took a file out of the cabinet behind him, extracted a glossy black-and-white photograph, and put in on the desk. Jake studied the open, smiling face. Nothing in it suggested she was capable of squashing a bug, let alone killing three human beings. Jake tried to read the face, but there was nothing there to grasp. He handed it back.

"Means nothing, of course," Peverell said. "She could have changed half a dozen ways."

"What's her name?"

"Planchet," Peverell said. He leaned back in his chair. "Marie-Ange Madeleine Planchet. Born Quimper, March 11, 1950. Solid parents. On the land, apparently. Educated in Quimper and Rennes. Enrolled at the Sorbonne in 1967. Mildly involved in left-wing politics, but nothing notable. Then, *les evenements de Mai*."

Forrester said, "Pardon me?"

"Paris student riots. Barricades, paving stones, dancing in the streets. Danny the Red. The administration overreacted, called in *Compagnie Républicaine de Sécurité*—

the CRS. Riot police. Unsubtle gentlemen, I'm afraid. In any event, Marie Planchet seems to have been among a group of students tearing up paving stones in Rue Gay-Lussac when a CRS unit jumped them. The CRS carry a rather nasty weapon called a *matraque*. Sort of truncheon. Some of them are wood, but the really unpleasant variety is made from plastic and weighted with lead shot. Knocks you silly, and after a bit of use the surface gets roughed up and very abrasive. One swipe can take the skin right off your cheek."

Jake thought Peverell said this with a certain satisfaction.

"They chased off the others, but Marie put up a fight. Rather silly of her. They beat her up rather badly. Then they dragged her into a house and raped her. Five of them. She was also very extensively brutalized; I expect they left her there for dead. She had a fractured pelvis. Internal injuries. Broken ribs. Lucky to be alive really."

"How do you know all of this?"

"Yes, that's quite interesting. Marie Planchet disappeared six months later. Dropped out of university. Didn't go back to Brittany either. There's some suggestion that she joined one of the free-lance pro-Palestinian groups. A girl something like her turned up in a training camp in Jordan in 1969, but the next positive sign of her was in July 1971. They hauled a man out of the Seine. He'd been . . . mistreated quite badly before he was killed. Most of his teeth had been pulled out, and some attention had been paid to his genitals. It's remarkable, you know, what one can do to a man just by isolating one testicle with a rubber band and simply flicking it with one's finger. . . ."

Jake flinched. Peverell smiled thinly. "You *did* ask. Well, the man proved to be ex-CRS. A week later, another body turned up. This time it was in a caravan in Mulhouse, up near the Swiss border. The man was a caretaker at the campsite. Had been ever since he left the CRS. Someone had gone to a lot of trouble to make him uncomfortable as well. In six months she got all of them."

"I didn't realize that," Mayo said. "Last time I checked, her score was only four."

"She got the lot. Or so we think. The last of them

came to the French police and admitted the whole thing. Asked for protection. They gave it to him, but it didn't make any difference. He died in his cell. Knife."

"That's when she went into business for herself," Mayo said from behind Jake.

"Yes. Exit Marie Planchet, enter Marie-Ange Borisot, Jeanne de Vigny, Françoise Martin . . . there are a dozen pseudonyms we know about. In 1973 she did a bombing over here. Iraqi journalist someone in Baghdad didn't care for. She specializes in particularly difficult work. Politicians, public figures. That cabinet minister who was blown up right in the Houses of Parliament parking garage in 1979. She did that on hire to the Irish. We actually nailed the man who set up the deal—or at least our colleagues in Dublin did. He told us about the payment terms. Sapphires. Always the best stones. Always six of them."

"Why sapphires?"

"Why kill people for a living? Don't make the mistake of thinking someone like Planchet is *normal*, old boy. Clinically I'm sure she's quite insane. A homicidal maniac. Intelligent, skillful, above all very, *very* careful. But mad. If you want my advice, it's this: Go back to wherever you feel safest, close the front door, turn out the lights, and just be glad she isn't interested in you."

Jake said, "Then you're sure the bomb in the car that killed Elaine and the shot killed Charlie Keble weren't meant for me?"

"This lady doesn't make errors. If your wife and Keble were killed, you can be sure those were the people on her list."

"The scaffolding in New York; what about that?"

"Not her style. No. I'd put that down to an amateur. If she wanted you, there were plenty of opportunities. For some reason, the person who's paying her doesn't want you dead. But that isn't to say they won't change their minds if you remain involved in this much longer."

Mayo said, "Mr. Forrester, believe me, the best way you can help us is to stay out of it. It's the quickest way to make sure we catch the murderer of your wife and friends."

Jake said nothing. He was thinking of that face. It had been a mistake to show him the photograph. It was personal now.

CHAPTER TWENTY

The in-flight movie was a new Don Siegel thriller. Jake
watched it with the earphones in his lap; it wasn't the
kind of film where one needed to follow dialogue. Burt
Reynolds drove his car through a brick wall, jumped out,
and demolished six hoodlums without mussing his hair.
The stuntmen took some fancy falls, lay on the ground
for a few seconds, then got up and bored in again. It
looked easy.

Kim slept in the seat next to him, arms folded, head on
his arm. The trust implied in that was infinitely touching.
He reached down and stroked her hair. When all this was
over . . .

But it wasn't over yet. It had hardly begun, though it
had taken a lot of hard talking with Mayo and Scotland
Yard to uncover the dimensions of the crimes in which he
was now unwittingly but inextricably involved.

He tried to order the facts in his mind and link them
up with his suppositions and suspicions.

First, Elaine had been involved in a blackmail plot.
Charlie Keble must have been her confederate, but Jake
suspected he was only a minor figure—perhaps even an
innocent outsider who happened to stumble on the
scheme and thus earn a bullet in the head. Were others
involved besides Elaine and Charlie? Again, he was convinced of this without any real evidence; Elaine's nature
didn't lend itself to intrigue. She would need to be led.

There was someone else in charge of the scheme—
someone who had Elaine and Charlie killed when they
wanted out. That was why Elaine behaved so oddly on
the day she was killed; she was nervous, ready to crack
and reveal everything. So was Keble. He had rung Jake
at the Treadway Inn to tell him about the plot, but Jake
was too busy to talk. Some part of Jake would never forgive himself for that; guilt about Charlie's death and

Elaine's drove him just as much now as when he had
assumed they died by mistake for him.

And now there was a third victim, Tony Stephens. Not
a conspirator this time, but one of the ring's *victims*. Why
did the ringleader—Jake tagged him X in his mind for
convenience—turn Marie-Ange Planchet onto Tony? Not
because he was getting ready to spill everything to Jake;
the killer was already at work when they met at Aberdeen. Was it because he knew the police suspected Tony
of the crime for which he was being blackmailed?

Or was it all much simpler than that? Had Elaine and
Keble been killed not because they were getting ready to
talk but because they knew too much about X? Was he
now, after having disposed of his confederates, turning to
the victims, any one of which, under pressure, might lead
the police to him?

Jake began to see X the ringleader in a different light.
This was not some greedy and ambitious money-maker
but a calculating businessman who dealt in murder as
routinely as any broker traded stocks and bonds. His killing was not indiscriminate; each death was planned, pro-
fessionally executed, untraceable to him. Jake remained
alive because he was not yet a direct threat; he had the
blackmail money, but as far as X knew, he could not
trace it to its source. One by one, the people who might
lead him to X were being snuffed out.

The plane trembled as it passed through a patch of
clear-air turbulence. Kim stirred on his arm.

Jake remembered the rumble that preceded the scaffolding that showered down on his head only a few days
before. *There* was an incident that did not fit into the
cool and efficient plan he had just constructed around
mysterious X. "Definitely an amateur," Peverell had
said. Hired by whom?

Clearly, someone who felt threatened by Jake. But X
had no particular reason to believe Jake was close to discovering his identity. And, if he had, it would be Marie-
Ange who would be called in to dispense efficient, untraceable death.

Had someone else entered the game? Was there a Y as
well as an X?

And what might Y's motives be to have Jake Forrester
dead? Y wasn't involved in a blackmail plot that Jake

might expose. But had Jake unwittingly, in his search for the killer of Elaine and Charlie, frightened someone else out of hiding? Someone with something to lose; someone with a stake in this game valuable enough to need protection by murder? Someone, perhaps, who needed *Sasori* to win?

He remembered Tom Needham's estimate of the homicidal tendencies of the big yacht men at the America's Cup Ball. Ryker, desperate for money. Fujita, ambitious and ruthless. Both were involved in the *Sasori* challenge—as was Tom Needham himself. Any one of them might want to protect his investment sufficiently to think of killing Jake, especially as he threatened to enter a boat of his own.

So now he faced two enemies: X the blackmailer and Y the yachtsman. Though they might prove to be the same person, Jake doubted it.

And as for fighting them, discovering their identities . . . Jake knew he could not hope to do so without embarking on a single-minded vendetta for which he was ill-equipped. He must search from inside the boat world, probe the weak spots (a few of which he had already targeted)—and, above all, persist with his attempts to find *Calinda* and enter the next America's Cup challenge.

Whether he found her or not was largely irrelevant; the fact that he was looking made him a constant irritation to X and Y, a potential threat that hovered just out of reach, as disconcerting but as impossible to destroy as a wasp buzzing around one's head. He smiled grimly; Halvorsen's creation would continue to embarrass the yachting establishment even though the old man no longer had any interest in it. Halvorsen would appreciate the irony.

Jake settled back in his seat. It was surprisingly calming to at least know the nature of one's enemy. Some logic was emerging from the chaos that had surrounded his life. For the moment, he was safe from X; that part of the game was in abeyance, and would be as long as Jake held the money X wanted. As for Y . . . Jake suspected he would soon be forced to show his hand. If they were met at Kennedy, if an attempt was made there to follow him, or to kill him, it would be Y who was responsible.

Closing his eyes, Jake slept, to dream of swimming

through dark blue waters, pursuing the faint pale form of a sea creature who beckoned him deeper and deeper into mysterious caverns.

He woke to a stewardess holding out a white plastic tray with an empty cup and a pastry wrapped in cellophane
"Tea or coffee?"
"Neither. How long before we land?"
"Forty-five minutes. What about your friend?"
Jake looked at Kim, still asleep on his shoulder. "Coffee. Light."
As she filled the cup, Jake asked, "Does this flight terminate at New York."
"No, it goes on to Washington, D.C."
"Can I extend my ticket to go on with it?"
The stewardess looked along the aisle at the stirring passengers. "I really don't know, sir. Why not speak to the cabin steward?"
When Jake came back ten minutes later, Kim was awake and sipping her coffee. That she could look like this, unrumpled and fresh, after sleeping for hours on an airplane seat, distinguished her even more from other women. It came, he supposed, from being young.
As he sat down, she took his hand and rubbed it against her face. "I thought you'd gone."
"No place to go."
"Oh, I don't know. I always wondered what happened up front, behind the curtain."
"It's just like coach, but with free champagne and a place to play gin rummy if you feel like losing some money."
She snuggled up to him. "I like it better here with you."
Feeling cheap, Jake took out the endorsed ticket and dropped it in her lap. "The plane goes on to Washington. I've booked you through on it."
"No!"
Her small face was pale, furious.
"Listen, Kim! I've got things to do in New York. There's no reason for you to be involved. Take the *Calinda* drawings and go down to Mobile. My mother will look after you."

"Jake . . ."

"Don't argue. Just do it. Please. Trust me. Do you really think I'd risk losing you now?"

She looked up at him for a long time. He wondered how often her father had abandoned her in the same way, how often *he'd* said, "Trust me."

Finally she picked up the ticket. "If you say so." She glanced at the endorsement inside. "Wouldn't you know it? Not even first class."

After England and the Orkneys, Kennedy's glaring spaces had a heartless vitality Jake admired almost as much as he disliked. You could respect the concrete brutality of the place, even as you squinted your eyes and choked on the gas fumes.

His London-bought clothes hardly filled a single flight bag, but he loitered in the baggage hall as if looking for more luggage until the customs lanes were crowded, then mingled with tourists as they hauled their bags out into the main terminal.

Jake looked around, scanning the faces that lined the metal barrier between customs and the terminal floor. One of them would be looking for him.

It had been a calculated risk to leave Kim on the plane. He doubted that anyone would pursue her, even though she might be able to provide some useful information on Jake's plans. The blackmailer he now thought of as *X*—the man who paid to have Elaine and Charlie and Tony Stephens murdered—was not interested in killing Jake; if he had been, the job could have been done a dozen times already.

No, it was *Y* he had to worry about now; the man who had tried to kill him with the scaffolding, who had something important to lose if Jake kept up his pressure against the *Sasori* challenge. Takeo Fujita? Vincent Ryker? Or someone else? Jake's mental image of *Y* was a good deal more detailed than that of *X*. A rich amateur who hired second-rate men; a man who sweated and panicked when the pressure was on. Jake had sailed with enough men like that—Sunday sailors with the right wardrobe for boating, but none of the guts—to know their faults.

Y would expect Jake and Kim to come off the plane together. He would have sent someone out to the airport to tail them to their hotel. But he'd be confused by Jake's lone arrival, as he'd been confused by his random, unpredictable act in swapping wallets with the dead pedestrian. Like a bad helmsman faced with a sudden savage squall driving him on a lee shore, he would panic.

All Jake needed was one moment of carelessness; once he was out of the airport, free in New York, *he* would make the running. He was almost looking forward to it as he straggled out among the passengers, threading his way through the knots of embracing new arrivals, checking the people who hung on the railings, craning for a glimpse into the customs hall as the doors hissed open and slid closed.

The watcher finally gave himself away. Just as Jake had decided he would have to make a move and watch for someone taking off after him, he noticed two women glance at the far side of a pillar and look hurriedly away. Circling in a long arc, Jake found a spot where the hidden side of the column was reflected in an Avis Car-Rental sign.

The chauffeur's dark uniform and dark glasses didn't disguise the skeleton shape or death's-head face.

Jubei.

Then *Y* was Fujita?

Jake found that the resolution surprised him. He thought the Japanese too smart for random violence—certainly too intelligent to send so obvious a sentinel to intercept him. In case the big man should be a plant, designed to spook him into making a run for it, Jake remained standing near the wall, watching for others who, like Jubei, loitered where they could check everyone going in and out of the terminal. Five minutes of this convinced him Jubei was alone.

The five minutes gave Jake time to plan his escape from the terminal building.

Through the glass wall, he watched cab after cab slide down the concourse and pick up new arrivals from the line that formed by the dispatcher's booth. He was that close to safety; only one man and half an inch of plate glass lay between him and escape. The man would be no

problem if Jake could only get a start on him. The glass
was another problem.

His eyes moved between the two sets of double doors,
one for passengers leaving the building, the other for new
arrivals. Both were the air lock kind—double sliding-
glass doors separated by eight feet of rubber matting that
covered a pressure switch. The first set of doors opened
as one approached and closed behind as those in front
opened.

Jake watched the main exit doors. People leaving the
building usually had porters to roll their baggage on a
trolley. They breezed through. Jake knew he could easily
slip by such a trolley. But so could Jubei.

He needed a way to delay the big Japanese. His eyes
moved to the entrance door and watched a couple drag
their half-dozen bags from the taxi towards the sliding
door. As they dumped them on the rubber mat and
looked around desperately for a porter, the outer doors
opened, but the inner set remained closed. Only when
they stepped onto the rubber mat did the second set
open.

Jake took a deep breath. A businessman, loaded down
with attaché case, plastic carrier with two bottles of duty-
free Scotch, a folding garment bag, and a camera case
shuffled across the sidewalk and onto the outer mat. The
doors opened. He almost stumbled inside. The inner
doors began to open . . .

Jake sprinted towards him. He watched the man's face
assume an expression of mingled fear and astonishment
as he grabbed him, spun him around, and, closing his
ears to the understandable protest, sent him reeling into
the terminal.

Glancing behind him through the closing inner doors,
Jake saw Jubei loping towards him, trying desperately to
avoid the heap of luggage and stumbling pedestrians he
had created. For an instant, Jake was trapped between
the two sets of doors; but another passenger was already
stepping unwittingly onto the pressure mat outside. As
the doors opened, Jake bolted out. He heard the furious
pounding of Jubei's fists against the glass, but it would
take him thirty seconds to decide he stood a better
chance of catching Jake by racing to the main exit doors,

and another fifteen to reach Jake's present position—right opposite the point where incoming cabs dropped off passengers.

Getting a cab at Kennedy is an orderly business. Arriving hacks drop off the fare and take their place in the pool of cabs; on a slow day, it can take an hour before they get called around to the dispatcher to collect another passenger.

The dispatcher was a dozen yards away, by the exit door. Jake ignored him and sprinted to the battered hack that had just left a family of puzzled Japanese at the curb.

"Manhattan." He wrestled with the back door, but the driver had both safety locks engaged.

"Get in line, pal. Take the first cab." He gestured over his shoulder towards the dispatcher.

"Fifty bucks." Jake tossed the bill into the front seat.

The driver said nothing, but Jake heard the locks click open. He dove in, and they roared away up the sloping concrete access road.

Jubei came out of the terminal and stood silent on the sidewalk. After half a minute watching the cabs come sliding down the ramp, drop off their passengers, and climb the access road, he went to where Jake had stood and waited. As the next cab came by, he stepped out in front of it.

Anthony Sognamillo had driven a hack in New York for seven years, first as an employee, then an owner. There was no aspect of human perfidy and intransigence with which he was not intimately acquainted. Hunching to squint at the figure leaning against his right front fender, he said, "Would you get the . . ."

Jubei's long arm reached in through the open window, across the front seat of the big Chrysler, and clamped the face of Sognamillo like a claw, four fingers deep into the curly black hair, thumb hooked under the bone of the jaw, flattening the carotid artery, applying such pressure to the nerves of the face that the man's throat choked in a gasp of agony.

The plastic screen separating a New York taxi's driving seat from the passenger compartment is designed to with-

stand the impact of a bullet fired at close range. Drawing
the man's head forward four inches, Jubei drove it back
hard against the scratched plastic. The crunch of splinter-
ing perspex mingled with the muffled squashing sound of
Sognamillo's skull caving in.

Jubei stepped back one pace, his arm rigid, hand still
around the dead man's face, dragging him away from the
driving seat as an alligator hauls the body of a trapped
animal into its lair by the grip of its jaws on the crushed
head. To anyone who had been watching, Jubei would
merely seem to have handed something in to the driver.
Not that anyone was watching; the next cab in the line
was still discharging passengers.

Circling the car, Jubei put his hand on the sill of the
open window and jerked. The safety lock snapped. He
climbed in, pushed the body of Sognamillo down into the
well, out of sight, and drove towards the freeway. His
eyes scanned the traffic in front of him for a yellow cab,
the trunk held closed with baling wire, and 720 as the last
numbers of the license. He caught it as they passed the
site of the New York World's Fair and shadowed it all
the way into Manhattan.

The new girl on the desk at *Yachts and Yachting* boasted
soft round breasts and a haircut even more brutal than
that of her predecssor.

"Sally Goldstone in?"

"I'll see, sir. Who shall I say . . ."

Before the girl could stand up to stop him, Jake
pushed through the doors and walked down the long editorial office. He interrupted Sally Goldstone as she
picked up her burring phone.

"Don't bother. It's only your playmate of the month
announcing me."

Not taking her eyes from his face, Sally said into the
phone, "It's okay, Candy. I was expecting Mr. Forrester."

Jake sat down. "Very friendly of you, Sally."

"Jake, I don't know what to say. First I read your obit
in *The Times*. Next thing, everyone's saying, 'Did you
hear about Jake Forrester turning up in London?' What
the hell's going on?"

"You tell me, Sally."

Her little eyes were suddenly nervous. "You lost me, pal."

"They say when you drown your life is supposed to flash in front of your eyes. Well, while that scrap iron was raining down on me, I had time to wonder about who set me up. Someone suckered me into that very spot on 44th Street. Someone who knew where I was staying, what car I was driving—knew everything about my movements, in fact."

"What was secret about the hotel you were booked into? And it doesn't take a Ph.D. to find out who rented a car. Anyone could have found out that sort of thing. Aaron Hart. Gerry Cornelius."

"You make a lousy conspirator, Sally. Who told you I talked to Hart and Cornelius? That was after I saw you."

"You said you were going to see them." Two spots of color glowed on her cheeks.

"No, Sally. I never even told you I'd hired a car. You were briefed after I left this office. By whom? Was it Fujita? Is he behind all this? His goon was at the airport to meet me. Did you set that up too? Did *you* set someone onto Tony Stephens? You gave me Halvorsen's location. Who else did you tell about me going to Britain?"

He surged across the desk, grabbed the front of her shirt, and hauled her out of her seat. The sick old lady's face stared a few inches from his.

"Goddammit, who? Or I'll take you onto that cute little balcony of yours and drop you into the street."

Someone battered on the door.

"Who?"

She croaked something, plucking at his hands. He realized he was strangling her and tried to relax his grip. The fingers wouldn't respond. He forced them open, one by one, with an effort of will. She sagged in her chair.

"Jake, I don't know . . ."

"The hell you don't." He reached for her again. She cringed.

"I swear. Sweet Jesus, I *swear*. Information . . . they buy information. Gossip. Dirt. It's been going on for years. Cash for anything they can use. All they hand out is a number."

"What number?"

"Four"—she tried to swallow—"four six seven double four."

"There must have been more than that."

"No. Nothing. Honest to God, Jake."

The door opened suddenly. The boy standing there, with a white-faced crowd behind him, carried a small fire extinguisher. He raised it threateningly as Jake turned on them.

"I wouldn't, sonny."

He stepped back. Jake pushed through the rest of them.

Nobody manned the front desk. He went through the doors into the main corridor and thumbed the elevator button.

He heard a noise. Thin and muffled. It sounded like a scream.

Except for the door of the magazine office and the two elevators, there was only one other—plain, wooden, with a plate marked Private. Staff Only. He pushed it open cautiously.

It was a washroom. There was a long mirror lit by flat fluorescent light, a machine that dispensed throwaway toothbrushes, face cream, sanitary napkins. The four stalls were divided by marble panels supported on metal shafts eighteen inches above the floor. From the door he could not see if any of the teak veneer doors were closed.

Another moan. He thought of animals caught in traps, of metal jaws sawing through flesh and bone.

He walked along the four cubicles. A narrow black back filled the third. As Jake stopped outside, Jubei turned and looked at him. His eyes had the uninterested glaze of a feeding shark. He straightened up, and Jake saw what he had been doing.

The blonde receptionist slumped on the lavatory seat.

She was naked to the waist because her blouse had been torn off to tie her arms, which were wrenched behind her, bound elbow to elbow.

This pulled her shoulders back and thrust her breasts forward. It was her breasts Jubei had used to bring her pain. They drooped softly, white except where crimson weals and bruises marked the skin. Both nipples were bruised and swollen, the color of ripe plums. There was blood on them and on the thighs of her white jeans.

She saw Jake and whimpered, "Make him stop. *Please.*"

"Leave her alone."

Jubei came out of the cubicle, smiling. The girl was just bait.

Backing away, Jake realized how successfully he had been set up. No chance here of surprise. No convenient chains. No cover. A killing ground.

Something touched him low on his back. He felt for it without taking his eyes away from Jubei. The edge of the washbasins. He fumbled across the smooth porcelain, looking for some kind of weapon.

A movement at the tips of his fingers. He groped for whatever it was, closed his hand over it. Smooth, oval. A cake of soap. Barely used. Jake calculated its weight. Four ounces? Too light to give weight to a punch. But some kind of weapon.

He shifted sideways quickly and pitched it straight at Jubei's face.

If the man had flinched, ducked, even closed his eyes for a second, Jake might have made it to the door.

Jubei just grabbed the thing out of the air a foot in front of his face. Nothing moved but his right arm.

He glanced at the soap, smiled, carefully closed his hand. White fragments pattered to the floor.

Then the air was full of them. Jubei had tossed the rest of them in Jake's face. He ducked instinctively, and the other man's foot lashed out with all the weight of his twisting torso behind it.

If his hard-soled shoes had not slipped fractionally on the terrazzo floor, Jubei would have killed Jake with the blow. A *tae kwon dō* punch or kick reaches its maximum force just *before* the limb is fully extended; the killer focuses his blow inside the body of the victim, to deliver the most powerful force at the surface.

But Jubei skidded as he threw the kick. Only two-thirds of its potential force struck Jake on the left shoulder.

Jake thought his shoulder was smashed.

He sat down hard on the floor, pain throbbing through his arm from shoulder joint to fingertips.

Scrambling under the shelter of the washbasins, he measured the distance to the door, bracing himself for one attempt to reach it, knowing that Jubei would be on him before he moved a yard.

The door opened. Not slowly. Confidently, with a squeal of its hinges. The newcomer sucked air as it eased shut after him.

The man grinned at Jake. Short, broad-faced, with a thick moustache, he looked Sicilian.

"Hi there."

He wore baggy white overalls. Jake took him for the man who replaced the towels, until he turned to look at Jubei. His face showed disgust and amusement.

"Well, look at this. Jubei. How come *I* get all the shit jobs?"

Jubei's smile faded.

"Well? You going to get out of here? Or do I have to throw you out?"

He strolled along the line of cubicles until he came to the one that held the girl.

"You okay, honey?"

The girl moaned something Jake didn't hear.

"Have ya outa there in a second." Over his shoulder he said to Jake, "Hang in there, pal, while I get rid of this rat turd. You know, this snake's so disgusting that even the Japs don't want anything to do with . . ."

Jubei swung his hand in a flat arc that should have chopped into the small man's head but instead swished through empty air. Before he could recover his balance, the other was under his guard, slamming two blows into his ribs with the edge of his right hand.

They seemed to have no effect. Sliding his feet in front of him as if feeling his way through ground strewn with obstacles, the Japanese edged forward, backing the little man towards the washbasins. As he felt the basins and straightened slightly, Jubei's right hand slashed at him. But he slipped under the blow and it hit the big mirror, which shattered with a flat crunch. Fragments of glass rattled into the washbasins. Jubei's hand came away bleeding.

The sight of his own blood seemed to enrage the big Japanese. With a roar he advanced, arms and legs windmilling. The little man reached behind him, clamped both hands onto the porcelain, and using the grip for added leverage, leaped up and out, both feet thudding into Jubei's chest. Jake heard the thump and the rush of breath as they connected.

Jubei was still standing, but the blow had done damage. There was blood on his lips, and he stood straighter, not using the muscles of his chest. The blow of the chain still hurt.

But pain made him cunning. He circled, looking for weaknesses in the other's defense. He found it when one of the crumbled fragments of soap made the other slip a fraction. Jubei spun, kicked, connected. Jake knew the pain of that blow and winced. He could see the man's face tighten each time he put weight on that side of his body.

Sensing victory, Jubei came on, not noticing that he was being lured towards the only cover in the room, the four lavatory stalls. When he did, he tried to head off his opponent, but before he could, the man was half inside the first of them.

With a smile, Jubei drew back his arm as he had the night he beat Sam Lewis, and drove it forward in a short jab. The marble shattered. Scraps clung to the metal pins holding the divider to the wall. The rest clattered and rattled across the floor.

One piece slid almost under Jake's hand. Sharp at one end, it broadened to six inches across at the other. Jake's fingers tightened around it. As Jubei moved in for the kill, he swung underhand, throwing the spinning spike of marble straight at his head.

Out of the corner of his eye Jubei saw it coming, but too late. The heavy slab struck him on the forehead with an audible clunk. Something seemed to happen to his eyes. He sat down heavily, rolled onto hands and knees, then stumbled to his feet and, fumbling along the line of marble tiles as if blind, finally found the door. Too exhausted to stop him, the two men watched him stagger out of the washroom.

Jake got painfully to his feet and helped the little man to stand.

"You okay?"

He felt his leg; obviously it hurt. "I'll live." Bending over with an effort, he picked up something from the floor on the end of his finger. A flake of color. "Contact lens. That bastard's half-blind without them. You really got him with that piece of marble. Must have blown them right out of his head. Always go for the face with Jubei."

"I'll remember," Jake said sourly. If, as now looked likely, the mysterious *Y* who planned his murder with the scaffolding was Fujita, this would not be his last meeting with the snakelike Jubei. He wasn't looking forward to the return match. Without the help of the man who'd come to his rescue, Jake would by now be dead.

But who did *he* work for? Jake had no time to ask. He disappeared into the stall that held the tortured girl and reemerged carrying her easily in his arms. She had obviously fainted.

"There a service elevator here, do you know?"

"I guess so."

"Let's get to it then." Still carrying the girl, he led Jake through the maze of corridors to the back of the building. The canvas-draped service elevator took them into the subbasement. Nobody took much notice of two battered-looking men carrying a half-naked girl.

In the alley at the back, a large black car idled. As Jake and the other man climbed down the narrow steps from the loading dock, two men in dark uniformlike suits slipped from the back seat.

"Why don't you get in back, Mr. Forrester," his rescuer said as he handed the girl over to them. "Few things I gotta do here before we leave." The three went into a whispered conference.

Painfully, Jake slid into the back seat and leaned back. A minute later he looked up as a second car drove into the alley. The girl and one of the men got into it, and it drove away along the narrow street, heading uptown. The remaining uniformed man took the driver's seat, and the small dark man with the moustache got in back with Jake. The car glided silently in the same direction as the first.

Jake said, "What's your name anyway?"

"Lew will do it."

"Well, Lew, thanks a lot."

"All part of the service, Mr. Forrester." He glanced at the intricate watch on his wrist. "Say, we aren't making bad time."

"Not making bad time towards what?"

"A meeting. My boss is kind of anxious to talk to you."

"And who's that exactly?"

Lew grinned. "I leave the explanations to him. Just relax. We'll be there in a few minutes."

Their chauffeur was talking urgently into a radio telephone, but the glass screen that separated them from the front seat blocked his voice completely.

The car pulled over to the curb. They were at Columbus Circle. Another man opened the door—a plumper, older man in a blue suit. Lew said, "Archie here'll take care of you."

The limousine pulled away, leaving Jake on the sidewalk. With a growing sense of unreality, Jake let himself be guided into Lincoln Center. Like a football player running interference, Archie cleared the way through ushers and program sellers.

Over his shoulder he said, "Please try to hurry, Mr. Forrester. Curtain's about to go up, and there's no admission until the first intermission."

They squeezed through the big doors at the back of the circle and followed the line of the wall until they entered a narrow corridor lined with numbered doors covered in red damask. Archie knocked on number 7, opened it, and motioned Jake inside.

The curtain went up almost as if his arrival had been a signal. Dancers dressed as Tirolean peasants sprang out onto the stage and whirled to music that sounded to Jake frantic, almost demonic. He vaguely recognized Stravinsky.

The box was sparsely furnished. Four chairs and a small table, on which stood an ice bucket drapped in white cloth and a plate covered in a napkin. Three of the chairs were empty. Takeo Fujita sat in the other.

"Please sit down, Mr. Forrester."

"What the hell *is* this?"

"*Petrouchka*. Let's talk in the intermission, shall we?"

CHAPTER TWENTY-ONE

Jake had been to the ballet less than half a dozen times in his life—usually to gala charity performances Elaine insisted they attend, which Jake dozed through, half-choked by stiff collar and bow tie. He saw even less of this performance. Each time he tried to concentrate, his mind wandered to the grotesque events of the morning. If Fujita was the elusive *Y*, the man who nearly killed him with the falling scaffolding, then why had Lew, who called Fujita his boss, rescued Jake from Jubei—*also* a Fujita man? Why had Lew turned up so fortuitously? It was obvious Jubei had followed him from the airport—so much for Jake's attempt to shake the tail. Had Lew been following him as well? And, if so, why?

From time to time, Jake glanced at the intent profile of Fujita. The jutting brow and bristling gray hair made him look like some old wild animal, an old coon who'd killed enough and been often enough nearly killed himself to know all the tricks. His eyes, black as marbles, never left the dancers. He might have been controlling them himself by sheer power of will, operating them like the marionettes they played in the story. As the music ended and the applause roared outside the box, Fujita turned to Jake with a look of relaxation that was probably as close as he ever came to smiling.

"An adequate performance, I think. No more than that."

Jake said drily, "I found it hard to concentrate. Just what am I doing here, Mr. Fujita?"

The door to the box opened. Archie came in, handed a note to Fujita, and began peeling the foil from the neck of the bottle of Bollinger in the ice bucket.

Fujita read the note and slipped it in his pocket. "The young lady Jubei mistreated will recover, it appears. She is being looked after in a private clinic we maintain for our employees."

"And Jubei? Who's going to look after him?"

Fujita took one of the glasses of champagne poured by
Archie and handed it to Jake. "We will talk of all this,
but in proper order." He inclined his head backwards
towards the now curtained stage. "This ballet. It has a
particular appeal for me. The *Bunraku* puppets of Japan
performed all the great traditional stories of our history.
I saw them as a child. A story like this *Petrouchka,* where
the puppets come to life at the will of their puppet-master—I often dreamed of that."

Jake thought of the dark-suited men who whisked
away the tortured girl, who brought him here to the theater—Fujita's puppets. "I should have thought a man
like yourself comes as close as anyone to having that
power."

"You think so?" Fujita looked out at the crowds milling in the aisles below them. "Which of those could I
direct? My men could enter that crowd, take one woman
from her seat, bring her up here, persuade her—pain,
money—to remove her clothes and offer herself to me.
Power of a sort, but not the puppeteer's power. He can
change minds, bring life to the dead, move the heart. All
the millions at my disposal could not do that, even to the
most stupid of these people." He glanced around the
huge auditorium. "On the other hand, I do have my influence; if I cannot animate the puppets, at least I can
build the theater where the performance takes place. Do
you know how much of this place is based on Tora technology? The lights and dimmer boards use our components. The upholstery of every seat uses a filiment
developed in our laboratories. The sensors in the sprinkler system, the torches used by the ushers, even some of
the musical instruments in the orchestra; we make a plastic violin with a tone as good as a Guarnerius. All Tora
products."

"And *Sasori*?"

"Yes. *Sasori.* By all means, let us talk of *Sasori.* Is she
not a fine creation?"

"From what I've seen, which is very little and under
difficult circumstances, she's a good boat."

"I would have been pleased to show her to you at any
time. Unfortunately, I put the matter of her introduction
into the United States into the hands of men who re-

spected my requirements for discretion perhaps a little too diligently. But until the New York Yacht Club passed the boat as fit to race, some secrecy was essential. Ryker is not a particularly subtle man, but he has the necessary contacts, and I left the matter to him. As it turned out, he did well."

"Your man Jubei did better. He nearly killed Sam Lewis when we tried to look over *Sasori*. He also murdered two of Ryker's men. This morning he tried to kill me. And I imagine he was the one who tried to drop a few tons of scrap metal on me a few days ago. You don't seem especially selective in your choice of employees."

"I told you. The puppet-master cannot always control his creations. Jubei worked for me at that time, true. But I loaned him to Ryker, and since then he has gone into business on his own."

Jake stared at Fujita. Was Jubei working for someone else— for *Y*? That would explain a lot. Why there was no reception party at Kennedy, but just Jubei alone; without Fujita's establishment behind him, he would have to do everything himself. And the reckless murder attempt with the scaffolding; that wasn't the scheme of someone with helpers, professional equipment, a guaranteed getaway.

"So you blame Ryker for these attempts on my life?"

"I didn't say that. He may be responsible. I do not know who Jubei works for. His activities are of no interest to me so long as they don't interfere with my own."

"And my death would have been . . . an interference?"

"Oh, yes, Mr. Forrester. Sooner or later, you and I must race to see who is the better sailor."

"I don't have a boat."

"You will find one. You are the kind of man who cannot live without sailing. I have watched your career for years. Of all the captains I know, you are the one I worry about most. You have the kind of anger that I thought only Japanese knew. There is a fire in you. But I will quench it."

A gong chimed somewhere. People began drifting back into the auditorium.

"You give me your word—Jubei isn't your man?"

"He is not."

"Ryker's?"

"Perhaps. You must ask him. We are opponents, Mr. Forrester. I respect you, but that is not to say I will help you. But to know a man, you must have looked him in the face. We have done that. We will meet again in Newport."

The lights began to dim. Jake let himself out of the door into the corridor and walked back down through the empty lobbies and into the real world. For half an hour, he walked through Central Park, thinking. Then he booked into the Plaza. The room he got was on the unfashionable side facing the air shaft, but he was not there to look at the view. Ordering a steak sandwich from room service, he started calling people.

He called his mother in Mobile and warned her to expect Kim. He called Sam Lewis at home. After more than a minute ringing, the phone was picked up, and a slurred voice said "Yeah?"

"Sam? It's Jake." A long pause. "Sam?"

"Jake. Hell. Where are ya, for Chrissake?"

"New York. Sam, what's the matter with you. Are you smashed?"

"I've been having a few, yeah. Jesus, man, I don't know whether to believe it's you or not. I heard all kinds of stuff. Your obit was even in *The Times*."

"I'll tell you all about that when I see you. Are you in shape for visitors?"

"I guess I can handle you. When will you be down?"

"Later this week. I want to talk to you about a couple of things."

"Like?"

"A boat called *Calinda*."

"Halvorsen's *Calinda?* What about it?"

Jake ignored the question. "The other thing is Fujita."

"That bastard's everyplace. You see *Time* magazine this week?"

Jake smiled to himself. "I've been sort of busy."

"Pick one up. You'll flip. What time will you get down here?"

"I don't know. Let me call you Friday. And stay off the booze."

He hung up and rang the drugstore downstairs to send up a copy of *Time*. Ten minutes later he was reading about Fujita's plans for a fleet of wind-powered light-weight freighters and tankers controlled by satellite. No wonder Tom Needham had insisted that a lot of people stood to make money from the *Sasori* challenge. If Fujita won, the way would be clear for a massive incursion into the whole world of shipping; who would doubt the credentials of a man whose boat had beaten the Americans at their own game after more than a century of world domination?

Jake closed the magazine. Now more than ever he needed to find *Calinda*. He dug out his notes, made from the plans that Kim carried with her to Mobile, and started serious work.

Sam's beige Mercedes was parked under the carport at the side of the house, but Jake saw no movement through the large picture windows. He was getting ready to press the bell again when the door opened suddenly. The girl had a spectacular figure, parts of which were confined inside a red bikini. Jake saw himself triply reflected in the silvered lenses of her sunglasses and the half-filled highball glass in her hand.

"Sam in?"

"Yeah. Sure." She stood back and let him in. "Sam," she called. "Visitors."

Sam looked up from his spot in the sun, where he'd established a snug headquarters—a tray with bottles, mixers, and an ice bucket, a heap of *Playboys*, and a pair of stereo earphones whose cable trailed off into the house. There was another sunbed beside his. Obviously the girl's.

"Hey, Jake. How are they hanging?" He sat up, the grubby bathrobe falling back from his short hairy legs. He wore nothing under it. "Susie, pour Jake a drink. Bourbon and water."

"How are you doing, Sam?"

"I'm getting there." He bent forward to show Jake the shaved patch on the back of his skull, covered in a dressing. "Arachnoid adhesions, whatever the fuck *they* are. Susie here's taking good care of me. Pretty good ass for a registered nurse, huh?" He reached over and stroked the tight fabric of her bikini pants as she bent over the drinks tray. She giggled.

"How long before you mend?"

"Hell, I'm mended now. But there's not much to do. Tom has *Andromeda* in production. They don't need me until the keel's laid and we start real building." He squinted at Jake. "What's this about Halvorsen's old boat?"

"You've seen *Sasori*. Nothing on the water now can beat her."

"*Andromeda* might."

"Okay. *Andromeda* might. We won't know until a year from now. I'd rather not leave it to chance. I want to enter a boat of my own against *Sasori*. The only one that seems to me might have a chance is *Calinda*."

Sam looked skeptical. "Twelve-year-old boat? Things have changed a lot since then."

"I was looking up the details of Halvorsen's other boats. You remember *Sprite, Loki, Sea Song* . . ."

"I forgot he built *Loki*. Some boat."

"Her record for Newport to Miami still stands, and that was in 1972. Even at the time, these boats were faster than the rest, and with the sort of sails and gear we've got today, they could be faster still. It's the hulls that gave them the speed; Halvorsen just had the touch. And he rated *Calinda* the fastest hull he ever built."

"So where is she?"

Jake sat back in his chair. "God knows. I spent two days in New York just going through *Lloyd's Register*. No boat called *Calinda* registered anyplace. Nobody knows who bought her after Halvorsen sold. Sam, I need your help. The people inside the boat business won't talk to me; Cornelius and the rest have put it around that I'm thinking of entering a boat. They think it's just a nuisance gesture. But on top of that business with Billy Weems . . ."

Sam said, "Sure. I'll ask around, pal. But . . . this whole deal; the Halvorsen boat. The Japs. I mean, who gives a fuck, huh? What are you going to do? Break yourself by going up against the whole NYYC, Tom, Fujita? Okay—maybe you've got some griefs with them. They owe you. But what's the bottom line? You lose your balls, that's what. They can take you apart with one hand. You're out of your league."

He waved his arm to take in the sun, the bay, the

beautiful girl. "Look, Jake; what more could you want? Move in, mellow out, take a load off your mind. Susie here will have you back in shape in a week. She's into yoga. Got muscles where you never thought there could be muscles."

Jake stood up. "Sorry to have bothered you, Sam. Hope you heal up soon."

He kept his cool until he got to the front door. Then he allowed himself the luxury of a thunderous slam.

CHAPTER TWENTY-TWO

The note of Peter Forrester's bicycle tires changed abruptly as they left the concrete path beside Forrester Marine and hit the wooden planks of the jetty. Stiffening his arms against the judder of the front wheel, he rode the bike halfway down the wharf, leaned it against the safety fence, and started down the steps to where the water sucked at the pilings.

"You lock that bike up?" Carl Bangsund stepped down from the yawl moored by Peter's boat.

"Who's going to steal it?"

"You think it's safe just because this is your daddy's place? Lock it up."

"Aw, gee . . ."

Bangsund frowned. Reluctantly Peter went back up to the wharf and locked the safety chain through the wheels.

He came back, heavy-footed and resentful. "Satisfied?"

"You think your father would thank me if I let your bike get stolen? A new Raleigh like that?"

"Okay if I take the boat out now?"

"Where you heading?"

"Battleship Park, I guess."

Bangsund looked down Mobile Bay. In forty years on these waters, he'd learned their every mood.

"Tide's making. Don't run aground."

"Have I ever?"

"First time for everything."

"I won't run aground." He was already untying the painter.

Bangsund watched him get the boat ready for sea and climbed back onto the wharf. Peter was like his father, a natural sailor, but stubborn. He'd drown rather than change his mind.

He saw Kim Ryker coming down the wharf towards

him. She wore a denim jacket and jeans. Her eyes were ringed with fatigue. When Carl's wife saw her for the first time, she'd said, "That girl needs about a year's vacation and a month of good meals."

"Morning, miss."

"Hi, Mr. Bangsund." She looked around the hazy sky. "Kind of a dull day."

"There's a good breeze. Want to go out? I could fix up one of the Lasers for you. Or young Peter's taking his boat down the bay."

She looked away. "I don't think Peter wants my company."

"Sure he does." He leaned over the dock "Hold up. Got a passenger for you."

Kim frowned. Peter had made his feelings more than clear in the weeks she had been staying at the house. She was the intruder, the interloper. These days, they hardly talked.

Reluctantly she climbed down the ladder. Peter sat at the tiller, adjusting the backstay. He saw Kim and looked furious.

"Take Miss Ryker down with you." Bangsund looked at Kim. "You seen Battleship Park yet, miss?"

"No."

"Ought to see that while you're here. Got the old *Alabama* down there. Fine ship. One of the sights of Mobile. Peter's going right by."

Peter looked sour. "I changed my mind. I'm taking her up towards town."

"You ain't neither." Bangsund spat in the water, watched the smear of spittle slide away from the side of the boat. "Tide's making. You go up there, you're stuck for the morning." He helped Kim into the boat and said pointedly, "Better get going pretty soon. No telling how long this breeze will last."

Kim slid into the well, facing Peter. "Let me handle the boom."

"I can do it."

She folded her arms as he set the sail and let the breeze fill it. Bangsund tossed the painter into the boat.

"Take care now."

Peter's face was set and hostile. Kim remembered thirteen herself. It was a bad age to deal with the world without parents to help out. He shoved off and turned the boat across the wind.

"This wasn't my idea," she said after a silent five minutes.

Peter didn't answer. The wind changed a point, and the sail began to rattle overhead. Before he could reach it, Kim loosened the sheet and twisted it around the cleat in a slippery hitch. For a moment she thought Peter would unwind the rope and retie it, but he just looked away.

They glided down the bay. The water was shallow, heavily dredged in the channels, only a few feet deep elsewhere. Artificial islands carpeted in green sea grass covered the mud flats where the dredgers dumped their loads, and the water was milky white with dissolved clay. The gray overcast blurred with the opaque water until the horizon disappeared.

"You needn't go to this Battleship place unless you want to," Kim said. "I'm happy just sailing. Sitting around the house drives me crazy."

"It's a neat place." He spoke without inflection, happy at the chance to contradict her.

"Okay. Let's see it then."

Conscious of having been outmaneuvered, Peter steered for the distant silhouette of the *Alabama*, moored stern out from the artificial island on which the park had been built.

His father used to bring him down here often when his mother was alive, to play on the old World War Two planes dotted around the island. He got to sit in the cockpit of the P-51 and climb over the wings of the C-47. They went down into the oily darkness of the submarine *Drum*, moored next to the battleship, and once the caretaker took him on a tour of the whole huge *Alabama*. He sat in the turret and looked through the ring sight at the far shore of Mobile Bay, under constant threat from the ship's silenced guns.

They were almost under the shadow of the battleship now. Peter's lips started to form the silent Boom Boom of that good lost time.

The speedboat came out of nowhere, rocketing from behind the gray steel cliff of the warship's hull. Seeing the dinghy, it turned sharply, throwing a fan of water that half-drowned the tiny boat.

Peter wrenched the tiller around, throwing the boat into irons. The sail flapped angrily as they rocked in the speedboat's wake.

"Did you see that? They could have smashed us to bits."

He looked towards Kim, his hostility forgotten in astonishment.

She huddled in the prow of the boat, arms wrapped around her ribs, knees drawn up to her chin.

"Hey. What's the matter?"

She didn't answer. Crawling to the bow, he put his hand tentatively on her shoulder. The face that turned to him was white and bloodless. Her lips were blue with fright. Tears matted strands of hair to her cheeks. She was trembling.

He squatted beside her until she stopped crying. His handkerchief was none too clean, but she took it when he offered and wiped away the damage of her tears.

"You okay now?"

"I suppose so. Sorry, Peter. It gave me a scare."

"Hey, me too. What a dumb thing. It was some kid. I saw him. I'll report him to the harbor master." He looked at her closely. "You want to go back home?"

"No." She sniffed. "I'll be all right in a minute. Let's go on. If you still want to."

"Yes. Sure." He smiled. "Would you like to go out a bit further? There's some good sailing down around Dauphin Island."

"Can we eat there?"

"There's a McDonald's on the pier."

"Okay, captain. My treat."

The weather broke just as Jake arrived in Mobile. He landed in a downpour and took a cab out to his mother's house. It seemed years since he had been back to the city. The rain, the dark, his own disorientation made once familiar streets seem alien and threatening.

He let himself in, shook the worst of the rain from his coat, and hung it on the old hatstand, a souvenir of his father that Elaine had always hated but which Jean refused to throw out. He heard voices in the parlor and opened the door.

Kim and Peter were cross-legged on the floor, playing Scrabble.

"*Wimp* isn't a word."

"Sure it is," Peter said.

"Well, look it up, then. But if it's wrong . . ."

She saw Jake in the doorway and sprang at him.

He had forgotten the difference in their heights. In bare feet her shoulders barely came up to his chest.

When he raised his face from kissing her, Peter was looking at them.

"Listen, if you give me five bucks, I'll go to the movies."

Jake reached out with his free arm and put it around his son. Peter wriggled in embarrassment, but Jake felt it was good-natured. Why had he ever imagined there would be a problem?

"Where's Jean?"

"Gone to some meeting. She left a message for you." He bolted towards the hall.

"You been all right?" he asked.

"Fine. What about you?"

"It's a long story."

Peter came in with a notepad.

"Jake, welcome home. I'd be there but I have an Arts Panel meeting. There's ratatouille and cheese in the frig. Jean."

"Jean been taking those cordon bleu cooking classes again?"

Peter grimaced. "Yeah. Kim and me sneak out for hamburgers when she's not looking. You want one?"

"Sure. A double cheeseburger." He fished for money and found a ten-dollar bill. "Some fries too."

As Peter bolted through the front door, struggling into his raincoat, Jake put his arms around Kim again. "Miss me?"

For an answer she held onto his neck, raised her slim body off the ground, and wrapped her legs around him. He could feel the warmth between her thighs.

"Let's do it right now. Standing up."

"Peter . . ."

"He has to learn sometime."

Jake gritted his teeth and peeled her off. "We can wait a couple of hours. And I've got some calls to make."

"Coward."

"How about some coffee to go with the burgers?"

He went into the living room and lifted the phone onto the big dining table. Beside it he spread out his meager file of documentation on *Calinda*. The scraps of information he had been able to pick up in New York over the last week, the suppositions and speculations about where she might be, who might be her owner now, made a thin bundle.

Lloyd's Register of Yachts had no registration of *Calinda* under that name since Halvorsen first entered her in their records. Owners were expected to advise the register of changes in ownership or of name; most were eager to do so for the pleasure of being on record as a yacht captain. But the new owners of *Calinda*, or whatever she was now called, preferred anonymity.

Eventually, he had turned up a name. It was scrawled on one of the letters Halvorsen gave him with the drawings. He had taken it for random jotting, but after half an hour with a magnifying glass, he puzzled out a name and address.

Riffling through the papers to find it, he turned up a list of dates and times scribbled on the back of a page from an in-flight magazine. It was the schedule of the America's Cup challenge he'd jotted down on the plane.

Selection of the America's Cup defender would begin in April of the following year. By then, the serious contenders should have been marked and assessed. After that came the grueling year of training, fitting, testing, and trials that culminated in the Newport races.

It would take Jake six months to train and season a crew, even before feeling confident to enter a boat in the selection process. Finding the crew alone would take two months—perhaps longer if he lacked serious sponsorship and official backing. Nobody wanted to be involved with a maverick.

Then there was money. He'd have to talk to the bank about a mortgage. An image of Elaine's safe-deposit box came into his mind. Those stacks of money, so carelessly jumbled in—from whom? For what? Somehow, he would have to solve the mystery of Elaine before he gave himself to the pursuit of the Cup and the defeat of *Sasori*.

But would he be allowed to solve the mystery? Fujita might have been removed from contention as a suspect, but Jake knew two people had tried to kill him: Elaine's blackmailing partner and the man who hired Jubei—*X* and *Y*. *X* remained as much of a mystery as ever. As for *Y*, the letter always conjured up Vincent Ryker's sweating face. If he was not *Y*, he almost certainly knew his identity.

To the problems of finding *Calinda* and, if he did find her, of preparing her to race, Jake added those of ordinary safety. The boatyard would have to become their fortress; high wire fences along the street line, security guards on the gate. He made a note among the jumble of papers and went back to his hunt for *Calinda*. It looked like his first stop would have to be Portland, Oregon.

CHAPTER TWENTY-THREE

The breasts of the big blonde were huge. They swung rhythmically as her head dipped and rose and dipped again, fellating the black man who sat negligently in the easy chair, one leg dangling over the arm.

"She's not bad," Billy Joe Cohen said, relighting his cigar. "Where did you find her?"

"You won't believe this. A schoolteacher."

"I believe it."

Proposition 13 had put a good bit of business his way. It was marvelous how the closing down of libraries and the firing of public employees had sent up takings in the adult bookstores and cinemas. He could also get all the help he needed in extending the shops, putting in peep-show booths, finding people to repair the worn films.

The girl turned, presenting her soft ass to the man. He slid off his chair and entered her from behind. They were obviously having a lot of fun. Cohen reached over and turned off the projector.

"It's good stuff. How much more have you got?"

"Six, seven reels. Depends how I cut them."

"You need some money?"

Tad Foden's country-boy face split in a wide grin. "You're kidding. When did *I* ever need money?"

Unlocking the lowest drawer of his desk, Cohen pulled out the cash box, counted out a thousand in new hundreds, and pushed them across the desk. Foden took them.

"You don't want a receipt?"

"We've done business before, kid. You know better than to rip me off. All it takes is a phone call."

Foden's smile faded. "Yeah. Sure, Billy Joe. I'm hip." He started to rewind the film.

Cohen swiveled his chair and looked down through his picture window at Portland, gleaming in the fall sunshine. It was a clear day. He could see Mount Hood on the skyline. If the weather held up, he might take Cindy and her kids down to Cannon Point for lunch on the weekend. Fresh clams—he could almost taste them.

The phone rang. He reached for it.

"Billy Joe?" Cindy. He visualized her sitting down in the office of Paris Cinemas Inc., with the Renoir prints and the framed certificate of incorporation and the wall-to-wall Wilton.

"Yeah, honey."

"Some man's been on the phone. Asking about a boat. You don't have any boat, do you?"

Cohen's spine stiffened. "What sort of boat?"

"A yacht. I wrote down the name; *Calinda*."

"I don't own any yacht."

"That's what I told him."

"Who was this guy? Did he give his name?"

"Yes. And address. Forrester. Lives in Mobile. Guess he got a wrong number."

"Yeah. Sounds like. Ring him back and tell him I never heard of it."

Her voice softened. "Am I gonna see you this weekend, Billy? Frank's taking the rig down to Salinas on Friday. Won't be back till Tuesday morning."

"I don't know, sweetheart. I'll get back to you." He was frowning as he put down the phone. Funny how old scams came back to haunt you. He'd thought the deal on the boat foolproof. Sell details and keys to someone, let them steal it, and claim on the insurance. Happened with cars all the time.

When Foden left, he mixed himself an Alka-Seltzer. His ulcer was nagging again.

Jake put down the phone. His hand was trembling. Mr. Cohen didn't own a yacht; had never owned a yacht. Especially not one called *Calinda*.

He knew she was lying. He looked at his hand and willed it to be calm. What ever happened to good old reliable Jake, placid, genial, unambitious? Maybe he drowned back there in the waters of the Rappahannock.

It was a very different Jake Forrester who rang the number for Portland directory information and began making inquiries about Billy Joe Cohen and Paris Cinemas Inc.

After two hours, he checked with the airlines. Eastern and American flew to Portland. He was on the first flight next day.

There was nobody in the outer office of Paris Cinemas. Jake pushed open the door marked: Mr. Cohen Private. The couple kissing sprang apart, the girl in the purple leisure suit struggling to zip up the front of her jacket. The man was short, bald, overweight, and red-faced.

"Who the hell are you?"

"Name's Forrester. You wouldn't talk to me on the phone, so I decided to drop in. I'm looking for a boat named *Calinda*."

"Cindy, just pick up the phone and call Captain Zeeland, will you? Tell him we got an intruder down here."

Jake dropped into the empty chair.

"Sure. Do that. Call up the papers while you're at it. I might have an announcement for them *and* the police."

Cohen looked wary.

"I did some checking after we talked. Quite a little enterprise you've got up here. Films, bookshops, a little dope . . ."

"That was never proved," Cohen said hurriedly. "They threw it out of court. Lack of evidence. And nobody's ever prosecuted over my other businesses. The First Amendment . . ."

"Mr. Cohen, I'm all in favor of free enterprise and free speech. I've got a business of my own. I know how damaging it can be if a citizen brings suit against someone in your very vulnerable position. A lot of unpleasant facts come out, even if it never goes to court."

He took out the notes he'd made the previous evening. "I had a talk with a Mrs. Susan Harris Zinnemann. Very pleasant woman."

"Meddling cunt."

"I don't doubt it. But influential. I see a lot of those Don't Californicate Our State bumper stickers around. She was delighted when I offered to finance a class action against you. Her attorneys think she has a dandy case."

Cohen subsided into the other chair. "Cindy, go get a coffee."

When she was gone, Cohen said, "Okay. I owned the

Calinda. Sailed her as the *Parisienne*. Got an advertising write-off that way."

"Owned? You don't still have her?"

"Who can afford a yacht these days? You should see my overheads. No, I got her through a broker when old what's his name—Halvorsen?—went bankrupt. Shipped her across by road. The cost of that alone . . . Anyway, I sailed her for a few months, but she was kind of bare, you know? I mean, not even a can? What do you guys do when you need to crap?"

"Generally we don't have the time. On training trips we carry a bucket."

"Yeah? Well, anyway, I decided to spring for some alterations. I sent her down to LA. This was in the fall of '77. And someone ripped her off."

"You mean *stole* her?"

"You got it. Took her from the marina where they were refitting her. Catalina Marine. They're in the book."

"And nobody got in touch with you about her?" Thieves didn't steal twelve-meter yachts unless they planned to hold the owners to ransom. They were as hard to hide and as difficult to handle as elephants.

"Naw. Insurance paid up. What the hell did I care? They probably sank the thing a mile offshore anyway. Listen, Forrester, I got work to do here. I told you everything. Give me a break, huh?"

Flying to Los Angeles was like a journey to another continent. Jake was sweating before he got off the plane. He hired a car at the airport and drove down to Long Beach with the windows closed and the air-conditioning roaring.

A young Chicano named Ramos owned Catalina Marine. He was stringy, tanned, and walked with the flat-footed sliding tread of someone who had spent a lot of time around boats. Jake liked him immediately.

"You living out here now, Mr. Forrester?" They were walking down the long jetty that jutted out into the gray-blue waters of the bay. "I don't know why you should—there sure isn't any boating worth your time. But we could do with some class."

"I'm looking for a boat. You did some work on it,

back in 1977. It came down from Oregon. Belonged to a man named Cohen."

"*Parisienne*. Sure, I remember. Who wouldn't? Some boat. When I saw what he wanted me to do to her, I cried, literally."

"How much work did you do?"

"A lot. Diesel—it broke my heart to cut up that hull. Sonar. UHF/VHF radio. We built a deckhouse over the main well, put in a galley, head, lots of fancy trim and brightwork. Big paint job. New sails. The kind of job you dream of getting in a small place like this. But I didn't enjoy it."

"Cohen said she was stolen."

"Yeah. Well, she disappeared. You can say that much. Stolen . . . I don't know."

"Meaning?"

"We'd done all the work. She was just waiting for the pickup. Cohen even paid for it, but I held onto her while the check cleared. He didn't look too straight to me. When she disappeared, I figured the check would bounce too. But it was good."

So Cohen had had the money to pay for all the work. Jake began to see the pattern. "A setup?"

"Had to be. Whoever took her would need to know the work was finished. He'd need the keys to the engine ignition, the schedule of the security men . . ."

"Cohen?"

"I figured. He'd been down here a couple of days before. Probably had someone watching the place, checking on the guards."

"Was there an investigation?"

"The LAPD don't even put it on the air unless someone's dead. A boat missing from a Chicano marina? A dead dog gets more attention." He looked closely at Forrester. "It's none of my business, but what's your interest in her?"

Jake felt he could trust Ramos. "Ever hear of a designer named Halvorsen?"

"Yeah. Sure. *Calinda*." He slapped the side of his head in mock rage. "*Parisienne*?"

"I tracked her here from the Orkneys." He looked out over the harbor, the water gray-blue and oily. She could be anywhere out there—Australia, Hawaii, Peru.

"*Sangre de dios*. Well, I hope you find her." He looked around the berths of the marina. It didn't seem to Jake that business was very good. "Mr. Forrester, we don't have too many celebrities down here. It would give me great pleasure to buy you some lunch."

"I'd like that."

"French dip sandwiches and a beer sound good to you?"

"Fine."

After lunch, Jake drove north up the Long Beach Freeway, cut northwest on Brooklyn Avenue, and let the climbing length of Sunset Boulevard carry him up into Hollywood.

The Day's Inn on Sunset was doing poor business, by the look of the empty loungers around the little swimming pool. Jake checked in, bought swimming trunks and a bottle of Gewurtztraminer at the supermarket opposite, took the wine out by the pool, lay in the sun, and drank half of it. Then he swam ten lengths of the pool and drank the rest.

When he climbed back up to his room and showered away the headache and smell of chlorine, his mind was clear.

The phone rang only once before a girl answered. "Ryker Industries. Electronics for a better America. May I help you?"

"Mr. Ryker, please."

"Who may I say is calling?"

"Jake Forrester. It's personal and urgent."

He expected another secretary. Instead, he got a man's nervous voice. Vincent Ryker sounded just the way he looked.

"Forrester? Where the hell are you?"

"LA. We need to talk."

"I guess we do at that."

"When can we meet?"

Someone muffled the phone. Jake could hear a murmur of voices. Ryker came on again.

"My house. Tonight. My secretary'll give you the address."

Jake waited a few seconds. Then a woman's voice said, "Mr. Forrester? That address is 18065 Glendower. Mr. Ryker suggests eight P.M.."

The wine had affected him more than he'd expected. He turned on the TV to take his mind off the problem of *Calinda* and woke up with a dry mouth and a ringing in his ears. The TV chattered on. A news show. He checked his watch. 6:33. For months, lapses like this had made up most of his life. Now they were rare enough to be disturbing.

CHAPTER TWENTY-FOUR

Glendower Avenue snakes up into the Hollywood hills, its houses perched on stilts or burrowed into the crumbling clay. As the cab's transmission whined on the switchback turns and the tires thrummed on the grooved roadway, Jake glimpsed the sunset over flat roofs and discreetly landscaped woodland. It was like watching flashes of a vivid travelogue between restlessly moving heads.

Number 18065 stuck out over the valley, a house that tumbled in terraces down a hill almost steep enough to be called a cliff. High chain-link fencing lined the road. Barbed wire ran along the top. The big metal gate was heavy and double-locked. Jake glimpsed gray junction boxes stenciled with crimson death's-heads on the tallest stanchions. Everything looked new, as if it had been installed that day.

"Friendly place."

The driver glanced at the fence without surprise. "This is Hollywood, mac. Thirty-five ninety."

The cab ground on up the hill. The driveway was too steep for normal walking; like everything else in Los Angeles, it had been built with cars in mind. Jake inched down, crabwise. Video cameras perched on the gateposts panned slowly to stare.

"Stop there." The voice grated tonelessly.

A man came out of the darkness. His face was invisible behind the gray perspex visor of his helmet. He wore padded clothing, probably bulletproof. The MAC II automatic cradled in his arms could riddle Jake in a second.

"Forrester. Mr. Ryker's expecting me."

"Step into the light."

One step brought him into the oval of illumination just in front of the gate. The guard shifted his gun to cover him.

"Wait."

Jake imagined the camera lenses zooming in on his face.

"Okay."

The gate opened three feet, the panels sliding slightly apart like an opening mouth. Jake squeezed through. The clunk when it closed was ominously final.

The main door of the house was closed; the square window set into it was dark. Leaves were piled against the weathered pine. It might have been locked for years.

He followed the guard down the driveway, leaning back against the slope. A heavy door on the second level showed a dim light.

"Wait."

The guard pressed a button. Jake waited in silence. Around the corner, he could see the roof of the next level—a large swimming pool lay, passive and glassy, its surface reflecting the purple of the late sunset.

Jake could feel he was being watched. The door clicked suddenly as an automatic lock was triggered. It swung open.

"Inside."

A long corridor. Bare concrete underfoot. The walls were made of cement block, mortar oozing out from the joints. New, clumsy work. He looked at the TV camera over the door at the other end of the corridor. The door behind him shut with the same ominous multiple click of oiled deadlocks.

The door under the TV camera opened. A square shape bulked against the light.

"I thought we said eight," Ryker grated.

Jake walked through the door under the TV camera.

"I decided to surprise you."

"I'm full up to here with surprises."

The corridor was obviously new. It jutted into what had been a spacious living room, with picture windows giving a spectacular view over the roof top swimming pool towards the lights of the city.

Ryker had turned the room into an observation post. Banks of TV monitors covered one wall. Jake counted eleven of them, stacked three high on metal shelving. The screens showed shadowy views of the outside world—the road, the grounds, the gate, empty rooms.

All the furniture was pushed back against the walls,

except for a few easy chairs. Dark blue drapes cut off most of the view. From their stiff folds, Jake guessed they were lined with something bulletproof—thick rubber woven with metal mesh.

"Take a seat." Ryker nodded towards the TV set in the middle of the room, the only free-standing TV in sight. A guard wearing the same uniform as the man at the gate was fiddling with the controls. The screen showed only snow.

"Marty, ring the plant. Tell them to send up another one. Tonight."

The guard went out through the security corridor, with a silent sideways glance at Jake.

"Drink?" Without waiting for an answer, Ryker poured Haig and Haig Pinch into a tumbler. "How's Kim?"

"She's okay. Staying with my family."

"She know you're here?"

Jake shook his head.

"I guess she's better out of it. Tell her Hi from me, huh?" He downed half his whisky and dropped into a chair. His face looked gray. He hadn't shaved for days.

"Anyone follow you here?"

"No." Ryker raised an eyebrow. "I would have noticed."

Ryker grinned without humor. "You hope." He pointed to the TV monitors. "Sometimes, late at night, I see movement out there, in the dark, under the trees. Nothing you can pin down. Just . . . movement."

"Call the police."

"You think I didn't? They came the first couple of times. Now you're lucky if you get a car before morning. I hired my own men. You won't catch *me* out there after dark."

"If they want you, they'll get you in the end."

"You sound as if you're enjoying it. How many shots have they had at you? Two? Three?"

"I'm not counting."

Ryker looked at him searchingly. "You *don't* care, do you? I like your balls, Forrester. But I can take a hint." He held up his left hand. For the first time Jake saw the bandage across the palm. "Last Thursday, some Chicano tried to mug me outside the plant. He cut me; when I ran, he didn't follow. Next day, the steering in my car went. I hit the safety barrier on the Sepulveda Freeway— I figure the guy with the knife was a lookout while someone fixed the linkage. I can take a hint. I moved in here over the weekend."

"Who?"

"God knows. I'm in deep to some people. They want money, and I don't want to pay. I guess that's a good enough excuse these days to total someone."

"These people you're in to. Was one of them my wife?"

Ryker raised his glass in a mock toast. "You figured it out at last, huh? Yeah, she was part of it. Her and at least one other person—maybe a dozen of them, for all I know. They sure as hell had good sources of information."

Jake thought about Sally Goldstone. They just want information . . . an answering machine . . . pay in cash . . .

"It was a dandy little business," Ryker went on. "God knows how many suckers in the yachting world were being milked. When you think about it, this game is a natural for blackmail. All that gossip, all that money; wives left alone for months on end while their husbands are out racing . . ."

"Were you and Elaine . . .?" Jake found he couldn't finish the question.

"Was I screwing her, you mean? Was *that* what they had on me?" He smiled. "Wish it was. I might have had some fun. No, nothing so glamorous. You know what the electronics business is like; the line between millions and zilch is infinitesimal. One new idea and you're rich. Someone managed to tap into the computer of another company out there. They offered me the information. I bought, and like an idiot I got drunk at a Deep Sea Conference bash and boasted about it. I still don't remember who was there. I was smashed. A couple of weeks later, someone got in touch. Ten thousand a month, or else the company I'd stolen from got to hear about it. About then, I heard Fujita wanted some help getting his boat past the NYYC. I offered to help."

"How much help did he need? Enough to be worth killing people for?"

"Nobody got killed," Ryker said uneasily.

"What about those two thugs of yours?"

"Levitt and Weisell? Yeah, okay. That freak Jubei totaled them, but it had nothing to do with me. Maybe Fujita told him to do it; I don't know and I don't care. I was on the other side of the world when that happened."

"Kim says Jubei came after her as well. You don't know anything about that, I suppose?"

For an answer, Ryker filled his glass again, to the brim. His face was haunted.

"Haven't you ever been in a corner, Forrester? Right up between the rock and the hard place? You don't think . . . hell, *anyone* seems expendable when you're desperate. I didn't seriously think any harm would come to her. Maybe they'd keep her out of circulation for a while; something like that." He drank down half the Scotch. "I'm not proud of it, if that matters."

"How about what happened to my boat and my mooring? Are you proud of that?"

"You were offered good money," Ryker said defensively. "Fujita was mad about secrecy. He thought news about *Sasori* would leak out before the club okayed her. If they turned her down, he didn't want anyone to know about it. He'd lose face and all that. And his own board wasn't too happy about pouring all that money into the Cup challenge. He's got some crazy plan to swamp the world with these wind-powered freighters built like the black boat. Hell, it might even work. Who would have imagined ten years ago we'd be spending billions of dollars on machines to record TV programs? Maybe airplanes will be as obsolete as zeppelins in twenty years' time, and we'll go everyplace in Fujita's black boats."

"What did you offer the club committee to pass *Sasori* anyway?"

"I didn't have to offer them anything! That's the joke. They would have passed *Sasori* if it'd been a rowboat, they were so anxious to get some new blood into the Cup. The British are broke; they can't enter a boat for another five years. The Australians have too much sense. The French do it for the fun of racing and getting smashed; you can't take them seriously. But *Sasori* . . . Jesus, it's like Muhammad Ali with sails. The boat business will go through the roof. *They* see it—Needham and

Hart and the rest. They're businessmen. You don't think they haven't started getting into Tora stock in a quiet way, do you? And whatever happens, Needham is going to end up as governor of Maryland; if he loses, he's the defender of the cup, gallant in defeat. If he wins . . . Jesus, they'll make him president!"

The intercom speaker over their head rattled. "Van coming up." On the nearest monitor, Jake watched the small white transit van turn into the light outside the front gate and idle there. The Ryker Industries emblem on its side was clearly visible.

Ryker lifted the control unit in his hand and said, "Check it out. That should be the new set."

Jake looked at the other monitors. Nothing moved on them. Was someone out there, watching, waiting to kill him? Or was it just the paranoia of guilt and booze.

Ryker saw him looking. "You see 'em, Forrester? They're out there all right."

"Who?"

"This'll make you laugh. At first, I thought it was you, taking over the business. I figured you and she were in it together. But I guess not, now. So your guess is as good as mine. Fujita? Your wife's old partner, afraid I might know more than I do? Some guy I screwed in business who's put out a contract on me? Lots of suspects, Forrester. But I'm staying here until they sort it out among themselves."

Jake stood up. "Can I catch a ride back to LA with your van?"

"Be my guest. I sure wouldn't walk around up here at night."

At the door, Jake paused. "Any message for Kim?"

But Ryker wasn't listening. Eyes moving restlessly from screen to screen, he scanned the silent monitors for a sign of movement, probing the darkness for a portent of his own death.

Jake went out into the dark. Further up the hill, a police helicopter followed the curve of Glendower, its searchlight drifting across the roofs, the pools, the silent gardens. Hollywood. He would be glad to get back home.

CHAPTER TWENTY-FIVE

Jean met Jake at Mobile airport. They drove home through the sort of sudden summer shower that often broke the heavy afternoons on the Gulf. Jake rolled down the window and enjoyed the moist evening air. It was almost as fresh as at sea.

"What's been happening?" he asked at last.

"Nothing special."

His mother was not usually so reticent. "Trouble with Petey?"

"No."

"With Kim?"

"No."

"When you say no in that tone, it means yes. You two not getting on?"

"She's a marvelous girl."

"I know that."

"Considering her background, it's astonishing she's turned out like she has. We've talked a lot these last few days. She's very . . . serious about you, you know."

"What's wrong with that? I'm serious about her."

"Jake, she's nineteen!"

"And I'm forty-eight. You're . . . what? Sixty-nine. Which means that, when I was born, you were twenty-one. How old were you when you got married? Twenty?"

"At least your father was only twenty-five."

"Don't you think you would have loved him if he'd been twice that?"

Jean looked sideways at him. "You could always talk your way around me, Jake. But I'm not convinced. Give it some time."

"I'll give it all the time I've got." At the moment, that didn't seem like much. He had eliminated Ryker as a possible threat, but where did that leave him? Without suspects, surrounded by dangers to which he couldn't give a name, enemies that never showed their faces. He could sympathize with Ryker now; the darkness was full of things that didn't like him.

But Ryker dramatized the danger of giving in to your fears. Jake had seen enough people gripped by their terrors—Elaine, Charlie, even himself for the months after Elaine's death—to see that it led only to weakness, helplessness, despair. He was not going to give in. If he kept up the pressure, something would crack. With luck, his enemies would reveal themselves while he still had the energy to defeat them.

As they turned into the driveway, Jake realized there was one fear he had not yet learned to face. He made a resolution then to do so first thing in the morning.

The bank manager was cordial. He could raise a loan of a quarter of a million on the marina and his other holdings with no trouble at all. Of course, interest rates were high, but . . .

It took a major effort of will to leave the manager's office and take the steps down into the basement.

"Both boxes?" the clerk said, looking at the two keys.

Jake nodded. When they were brought, he emptied the contents of both into the small suitcase he'd brought with him. The bundles of bills and certificates barely fitted in; there were more than he had ever imagined.

Back home, he cleared the big table in the parlor and emptied out the suitcase. For the first time, he realized the box contained more than money. He found half a dozen diaries, tied with tape, and a number of envelopes, bulky with papers. Names were scribbled on them—*Calypso, Cowboy.*

Choosing *Calypso* at random, he cracked the flap. Inside were Xerox copies of letters, check records, bank statements, showing large sums of money being transferred from account to account until they ended up snugly in Credit Suisse in Zurich. The payer was a large Swiss sports equipment firm. And the payee? Stapled to the financial reports was another envelope containing photographs taken with a long lens of two men chatting in a park. Jake recognized one of them as an adviser to the Olympic Yachting Federation.

Jake pushed the diaries and envelopes to one side and started on the money. Separating it into neat piles, he counted it methodically. As far as he could tell after an hour's counting, there was almost $400,000; some in negotiable bonds, some in banker's checks, but the bulk in currency. The American bills were all used, without consecutive serial numbers, but the British, French, German, and Swiss notes remained in their wrappers, easily traceable. Elaine and her collaborator must have known they were immune from harassment.

After sorting the money, Jake reached for the bundle of diaries. He hesitated as he untied the tape, then went to the sideboard, found a bottle of Old Harper, filled a glass, and took a swallow that burned all the way down to his stomach.

He pulled apart the bundle, and a small white envelope lay among them. He tore it open.

Dearest Jake—

I don't know what you will make of all this, if you ever get to read it—and I hope you never do. There's only one circumstance in which you might read it, and that's if I'm dead. In that case, none of it will matter anyway, so I don't know why I'm worrying.

It was never meant to become so serious, Jake. I wish you'd remember that. At first it was a game— you know how kids like secrets. I guess I never grew up when it came to gossip.

After a while, I saw a way to help you with what I'd learned. You won't like hearing that, I know; you never cared for me getting involved in your work. But if I hadn't, you wouldn't be where you are, sweetheart, and I'm not sorry for that. I loved to see you getting the breaks and the boats. You deserved them.

So I never meant to get involved. But once I did, there was no way to stop. I depended on the money, and by then other people were mixed up in it. You'll know who by now.

All through this, you were the only one who mattered. Don't doubt that—ever.

It was signed in her usual scrawl.

Jake folded the letter and put it in his pocket. He had hoped Elaine now belonged in the world he'd left behind, the world of the old Jake Forrester, abstracted and indecisive. But he knew from the thickness in his chest that she had stayed with him, occupying the part of his soul she owned in life. Her memory could not fill all of it, but like a light left burning in an empty apartment, some part of her remained there. It always would. He knew that, just as he knew that only by discovering her murderer would he ever find it bearable to live with that silent presence.

He started to read the diaries with a sort of savage concentration.

It had begun in 1979—the year he skippered *Quester* in the Admiral's Cup and spent most of the year in England.

Elaine was having an affair. Nothing in the diaries told him, but Jake could gauge from the cryptic notes of meetings that she was seeing someone. He had always known that a part of her emotional life was closed to him, as that part of his dealing with boats and sailing would always be closed to her. By tacit agreement they never talked about these things.

That must have made it harder for her to tell Jake that she needed money and that her lover had given it to her.

It hadn't been much. A bank statement tucked in the bottom of the box told the story: rising rent on the boutique, business falling off. Then, overnight, a new healthy balance, and an entry in her diary—"Traven. $2400."

It was the first of a dozen. Then, abruptly, they ceased. Jake could sense the moment when what had been a favor between lovers suddenly became business. Were they in bed, Elaine and Traven—the man up till now Jake had thought of as *X*? Did he casually point out there was a simpler way to satisfy her need for money? Perhaps Elaine was relaying some juicy piece of gossip, and he had said (being careful not to make it too serious a suggestion), "Hell, wouldn't his wife he upset if *that* got around!"

Elaine, with her love of conspiracy—it was typical she identified even her lover with a pseudonym—would have gone along with the game, planning the anonymous letter, discussing with giggles what they might charge for keeping quiet. Never thinking for a moment Traven meant to go through with it.

And when he did . . . Elaine was weak, ambitious, broke. There was the money; untraceable, waiting to be picked up. She took it, as she took the next payment, and the next. . . .

"After a while, I saw a way to help you . . ." She'd come to England in the spring of 1979—an unexpected visit that must have been financed by the first payments from the blackmail victims. If the visit had not been idyllic, she might have changed her mind; might even have confided to him the mess in which she had become involved.

But that had been one of the happiest summers of their marriage. He could remember how delighted he was to see her get off the plane at Heathrow. How they hugged and kissed in the terminal, watched by disapproving English travelers; how, the moment they got back to Southampton, they made love in the little hotel overlooking the harbor. Every moment of pleasure must have seemed an endorsement of what she was doing.

And, after that, the boats and breaks started. Opening envelopes, he found the faces of men and women who had helped him; how they must have hated Jake as they smiled and offered him the sponsorship he thought had been won by merit and worth. He pushed the papers away from him convulsively, filled with loathing of himself, filled with guilt no less painful for having been unearned. It *was* his fault that Elaine died. *I'll make you a success if it kills me. . . .*

It had.

Because, finally, Elaine had rebelled. What had caused it? The diaries offered no evidence, but Jake guessed it was a combination of guilt and guile. The payments were becoming more substantial, the operation an international one. Traven's web of contacts reached into every corner of the yachting world. Sooner or later, someone would crack and go to the police.

And, she must have thought with her prim little smile, Jake had what he wanted now; captaincy of the America's Cup defender, an unassailable position in the yachting hierarchy. She could retire, still ahead of the game.

That was when Traven called up Marie-Ange Planchet and gave her the six star sapphires that were the price of two lives.

A few fingers of bourbon remained in the bottom of the bottle; the rest was in his belly and his head. Spilling the liquor across the scattered papers, he lurched into the kitchen for a box of matches and, returning, struck one over the heap. Blue flames wavered above them, but none caught fire. He was trying to strike another match, fumbling with the box, when the phone rang.

He ignored it. After a minute the ringing stopped. He sat down heavily and leaned on his elbows, carefully bringing the match to the striking surface and pressing down hard. The match broke. He was trying with another when the phone rang again.

Frustration and rage boiled up in him like vomit. He tore the phone from its cradle, the receiver like a soft toy in his numbed hand. Not waiting to find out who was at the other end, he roared his rage into the mouthpiece, then threw it the length of the room. The cord caught his ankles and he fell headlong. He didn't remember much else.

"How are you doing?"

He opened one eye painfully. Kim was bending over him, her hair pulled back in a pony tail.

"Not so good." His voice was a croak. His head throbbed.

"Could you use some coffee?"

"Maybe. Water first though."

She came back with a glass of water. Two white tablets fizzed and bubbled in it.

"Alka-Seltzer. Good for hangovers."

Nothing less than a bullet in the brain could cure *this* hangover, Jake decided, but he choked down the mixture. It seemed to clear his nasal passages, because he smelled the choking stink of alcohol. He retched.

"It's bourbon. You spilled some on your papers."

He turned his head gingerly. The table was clear.

"You did a lousy job. I put them away."

"Look at any of them?"

"A few. How about that coffee?" She went back into the kitchen.

Jake got up from the couch and took a deep breath. It rasped in a throat that felt constricted to half its normal diameter. Trying to touch his toes sent waves of pain throbbing through his spine and skull. But he kept it up, bending and straightening until the blood started to circulate and the body purge itself of poisons.

He was running in place when Kim came back with the coffee.

"Who are you? Superman?"

"I've got things to do." He took the coffee and stopped to drain the cup. "How about getting my sneakers from the closet upstairs?"

Ten minutes later he pulled open the front door. The street was cool and clean in the early morning. Sprinklers hissed on lawns; kids raced their bikes up and down the sidewalk, yelling.

He tottered down the steps and along the sidewalk to where a sprinkler fanned its spray out over the concrete. Standing under the mist of water, he let it soak his hair and face. Then he started to run.

Kim and Jean were in the kitchen when he staggered back half an hour later.

"Heavy night?" Jean asked.

"Sort of."

His head still ached, but life was returning to the rest of his body. He might even eat something.

Jean said, "You'll be sorry to hear you didn't break the phone. Not permanently, anyway." She nodded to a note on the table. "You had a call."

Jake vaguely remembered the phone ringing in the middle of the night. It had a fresh chip on one edge. His work, he assumed. He read the note.

"Isn't this Sam Lewis's number?"

"Looks like."

Jake dialed the familiar codes.

"Lewis." It was Sam's grating bark.

"I hear you called me."

"Yeah. Twice. Don't know why I'm talkin' to you after that stuff you fed me last night."

Jake ran his fingers through his hair. "I don't remember much of that. Tied one on last night."

"You could have fooled me. Listen, are you in a fit state to talk?"

"Try me."

"You still looking for Halvorsen's boat?"

"Trying. I tracked her to Oregon, then to Los Angeles. Someone stole her from a marina there about five years ago. After that, nothing."

"Well, hold onto your hat, pal. Because I found her for you."

"You *what*? The *Calinda*?"

"No, dummy—the *Queen* fucking *Elizabeth*."

"But how? Where is she?"

"How? Well, after you came by, I started thinking about what you said. Didn't seem much percentage in sitting there getting drunk as a profession. So I called in a few favors. I still got some pals from the service who hang around the rackets. One of them happened to know about a fast boat being operated by someone in the dope business. Couldn't really be anything but *Calinda*."

"Sam, get to it. Where?"

"Yeah, well that's a problem. She's in South America. Colombia. And the word goes she's a wreck."

CHAPTER TWENTY-SIX

A hot wind from the sea carried the smells of Cartagena into the center of town. As Jake crossed Plaza Bolivar, he identified them one by one. Salt from the sea and the old harbor. Hot stone from the walls of the Palacio Inquisicion that took up one whole side of the square. Smoke and spices from the little stalls selling grilled fish and meat along the sidewalk. Sweat and gas fumes from the stalled traffic and the tiny motorcycles, always with at least two riders, that wove through the jam.

He passed a stall piled high with round pink objects the size of tennis balls. The woman behind it, recognizing a tourist, held one up invitingly. It was a skull made from pink candy, teeth and eye sockets realistically outlined with black dye. For the first time, he realized the date. Halloween. The day of the dead.

Further down the street, there were more candy stalls with the same display. Others sold toys. Skeleton dolls and puppets, and a particularly realistic variety of rat made from gray fur, which twitched and darted around the sidewalk dragging a limp pink tail when the owner squeezed a rubber bulb. Some had tiny bead eyes that lit up, dark red and glowing.

Jake crossed the road and walked along the tree-shaded street under the jutting metal balconies until he found number 90.

Portago's office was on the second floor, at the top of a winding stone staircase. His secretary had a tiny room two flights lower. Jake followed the girl up the narrow stairs with something like awe. The trim buttocks just in front of his face moved with liquid precision. Her perfume in the cramped stairwell was dizzying.

"Please go in, señor." She smiled. No wonder the buccaneers had used Cartagena as a base, if her great-great-grandmother was anything like her.

Portago leaned across his desk, hand outstretched. He

was thin, fortyish, with the matinee idol looks Jake was fast taking for granted in Colombia. Everyone looked like Gilbert Roland's younger brother.

"Señor Forrester, welcome. Did you have a good flight?"

"Good enough." His brain had been whirling too much to take it in.

"Your first visit to Colombia?"

"Yes." He could see out the window to the plaza. Even through the closed window, the noise was audible, but Portago was unconcerned.

"Coffee." He said it without a question mark, reaching behind him for the electric pot that stood on the windowsill. "I got the habit in the States. Now I cannot work without it."

"Thanks. I didn't get any breakfast."

"Frankly, I didn't expect you so soon. There hasn't been time to do much since you called." He pulled a file towards him. "However, I have discovered this man Bordón, in whom you are interested. He is in the state prison." He nodded over his shoulder. "Perhaps ten blocks."

"I'm not so much interested in him as in a boat he owns."

Portago read down the top paper in the file. "He was arrested in a boat. A yacht called *Bruja*. The witch."

"I imagine that's it. Where is it? I understand it was damaged."

Portago shrugged. "I have no information. He was arrested at Isla Tierra Bomba, about six hours up the coast. A quiet place. Excellent for his purposes. Could I ask—and anything you say is without prejudice, of course—are you an associate of Mr. Bordón?"

"I've never met him."

"That is not quite an answer, Mr. Forrester. These days, men are often in business with nothing between them but a telephone line. I think I should make it clear, however, that the cargo Mr. Bordón was carrying—about five hundred kilos of cocaine—is now confiscated and in bonded storage as evidence. It is not on *Bruja*."

"All I want is the boat. She's a racing yacht—a very special one. I want to race her. If you need credentials,

you might ring a Señor Zarzuela. I hear he's something
in the government down here now."

Portago's eyebrows rose. "*Ramon* Zarzuela? You
know him?"

"We raced together when he was with your embassy in
Washington. I'm sure if you ring him . . ."

"No. That won't be necessary." There was a subtle
variation in Portago's tone. "Let me make some calls."

Jake understood one word in three of Portago's rapid
Spanish. His first conversation was brusque, the second
conciliatory. By the fifth he was fawning. He hung up
after protracted protestations of respect and admiration
and wiped his forehead.

"We are getting somewhere. Bordón was arrested
more than a month ago, on the twenty-fifth. He was taking on his cargo when the police ambushed him. Bordón
and eight of his crew are in custody. During the raid the
boat apparently ran onto rocks. It is still there, under
guard."

Jake had learned most of this from Sam Lewis. He
wouldn't tell Jake his source. "Just a guy I knew in the
army. Not the sort you invite to the house, but we keep
in touch."

"How bad is the damage?"

"My information is, extremely bad. One person insisted the boat had sunk, but I doubt that." He tapped
his pencil on his pages of notes. "This is all a little
strange."

"Strange how?"

"Bordón is no amateur. I recall his name from the papers. He has been in business for some time. To stay
alive that long, it is necessary to pay people, and pay
them a lot. Yet here he is, under arrest."

"Maybe he let the payments fall behind?"

"Possibly. Though that is a good way to end up dead
down here. A better guess is, someone paid more."

"To wipe him out? Who?"

"Competitors. Enemies. Who knows?" He stood up
and put on a paper-white Panama. "Bordón is the best
man to help us there."

"We can go and see him?"

"For a few dollars, one can see any man. Even the

president. We will offer a little expense money to the *jefé* at the prison."

"It's that easy?"

"Señor, the wonder of this country is that there are any jails at all."

Jake's conception of a Colombian dope dealer needed revision after meeting Alfonso Bordón.

No drooping Zapata moustache. No crumpled white linen suit. No gold chain and medallion dangling on hairy chest. No shifty eyes and bitten fingernails. He looked like an accountant, about forty-five, balding, with candid blue eyes that only shifted if one looked at them obliquely through his thick, rimless spectacles.

He shook hands formally with Jake and Portago and indicated the two battered wooden chairs of the prison interview room with an apologetic shrug.

"The facilities are not all I could wish, gentlemen, but they are at your disposal. I regret the only refreshment I can offer you is a little *aguardiente*."

He nodded to the guard, who waddled off, returning with a bottle of smoky liquor and two cracked cups. He poured the drinks with the solemnity of a head waiter.

"You aren't joining us?" Portago asked.

Bordón put one hand on his stomach. "I regret. An ulcer. But one can enjoy one's vice by proxy."

Jake tried the drink. It was good but powerful. He sipped while Portago went about the business of extricating *Calinda* from Bórdon.

"The fact that the boat is damaged and impounded by the authorities must, of course, influence my client's attitude to a purchase."

Bordón smiled sleepily. "Indeed. But Señor Forrester would hardly have come so far and"—he bowed slightly to Portago—"retained so distinguished a representative if his interest was not serious."

Jake could see this fencing taking all day. "I'm sure Señor Portago will forgive me if I speak plainly. I want the boat." He felt Portago wince. "I have money. Not as much as you may think, Señor Bordón. All boat owners are not millionaires, contrary to the publicity. It will cost me a great deal to get this boat back to the United States, and to refit her. If I must pay excessively, it might be best for me to abandon the plan right now."

"Since you have spoken plainly," Bordón smiled, "I am sure you will forgive a question I would not normally ask. What is so special about *Bruja* that you are prepared to pay at all? You are perhaps well acquainted with her already?"

"I've never seen her in my life. But I have my reasons for being confident she is the boat I require."

Jake didn't describe how he had spent the last three weeks. Deciding that if Sam could pull in a few favors, so could he, Jake called an old friend at one of the City Island boatyards—one with contacts in the defense industry. With his help, he had run the data on *Calinda* through the big IBMs at the Brooklyn Navy Yard. In these days of computer simulation, it was no longer really necessary to tank-test a hull; Jake fed in the parameters of Halvorsen's design, based on his drawings and the scale model, punched up a variety of data to duplicate the boat's potential when it was fitted with the newest continuous-film sails, lightweight winching, and low-drag mast, and ran the resulting model through the program originally designed to test a new boat against a wide variety of sea and weather conditions.

The results were exhilarating. There was no way one could truly test a boat except on the water, but Jake flew to Colombia confident he had not made a mistake in staking so much on *Calinda*. Halvorsen's boast of having designed "the ultimate twelve" was not just talk.

Bordón watched Jake's face for some sign of evasion. What did he suspect? Someone trying to buy the boat and take over his old business? A legal maneuver to force him to admit ownership of *Bruja* and thus incriminate himself? Finally, he smiled.

"I see you are an aficionado, sir. She is a special boat; even I, no expert, sensed that. When I . . . acquired her, the understanding was that she could outrun and outsail any comparable craft in these waters. I am bound to say that this proved an accurate forecast. Even with the idiots who crewed her, she was incomparable."

Portago tried to take charge of things again. "Mr. Forrester feels . . ."

Jake stopped him. "I want her. Name your price, Señor Bordón. If I can afford it, I'll pay."

Bordón smiled dreamily. "You have no idea, Señor Forrester, how refreshing I find your attitude. This traditional haggling so beloved of my countrymen is often an excuse for wasting time and drinking a great deal of expensive cognac. Very well. The boat *is* valuable to me"— he gestured around the jail walls—"but in here I have little use for boats. If it remains at Tierra Bomba much longer, the local people will remove everything detachable. I will accept from you what I paid to the agents of Señor Cohen. One hundred and fifty thousand American dollars."

Jake reached for his checkbook.

The ancient diesel engine choked and coughed as the fishing boat labored around the point. Heat seemed to have dazed the air into exhaustion. Not the slightest touch of a breeze marked the oily sea. The high forested cliffs around the bay trapped the air, and the sun heated it as if in an oven.

Portago had taken off his coat and tie. He sprawled in the front of the boat.

"You should get further back," Jake said. "The swell is always worst forward."

"But the smell of fish is less. Also that of the engine."

"I suppose." Jake was too tense to notice either. "How far is this place?"

Portago straightened up and looked around. "We are here."

Almost immediately, Jake saw *Calinda*, a quarter of a mile away, lost in the tumbling greenery of the cliff.

With her long hull heeled over and the mainsail run up, she might have been reaching at full speed in a good wind. But the air was motionless, and the sail sagged heavily in the hot air. As they came closer, Jake saw the dark shapes of rocks just under the surface of the green water. She was hard aground.

They bumped alongside. The fishing boat's gunwhale added a few more scars to the weathered white paint, but there were plenty to precede them. *Calinda* had seen hard times.

Portago looked dubious. "One hundred and fifty thousand dollars—for this?"

She was down by the stern. Water lapped over the counter and filled the cockpit. As Jake jumped aboard, something scrambled inside the cavity. A cormorant, a fish struggling crosswise in its bill, flapped heavily into the air.

He looked down into the cockpit. Fishbones and bird droppings caked the coaming. At high tide it became an effective fish trap, which at low tide the birds plundered at their leisure.

Rotting fish and guano weren't the only smells. Soaked and decaying upholstery and woodwork have an odor all their own, as persistent and distinctive as the stink after a fire. It filled the air now.

For the first time, Jake could appraise the extent of Cohen's so-called improvements.

There was solid teak decking under his feet and a deckhouse where in a racing yacht there would be only the open well. Ramos had done a good job. The woodwork felt solid, even though it had been sadly neglected. It was years since anyone had treated the deck with linseed oil and varnish or washed down the brasswork. Salt water pitted almost every piece of metal in sight—those that had not been removed already. A number of blank spots and empty screwholes showed that, as Bordón had suggested, the locals had wasted no time.

He slid back the hatch leading down into the cabin. The smell of decay billowed up at him, making him gag.

Three feet of water filled the cabin, submerging the bunks on the port side and leaving those on the starboard only a few inches above water. The hull must be breached. If *Calinda* were floated off now, she'd probably sink like a broken bottle.

He waded down the steps until the water, warm as a bath, came halfway up his thighs. Plastic containers and scraps of debris bobbed against his legs. The water felt greasy, the floor slimy underfoot. Something living tickled his leg. He thought about watersnakes.

But his feet finally found solid metal under the matting that covered the floor. Ramos hadn't ripped up the old metal deck, just built on top of it. Under the improvements *Calinda* was intact.

Jake climbed back into the air and squeezed the worst of the water from his trousers. In the heat they would dry in a minute or two.

"Ask him when is high tide."

The fishermen looked surprised at Portago's question. He spoke volubly for almost a minute.

"He says it is high tide now. And again at ten tonight. He says that if the tide went higher than this, the boat would have floated off and sunk long ago. He says his friends have tried to get her off but failed. He says it is doomed." Portago turned away from the smell of rotting fish. "I think he is a very sensible gentleman."

Jake scanned the bay. He didn't see what he had hoped to.

"Are there any other big yachts around here?"

Portago quizzed the fishermen. "Not around here," he said at last. "Just fishing boats. Like this tub. The big boats go to Barranquilla or the yacht harbor at Cartagena. Why do you ask?"

"It's not important." Jake dropped back into the boat. "Let's get back to town."

If Jake had squinted his eyes, the yacht harbor of Cartagena might have been any one of a hundred in the Carribbean. Key West. Bimini. St. Lucia. Even its boats were the same; the smart yawls and ketches with Newport and Key West registrations, the dozen or so motor cruisers fitted out for the cocktail set, and a handful of old wooden boats with peeling varnished masts and canvas sails, on their way from nowhere to nowhere.

He went past the dockside restaurants with their sun umbrellas. Sunday sailors sipped Harvey Wallbangers with half-naked girls whose tans seemed to have been sprayed on from a very expensive can. Further down the yacht basin, where the asphalt gave way to splintered railway ties laid over gravel, he found the bar he wanted.

The air smelled of gas from the pumps nearby, and of drains from the stormwater channel that emptied out just under the dock. A dozen kids were damming the flow with cans and bits of wood.

Jake went into the bar. The bartender swabbed down the zinc top with a gray rag. "*Señor?*"

"Cerveza."

"American ou Colombian?"

Jake looked around at the only other American in the room. He was drinking at a table by the window.

"Medellin's okay," the man said.

The bartender gave him a cold bottle of locally brewed lager. It tasted passable. He took it over to the man's table.

"Mind if I sit down?"

"Be my guest." He held out his hand. "Burt Grale."

Jake said, "Tom Summerville. You are a sailor, Mr. Grale?"

"Occasionally." He nodded through the window. "Came down as crew on that two-master out there. Owner ran into some trouble, decided he'd be happier in Miami. Been here ever since."

Jake looked along the dock for the two-master. It was huge, near enough to a topsail schooner. Only one sort of cargo made sense on a boat like that. People.

Grale followed his thoughts. "Yeah. This guy had some good contacts here. Claimed he could get five hundred bucks a head for the trip to Miami. I don't doubt it, but I guess someone else has the wetback concession. Colombian Coast Guard nailed us the moment we came inside the twelve-mile limit." He smiled. "Not the kind of sailboating you're used to, Mr. Forrester."

Jake smiled and drank some more of the beer.

"You've got kind of memorable face. I hung round the twelve-meter scene a bit, year or two back. If it isn't a rude question, what the hell are you doing down here? This is kind of far back in the hills for you."

Jake wondered how much to tell Grale. Tropical ports attracted drifters. Some would sign on to crew a boat, murder the owners, and sell it to the smugglers. Grale looked honest, but . . .

"You carry a knife?"

"A knife? Sure."

"Mind if I take a look at it?"

Grale slipped a sheath knife out of his belt and laid it, hilt toward Jake, on the table.

A sailor's knife is his most important tool. His life can depend on its sharpness, on the ease with which it can be flipped from a sheath to cut free a trailing piece of rigging or slit the cloth over a broken leg.

Tackle shops carry a hundred kinds of knives: folding and flick blades; knives with pliers and marlin spikes built in; knives with smooth hilts, scored hilts, hilts shaped like naked women; knives with three-inch blades, six inch, nine inch . . .

From experience, Jake knew only one kind of knife was worth a damn in an emergency.

The blade needed to be between three and six inches long, and broad, otherwise the metal might snap under strain. The hilt should be scored, to give a good grip in wet weather, and stubby, so that it didn't dig into your ribs when you bent over. Only stainless steel kept its edge under the corrosion of saltwater. And the smart crewman ground his knife on a grinding wheel rather than with a whetstone. Stone grinding gave the blade a slightly serrated edge that cut through rope better than razor sharpness.

Grale's knife was a five-inch Swedish stainless, its hilt bound with twine, the blade sharp but rough-edged; whatever else he was, Grale was a professional seaman. Jake gave it back to him.

"I've bought a boat. I need to get it back stateside. Quickly and quietly. You interested in a job?"

Grale slipped the knife back in its sheath. "What kind of boat?"

"Twelve."

"In good shape?"

"Pretty bad. Breached below the waterline, aground, flooded. Rigging looks okay, but I don't know about the sails. It's been used for smuggling, so we might run into some trouble getting it out of the country."

"Is that all?" Grale grinned. "Sounds like a rerun of *The Wages of Fear*."

"I'll pay top money. Hundred a day until we get back to the U.S. I'll need a few more men too."

"I know some people. Count me in."

"What about the two-master?"

"The bastard's probably already reported her sunk and collected the insurance."

He got up. The bartender strolled over. "Two hundred pesos, señor."

Grale grinned. "That's a hundred a day plus expenses, right?"

Jake dug into his pocket. It wouldn't be the first time that day.

Grale proved invaluable. He knew everyone. From the bars of the Boca Grande, he dug out two more crewmen with experience in twelves. Phil and Charlie Weselowski had sailed down as crew on a catamaran that flipped and sank in a hurricane off Santa Marta, killing the owner. They had been on the beach two months, waiting for a berth back stateside. Both would have worked for nothing just to get back home. Their conversation was exclusively of New York—food, air-conditioning, Coors beer, girls, more food.

The fisherman who had ferried Jake and Portago to Isla Tierra Bomba was more than happy to repeat the trip. He chattered in staccato Spanish as he helped the four men into the boat and settled their new gear around them.

"I got about half of that," Jake said.

"He's offering to sell you his boat outright. Says fishing isn't good and he wants to retire. I guess he thinks you like this trip."

"Tell him I'll think about it." No point in alienating the man. They would need him to ferry more equipment to the stranded *Calinda*.

They rounded the point into the bay just as the sun sank over the lip of the encircling hills and shadows began to slide over the green water.

Phil Weselowski focused his binoculars. "That her over by the shore?"

"Yes."

"Then we've got company."

The launch moored to *Calinda*'s bow had already rubbed another large scar on the bruised paintwork. Two men in faded khaki uniform and peaked caps stood self-importantly on her deck.

They waved the launch away with a stream of Spanish.

"Coast Guard," Grale said. "Or what passes for it down here. I'm surprised they even have a boat."

"What do they want?"

"At a guess, money. You laid out any cash yet?"

"No."

"Got any?"

"Some."

"You want to offer?"

"That a good idea?"

"You're south of the border now. It's no pay, no play."

"See what you can do."

The bargaining took half an hour. While Grale haggled, Jake and the others pulled their launch around to the shady side and used a snorkel mask to examine the reef on which *Calinda* was stuck. There seemed to be rocks everywhere.

Grale climbed up the sloping deck and leaned over.

"Someone's been spending a lot of money around here. Who owned this boat?"

Jake explained about Bordón.

"Well, sounds to me as if someone outbid him and got him nailed but good. These guys claim the boat's impounded until the end of time. Nothing short of a judge can shake it loose."

"They won't take money?"

"I didn't say *that*. They'll take a little something to leave us alone, for now. But getting her out of the bay— that will take some doing. You got enough to buy a judge?"

"No."

"Well, better take what we can get. Have you got five thousand pesos?"

Jake counted out the notes from his diminishing bankroll, telling himself it was less than a hundred dollars.

Ten minutes later, the Coast Guard launch chugged away, taking the old fisherman with it and leaving behind his boat, now Jakes's. He climbed on board and helped the others lift on the gear.

"It'll hold them until tomorrow," Grale said. "Maybe we'll think of something by then."

The bay by night was hotter and more oppressive than by day. Damp air flowed from the mountains and hung over the water like a sodden blanket. Tiny insects swarmed to the slightest light. Their bites were like hot needles and left hard swellings that itched. Finally the men climbed into wet suits, diving overboard every five minutes to drain off the heat.

Jake hung over the side of the boat, holding a flashlight just below the surface. The beam wavered eerily in the still water. Tiny shrimp rose inquisitively towards it, circling, fondling it with their antennae.

A bow wave thrust them away, and Charlie's head surfaced by the light. He pulled back his mask and blew the water from his nose.

"She's stuck real fast. Two rocks, like a vise. The water's coming in through a crack between two plates just forward of the rocks."

"How bad's the hole?"

"Eight inches long. A foot maybe. Plate's peeled back. I can hammer it from inside, seal it with a patch, but the weld won't stand too much pounding. If we run into bad weather . . ."

"Let's worry about that when we come to it. Do you think we can get her off?"

"With a tow. Not otherwise."

Jake looked around the silent hills. The sound of an engine at night would bring the Coast Guard around in minutes.

"No tow."

Charlie hauled himself onto the deck. Phil and Burt came up from the cabin, each dragging a plastic garbage bag filled with ruptured tins, rotted matting, decaying woodwork.

"What's it like down there?"

"It ain't gonna win no *Good Housekeeping* award. But we could maybe sleep inside if we get the water out."

"How about the engine?"

"That looked okay," Grale said. "They probably ran her mostly on the engine unless they wanted to be quiet. Plenty of gas, and the water didn't get into the electrics either."

"I guess that's something," Jake said.

The four squatted in a circle on the deck, swiping at the mosquitoes that homed on their warmth with a greedy whine.

A distant flash lit the sky. For an instant the peaks of

the surrounding hills were outlined against starless
darkness.

"Might get some rain," Phil said, unzipping his wet
suit.

A feather of breeze brushed over them. The insects
were suddenly gone. And there was another change. The
croaking of frogs, the whirr of cicadas, and the rustle of
night birds in the overhanging trees cut off in unison, as
if a tape had come to an end.

Another flash of lightning. This time they heard the
thunder as well—an echoing crack, like the snap of a
wooden plank, followed by a long rolling rumble.

"Wouldn't be surprised if it didn't . . ." Grale started
to say.

Then the storm was on them.

The first gust whipped waves from the surface of the
bay and sent them splashing into the cockpit. Underfoot,
the deck shuddered, shifting an inch as the wind heaved
against the *Calinda*'s exposed hull.

Something grated deep underwater as the hull rocked
in the swell.

"Get the sail onto her!" Jake scrambled up the deck,
groping for the sheets. "She's shifting." If the storm
broke her loose, they might get away under cover of the
rain. Already he could barely see a yard.

Something squashed underfoot. A bag of garbage. He
heaved it into the darkness.

"Get all this overboard. Anything we don't need. The
sails."

Four spare sails stored in the bilges had rotted to pulp.
They had been brought on deck in the hope that the cable clamps and jib track cars could be salvaged. Jake levered the fat roll halfway over the side and watched the
weight drag the rest into darkness.

The rain began. The sky seemed to have ripped open.
Jake felt his back bent by the weight of water. Lightning
fizzed and exploded overhead, and the thunder was like
artillery, incessant, deafening.

Grale grabbed his arm. He had to yell to make himself
heard.

"We might get her off now, with the engine. Do you
want to try?"

Jake nodded. She might sink. But it was their only chance.

A moment later, the whole boat shuddered as the engine caught. The gears engaged with a grating clash. *Calinda* quivered. A vibration built up in the metal of the hull until Jake could feel it through his feet. The skin of his soles itched with it.

She didn't move.

He caught Grale's eye as he looked back from the engine controls in the cockpit. The rain had plastered his hair over his forehead, but Jake could understand his expression.

Maybe if they could shift the balance a little more.

Jake grabbed Phil Weselowski by the shoulder and pushed him towards the stern. They scrambled into the cockpit and out the other side, onto the counter, right over the propeller.

He nodded to Grale. The engine roared again. Over the stern, Jake saw water foaming as the big screw dragged *Calinda* away from the reef. The rocks would not give her up. He visualized the hole in the hull torn open even more as she was shaken and dragged from their grip.

Then she seemed to leap backwards. The stern dipped deep into the water, throwing all four men into the cockpit. The whining vibration turned to a deep throb.

Grale leaped for the engine controls, disengaged the gears, and put her into neutral.

"Back her away. Half," Jake yelled through the rain.

He grabbed the big wheel, turned it, and sensed the rudder biting. Swinging it, he felt the boat back in a circle, turning her bow towards the open sea.

"Half forward." He waved the Weselowskis towards the bow. The howling wind of the squall would give enough power to sail her out of the bay, using the engine as an auxiliary, if they could get the mainsail set.

The squall had thrown up three-foot waves. One of them hit *Calinda* broadside. She wallowed like a log. Water must be pouring in through the hole below decks.

It was impossible to make himself heard. He pointed emphatically at the companionway. Grale left the engine and dived below. He would know what had to be done.

If he could plug the gash in her hull, if they could pump out the hundreds of gallons of water, if the storm didn't rip the rotten sail . . .

The lightning flashed again, showing the heads of the bay dark across the foaming water. He spun the wheel and drove towards them.

CHAPTER TWENTY-SEVEN

The storm of the night before had swept the sky of everything but a plume of cirrus like a brush stroke in the west, where the last scrap of wind hovered in a standing wave of ice crystals, high and cold.

Kim's visit to the boatyard before breakfast was becoming a morning ritual. For the first week, the absence of good news had disappointed her. Now she was grateful for it. In another few days, she would begin to expect the worst news of all.

Nobody challenged her as she walked through the gates and along to the jetty. Someone usually called hello—Carl Bangsund or one of the workmen. Today, she saw nobody.

She began to run. Her sneakers rattled the bolts holding the old ties in place. Through the cracks she caught glimpses of green water.

Carl's gleaming bald head appeared above the level of the pier just ahead of her. She skidded to a stop.

"I was just going to call you. It's down here."

She was trembling as she walked to the edge of the jetty and looked down. Into the *Calinda*.

It was a wreck.

The mast ended twenty feet above the deck in a jagged raw-edged break. What remained of the mainsail was rigged to the broken mast, with the boom swung way outboard to give the boat some sort of sail power, but the sail hung in gray tatters from the rigging.

The rest of the deck was splintered wood, bent stanchions, rigging spiky with snags in a dozen places.

Then Jake stuck his head out of the companionway and smiled tiredly up at her. After that, the ruin of *Calinda* didn't matter at all.

She threw herself at him from halfway down the ladder and kissed him for so long she thought she would drown in it.

Wearily he unwound her arms from around his neck and settled her back on her feet.

"Sweetheart, right now, my clothes are doing most of my standing up for me. I'm so dirty I may even be contagious."

He plucked at the salt-stiff shirt. In the morning warmth it had started to smell.

"Come and have a bath. I'll scrub your back."

"A bath? There's no such thing."

His face under a week of beard was haggard. Sun-burned skin peeled from forehead and nose. The glint in his eyes was mostly exhaustion, but there was triumph there too. He leaned over the rail and looked down at the boat.

"You guys coming up or do you want to live on board?"

The three men who hauled themselves up the ladder looked as bushed as Jake. They collapsed on the jetty and leaned gratefully against the rail. Bangsund followed them up and stood at the top, wiping grease from his hands.

"You brought *that* across the Gulf?"

"And through the fringe of a hurricane." He nodded at the three men dozing in the sun. "They're good boys."

"They're supermen, if you ask me. What's wrong with the hull?"

"Sprung plate. We didn't dare hammer it. The whole thing could have come out. We stretched part of a sail over it and wired it on. It kept the leak down so that the pumps could handle it. But you'd better get her out of the water right now, or she'll sink."

"Might be the best thing for her."

"Carl, we brought that boat through seas twenty feet high. Until the mast went. And even then, with half a mast and all that top hamper *and* the drag of a screw, she still moved like a dream. There isn't a boat like that in the world."

"You're the boss," Bangsund said. A knot of workmen had gathered on the dock. "Okay, get out the tender. Tow her over to the cradle and haul her inside."

Jake looked around the boatyard. He had to see it with new eyes now, as a base, and perhaps a fortress.

"Couple more things, Carl. Get someone in to build a

fence along the frontage with the road. Hire some security men. I don't want anyone in or out unless they've
got business here." He looked along the jetty at the
moored boats. "How much work have we got on at the
moment?"

"A month's worth, maybe. Been a good summer."

"Lay it off. Give it to Sam Minetti. He'll be glad of it."

"That's fifteen, twenty thousand dollars worth of
business!"

"We'll have plenty to do, don't worry about that."

He whistled sharply. Grale and the Weselowskis
opened their eyes wearily.

"Lady here's promising breakfast, a bath, and bed.
Any takers?"

Phil said, "Ask me in a week," but he joined the others in straggling up the jetty.

Jake lagged behind to watch the yard tender link up to
the bitts in the bow of Calinda and tow her towards the
slipway. She was down by the stern with the weight of
water in the bilges. The paintwork was a ruin, the remains of the jury-rigging trailed in the water, and the
sheet of gray canvas bound across the bow looked like
some ridiculous bandage.

He could not remember seeing anything more beautiful in his life.

An hour later, Jake roused himself from exhaustion just
as the soapy water of the brimming bathtub lapped
around his nose.

Kim sat on a stool by the bath, staring at him with little
girl fascination.

"Guess I went to sleep."

"Right in the middle of a sentence."

"What was I saying?"

The pad on her lap was covered in writing. "I'm to
make sure Carl gets the security guards and starts on the
fence. I'm to write Mr. Halvorsen and tell him you've
found her, and get the number of a man named Hubble.
A welder. I have to make an appointment at the bank,
and remind you to get something out of a safe-deposit
box. You didn't say what."

"Securities." It would cost a quarter of a million to do
what had to be done to Calinda. "What else?"

"Call Sam Lewis."

"That sounds like the lot."

She put down the pad. "Want me to wash your back?"

Her insistent hands coaxed the last fatigue from his muscles. When he fell into bed, it was to sleep in total contentment for twenty hours.

What woke him was a familiar grating laugh. He went downstairs. Sam Lewis and Kim sat side by side on the couch, while Jean poured out drinks. Sam took only ginger ale.

"You didn't waste any time."

"Hey!" Sam grabbed his hand, wrung it energetically. "What are you doing up? I heard you were just about finished."

"I heard that too." He sat down opposite. "Never believe rumors. What do you think of my baby?"

The *Calinda* plans and the hull model lay on the table. Sam picked up the model and caressed it with loving attention.

"Jesus, just feel that!"

"Better than you could build?"

"Hell, I didn't say it was *that* good." His finger followed the long blade of the bow as it swelled into the hull's smooth curve, then cut back into the narrow counter. "Well, okay. Maybe that crazy old bastard knew a few things I don't. Is the hull really as thin as he says?"

"It's an eggshell."

"Eggshells don't sail worth a damn."

"This one does."

Sam stood up. "Okay. You won't be happy until you show us, I guess. Let's get it over with. Maybe then I can go back to drinking."

The yard was bustling. A barrier of two trestles and a plank barred the main gate. Two heavy men in brown uniforms with lightning flashes on their sleeves and .38 police specials in open holsters walked up to the car as it halted.

Jake rolled down the window. "I'm Forrester."

"Got some ID, Mr. Forrester?"

He was reaching for his license when Carl Bangsund came out of the office. "He's okay." He leaned in the window. "You sure you need all this?"

"Every bit. How's the fence coming?"

Carl looked up the road. A post-hole digger on the back of a small tractor was drilling pits along the edge of the grass. "Have it up in three days."

"I want barbed wire along the top. And an alarm system. You get in touch with the customers?"

"Most of 'em. Some aren't well pleased, but Minetti sure is. Says he's sending you a case of Jack Daniels."

"We'll need it." He waved aside the barrier. "I'll be down at the slip."

A smell of rot and damp filled the boathouse. Brackish yellow water gurgled out of the hose hanging over the *Calinda*'s side. Heaped on the concrete, the remains of her sails made a tattered and dirty pile in the sunlight.

The hull was no better. A fur of green slime covered it from the waterline, except where rocks had cut long scars, exposing raw aluminum. For the first time, Jake saw the crushed and torn dent on the bow that had almost sunk her; it was like a compressed fracture, with four or five plates bent and crumpled. The whole area would need to be replaced. In half a dozen other spots, lines of corrosion showed failed welds. And he didn't dare examine the stern, where large areas of metal had been cut away when the engine was installed.

Even Sam was speechless. Jake felt Kim's hand in his. He squeezed it.

Squatting, Sam ran his hand across the slimy hull.

"Jesus. Feels like the bottom of a cesspit." His thumbnail scratched through the encrustation. "What the hell did they paint her with?"

"Looks like ordinary marine white. They weren't racing her."

"Get that off for a start. Must be a hundred pounds of it. Hull okay?"

"Except for the holes."

"There's really no filler?"

"Feel for yourself."

Lewis dropped on all fours and scrambled out of sight under the boat, examining it from end to end. For minutes he scraped, poked, and slapped the curving shell of metal, then straightened up, wiping his hands on his jeans.

"She isn't bad. We might do something with her."

"How do you mean 'we'?" Jake asked. "What about *Andromeda*?"

"Just because I built her doesn't mean I have to sail in her. Of course, maybe you've already got a caller in mind."

"I was just going to say I don't think we could do it without you."

"Damn right you couldn't," Sam grinned. He peeled off his jacket and tossed it on deck. "Let's get to it."

CHAPTER TWENTY-EIGHT

Hatton Garden runs in a cranky curve from High Holborn to Clerkenwell Road, delineating the interface between the new commercial London and the old.

Almost every building on the western side is new. Blank glass facades clash with the unexpected gaudiness of the jewelry stores that occupy the street level, where bright golden light gleams on a thousand rings, on yards of black velvet strewn with diamonds, on the thick arrogance of armored glass.

Across the road, nothing has changed since Victorian times. The old buildings still crowd together, their brownstone frontages running one into another, the bas-reliefs of Commerce and Industry turning their faces away from the vulgarity opposite.

Diamond House at number 38 was built before the Great War; most of the tenants whose names appear on the close-packed white bakelite plates inside the vestibule took up their leases when the building was new and have remained ever since. The old wooden doors squeak, the tile floor is uneven and much repaired, the staircases are narrow and poorly lit. Some members of the jewelry trade see no reason to advertise their wealth, though the Rolls Royces parked up and down the street outside are an indication in themselves.

Meadows's clerk left his visitor in the outer office and used the phone on his employer's desk to ring the London Diamond Club, diagonally opposite number 38.

Meadows received the message just as he was getting ready to complete the day's fourth rubber of bridge. He laid down his cards without comment and took his coat from the back of his chair.

He was partnering Nikolides. The big Greek was astonished. "Alex? In the middle of a hand?"

Meadows put on his coat. "Sorry, gentlemen. Important customer."

He didn't like to say how important. For maintaining a discreet silence to the police about the nature of her holdings, this lady paid Meadows a generous ten percent over the value of what he handled. Gem dealers get used to secrecy; so much illegal and unofficial money passes from country to country in the form of precious stones that a company would remain in business barely a week if its owners let slip the source of its merchandise. For centuries, the dealers and clients of the little holes in the wall along Hatton Garden had worked out a convenient modus vivendi: The client undertook not to offer any gem so obviously and recently stolen that its possession would be a positive embarrassment; the dealers, for their part, turned a blind eye to anything that had been decently disguised.

In Europe, vexed with nosy bank officials, the gem business labored under great difficulties. England was far more discreet. This lady was far from Meadows's only continental client.

As he came back into his office, the woman in the black dress put down her copy of London *Vogue*.

"I didn't expect you this month, madame."

Marie-Ange shook his hand. "I was in London. Two birds with one stone, as you say."

They went into his inner office.

It would have taken an expert to recognize Marie-Ange. She wore a light shade of Clinique makeup, a cosmetic designed for people with sensitive skins. The slightly opaque cream made her skin look sallow, even unhealthy. This, and her dress, a Balmain copy a year or two out of date, combined to give her the look of someone who spent most of her life indoors—the owner of a smart dress shop or the manager of a small company.

Meadows had his private theory. She probably owned one of those select brothels in Paris one heard about—for Arab sheiks and cabinet minsters only. That would certainly explain the business they had together.

"I suppose you'd like to see how things stand?"

"Yes."

He unlocked his desk drawer with one of five small silver keys he kept on a watch chain and took out another set of keys. Sliding back an oak panel in the wall, he fitted one of the new keys and one from his chain into a small safe set in the wall. Twenty-five flat trays filled it. He unlocked the fifth and carried it back to the desk.

It contained forty-three sapphires, ranging in size from eighty carats to one of more than two hundred. They varied in color from a vivid aquamarine, as transparent as the Carribbean, to deep purple, hazy with the whitish sheen experts called "silk." There were five superb Kashmiri stones, oval cut to show the twelve-rayed star at the center of each. Properly mounted, they would make an incomparable necklace. Meadows never looked at them without regretting his client's peculiar wish never to have the gems set.

"Still quite a few," he said, "even after the last sale."

Marie-Ange moved the stones around with her finger. There was something dreadful in their brilliance. They were the souls of men. A death for each. She could almost identify them. The Englishman on his way to her bed again when the device she had planted in his Porsche blew him through the roof. The Arab with sweaty hands who never knew what stabbed through the nape of his neck, severing the spinal cord.

She opened her handbag and gave him a small box. "I have these for you."

Meadows took a square of black baize from his drawer, squared it on the desk, and tipped out the stones. Eighteen of them. Various sizes. Some looked very fine. He screwed the loupe into his eye and bent over them.

For ten minutes he sorted among them. Marie-Ange watched his fingers, trickling the glowing blobs of deep blue with those neat white hands. If he had looked up and met her eye, many of his assumptions about the lady from Paris would have been revised. Her eyes were heavy, almost closed, her skin perspiring under the thick *maquillage*. Her nipples throbbed almost painfully, and the hair between her thighs was moist and hot. . . .

She had thought they were finished with her, the thugs from the CRS.

The little room in the pension smelled of wine and oil and bread and drains. A sting of the tear gas lingered in eyes and nose. Everything flared and swam through her tears.

They had stripped her naked.

Her shame impinged only on the surface of her consciousness. The ache in her head drove out almost everything else. Her skull was full of pain. Brimming with it. It slopped over if she moved.

She could feel something hard under her back. Wood. Something sharp, like gravel, dug into the skin of her buttocks every time she moved. It must be sugar from the spilled packet she could see from the corner of her eye.

She tried to raise her hips from the discomfort.

Impossible.

They were holding her down. By the ankles. The wrists. Her legs were wrenched wider apart, her thighs levered down over the table's hard edges, bringing her spread hips to the very end.

She screamed with the pain. The scream died in her open mouth as a hand struck her savagely over the ear.

In a daze she watched one of them bend over her, mumble words that were blurred by pain and made incomprehensible. He waved something in front of her face. Stroked her breasts. Rough. Sharp. Scratching her nipples.

No. No more. Please. No.

She knew what it was. The thing they beat her with. The *matraque*.

Lower. It touched the place where she was already bruised, throbbing, oozing. Where they had taken her— all five of them—hard, brutal, while the others watched and laughed and held her down to the table.

The grating tip of the *matraque* dragged over her belly and touched her where she was tenderest, swollen . . .

Then he thrust it into her.

Pain. More pain than she knew could exist. Jagged blades through hips, stomach. Her back arched off the table. Behind the shape bending over her, beyond the shoulders, she could see the tiny skylight that let brightness into the little kitchen.

The sun came out, and the panel of glass glowed, showing its vivid colors. Tendrils of green vine curled against the yellow background around a central disc of deepest glowing blue, as bulbous as an eye, all seeing, all welcoming. She opened up her body to the blue and flowed into it, away from all pain, all fear. . . .

Marie-Ange opened her eyes slowly, unwilling to acknowledge the throb and warmth in her thighs and stomach, the sense of satisfaction that filled her.

Meadows was watching her. "Are you feeling unwell, madame?"

"No. It's nothing. I think I dozed a little." She saw he had arrangd the stones in two groups on the baize; one of twelve, the other of six. "What do you think about these?"

He looked uncomfortable. "With your permission, I'd like my assistant to have a look at some of them."

"Why?"

"Just a precaution." He lifted his phone.

The man who came in might have been a successful stockbroker on his way up. He smiled at Marie-Ange, bowed slightly.

Meadows gave him the loupe. "Take a look at these, will you, Adrian?" He pointed to the small group of six stones set apart from the rest.

Adrian took more than a minute over the first of them, even taking it to the window to examine the stone in natural light. He came back, put it with the rest, picked up the second and glanced at it through the eyepiece.

"Yes. I see. They're excellent."

"But . . . artificial?"

"Oh, yes. Without a doubt."

Marie-Ange went white. "*Faux? C'est vrai?*"

"*Oui, madame. Je regrette.* You didn't know?"

She shook her head.

The young man said, "A lot of firms do them these days. For industrial gems. If you use a fine enough grade of alumina power and heat it to two thousand degrees centigrade, it's possible to create a very smooth stone." He picked up one of the fakes and looked at it critically. "Of course, someone's gone to a lot more trouble with these. The silk's very fine. I would imagine they used radiation to get the rutile needles to form. Best I've seen, but then I'm not right up to date on the new technology. I understand the Japanese are very advanced in this area."

"Are they worth anything?" Marie-Ange asked.

Meadows said, "The second group is excellent. Roughly fifteen to twenty thousand pounds on the market at the moment. The fakes . . . well, perhaps a thousand. Do you want me to offer them for sale?"

She held out her hand. "Not at the moment."

CHAPTER TWENTY-NINE

Gradually, it all became routine. Even the most pleasurable things become, in the end, a routine. Peter Forrester realized this on the fifth or sixth day of work on *Calinda*. It was a revelation of a sort, and one he quietly prized.

His father seemed to be everyplace at once, as if the boat could be brought back to life with energy alone. The team began work at seven in the morning, with the mist still on the bay, and finished when the chill made fingers clumsy and tempers short.

But often Peter came down to the boathouse after watching TV to find Jake still deep inside the hull, working by the light of the caged lamps that hung all over *Calinda* like lights on a Christmas tree. Kim was usually there. That was something he had not yet made up his mind about. If he saw her on those nights, bent over a cracked weld, probing out the corrosion, or grinding the last of the paint from the hull, he slipped away to walk back up the jetty and through the quiet streets to the house without telling anyone he had been there.

Most of the time, he was too busy to be resentful. Everyone had a job. Peter found himself in charge of the commissary.

Jean made boxed lunches for the first few days until one of the Weselowskis peered into his and asked politely, "I'm not saying I can't eat it. I'd just like to know what it is."

Peter looked over his shoulder. "Duck à l'orange. We had it for dinner last night."

Weselowski inserted a finger to lift the withered meat in its gummy sauce. "What the hell's this stuff underneath?"

"Wild rice."

"Wouldn't be the same without wild rice," his brother said, deadpan.

"Hasn't anyone up there ever heard of bologna? Hamburgers?"

The next day, Peter set the alarm for six and spent an hour in the kitchen. At lunch break the crew opened their bags with trepidation, then beamed and dived in.

"New chef?" Phil said, watching Burt Grale trying to get his mouth around slabs of ham and rat cheese on half-inch slices of bread.

After that, Peter had a new responsibility.

Day by day, *Calinda* changed. At first, so much stuff was heaved out to lie in a tattered heap on the slipway that he wondered what would be left.

The deckhouse disappeared. So did the wooden deck and everything below. Stoves, a vacuum lavatory, even radio equipment.

Carl Bangsund rescued the radio gear. "You aren't scrappin' this, are you?"

Jake looked up from supervising the removal of the drive shaft and propeller from the hull. The engine they had hauled out the day before sat leaking oil on the concrete. "No, I guess we can get something for that. Put it in the bargain shop."

Peter said, "Don't you need a radio?"

"What for? On race days, there'll be a thousand boats in sight."

"Oh. Yeah."

Carl handed him the set. Peter sagged under the weight. "Feel that. Fifty, sixty pounds. Could cut a second off the speed. Not worth it."

Sam Lewis draped his legs over the edge of the deck. "Remember when we used to race under the old rule, Jake?"

Jake looked up from the greasy drive shaft. "Do I? Every boat fitted out with the essentials for cruising. All that balsa wood furniture. Just as well we never had to sit on it. Then there was the paneling. In '78 they decided we didn't need wood paneling right through the boat; just a proper wall covering. The Australians put in plasterboard, so I put in Formica. They tore out the plasterboard and put in wood veneer."

Sam guffawed. "Hell, yeah. I remember that. *You* tore

out the Formica and just glued paper over the walls. The
hardware stores were going crazy. We had wood and veneer and plastic sheet piled up everyplace."

There was an ominous clunk from the rear of the boat
as a large piece of metal landed on the concrete. Burt
Grale unbent painfully and dropped his monkey wrench
beside the greasy and scored length of drive shaft.

"It's a real pleasure to stand about here listening to
you two grand old men of the boat scene, but can either
of you tell me what the hell we're going to do with this
goddam hole?"

Jake went to the stern and looked through the gap cut
in *Calinda*'s stern to install the engine. The entire length
of the gutted boat was revealed. Light lanced into the
dark interior in a dozen places where plates were sprung
or welds cracked.

"We could sure use that welder," Jake said.

"What do you hear from him?"

"Said he'd be here this week. I couldn't pin him down
to a day."

Peter paused with an armful of waste paper on his way
to the endlessly smoking incinerator. "Mr. Bellero down
on Sackville does welding. He's fixed boats. I've seen
him."

"This is a special kind of welding, Petey. Only a couple
of people in the country can do it right. This is the man
who made the hull in the first place. I don't want anyone
else touching it."

Grale said, "He'd better get here soon. Otherwise
we're up the creek without a paddle. Or an engine."

But the welder arrived that afternoon. He wasn't what
any of them expected.

They were sitting around, eating lunch—cold turkey,
pickles, soup—when Carl rang down from the main gate.

"Couple of fellers here say they've come to see you.
One's name of Hubble."

"That's our boy." Jake swallowed the last of his sandwich, dusted off the crumbs, and doubled up the path
towards the gate.

Two men stood outside the fence, watched warily by
the guards. One was about forty-five, with a long beard

streaked with gray. He wore sandals, bib-front dungarees, and a lumberjack shirt. The other was in his middle thirties, with jeans, denim jacket, and a Zapata moustache. A large motor-drive Nikon hung around his neck. Neither looked like a welder.

Jake looked from one to the other. "Uh, either of you gentlemen Ray Hubble?"

The older one straightened up marginally. He was scowling.

"You Forrester?"

"Yes. Been expecting you."

Hubble waved at the fence and the guards. "What's all this shit, man? Goon here asked for some ID. I don't carry no ID. What sort of fascist setup you got here?"

Halvorsen had prepared Jake for temperament. *But that guy's an artist. You look at Calinda and tell me if you can imagine anyone doing it better.*

Jake swallowed his irritation and opened the gate. "I'll tell them to let you and your friend in and out anytime."

As Hubble walked down the slope towards the boatyard, his companion stopped and held out his hand. "Tom Santchini, Mr. Forrester. I'm doing a story on Ray."

"I don't want any publicity on *Calinda* until after she's launched, Mr. Santchini."

"Don't worry. It's for *Arts Forum*. A quarterly. This issue won't come out until next fall."

"*Arts Forum*? I didn't think a painting and sculpture magazine would be interested in boating."

"We've done quite a bit about Ray's work in *AF* over the years. This will be the first full-length piece though."

"About a *welder*?"

Santchini lifted the camera and snapped a picture of Jake's puzzled face. "Nice light down here by the water. No, Ray isn't exactly a welder. He's a sculptor. Got work in the Getty, MOMA, a couple of big pieces out west. Colorado State. The Tate did a retrospective on him a while back. That's in London."

"I know where the Tate is, thanks. What the hell is a sculptor doing working on a boat?"

"As I understand it, this man Halvorsen approached Ray after the Tate show. Said he looked like the only man who could do the job he wanted. Paid him a lot of money for it. He used it to study with Marini in Florence."

Jake revised his memory of the conversation with Halvorsen. When he had said, "that guy's an artist," he'd meant it literally.

"He can be a pain," Santchini said. "But he gets the work out."

When Jake and Santchini arrived on the slipway, Hubble was on deck, prowling up and down, and frowning.

"What the hell have you done to it? Goddam holes everywhere." He squatted and stuck a finger through one of the holes drilled to anchor a vanished deckhouse. "You've really screwed her up, man."

"Can you fix it?"

"Shit, man, I don't know if I want to get involved."

"We'll pay top money."

Hubble looked scornful. "Money. Answer to everything, right?"

Santchini took another picture. "What about that Henry Moore? What did they want for that?"

"Ten thousand." Hubble looked thoughtful. He glanced at Jake. "Worth that to you?"

"If you do it in a week."

"I'll do it in less than that. Think I want to spend any more time around this toilet than I can help?" He stamped his foot on the deck to test the reverberation. It rang hollow. "The whole spatial concept's shot to hell, man."

"Well, we got our welder," Grale said that evening as he and Jake sat in Jean's parlor, checking over the day's progress. "What next?"

"You know the boat world pretty well, don't you, Burt?"

"I've touched base here and there. Why?"

Jake took a sheet of paper from his shirt pocket. It had cost him a week of phone calls and a lot of favors.

"I've been thinking about the opposition. Most of the entries must be settling down now. I figure there are about six possibles for the defense. Ted Turner, Du Moulin, Needham . . ." He gave Grale the paper. "They're all listed there, along with places, schedules

where I could find them out, sponsors. Take a little trip.
See what they look like. See if you can spot the real
threats."

"Anyone in particular?"

"Sam told me about the work he did on *Andromeda*
for Needham. She sounds like a sweet boat."

"What about crew? Are you recruiting?"

Jake grinned. "Seems I've got a pretty good team right
now."

"Anyone wants my spot, I'll wrestle him for it," Grale
said.

"It'll be waiting for you when you get back." He could
afford to be generous. By now, the front-runners had
their teams in training, helped by the generous sponsorship of the big companies anxious to cash in on America's Cup prestige. If any crewmen of quality were left on
the loose, they wouldn't be drawn to a wrecked boat
skippered by a known eccentric.

But Jake underestimated Grale. Three days after he
left, the security man sent down a message that someone
wanted to see him.

The man was forty, balding, and spare, almost gaunt.
He wore a leather jacket, faded jeans, Decksiders, and
carried a tightly packed duffel.

"I hear you're looking for crew. I'm Pete Carraway.
Burt Grale told me to look you up."

Jake raked through his memory. "Seems I know your
name, Mr. Carraway."

"I crewed for old Halvorsen once, on *Loki*, when I
was a kid. Deck boss on *Constellation*. Crewed on
Intrepid." He reeled off a score of berths. Jake was
impressed.

"I thought maybe you needed a caller."

"Sam Lewis's calling for us."

"Yeah? Good man."

"We think so."

"Anything else open?"

They badly needed an experienced deck boss. Carraway would be ideal. But there was something . . .

"What have you done this year?"

Carraway smiled thinly. "Cleared a lot of brush
mostly. I've been in the slammer." He picked up his
duffel. "Nice talking to you."

"Hold up. Mind telling me what you were in for?"

"Nonpayment of maintenance." He grimaced. "I married a bitch, Mr. Forrester."

Jake signaled for the guard to open the gate. "Come on in and have a cup of coffee."

Word got around. Before the end of the week, five more men turned up. Jake took on three of them. As soon as Hubble had finished his work, it would be possible to get *Calinda* into the water and try a shakedown cruise. He was thinking about the possibilities of making that his own personal Christmas present to himself when Burt arrived back. None of his news was good.

He slumped down in the easy chair and put his feet on the coffee table. "Is there a drink in the house? I've looked at boats until I'm seasick."

Jake put a bottle of bourbon and a water jug down beside a glass. "Let's hear it."

"It'll be a strong year. No doubt about that. Turner's new boat is a honey. I've got the figures . . ." He patted his pocket. "Had to drink a few guys under the table to get them." He downed half of a large bourbon and water. "I wouldn't worry about Du Moulin. Looks too old-fashioned for this company. And they've got money trouble. All the smart sponsorship's going other places. For instance . . ." He fished out a press clipping.

AMERICA'S CUP CONTENDER
COMPLETED IN RECORD TIME.

Jake stared at the photograph of three beaming men clasping hands Three Musketeers style.

Syndicate chairman and Mayor Thomas Needham III, Harriman Aluminum VP Tyler Caldwell, and Baltimore Chamber of Commerce President J.L. Prinzheim after making the joint announcement of a grand unveiling and christening for the million-dollar boat this December 26. Among guests expected to attend are . . ."

"Didn't waste any time, did he?" Jake said.

"Get that list. Five senators—*and* Jane Fonda. Now

he's made mayor, there's a murmur Needham wants the nomination for governor."

Jean came into the room just as Jake and Burt headed for the front door.

"You aren't going to work *tonight?*"

"Be grateful, Mrs. Forrester," Grale said. "We're saving the country from Tom Needham. Without us, he's likely to end up president."

In the car, Grale asked, "How are we doing, anyway?"

"Not bad. Hubble's about finished. All the gear's arrived. Sails too. We still don't have everything we need, but the cupboard's bare."

"We'll stir up some sponsors as soon as they see what she can do."

"I hope so."

The streets were empty along the bay front. A cold night wind buffeted the car as Jake turned into the boatyard entrance and stopped at the gate. He honked. After a minute Carl Bangsund appeared from the office, fumbling with the keys.

Jake drove in and stopped. "What are you doing up here, Carl? Where's the security man?"

"Night guard didn't show. I can take care of things okay."

A small alarm bell rang somewhere in Jake's mind, but too many other problems occupied his attention for the warning to register. He drove through to the boathouse while Bangsund pushed the gate closed behind him.

Half a block down the street, the man who had been watching the yard most of the day made a mental note of Jake's arrival. Everything was lining up nicely. Slipping out of the car, he shoved his hands into the pockets of his windbreaker and ambled up the block to the gas station where there was a public pay phone.

Feeding in his coins, he punched out the number and waited for the expected four rings. After that, the answering machine cut in; by now, he recognized the faint hiss of the tape. He gave his information quickly and precisely, then read off the number of the pay phone and hung up.

Three minutes later the bell rang inside the plastic hood. He picked up the phone.

"Tomorrow." The voice was uninflected, almost mechanical. "Four P.M. In the morning, go to the general delivery counter at the Government Boulevard Post Office and pick up a letter addressed to J. Brosnan. That's B-R-O-S-N-A-N. It contains a parking check for the Bienville Garage on North Royal. A blue Ford truck." The tape hissed for a few seconds. "Don't take any chances this time. We don't want a recurrence of what happened in New York. Follow your orders and there will be no trouble."

The phone clicked.

Jubei looked at the disconnected phone and grinned without humor. His hand clenched, the bony fingers tightening like thin knuckled pieces of bamboo, and the plastic cracked, flakes of its shell rattling onto the concrete. He carefully hung up the broken-backed phone in its cradle.

CHAPTER THIRTY

Jake drove back slowly from the bank. Visits were becoming more frequent, and the balance in his account, lower. Soon he would have to make the crucial decision about whether or not to use the money in Elaine's box. He relished the opportunity for revenge in doing so, but something held him back. To spend that money would commit him totally to a cover-up of her activites and those of her confederate.

And, sooner or later, the confederate would come looking for his $400,000. While it existed, Jake was safe. Only he had access to the money, and whoever had employed Jubei and Marie-Ange knew that. There had been no more attempts on his life since he had talked to Ryker; the killer knew that Ryker would have told Jake all he needed to know.

Traffic was better than Jake expected. He arrived in front of the marina at 4:15. A new guard opened the gate.

"Anything new?"

"All quiet, Mr. Forrester. Couple of kids stopped opposite, tried to look through the fence. We moved 'em on. Only person who's been through was the guy delivering acetylene."

"Okay." He stopped, chilled. "*Acetylene*?"

"For the welder. Ten tanks. He had an order signed by you."

Hubble didn't use acetylene. Aluminum welding needed argon shielding to prevent oxygen from interacting with the melted metal.

"When was this?"

"Few minutes ago."

"What's he look like?" Jake was already reaching for the gear shift.

"Black guy. Tall. Wore shades. I guess he's still down

there, if you want to see him. The truck only came through about three minutes ago.''

Jake clashed his gears trying to get the car into instant motion. He left behind a cloud of burned rubber as he accelerated down the road towards the boathouse.

As he rounded the end of the building and drove onto the slipway, the blast hit him.

The windshield suddenly became a milky white, and he held up his hand to protect his face as fragments of glass avalanched into the front seat. The car lifted onto its left wheels, slued, and crashed to a halt against the concrete retaining wall.

Jake clambered out.

The remains of a wrecked blue Ford truck burned with gusts of orange flame in the center of the slipway, fifty feet from *Calinda*'s hull. As he watched, another blast racked it, sending fragments showering into the bay.

Santchini, the photographer, straightened up slowly from behind some oil drums by the boathouse. He held a .45 army Colt automatic with professional precision in both hands.

Jake stopped abruptly. Santchini saw his alarm, waved, and shoved the gun into his belt. From behind him, Sam, Peter, and others inched into the light.

"Someone mind telling me what's going on?"

Santchini said, "We had a visitor. Supposed to be delivering acetylene. I heard him drive up, but when nobody came into the workshop, I got suspicious. I came out here just as she blew up. Must have had it rigged."

Jake looked at the pistol. "That regular issue for photographers?"

"Mr. Fujita thought you might be able to use a little help down here. Could be he was right."

Hubble came out of the boathouse looking pale. "What the hell's going on here?"

"Someone doesn't want *Calinda* launched. How is she?"

"Not even touched."

Jake measured the distance from the burning wreck of the car to the boat. The heat hadn't even singed her.

"Guess he got cold feet," Burt said.

That was possible.

Or . . .

Jake felt cold. He counted heads again.

"Where's Kim?"

Sam said, "She was here just before he came down. Maybe she went back to the house."

"No," Peter said. "I was helping her clean the cockpit."

The security men on the gate knew nothing. She had not left the yard.

Jake drove to the house with a growing certainty of what he would find there.

The envelope lay on the doormat. Plain manila, without any name. Inside was a tape cassette. He shoved it angrily into the car player.

The voice seemed to come from far away, through echoing caverns of static and interference. He might have been talking from the moon.

"We have your friend, Mr. Forrester. Kimberly Ryker. She will be hurt very badly unless you fall in with our requirements." A long pause as the static hissed and roared. "The documents and money collected by your late wife must be gathered and prepared for delivery to us. Everything. You will be advised where they must be deposited."

The tape wound on, but the rest was blank.

So now the gloves were off. The enemy had made his move. Jake would need all the friends he had if Kim's life was to be saved.

"BASF." Santchini turned the cassette over in his hands. "Buy them anyplace."

"What about the voice?"

"Vocoder—computer distortion. Plus a lot of white noise. Kid stuff. You can find the gear to do it in any hi-fi store."

Grale came in with the Weselowskis. "He had a boat waiting. He got Kim while we were worrying about the fire. You want me to call the cops?"

"No." He slipped the tape into a portable recorder and played it.

"What's all this stuff they want? Documents and money? I don't get it."

Jake brought out the suitcase and dumped the contents. Grale twitched a photograph from the heap, looked at it without reaction, and laid it facedown among the rest.

Jake sat down heavily. "She got into blackmailing some of her friends. With an accomplice. She wanted to pull out. He hired a professional killer to murder her, and anyone else who knew what she knew. I was lucky— Elaine had been very careful to keep her activities from me. But young Charlie Keble knew, for instance. He was ready to tell me about it. So they shot him. Tony Stephens as well."

Sam said, "Christ. I thought maybe Fujita . . ."

Jake glanced at Santchini. "So did I, at first. Then someone put me straight. Whoever hired the killer also turned around Fujita's man Jubei. That's who kidnapped Kim."

"He says 'money,'" Grale said.

"Four hundred thousand. The payoffs. It was in the bank."

"Well, *give* him the stuff," Grale said.

Santchini said, "It's not really my business, but I wouldn't do that. Kim would have seen who snatched her."

He didn't have to spell it out. Hostages who knew too much had only one possible fate.

"What then?" Jake asked.

Santchini picked up one of the diaries. "Whoever your wife was working with, he's in here. Someone involved in the boat world. Someone you know. It's going to mean some grief for you but . . . well, let's go through this stuff. Somewhere, we'll find a name, a clue."

Quietly Sam said, "Do you have the diary for 1979?"

Jake dug it out. "Why?"

"I really liked Elaine. You know that."

"She's dead, Sam. Nothing you say can hurt her now."

"Okay. I saw her once, in New York. By accident. September second. That's why I remember the date. My birthday."

"So?"

"A couple of the guys took me to Trader Vic's for lunch. As we went in, I noticed Elaine and some guy. I thought it was you, but then I recognized who it was." He paused. "Well, I thought, what business is it of mine?"

Jake thumbed through the diary to September 2.

"*11 A.M. Nails. 12:30 Lunch. Tr. Vic. 2:30. Traven. $1000.*"

"Who did she meet?" Jake's throat was tight.

"It might have been a coincidence . . ."

Who?"

"Tom Needham."

His birthday was in Apr earlier in this street 8 mo after Elaine was killed, when he went to visit Jake & told him to come stay with him & celebrate his birthday. remember?

CHAPTER THIRTY-ONE

Snow began to fall over Baltimore at 5:17 P.M. By 6 it was starting to settle, and Wally Burgess, weatherman on Mediametric's Evening Action News, came on dressed as Santa Claus to announce with the ringing of a hand-bell and a great deal of ho-ho-ho that all signs pointed to a white Christmas.

Tom Needham looked down the long conference table in the corporation's penthouse boardroom. The seven people of the *Andromeda* team, skimmed from his top personnel to do nothing but smooth the media launch of his new boat, watched him warily, flipping through their mental card files for some detail they might have missed, some provision not thoroughly nailed down. TN had a way of finding the loose shingle and using it to tear down the whole house.

Harvey Hardenbergh, the weather chief, looked over his shoulder at the indigo evening sky swirling with the white powder of windborne snow and felt a sense of personal indignity. How could the weather do this to him?

"Well," Needham asked, "what's the story, Harvey?" Someone down the table laughed at the imitation of news anchorman Artie Carver's voice. Hardenbergh wasn't amused.

"Looks worse than it is, Tom. There's a ridge of high pressure . . ."

"Don't give me that weatherman stuff, Harvey. I can get that by turning on the monitor and listening to Burgess. Just tell me what we can expect for the day after tomorrow."

"Well . . . cold, Tom. Maybe a little snow. But clear."

"No rain?"

"Rain? No. I doubt it."

Tom weighed this news. Cold. Clear. Sure, why not? It was always cold during presidential inaugurations, and they were among the most successful of all media events.

A boat launch in the snow . . . he saw himself in a good Harris tweed topcoat, maybe even a hat. Solid, indestructible, statesmanlike.

He turned towards Hannah Klein, his personal publicist (Personal Assistant—Media Relations read the plate on her door). "What about it, Hannah?"

The elegant Ms. Klein lifted her pen from the pad where she had sketched a triangular outline like that of a yacht sail and filled it with diagonal stripes of red, white, and blue. "No problem in general. It might be a good idea to bring in more heaters, maybe give the TV people some extra time to warm up."

"Change the photo call from eleven to ten thirty. That be enough?"

"Fine." She lettered Hail To The Chief under the sketch and started embellishing it with cherubs blowing golden trumpets. Ms. Klein had majored in art history at Sarah Lawrence before going into TV.

Needham swiveled in his chair. "So that only leaves you, Bobby."

Bobby Seitz, borrowed from the news crew to organize the preliminary events, moved guiltily in his chair. "We've had a few problems . . ." He shuffled among his papers, conscious of the noise they made in the suddenly quiet room. Looking around the rest of the group with a conciliatory smile, he met only stone faces and swallowed. "One thing . . . the parks commissioner is dragging his feet on our request to put up a marquee."

"Saunders? Well, that makes sense." Saunders, the parks commissioner, belonged to the out-going administration. He knew that one of Tom Needham's first pleasurable tasks as mayor would be to fire him and everyone else who supported the old regime. "Look, Bobby, put it up anyway. If they give you any trouble, refer them to me." Let them cite him for a violation of the land-use codes; he could use it as a club to attack outdated rules about public amenities. They'd be sorry they ever took him on.

And by then *Andromeda* would have been well and truly launched.

"What about the ticker-tape parade?"

Seitz squirmed. "Little problem there too, Mr. Needham. Most buildings in the business district don't have the kind of windows that open. It's the air-conditioning. We plotted those that do and routed the motorcade past them."

He handed Needham a marked map. The route wound through a dozen side streets, some of them hangouts of derelicts.

"This is no good. What about Hanover, West Fayette, Baltimore?"

"All the wrong kind of building, Mr. Needham. You can't throw out ticker tape if the windows don't open."

"Bobby, Bobby . . ." Needham sounded avuncular. Older and more experienced employees round the table glanced at one another. "You haven't thought it out." He pointed through the windows at the building opposite, where men in window-cleaners' cradles were wiring up a gigantic electric Christmas tree. It spread out across the frontage in a network of colored lights.

Bobby looked blankly at the scene. "Uh . . . I'm sorry, chief . . ."

Hannah Klein looked up from her doodling. "What Tom means, I think, is why not hire window-cleaners to throw down the ticker tape? They can hang their cradles outside the buildings. You don't need to open the windows."

"Gee, I don't know, Mr. Needham. The day after Christmas . . ."

"Oh, Bobby, you're underrating yourself. I know you can swing it. I'm really confident. I mean, if a man can't rise to a challenge, he might as well be hustling cables, right?"

Bobby swallowed. He'd done enough hustling cables around Mediametric studios in his early days. He didn't want to go back to that—ever.

"I'll get right onto it, sir."

"I knew I could count on you, Bobby." He looked around the table. "Anything else? Okay, I'll be home after nine. Before that, I'm checking out the hall."

"Anything?" he asked his secretary when he returned to his office.

"Not that you need worry about. Have a nice weekend, Mr. Needham."

"You too, Helen. I'll see you at the launch, won't I?"

"Well, sure, Mr. Needham. Wouldn't miss that."

The private office felt still and quiet. Looking out over the darkening skyline of the city, he experienced a brief moment of wonder as a handful of white flakes eddied outside the glass. A white Christmas.

The phone rang. His private line. Maybe a dozen people knew the number. He locked the office door from the inside and picked it up.

Below, in the street, Jake looked up towards the office.

The Needham Building climbed into a sky of sulphur and ink, the last five stories lost in the overcast. A flake of snow settled in Jake's eye. He blinked it away.

The cold had begun to eat through to his shoulders. He should have brought a heavier coat, thick boots, gloves.

Like those Needham's chauffeur wore. His name was Fennimann, and he had driven Jake a dozen times. Jake stayed well back in the shadows, watching Fennimann stroll up and down on the sidewalk opposite, next to the burgundy Corniche that replaced the Phantom VI burned at The Breakers.

A stream of people spilled from the revolving doors onto the slippery sidewalk. None of them was Needham. Jake watched Fennimann as the flakes settled on his black uniform and the shining visor of his cap.

In a minute Needham would leave his office and step into the car. After that, he was lost. Every cab that crawled by in the slush was occupied. The buses were jammed.

Jake looked up and down the street. A few doors down, diagonally opposite the Needham Building, a motorbike showroom was doing good business. They'd opened up the big windows and put half a dozen bikes on stands. People were stopping to admire. A boy climbed astride a big Suzuki and made *brrrrm brrrrrm* noises while his parents smiled.

It was worth a chance. Jake sprinted down the street, stepped into the showroom, and buttonholed the first salesman he saw.

"How much are the scramblers?"

"Well, that depends." He put his hand on the saddle of a Yamaha in green and gold. "A bike like this costs a little more than most, but it puts more power under your foot than you'll find in a few cars I could name. It comes . . ."

"How *much*?"

"Uh, well, with city tax, this baby sells for one thousand nine hundred and seventy-four dollars. But we can write you a dandy deal over twenty months that, with charges and everything included . . ."

Jake took out his credit cards. "You take American Express? MasterCard?"

"Well, any of them, sir, but of course on a purchase of this size, I'll have to check your rating."

Jake gave him the American Express plate. "Okay. Make it snappy."

He looked back to the Needham Building just as Tom Needham came through the revolving doors. Fennimann opened the back door and put his fingers to his cap.

There was no sign of the salesman. Jake kicked away the front wheel stand, threw his leg over the bike, and fumbled for the hand throttle, praying they kept the bikes gassed up.

The engine blatted. Everyone in the showroom looked up. The salesman stuck his head out of his office door. One hand held the phone, the other Jake's charge plate. "Sir, I'm afraid you can't . . ."

But then the wheels squealed on the linoleum floor, and Jake tobogganed down the ramp in front of the store through the evening pedestrian traffic. People scattered in front of him. He saw the Corniche slide by, Needham's profile leaning back in the seat, and gunned the bike after him.

For the next twenty minutes, only the red taillights of the car existed for him. He wove through the traffic, hanging back, keeping two cars behind until a sudden gap put the Rolls right in front of him. Then it stopped suddenly to avoid a pedestrian and the red brake lights flared in his face.

He twisted away, fiddled with a side mirror until a honk behind him made him look up again. He just caught the car's taillights swinging left, almost lost in the thickening snow, and slithered around the corner after them.

Snow built up on his face. His ears began to freeze. All feeling had left his hands. But he hung on. There were fewer cars around, and finally just one. Dousing his headlamp, he followed it from a hundred yards behind and, when it stopped, coasted by to turn at the next corner.

He was in a narrow side street hemmed in by blank-faced warehouses. The ruts of old trolley tracks gleamed with ice from the middle of the street. Somewhere nearby, water lapped.

Snow turned the sky a powdery yellow-orange as it floated down through the streetlights. The end of the street framed a patch of water—the inner harbor. Across the gray water he glimpsed lights and an impression of low glass and metal buildings.

He knew now where Needham had been heading.

Tom had boasted to him once how his grandfather had owned all of Baltimore's waterfront. When the docks and warehouses became too run-down, derelict, and rat-infested to be profitable, he presented them to the city. As a result, he was given the Freedom of Baltimore and died respected as well as rich. It took more than twenty years for the city to find any use for the old ruins. Those across the inner harbor basin were torn down to create Harborplace, a dismal Disneyland of fake history, with shops, restaurants, and asceptic waterside walks.

The old warehouses on the unfashionable side remained empty. Tom had bought one back from the city and turned it into a TV studio.

When Jake turned the corner, the car was no longer parked outside. For a moment he almost believed he'd lost it. Then he saw a needle of light shining between huge doors. A banner hung across the frontage, plastered to the corrugated metal cladding by snow. Andromeda—Press Preview.

From here, after the grand unveiling, *Andromeda* would be drawn in triumph through the city to her launching in the main harbor.

The door rumbled open with a muted roar of oiled bearings as Jake put his shoulder to it. He slipped inside.

He'd been here before, for interviews and talk shows. It was usually cluttered with props, scenery, camera gear, but all that was gone.

Every light bar now hung fifteen feet above the floor, some to shine on the long refreshment tables, the rest to illuminate the towering triangular shape shrouded in white cloth that filled the far end of the studio. Tom Needham stood with his back to Jake.

Without turning around, he said, "Hello, Jake. That was quite a performance on the bike. A couple of times I almost got out and offered you a ride."

Jake shook the snow off his clothes. The studio was blessedly warm. "I would have taken it."

While he spoke, he inched forward, the strip of red carpet that led to the dais muffling his steps. He stopped as Needham turned around, a long-barreled pistol in his hand.

"This is where you're supposed to say, You won't be crazy enough to use that thing. Isn't that the line in the thrillers?"

He lifted the pistol, holding it in both hands at eye height, and fired before Jake had time even to flinch. The sound was hardly louder than a snapped twig. Something flicked Jake's collar. He fingered the upturned lapel of his leather jacket and felt a neat hole.

"Browning Target," Tom said. "Best point twenty-two in the world. And I know how to use it. Pistol shooting's like sailing—an accomplishment a gentleman needn't be ashamed of."

"People know I'm here." Including, Jake thought, someone who had warned Needham he was coming.

"Yes, I'm not saying it's the most convenient method, but I think I can get away with it. A stranger, shot in this area? Not too unusual." He smiled. "There are more murders down here now that the place is infested with tourists than there were when it was docks."

Jake looked past him at the shrouded shape on stage. "Do I get a look at her?"

"Playing for time, just like the novels. Well, there's plenty of time, Jake. Sure. Take a look. The button on the lectern."

Jake pressed it. Cables lifted the canvas covering up into the ceiling shadows.

It was a beautiful boat. Low-lined, flatter than usual so that its hull would skate across the water, rather than carve it like *Calinda*. Sam had gambled on calm weather in the Sound in September and on good conditions for a light boat. When the mast was erected *Andromeda* would be breathlessly beautiful.

"So you see, Jake, you won't miss out on anything by not being in the Cup. There isn't a better boat in the water than *Andromeda*."

"You really want to win that much? Enough to kill for it?"

"To win? No, I could do without being one of the best sailors in the world. How long does it last? One season? Two? But it's a springboard. I told you once that it counted for something in the boardroom and the market. That goes for the statehouse as well."

"And that's why you killed Elaine and Keble and Stephens? So you could run for governor?"

"*I* didn't kill anyone."

"You had them killed. It's the same thing."

Unexpectedly, Needham laughed. It had a nervous edge.

"What have you got? Recorder taped to your back? Mike up your sleeve?"

"No recorder, Tom. Just you and me."

He took one step forward. Needham backed away, raised the gun. "You know how good I am with this."

Jake took another step.

Needham began to sweat. Jake could see the tremor shaking the sharp creases of his trousers. He took two quick steps, knocked aside the barrel of the Browning and slammed his fist into Needham's belly. He choked and fell to the floor, the gun sliding from his hand. Jake picked it up wearily and helped Needham to his feet. Jake had expected the punch to relieve all the suppressed tension inside him, but he just felt empty.

"You knew, you bastard," Needham said, slumping onto a chair.

"You aren't the killer type, Tom. Why hire someone like Jubei to do your killing if you were capable of doing it yourself?"

"Very clever. Jake Forrester, the all-seeing, all-knowing. You think you've figured it all out for yourself, don't you? It took you long enough."

Jake said, "I don't take credit for it. If Sam hadn't

remembered seeing you and Elaine together, we'd never have connected you two."

"Sam," Needham said. "Well, that was careless of me."

Jake wanted to ask a thousand questions about the blackmail scheme, about Elaine, Marie-Ange, about motives and methods and ambitions, but one seemed to outweigh all the rest.

"Where's Kim?"

"Oh, Christ, of course. Your child bride."

Jake pulled back his fist. Needham turned his face away.

"You think I mind? You don't frighten me anymore, Forrester. I'm past it."

"What have you done with her?"

"She's at Battleship Park. That gorilla Jubei has her. Try getting her away from *him*."

"Call him off."

"No. Get the hell out of here." He lurched towards *Andromeda*. "I've got things to do."

Jake shoved the gun inside his jacket and went out into the snow. He had not been able to save Elaine when she had needed him—but Kim was still alive.

CHAPTER THIRTY-TWO

The hour before dawn. It has a smell all its own: of damp, sweat, and—on this morning—iron.

Through the low grass, Jake could see the *Alabama* as a black mass anchored in the infinity of the night. Squirming forward a few inches, he picked up the top of her mast against the marginal lightness of the sky to the east. It gave him a sense of direction but not much else. He could not see more than an inch in front of his face.

He itched inside his black sweater. It was years since he'd worn it. Under the black shoe polish, his face felt greasy.

Something rustled behind him. He rolled on his shoulder as Santchini wriggled up level with him.

"Nobody about. The only guard's the one on the *Alabama*, and he'll be asleep. Here."

Jake felt something cold and metallic.

"Wire cutters. They'll get you through the fence. You want a gun?"

He felt the shape of the Browning .22 he'd taken from Needham hard against his stomach. "I'm okay."

"I brought something else you might find useful. Put 'em on."

Jake wrestled the elastic band around the back of his head and fixed the goggles in place. They stuck out almost an inch, like the rounded eyes of pop-eyed goldfish.

He blinked. Suddenly he was looking at a world he could see. A white-on-black world, like a chalk sketch on black paper.

He could see the hill now. It fell away in front of him like a slope of dirty snow. The wire fence was a zone of shimmering shadow against the pale gray of the park beyond.

The water of the bay shifted and eddied, crawling with restless patterns. The *Alabama* was outlined against it with the harsh certainty of a cutout silhouette.

"They take some getting used to," Santchini said, "but they work."

"What am I seeing? Heat?"

"Yeah; hotter it is, the lighter it is. Easier to read than infrared. Hold your hand in front of you."

His hand was a ghostly shape outlined against the dark. Patterns crawled over the skin, white where the blood was close to the surface, darker at the edges where heat bled off into the cold air.

"Thanks. They'll help." Unless Jubei had a pair of his own.

"If I hear shooting, I'll come running."

"I'd appreciate it." Jake picked up the wire cutters and scrambled down the slope towards the fence. Working down low, he cut a hole close to the ground, wriggled through, and bent the strands back to cover the damage.

Cinders crunched underfoot. This was ground reclaimed from the bay, bulldozed and leveled. He looked over his shoulder and saw ghostly white footprints marking his trail. They faded as he watched, the ground absorbing the heat from his shoes.

Something bulked to his left. A P-51, snout aiming towards a phantom enemy. Beyond it, he could see the old C-47 where he'd taken Petey to play. The *Alabama* began to blot out the lightness of the sky. He moved towards the gangplank . . .

Something burst out of the ground in front of him, a clattering white shape, screeching and clawing.

Jake fell back on his haunches, the gun in his hand, and waited for his heart to stop pounding. The gull on which he had almost stepped flapped away into the dark, cawing irritably.

He waited for five minutes, motionless, but nothing stirred on the ship. He crept the last few yards, slipped the chain at the bottom of the wooden gangplank, and climbed into the iron blackness of the battleship.

At first, cold iron deadened the glasses. He saw only utter blackness.

But here and there heat scraped a mark on the darkness. Power cables strung along ceilings retained enough heat to leave a pencil-thin line. Wooden patterns on the floor were grids of pale gray over pits of darkness. He moved through a doorway into a larger room and nearly collided with a pale shimmering object as tall as a man. His fingers felt scraps of shiny cardboard. A postcard rack. He was in the main souvenir shop.

Jake tried to recall his few journeys on navy ships, mainly the rolling troop transports that had put his unit ashore at Inchon. It had been more comfortable, he remembered, above the waterline than below.

Jubei would want comfort. Jake slipped another rope and moved quietly up the wide staircase towards "officer country."

For ten minutes he navigated mostly by touch, groping along the bare metal corridors, but two decks higher the metal underfoot gave way to carpet, the walls to wood paneling. He walked in a world that was like a photographic negative; doors and walls were pale gray, metal fixtures, knobs, and locks dead black, like the ceiling above him.

He turned a corner, and stopped. Halfway down the new corridor, a blob of darkness marred the pale walls. A metal door, probably protecting some piece of equipment.

But this one was disfigured by an irregular blot of white in the center.

Heat from a junction box might warm metal in that way. So might Jubei, pressed against the metal, listening.

The gun butt felt greasy in his hand. He slipped the safety catch, felt for the door handle, and flipped it back. The door sprang open, and something rolled at his feet.

It was a grotesque parody of a human body, as featureless as something molded out of dough. Stubby legs, a lump of a head, a bloated torso.

Jake yanked off his glasses and risked a flash with his torch.

The man wore working clothes and a baseball cap. The round time clock locked to his wrist ticked and whirred in the silence. His neck was broken. Jubei must have surprised him on his rounds, killed him, and shoved the body into the cupboard. From the amount of heat still radiating from the thicker parts of the body, he could not have been dead too long.

Jake turned off the flashlight, slipped his night glasses on. Out of the confined closet, the man's body was losing heat more rapidly. The head was almost invisible now, a bump on his shoulders. He stepped over him and went on down to the next intersection.

All the doors on the next corridor were wood, pale oblongs against the darker walls. All but one, so sharply outlined that it might have been lit from above. Heat streamed through it.

He stood in the center of the corridor, listening. There was no sound from inside the room. He started forward . . .

The air seemed brighter—slightly hazy. Warmth from the room? It would hardly be enough to heat the whole corridor.

He looked up. The ceiling was becoming lighter as well. From the circular zones that he now recognized to be light fixtures a paleness spread across the roof.

If the fittings were becoming warmer . . .

He tore off the night glasses. He was standing in a brilliantly lit corridor.

Something hit him on the back of his neck.

He'd been half crouched when the blow hit him. That saved his life. He crashed against the door at the end of the corridor, rolled over, and groped for his gun.

His fingers refused to close over the butt. The shock to his spinal cord had left him rubber-legged, almost helpless.

Jubei grinned and came slowly towards him. He had to bend to avoid scraping the roof with his shaven head. He was bare-chested. His skin looked like dirty suede.

Jake leveled the pistol and tried to aim. His hand wavered and the muzzle drooped as he pulled the trigger. The bullet went low, whining off the metal wall.

He struggled to lift the gun higher. His muscles were like rubber. Jubei grinned. Two more long steps . . .

The second shot went high and wide. A light fixture down the corridor shattered.

The light fixtures. Always go for the eyes with Jubei.

Jake acted out of desperation. The light fixture was just a few feet over his head. He steadied the gun with both hands and put three shots into the center.

Glass showered down on his head. There was the glaring arc of a short circuit, and the lights in the corridor went out.

Scrabbling the night glasses back over his eyes, Jake

struggled to his feet. Jubei had stopped six feet away, momentarily blinded by the flash of the short circuit and confused by the dark. Jake saw him as a skeletal figure, wavering with heat, the death's-head face weaving as he listened for movement.

Three more bullets.

Jake raised the pistol, sighted down the barrel. The metal, hot from the last shots, was fuzzed. He couldn't see the sights. He pulled the trigger.

Jubei growled, took a step forward.

He fired again. Jubei rocked, grabbing his neck. A graze. Jake saw blood, white with heat, splash down his chest.

The last bullet. Jake pulled the trigger.

The pain in Jubei's neck made him flinch to the right. The bullet hit him just below the left eye.

His face seemed to disapapear as the shock drove blood from the tissues. Then it swam back out of the darkness, with a white blossom like a grotesque third eye on his cheek.

He swayed for a moment, mumbling, feeling across his face.

And came on.

Jake had no escape. The door behind him was locked. Once those enormous hands were on him . . . He reversed the gun and grasped the barrel, ready to hack at the injured face with the butt.

Something roared in the narrow corridor.

The whole of Jubei's body seemed to expand. For an instant, every finger was visible, every inch of the skin from navel to forehead almost blinding white, as if lit by an electronic flash.

His body crashed against Jake, pinning him to the door. When he didn't move, Jake rolled him away and stood up shakily. In the middle of Jubei's bare back, a hole pumped, glowing with blood.

What he had seen was the hydrostatic shock as the impact forced blood into Jubei's tissues.

Santchini shoved his .45 back into his belt.

"Howza boy?"

Jake tried to grin. Then he remembered why he was here.

As he pounded on the locked door, he could only

think of the tortured girl in New York, bloody, mutilated.

Santchini pushed him aside and blew the lock away. The door yawned. As Jake went inside, he was trembling.

The turnout for Tom Needham's *Andromeda* press preview was excellent. It lacked only the guest of honor.

"Where *is* he?"

Birdwell looked at his watch. Hannah Klein crossed off the last in the row of ten tiny strokes inked on her sketch pad and drew ten more.

One of the pressmen wandered over from the table where his colleagues were gathered around the breakfast buffet. "We going to get this show on the road soon? I've got a noon deadline if you want to catch the evening news."

"He'll be here, Hal. Don't worry about it. The snow . . . you know how it is."

"Yeah. Sure." But he looked unconvinced.

"Have some more coffee. Anything else you guys need? More muffins?"

"Food's fine. Some of those freeloaders won't need to eat for a week. But I'd like something to shoot."

He strolled back to the table. Birdwell looked at his watch. 11:08. Hannah crossed off another stroke.

"Start without him?" she suggested.

"Are you kidding? He'd have my balls. This thing is all for his benefit. Who the hell cares about his boat except him? Nobody else stages all this hoopla."

"Nobody else wants to be governor."

Bobby Seitz came in. Since being threatened with demotion to cable shifting, he had became the eagerest of them all. "No sign of him at the office. He's not at his house either."

Birdwell gnawed his lip and looked at his watch.

Seitz said, "They're going bananas downtown. Cops are stopping traffic. If we don't get on the road soon . . ."

"Maybe he's gone directly to the harbor," Birdwell said.

"It's a possibility."

Birdwell seized on this. "He wouldn't want to miss out on the media coverage or the ticker-tape parade. Even if he's not here." He had almost convinced himself.

Two more journalists came over. "Is this thing going to get started? The DA's got a press conference at one on this freak who's been cutting up the hookers. We'll have to leave in ten minutes."

"Mr. Needham'll be here any minute now."

"Sorry. We're packing up."

Birdwell made a decision. He took his place irresolutely behind the lectern. Hannah crossed off thirteen, fourteen, and fifteen while the journalists gathered below the dais.

"Ladies and gentlemen, I'm sorry Mr. Needham isn't here to greet you personally. I'm sure he's been held up by circumstances beyond his control. And I know that he would want me to say that he looks forward to talking to all of you in the days to come as this wonderful boat makes its triumphant way towards victory in the America's Cup."

He cleared his throat, still worried that Needham would step out from behind the dais and snatch the microphone from him.

"He would also want me to say, I know, that he represents only one part of a great team that has made this boat possible. Sam Lewis, the designer, Mr. Needham's colleagues in the *Andromeda* syndicate, the many commercial sponsors whose generosity has helped make the project possible: the Coca-Cola Company, Sony Electronics, Nabisco, Rolex . . ." He improvised freely, one eye on the doors, in case Needham should hurry in at the last minute. Finally, with the press people fidgeting and looking at their watches, he knew he couldn't maintain the facade any longer.

He reached resignedly for the red button. Cameras were raised.

"So now, ladies and gentlemen, I give you"—he swallowed and pushed the button—"*Andromeda*."

He heard the whirr of the motor as the cable wound up and the shroud lifted with a rustle.

"Jesus *Christ*!" someone said.

And the cameras started flashing. Looking around their faces, Birdwell saw astonishment, almost fright.

Cameramen were shouldering forward, ENG gear strapped to their shoulders. He saw pressmen struggling to get closer, jostling one another. Some even tried to climb onto the dais.

He hadn't expected this kind of reaction. He turned to look at the boat for the first time, and his jaw dropped.

Tom Needham, head canted at a horrible angle, tongue protruding, face bulging with blood, hung from the mast-top of *Andromeda*, the crisp white cord of a flag halyard cutting into the flesh of his neck.

CHAPTER THIRTY-THREE

Kim was sitting up in the hospital bed and reading when Jake came in. He kissed her above the dressing that covered her bruised right eye and sat on the edge of the bed.

"Did the doctor say anything about holding hands?" he asked.

She grabbed his hand and kissed the back of it. "I can feel it doing me good already." She guided it to her breasts, hard and erect under the shapeless hospital gown. "It would do me a lot more good in other places."

Jake removed it. "You're supposed to be sick."

"I'm okay. A few bruises, and the effects of whatever it was he shot into me to keep me quiet." She looked away. "He never . . . did . . . anything to me."

The tremor in her voice betrayed her calm. The real injuries were inside her head; they would take a lot longer to heal than bruises.

"You didn't tell me about Tom Needham," she said at last.

"What about Tom Needham?"

"Oh, Jake, they let me read the papers, you know. It's all there. They don't mention your name, but it's obvious you found out where I was from him. Why else would he kill himself?"

"I didn't want to worry you."

"What is there to worry about now? You've solved the mystery! You know who killed Elaine and the Keble guy and Tony Stephens." She threw her arms around his neck. "Come on. It's New Year's! Cheer up."

Hearing raised voices, the nurse came in. "Visiting hours are over," she said pointedly. Jake kissed Kim again and left.

As he walked towards the parking lot, he thought about what she'd said. "You solved the mystery. . . . You know who killed Elaine and Keble and Stephens."

He did know, it was true. But there were still a lot

more loose ends to be tied up before the whole tangle of Elaine's life was really unraveled.

And that was far from the only thing on Jake's mind.

On the last day of the year, he had called together the crew and the yard staff and explained the situation.

"We're broke."

The few who had known what *Calinda* was costing to refit and rebuild nodded; this was nothing new to them. For weeks, creditors had been more and more pointed with their demands. A few had even refused to supply more materials.

"How about the yard?" Carl Bangsund asked.

"Mortgaged. I'm not sure we can even meet the payroll for more than another month."

Bangsund said, "Well, Mr. Forrester, I thought maybe this would be a problem, so I had a word with the boys and girls. They can get by through January and February without salary, if that's any help."

Jake felt a thickening in his chest. He coughed. "That's . . . very kind of them, Carl. I hope it won't come to that." He looked around the group. "Thanks—all of you. I . . . well, I appreciate it."

"What about sponsorship?" Burt Grale asked. "Seems like we should be getting some nibbles, even if the biggies won't touch us."

Sam said, "I had an offer from a hot dog store downtown. Two hundred bucks if we wear jackets with Archie's Chili-Dog Heaven on 'em."

In the laughter Phil Weselowski said, "Take it. And see if they'll throw in all the dogs we can eat."

Jake let them laugh. That they could showed the spirit was still there. They had done miracles in the months since he had brought *Calinda* back from Colombia. She was fit for sea now, all her basic equipment installed, her sails fitted, her rigging strung.

But that was only the first part of an America's Cup challenge. Some of the most expensive gear—the electronics, for instance—still remained to be bought. And, though more than eighteen months separated them from the next Cup tie, those eighteen months were the most crucial and the most expensive.

Soon, all the boatyard space in Newport would be booked up. So would most of the technicians *Calinda* needed for the long period of refining and perfecting that led up to the eliminations. In that process, a great deal of what had already been done to *Calinda* might have to be redone. Sails revealed their deficiencies only after long grueling weeks of test sailing. The balance of a boat could add or subtract half a knot from her speed; during the next year, Jake would sail *Calinda* up and down the coast off Rhode Island, trailed by three powerboat tenders on which video cameras made second-by-second records of her trim. Viewed and analyzed, those tapes would give him the information he needed to make the minute adjustments in weight distribution that gave one boat a winning edge over another. On top of these, the crew had to be fed, clothed, transported, as did *Calinda* —just to ship her from Mobile to Newport would cost thousands of dollars.

In a traditional challenge, these expenses were taken care of by the syndicate backing the boat—rich men with money to spare for the kudos of being associated with a potential prizewinner. They supplemented this with contributions from commercial companies who shared that ambition; everything from sails to breakfast food came courtesy of eager sponsors.

No sponsors had approached Jake. None, he knew, would. *Calinda*, the maverick boat with its unstable captain, could do more damage than good to a corporate image.

At the meeting Jake had told them the hard facts and left it up to them.

"What exactly are you saying, Jake?" Sam asked. "Are you asking us if we want to quit?"

"I guess that about sums it up."

A murmur of disbelief ran around the room. Sam said, "Maybe I'm speaking out of turn, but as far as I'm concerned, we quit when the courts move in and start sticking labels on the furniture." He looked at the others. "Any dissenters?"

Nobody raised a hand. Jake nodded and stood up. "Well, I guess we know where we stand. Thanks, everyone."

He appreciated the vote of confidence. But the problems remained. He had just been asked to postpone facing them.

He was letting the endless strings of figures weave them-selves into a web inside his head when he turned into the street in front of the house and saw the cars drawn up along the curb.

Two men in tweed overcoats stood talking on the porch. As Jake parked, doors slammed up and down the street as others left the warmth of their Jaguars and Mercedeses.

A tall man with iron-gray hair held out his hand. "Hello, Jake."

Jake shook it. "Aaron."

"Hope you don't mind us dropping in on you like this. We'd have approached you at Tom Needham's funeral but. . . ."

Jake looked around the group. "Can I offer you gen-tlemen a drink?"

Aaron Hart said, "Your mother's already been more than generous in that regard. We really came down to talk."

"What about, I wonder?" He looked from face to face. Aaron Hart, chairman of the NYYC Race Committee, Gerry Cornelius, commodore. Archie Crooks . . . "I thought you were in the *Andromeda* syndicate, Archie."

Crooks frowned and looked away.

Jake continued around the group. Steve Kahelli, Mark Samuelson . . . he stopped. "I don't think I know this gentleman."

He might have been seventy, but Jake decided he was older still. He stood straight, but with a slight indication of effort, as if he leaned into a high wind.

"That's a deficiency I'm glad to remedy, Mr. Forrester. I'm John Ollinger."

Jake took the thin hand carefully. It was worth a bil-lion dollars. "It's an honor, Mr. Ollinger. You've always been just a name on the club letterhead. I'm happy to know you really exist."

Ollinger smiled thinly. "It's a near thing. This trip may tip the scales. But I wanted to make it just the same."

"I hope it hasn't been wasted."

"We'll see about that. I don't know about the rest of these gentlemen, but what I want to see is this damned boat of yours."

"You don't *mind* if we look, do you?" Crooks asked sarcastically.

Jake fished for his keys. "Follow my car. It's not far."

The Weselowskis rolled back the big double doors. *Calinda* was a long silent gleam in the dark of the workshop. Jake waved his arm, and Carl started the cable winch. She rolled out into the winter afternoon sun, steely and silent on her cradle.

He heard their intake of breath.

"Oh you sweetheart," Kahelli said reverently.

She was seventy feet of gleaming polished aluminum, buffed to a mirror so that the shapes of the men, elongated and distorted, were etched as sharp as photographs on the sweet curve of hull into keel, keel into fin.

Of the damaged plates, the thick paint, the heavy wooden deckhouse, no sign remained. Everything that might slow her had been ruthlessly discarded.

The rolled sails on her deck were the plastic white of a toothpaste tube. At the last minute, on Sam's urgent recommendation, Jake invested in continuous-film sails. The $150,000 for a full suit of sails had emptied his bank account and exhausted the last of his credit. But in the first trials with her new sails, *Calinda*'s response had been phenomenal.

Hart and Crooks had already hauled themselves on board.

Ollinger said, "Very pretty. But can she sail?"

"More to the point," Cornelius said, "can she win?"

"She can win," Jake said.

"You haven't seen that black bastard."

"I've seen her. *Calinda* can win."

Ollinger screwed up his eyes. "Or do you mean *Sasori* can lose?"

"That, too. But she can win."

Crooks looked down from the deck. "Talk's cheap, Forrester."

Jake looked at the sky, judging the wind. A nice offshore breeze. "Only one way I can think of to convince you. We could take her for a run, if we had a crew."

Kahelli climbed up onto the deck with the others.

"Hell, I can handle a sail. Get out your tender, Forrester."

An hour later, as *Calinda* heeled in the stiff twelve-knot breeze, Jake looked down the length of the boat at the miscellaneous crew scattered around the deck.

Hart and Cornelius sat with their feet on either side of the columns that held the twin six-speed Lewmar winches. Kahelli and two others made up a scratch fore-deck crew. Over their head, the eighty-foot mainsail thrummed in the racing wind.

Jake glanced at Ollinger, who stood beside him in the cockpit, studying the wind, water speed, temperature, and barometric pressure dials on the auxiliary computer display, a duplicate of that in the tiny cockpit aft of them in which the race electronics man would sit on a normal trial. So far, they were just dials, unconnected.

"Any time you like, commodore."

Ollinger smiled. In his borrowed sweater and life jacket, he looked like a child. "Mr. Forrester, it's your boat."

Jake turned the big wheel experimentally through an eighth of its circle, feeling for the groove.

Every boat has a fractional angle to the wind and the sea that is perfect for the day and the conditions. A computer can advise the helmsman about wind speed and temperature, the strategist can suggest how one sail might function better than another, but in the end it's the feel of the wind on the helmsman's cheek, the look of the foam creaming past the dipping hull, the flatness of the sail overhead that tells him what to do. At the helm he is deaf and blind, creating the race from instant to instant.

An eighth was too much. Jake felt back along the arc, waiting for that fractional change in feel that marked the right, the exact point of balance.

Then something happened to *Calinda*.

As a plane is, at one moment, lumbering, fat and loaded, along the runway, and the next magically air-borne, so *Calinda* changed in a second from a dead weight dragged by wind through the water into a gliding swan.

Flowing into the slot between the two sails, air mole-cules turned from a random milling mass into a seamless current that sucked vacuums in the bellying hollows of the fabric.

In the deck well, flat on the bow, hunched over the wheel in the cockpit, every man sensed the instant and felt a thrill that surged along every nerve.

Calinda turned her bow to the open sea and flew.

Much later, something pricked Jake's concentration.

He sorted through his senses, isolated hearing, identified the sound, straightened up, and looked around for its source.

John Ollinger smiled in embarrassment and held up a small bottle of white pills. The metal cap rolled around underfoot.

"Sorry. I have to take these every two hours. Doctor's orders."

Jake was suddenly aware that his back hurt. Every muscle felt like wood. His feet ached. One cheek felt seared. He could drink a quart of water. And he needed very badly to take a leak.

"How long have we been going?"

Ollinger looked at his watch. "Best part of an hour?"

The other men were still much where he last remembered seeing them, but they were looking at him now. There was something in their eyes—something that had not been there when they set sail.

Respect. Even awe.

"Quite a boat," Cornelius said.

Jake stood back from the wheel and looked at Ollinger. "Like to take a turn, sir?"

Ollinger licked his lips. "Mr. Forrester, it would be an honor."

Jake went below and relieved himself in the bucket. Tucked behind a rib, he noticed a six-pack of Coors beer, left over from the last days of the overhaul. He cracked one can, took the rest on deck, and handed them around. To the sound of fizzing beer cans, and with the commodore of the NYYC at the helm, looking as delighted as a small boy steering the family car on his father's knee, *Calinda* headed home while the men on deck talked millions.

CHAPTER THIRTY-FOUR

Twenty months later Jake walked the streets of Newport at three in the morning and tried not to throw up. A few people were still around. None of them recognized the hunched shape in the dark blue windbreaker—or, if they did, refused to believe that the captain of the America's Cup defender could spend the night before the first race wandering sleeplessly around town.

Jake could have told them differently. He remembered Ted Turner barfing repeatedly on the dock before a race. Other skippers had an overwhelming urge to empty their bowels that lasted until the starting gun cracked.

Jake hungered for that moment. The hours by which he was separated from it stretched endlessly.

Half a dozen late celebrators reeled up the lane that led to Newport Offshore, where the French boat berthed. The French could afford to celebrate. *Sasori* had knocked out *Hirondelle* in the second series of match races. Out in the wide bay, Jake could see the masts of *Shenandoah*, Baron Bich's schooner, from which those party guests still sober would watch tomorrow's race after a lavish lunch in its wood-paneled saloon. The rich liked to enjoy their racing in comfort.

Money.

It all came down to money in the end. Aaron Hart had been blunt when they discussed it.

"Jake, you don't have a prayer without our help. Tom Needham's suicide frightened off a lot of sponsors. You can swing some of them over to *Calinda*, with our help. Otherwise, just drop out right now. You don't have the backing to handle a challenge single-handed."

"What's your interest in all this?"

"We need a hero. Tom's death did the sport a lot of harm. You're unblemished. Good credentials. Good boat. Okay, you punched out Billy Weems. We can fix that—set up a photo call with both of you. Big handshake; old pals; tremendous strain of wife's death. They'll buy it. Frankly, I don't much care if you can beat the Japs or not. An honorable defense where the best boat wins . . . well, it's better than nothing. Are you in or out?"

Jake didn't have to think about it. "In."

Hart kept his part of the bargain. The money rolled in. Five thousand dollars to use Budweiser, ten thousand to use Rice Krispies, twenty-five thousand from Reynolds Aluminum, advances for TV and film rights, for the book a journalist was all set to write about the defense. Free Swiss chronometers, free Japanese cameras, free wine, free food, free clothes. His windbreaker with *Calinda* and her sail number sewn on, his handmade deck shoes and hand-cut slacks all came from sponsors. He was co-cooned in wealth.

Money gave them the luxury of time. Sam worked on tactics until Jake, to Kim's distress, mumbled routines in his sleep. Burt Grale had turned into a superb sailing master, and Carraway had welded the randomly accumulated crew into a smooth team. After a spectacularly sailed elimination race against the last challenger, *Freedom*, in which Sam ordered a tack three minutes from the finish line and cut across her bow ten seconds ahead, Jake allowed himself the luxury of thinking they could win.

Then they watched *Sasori* at work in the first races to decide on a challenger.

She was racing Bengt Holm-Jensen's *Stockholm*. *Calinda*'s tender passed the Swedes on the way out to the course. They waved and made beer-drinking gestures, the promise of the usual postrace party.

Sasori was already waiting at the starting line. As *Stockholm* was towed abreast of her, their cheerfulness drained away. After one long look at the silent black hull, the bare mast, Holm-Jensen's crew moved to their places, efficient and unspeaking.

There was no prerace maneuvering, no fencing for position. *Stockholm* set her sails and cruised in a slow circle as the ten-minute and then the five-minute gun cracked from the committee boat.

Sasori remained motionless. Even when the starting

gun was fired and the race flag raised, she lay as still as if anchored.

Stockholm crossed the line and set off down the first leg of the course, a puzzled afterguard staring over its shoulder.

She was a hundred yards down the course when *Sasori* began to move.

There was no signal, no sign of movement on her deck. One moment, the black boat was still, a light swell breaking against the oily darkness of her hull. The next, her silky sails were sliding up the rigging, her bow was turning towards the line as she picked up speed.

Jake could think only of a shark. The knifelike blade of her hull cleaved the water so cleanly that no speck of white foam marred the cold impersonality of her lines.

She glided by *Calinda*'s tender, no more than twenty feet away. For an instant, Jake looked into her cockpit. Takeo Fujita stood at the wheel. He wore the same green windbreaker and black trousers as the rest of the crew, but there was power in every line of him. For an instant, he turned and met Jake's eye, and Jake knew what this display meant. Watch. This is what we will do to you.

Sasori caught up to *Stockholm* within a mile. After three miles she was two boat lengths ahead. She won by a humiliating twenty-seven minutes, leaving the Swedish boat to limp home with a crew exhausted by a race in which Holm-Jensen had tried every trick he knew. Not one had reduced by a yard the effortlessly lengthening gap between the two boats.

Each race repeated the formula. *Sasori* sailed like a machine. Fujita exploited every error, capitalized on every deficiency of strategy and skill. She never lost a race.

Jake realized he had been walking faster as he reviewed the races of the last few weeks. He was beyond Thames Street now, out in the empty, modern spaces of the new town. He cut across the landscaped traffic island in front of the post office and walked to the little park edging the bay.

Opposite, he could see some of the mansions of Jamestown, silent and solemn in the early morning. A few still showed lights; people getting up to make an early start out to the race. By dawn traffic on the bay would be worse than the New Jersey Turnpike on Fourth of July.

But now, for a few minutes, the whole town was still, with the hush that falls on an audience as they sense that the play is about to begin. Even the breeze seemed to fall.

Jake sniffed. There was something odd about the air. The hair on the back of his neck prickled.

He looked quickly over his shoulder. Nothing moved. He was alone in the empty, motionless town.

He told himself it was ridiculous and, shoving his hands into his windbreaker pockets, turned to leave the park when, away beyond the line of houses across the bay, a light flared, outlining the crenellations of the big houses briefly against a curtain of purple clouds.

Jake waited, listening for the answering crack of thunder. It didn't come. Heat lightning? There should still be thunder. He stood for another minute, watching the sky.

But his passive nervousness was disturbed now. It had a focus. He walked back up Thames and turned down the lane that led to Deepwater, and *Calinda*.

Under the light at the gate, he pushed the bell. The guard relaxed when he saw who was ringing.

"How's it going?"

"Pretty quiet, Mr. Forrester. The lady's still down there."

Jake froze. "Lady?"

"Yeah. Miss Ryker. Came down an hour or so back. That was okay, wasn't it?"

"What? Oh, sure."

He walked towards the waterside. Between the gate and the dock, two more guards challenged him. Another sat on the end of the dock, sweeping the water occasionally with a torch to check for scuba divers.

He climbed the gantry that held *Calinda* out of the water and looked down into the cockpit.

"Hi."

Kim stirred sleepily under the blanket she had wrapped around herself. "I wondered how long it'd take you to get here."

"When did you know I was gone?"

"About ten seconds after you thought of it."

"Why didn't you tell me you were awake?"

"You're pretty dumb for a man old enough to be my father."

He jumped down into the cockpit. She lifted the blanket. He slipped into the warmth under it.

"Ever made out in the cockpit of a twelve?" she asked.

"Is it anything like the back seat of a '54 Ford?"

She felt around with her feet. "Harder."

"Then I don't think I'd like it."

Her small hand stole under his sweater and stroked his chest. "Let me persuade you."

After an hour the eastern sky paled. There was a bustle in the yard, shouts, and the chime of rigging against masts. It was race day.

"Jesus, listen to them howl!"

Sam Lewis leaned his head back over the edge of the cockpit and drank in the bedlam of sirens, shouts, whistles, and cheers as the tender drew *Calinda* out of her berth and headed down the bay towards the open sea.

Every rowboat, speedboat, cabin cruiser, ketch, yawl, sloop, and dinghy seemed to be out. Coast Guard cutters raced back and forth, blue lights flashing, sirens howling, as they bullied the boats back from the hundred-yard lane down which *Calinda* was towed. Occasionally, some speedboat, cheekier than the rest, darted through the cordon, zoomed past the twelve, and its crew, already glowing with sun and booze, yelled their good wishes before the cutters herded them back into place.

Jake got tired of waving. He settled down in the cockpit and looked around at the sky. There was a faint copper tinge in the blue, and a smeary yellow horizon.

"How's the weather feel to you?"

Sam sniffed. "I wondered about that. Bit heavy." He checked the readout from the weather computer. "Wind six knots from the southeast."

"More like seven," Grale said. Almost as if it had heard him, the gauge climbed to seven and hovered there.

"I saw lightning last night."

"So?" Sam said.

"No storm came inland. Might be something hovering out there."

"Nothing on the satellite picture." Someone had driven down from the newspaper office at dawn with the overnight satellite picture. It was hazy but clear enough. No heavy fronts. No incipient swirls of cloud out over the Atlantic that might signal squalls or a storm.

But Jake distrusted satellite pictures. The germ of a storm might hover between air masses, expanding and contracting as they moved, ready to create a tiny whirlwind or a freak shower of hail. He'd seen waterspouts rise out of calm seas, a draft of hot air drawing first vapor, then thousands of gallons of the ocean itself into the air until a tower of green water, solid as a twenty-story building, swayed at them across the sea like a drunken giant.

"I guess I'm just nervous."

Kim ran down the deck and dropped into the cockpit. "Carraway says what genoa?"

"Six ounce?" Jake asked. Sam noddded. She scampered forward again. She was enjoying herself. Ten years ago, a woman crewmember on a racing yacht would have been unthinkable; this year, there were a dozen of them.

It took almost an hour to reach the committee boat. Two miles back from the start line, the Coast Guard cutters smoothly divided the spectator fleet. Boats flying the Privilege flag followed *Calinda* to the starting point. The rest were shunted two miles back, where they would see almost nothing.

One audacious speedboat left the crowd and circled slipping under the bow with only a few yards to spare. Jake glanced down at the girl holding the tiller and waved. Her face was turned away, almost as if she didn't want to be seen. Odd . . .

Then his mind cleared as they came up to *Sasori*.

It was like a replay of the *Stockholm* race—of every race in which *Sasori* had competed. The silent boat. The bare mast.

Grale watched it over the narrowing gap of water.

"Bastard gives me the creeps."

Sam said, "Don't fall for it like the others, pal. That's what they're waiting for."

For weeks, the team had discussed *Sasori*'s strategy. It

was Pete Carraway who finally isolated its particular power.

"You ever seen a good karate bout? Olympic level?"

"No," Jake said truthfully.

"Yeah. Well, you never will. They just don't last long enough. Unless you use slow-motion film, the whole thing goes by so fast the mind can't analyze it. The real interesting stuff takes place before, and that can't be filmed. That long silent time when the two just stare at one another. *That*'s when the work's done. Fujita knows there's nothing like silence to psych out another boat."

"So he psychs us out," Phil Weselowski said. "Not much we can do about it except take it."

"I don't know," Jake said. "Maybe we can do a little psyching ourselves."

Now they had five or six race plans, as carefully worked out as chess openings.

Jake watched *Sasori* and looked around at the weather. "Number two?"

"Sounds good to me," Sam said.

Jake looked forward and held up one finger on each hand. Carraway nodded.

The ten-minute gun cracked from the committee boat. Jake picked up the radiophone whose tuner was locked on the judging committee's frequency. It would be used during the race only in emergencies—to call off the race if weather conditions deteriorated or there was a serious accident.

Aaron Hart answered. "Checking radiophone," Jake said.

"Sounds fine, Jake. No problems?"

"Are you sure about the weather, Aaron?" He stared towards the horizon, where the distinction was becoming less sharp. He might have been looking at solid land out there.

"Nothing that should worry you, *Calinda*. A minor low is showing up on our radar. Very local situation."

"Couldn't be anything worse? A squall maybe?"

"Not in our judgment."

"Okay." Jake hung up. There would be no more time to worry about the weather. He waited for the five-minute gun. That would be the signal for *Calinda* to begin her race. It roared before he expected it.

"Here we go," Sam said, as the crew, working to the race plan memorized weeks ago, surged into action. *Calinda* turned her back on the starting line and headed back the way she had come with every sail set.

Jake could almost hear the yells of surprise from the committee boat. Looking back, he saw the rail crowded with watchers, some with binoculars trained on him. He ignored them.

They swept past the Privilege fleet, leaving behind astonished faces. Someone trying to lean out too far from a big cabin cruiser to see what was happening fell in with a splash.

"Watch that clock," Jake said to Burt Grale.

"Two minutes ten. Tack in one fifty."

They were beyond the Privilege fleet now. A mile ahead bobbed the main spectator crowd, a yellow haze gathering over them from the idling engines of the motorboats. Helicopters circled above, and a light plane dived towards *Calinda*, a cameraman hanging out of the window to film them as she went overhead.

"If one of those helicopters comes anywhere near us," Jake said, "give him a flare."

Grale nodded, not looking up from his watch. The downdraft from a helicopter could rob a boat of wind and leave it wallowing helplessly. But *Calinda*'s unexpected maneuver had confused the cameramen as much as everyone else. None came near her.

"Ten seconds to tack," Grale said. "And counting."

They had sailed half a mile with the wind at their backs. *Calinda* moved easily, but running before the wind was not her best point. She achieved her highest speed while reaching at an angle to the wind, the air streaming through the slot between her sails with a force that drew her forward as the vacuum around a wing pulls a plane into the air.

"Anything from *Sasori*?"

Phil Weselowski in the computer cabin behind the cockpit said, "Hasn't stirred."

". . . three . . . two . . . one," Grale chanted.

Jake took a deep breath. "Tack."

He threw the rudder over as the big Lewmars whirred, shifting the sails into the new angle that would bring her around through the wind. Jake felt the rudder and trim tab bite at the exact instant the sails came over, and she spun like a ballerina.

Calinda leaped back towards the starting line.

"Too fast," Sam hissed.

"No."

Exact timing was crucial. If she crossed the line before the starting gun, she was disqualified. If she waited too long, *Sasori* would take a lead they might never make up. But Jake could feel the boat under him; some days she glided across the water. On others, he sensed a resistance. It was there today. A vital factor in his timing.

They seemed to hurtle towards the gap between the committee boat and the block of Privilege boats. He could already make out people at the rail of the *Shenandoah*, lured up from the saloon by *Calinda*'s inexplicable behavior.

"Forty-five seconds to start," Grale said.

The committee boat was closer still. He was cutting this very very fine. *Sasori* still hadn't moved. . . .

But as his mind registered this, he was astonished to see her mainsail creep up the mast and her silhouette lengthen as the wind brought her round at a slight angle to the starting line.

Sasori was changing her tactics.

"Oh, *great!*" Grale groaned. "She's under way."

Sam left the second wheel and sprawled along the edge of the deck, the water racing only a few inches from his shoulder, to see better.

"How the hell can she be that close to the line? She'll be over before the start. Fujita isn't that crazy."

Jake watched the boat glide at an angle almost parallel to the starting line, like a panther prowling the limits of its cage. The gap between *Sasori*'s bow and the committee boat narrowed to a hundred yards. The gap through which *Calinda* must pass to cross the line.

"He's trying to cut us off," Grale said. "He's playing chicken with us."

"How long?" Jake asked.

Grale looked at the watch. "Ten seconds."

Sasori turned now and headed for the line. The high stern of the Japanese boat was almost dead in front of them. Jake could slide to the left of it, but that put him at an impossible angle to begin the race, heading across the

wind and forcing him to waste precious minutes tacking
to bring him back parallel to the other boat.

But if he slid to the right, he would be running side by
side with *Sasori*, with the committee boat dead ahead. At
best, a brush with *Sasori* and disqualification. At worst, a
three-boat pileup and the end of the entire series.

Jake had a second or two in which to make up his
mind. And as he balanced the two possibilities, the wind
dropped. Just a fraction, but he had sailed on the Sound
often enough to know what that slight lull meant.

Wind moves in cells—areas of disturbed air that push
one another along like railcars, with fractional breaks between them. A cell had just passed over *Calinda*, and for
a second the air was dead calm. Soon it would reach
Sasori. . . .

Jake knew what would happen then.

Sasori was fast, but speed meant vulnerability. Like a
flyweight boxer in lead boots, she could be easily
toppled.

Calinda's bow inched up level with *Sasori*'s stern and
started to overtake. Then the dead spot in the wind hit
Sasori.

Her mast straightened perceptibly towards the vertical
as the wind disappeared. The helmsman swung the wheel
a few points, looking for the new groove—and the wind
returned.

Sasori heeled over. For a few precious seconds the
boat fell away from the critical path. Waves broke over
her bow, deadening her speed, killing the streamlining
effect of her hull.

Calinda slipped past her bow ten feet ahead and fled
upwind, over the line at almost the same instant as the
starting gun roared.

Behind them streamed the long pennant of spoiled air
that would interfere with *Sasori*'s sails, impair their efficiency, and make the stern chase ten times harder. The
first boat over the line in the America's Cup almost in-
variably won.

Sam pounded on the edge of the cockpit in delight.
"We screwed them!"

They were fifty yards ahead and moving away. *Sasori*
settled down just short of the dirty air from *Calinda*'s

wake, waiting for the first turn, when a tack might allow them to cut across *Calinda*'s bow and shorten her lead.

Jake bent over the wheel, trying to clear his mind for the job of sailing the boat. But two images insistently returned—the black shape hovering over his shoulder and the dark line of weather that loomed ahead.

CHAPTER THIRTY-FIVE

Out over the ocean, the cell of turbulent air whose clouds had boiled twelve hours earlier with the fury of a sudden heat-storm roiled and tumbled, caught between the high inversion layer of cooler, fast-moving winds and the flat sea. As the sun warmed the water, warm wet air began to rise, the fat balloons of vapor pushing up through the invisible membrane that separated the layers of air.

A chisel of cold air probed downward, hit the hard upper surface of the storm and ricocheted away, but not before giving the squall the motion it desperately needed to break from its prison. Powered by the blast of cold air, it rolled forward from between the imprisoning fronts and gathered momentum.

"Turn coming up."

Jake lifted his head from the instruments and watched the orange buoy sliding towards them. They had covered the first four-and-a-half-mile leg of the course in less than thirty minutes. A good time.

Over their shoulder, *Sasori* hung in the same station, six lengths behind, bucking against a sea noticeably heavier that when they crossed the line.

"Blowing up a bit," he said to Sam, who had taken the second wheel while Jake made his calculations.

"Yeah. Wave pattern's a bit different too."

Jake had noticed that as well. Every fifth or sixth wave was a cross-swell that shuddered through the boat. They had taken a lot of water across the deck. Most of the crew were soaked.

They rounded the buoy cleanly, and for the next three minutes Jake's mind was occupied with the intricacies of plotting a track with the wind forty-five degrees on their starboard quarter. When he had time to look at the gauge again, the wind was up to eighteen knots.

The smear on the horizon was nearer now and changing color. It was darker, almost blue-black, like a bruise.

"Burt, let me have the readouts."

Grale tore off the strips of paper. Jake tried to turn the numbers into a picture of the weather that surrounded them. He failed. It was like nothing he had ever experienced in these waters. Except perhaps once.

"Sam, were you up here in 1970?"

"*Gretel II* and *Intrepid*? Hell, yeah. So were you. Don't you remember, we decided to help out Bill Ficker by getting the Aussies drunk?" Sam, Jake and the crew got crocked every night for a week; the Australians were ten times worse. Only after *Gretel II* nearly took the cup did Jake and Sam realize the Australians had been sending down the relief crew to drink with them while the first team went to bed at ten.

"Remember anything about the races? The first one, for instance."

"I remember there was a bit of wind."

A bit of wind. Jake had been out with the spectators. An eight-knot breeze blew up into a twenty-four knot gale almost before anyone knew it was happening. In gusts between twenty-five and thirty knots, the Australian boat battled itself into a near wreck. Waves washing over the deck sluiced lubricant out of *Gretel*'s winches, and the foredeck boss slipped on the greasy surface. They lost two minutes fishing him out of the rising seas.

Since then, the rules had been changed. If the wind rose over thirty knots, the committee automatically called off the race.

"I don't like this." He looked around. Sam Lewis was still in his place, hands resting on the second wheel, as if hypnotized by their speed. The boat shuddered in a heavy swell.

"Sam, you're pushing her too much."

"She'll be okay."

"Not in these conditions."

"You brought her through a goddam hurricane, didn't you? You think she's going to sink in half a gale?"

"It's more than half a gale." He could see the storm clearly now, the low black cloud base, the trailing veils of rain that whipped the ocean to froth. It was less than a mile away.

"I'll take her." Sam reluctantly stepped back from the wheel.

Sasori was using the high winds well. They had closed the gap between the boats to less than a hundred yards. The crew was permanently at the winches, increasing and decreasing tension on the sails minute by minute. It was exhausting work, but it paid off. Jake could see the gap narrowing inch by inch.

They were coming up to the second turn. *Sasori* would slip through the gap between *Calinda* and the buoy if Jake let her. He trimmed the rudder, aiming for the orange marker that was invisible for seconds on end as the waves buried it in green water. He had a fleeting memory of the moment three years ago when rounding a similar marker had been the signal for murder. A premonition of more danger nagged at him now.

The wind pouring over his shoulder was a gale by now. Jake hung onto the wheel and bent his head to avoid being thrust sideways by its force. He looked up and saw the mast flex as it took the full weight of the pouring wind. The anemometer at the masthead was spinning too fast for its cups to be visible. Jake looked at the gauge: twenty-eight knots. As he watched, the needle crept to twenty-nine.

"This is getting dangerous," Grale said. *Calinda* was leaping out of the water now, sliding down the slope of the long swells and hitting the next wave with a thump that shuddered through the hull.

Sam Lewis grinned, clinging to the second wheel. "Jesus, what a boat. Listen to her go!"

Jake and Grale exchanged a glance.

Almost as if to coincide with their alarm, the radio beeped. Grale lifted the hand-set. Only one person could be on the other end during a race—the marshal in charge of the course.

He listened. "Okay. Acknowledged."

"Calling it off?" Jake asked.

"Wind hit thirty-two knots down there. They're running for home."

With a sense of anticlimax, Jake looked over his shoulder at *Sasori*. It had made up its loss at the buoy and hung just clear of *Calinda*'s wind shadow. The heavy weather shook her far more than the American boat; as he watched, a wave almost buried the prow in foam. But, though she must have received the marshal's message when *Calinda* did, she showed no signs of slowing.

"Better get the sails off her," Jake said to Sam. "Should we take a reef or set a heavier main?"

All through the exchange Sam had remained standing by the other wheel, eyes fixed on the taut mainsail. Now he turned and glared at them. His expression was obsessed.

"You're going to pull out?"

"Race's off, pal. We'll get them another day."

"We've got 'em now, goddammit! We'll beat 'em by a mile."

"Sam, it's off."

"The hell it's off." He groped inside his windbreaker, and when his hand came out, it held the .380 automatic Jake had seen before.

"Come on, Sam, we can't do anything now. There isn't any race. Put that away."

He took one step towards Lewis. Without sighting, Sam put a shot six inches from his ear.

"You know I can do better than that, Jake. Back off."

"Sam, what's the point? The race's canceled."

"And we just walk away from those bastards, right? Like we did in Korea and 'Nam. Let them keep the marbles. Not this time. Where are they?"

Grale looked over the stern. "Two lengths behind."

"Are they pulling out?"

"Should I ask them?" Grale said acidly.

Jake picked up his binoculars and focused on *Sasori*'s deck. The crew remained at their places, clinging to the deck as she plunged through the waves. Fujita was almost hidden in the cockpit, but his shape was unmistakable behind the big wheel.

"They're still after us," he said.

"You bet they are. They don't quit. Not those mothers. We'll quit when they do."

"Sam, the boat won't take it."

"Let's see if you're right. Don't shorten sail. And when we go around onto the third leg, put up the kite."

"You're crazy," Grale said "A spinnaker would take the mast right out of her."

The buoy was racing towards them. The next turn would bring them back to the last side of the triangle, sending the boat down a long reach with the wind on the port quarter that would end at the committee boat. There might be time to distract Sam, to get the gun away from him.

But they would also be running before the main fury of the squall.

Kim came scrambling down the deck, bent double against the wind. "We can't . . ." She stopped as she saw the gun in Sam's hand.

"Get down here."

As she slid into the cockpit, he reached out, grabbed her sleeve, and dragged her close to him, pressing the gun against her head.

"Now put her around the marker. And get the spinnaker up."

For a second as they turned, Jake thought the mast must snap. It actually groaned, and the metal bowed visibly. The sails had become too tight even to vibrate. They hovered on the interface between super efficiency and total collapse.

Sasori rounded only a second or two behind. They were almost level at the start of the third leg.

"Spinnaker," Sam said. He pushed the pistol against Kim's head. "I'll blow it off. So help me God I will."

Grale and Jake exchanged a glance, then looked over the stern at the squall.

There was something frighteningly effortless about its progress towards them. It drifted, shadowing the sea beneath, thrashing the surface into froth. Gray veils of rain wavered and swung like tendrils in the downdrafts from the cloud. They could imagine the wind force in there.

Jake could see Grale measuring the distance between himself and Sam. He shook his head.

"Okay, Sam. You win. Better go tell them, Burt."

Grale crept forward, sliding on his belly part of the way to avoid being blown overboard. Jake could see the looks of incredulity on the crew's faces as they heard the order to raise the spinnaker, but a few seconds later three men were struggling to haul the big sail out of its cover and link it to the rigging and spinnaker pole.

The freshening wind had cleared the sky. Far ahead,

Jake saw the blur of the spectator fleet. This breeze would be putting a panic into all those Sunday sailors. And when the squall hit them . . .

"Sam, let Kim loose."

"She's fine right here."

"I want her to call the committee boat. They ought to be clearing out the spectators."

"Fuck them. That spinnaker up yet?"

Jake looked forward. As he watched, the blue balloon of the spinnaker bulged out over the prow of the boat. Almost instantly, *Calinda* surged. He looked at the speed indicator in blank astonishment as it wavered up to twenty knots.

Sasori must have seen their preparations, because a second later her own spinnaker went up, black and gleaming. The Japanese boat bore down on them, and at the same moment the first fringe of the squall caught up with both boats.

The air became dark and cold. Jake smelled ozone, salt. There was a sense of electricity in the air. He saw the crew staring at the masthead. Blue sparks played over the rigging, and a fat bulb of ball lightning like a glowing blue basketball hovered around the forestay for a second before fizzing out of existence against the sail.

Sasori was like part of the storm. He caught one glimpse of her long black hull, dragged half out of the water by the power of its sails. A crewman struggled towards the forepeak, flat against the deck to avoid the worst of the water exploding over her bow. He carried something long and gleaming.

Jake recognized the long curved blade of polished and folded steel. The crewman lashed it so that the blade jutted out like a bowsprit, razor sharp—a gesture of defiance.

Grale crawled back into the cockpit.

Sam grinned. "A sword on the bow? The bastard feels it too. A battle to the death."

Jake looked across the fifty feet separating the two boats, searching for Fujita, but the rain swept over them. She was a shape in the gray storm, a shadow pacing them wave for wave in a race to nowhere.

Yet Jake felt an insane excitement. He had never sailed a twelve like this before. He never would again.

Eventually, some component had to fail. As he met each surge and felt the hull of *Calinda* groan with the strain, he waited for the explosive snap of a plate or the grinding crash of the mast and sails collapsing overboard, but when the sound didn't come, he braced himself with a grin for the exhilarating glide down the wave, and the sense of the boat leaping out of the water under him.

The end came suddenly. One moment, *Sasori* raced beside them. The next, she seemed to stagger. The bow inched towards them.

"What's she trying?" Grale said. "She wouldn't ram us."

"He's lost his rudder," Jake said quietly.

He could remember the 1980 Fastnet; the dozens of boats caught in the storm between England and Ireland whose carbon-fiber rudders had snapped clean in half, putting the boats utterly out of control.

She was only thirty feet away now. Jake spun the wheel.

Not expecting it, Sam fell sideways onto the deck. Grale stamped his foot on his wrist, dragged the pistol from his hand, and pulled him upright.

"You crazy bastard, you've killed all of us!"

His punch split Sam's lip. He'd hauled him upright and was pulling back his fist for a second blow when Jake yelled, "Leave him alone. Keep the gun on him." He glanced at *Sasori*. "And hold on."

The boats collided.

It was a glancing blow, but the shock was like an explosion that shuddered through *Calinda*. *Sasori* rebounded two yards in an instant, and Jake saw three of its crewmen flung overboard into the foaming water. Out of control, she surged ahead, and for an instant Jake looked into the cockpit.

Fujita stood erect at the wheel, looking straight ahead. He might have been on an afternoon cruise. The computer displays around him were untended; piles of soggy paper lay around his feet, and the machines continued to chatter out their useless data as he raced forward into the overcast.

Something whirled by in the water between them. A dinghy, overturned. A life preserver followed it, then a body, floating face down.

The rain drifted away from ahead of them. They saw the spectator fleet—or what was left of it.

It was like the wake of a hurricane. The ocean was littered with boats. Most drifted helplessly, sails and rigging trailing overside. Cabin cruisers had capsized entirely. Everywhere people struggled, clinging to any piece of debris in the foaming chop of the storm.

The Coast Guard cutters roared through the rain, lights blazing, unable to do more than protest the destruction. They were too busy to notice the two yachts that drove out of the gray storm right under their bows.

Jake watched the whole tragedy with a sense of hopelessness.

At the last moment, *Sasori*'s mast snapped a foot above the deck. In an instant she became a wallowing wreck, half-submerged by the weight of the dragging mast and sails.

The high bow of the Coast Guard cutter hid her entirely from view. Her engines were going at full speed when she sliced into *Sasori* just behind the stub of the mast.

The black yacht leaped out of the water, thrust ahead of the cutter by the momentum of the collision. Then she snapped in half. The rear half, dragged down by the twenty tons of lead in the keel, sank instantly. Jake did not see Fujita go. It was as if the waves had swallowed him and his boat whole.

Held up by air trapped in the forepeak, the front half stayed afloat a few moments more, long enough for the surviving crewmen to swim away to safety. Then it tilted, slid backwards. The last thing Jake saw was the samurai sword gleaming on the prow as the sinking hull dragged it down.

CHAPTER THIRTY-SIX

After disaster, there's always a quiet time, when the dust begins to settle and the cost is counted. Jake remembered that, in Korea, it took only a few minutes after a bombardment for the birds to start singing and the flies to settle on the faces of the dead.

Calinda rolled at rest among the remains of the spectator fleet, moored to the committee boat. Their tender was somewhere in the chaos of shattered, dismasted, and half-swamped boats that had limped to the shelter of the Coast Guard cutters.

Jake put the crew on board the committee boat. Only Sam refused to go. Alone in the cockpit, Jake watched the motionless figure sprawled in the well, back against a winch, staring at the clearing sky.

Picking up the pistol, he went forward. Sam glanced up at him. He was smiling.

"We showed the little bastards, huh?"

"I guess so, Sam."

"I don't know what came over me back there." He felt the back of his skull. "Maybe that thug of Fujita's shook up my brains. I mean, I hardly believe I put a gun on Kim. You know I love that kid."

"It won't work, Sam."

Lewis looked puzzled. "Huh?"

"The crazy bit. I know why you pulled that stunt. You wanted a diversion. What would you have done if the weather hadn't blown up? Rammed her?"

"Jake, you're crazy! Until that moment out there, it never occurred to me . . ."

"I've known for a long time, Sam. You gave yourself away more than a year ago. I didn't figure you'd run until we'd sailed in the Cup. If you had tried to pull out, someone would have gotten suspicious about some of the loose ends in Tom Needham's suicide."

Lewis squinted up at him. "You lost me, pal."

"Come on, Sam. I know you killed Elaine and Charlie Keble and Tony Stephens—or at least hired that girl to kill them. You were Elaine's partner in the blackmail scheme, not poor Tom Needham. You thought it up. You're Traven."

Sam grinned. "You've got a lousy memory. Tom Needham hanged himself, remember? What's that if not a confession of guilt?"

"I always knew there were two people involved with Elaine. Tom put up the money, didn't he? He kept Elaine and you moving around in the yachting world, looking for news. He financed the information-gathering network. And when you decided that Elaine needed to be killed, he paid for Marie-Ange Planchet to do the job. But then Tom got worried. You had covered your tracks very well, but *he* felt exposed. I wouldn't play the grieving widower, as you'd all expected me to. He hired Jubei away from Fujita to get rid of me. That just made things worse. His last chance was to kidnap Kim and get hold of the evidence."

"It all sounds fine; I guess that is how Tom did it. But how the hell do you involve *me*?"

"You involved *yourself*, Sam. You gave yourself away at least twice. Tom didn't tell you he planned to kidnap Kim, and for a little while after that tape arrived, you must have been going up the wall. You had to act on the spur of the moment, and you made a couple of mistakes. First, to stop us from going through Elaine's diaries and maybe figuring out that you were involved, you shifted the suspicion to Tom by remembering a fake meeting between Tom and Elaine."

"What do you mean, fake?"

"You said it was on your birthday; that's why you remembered it. September second."

"So?"

"Don't you remember when you came down to Mobile and we went back up to your house? That was April. You had your birthday that weekend. It was clumsy, but you might have gotten away with it if you hadn't guessed Tom was behind the kidnapping and rung him to warn him that I was coming to Baltimore. He was expecting me, had a gun, and was ready to use it. Nobody could have warned him except you. Only his confederate would know who had organized the kidnap."

"It all sounds good, buddy," Sam said. He seemed unalarmed.

"I can understand why most of the people were killed. Elaine because she got tired of it and wanted to pull out. She took the money with her to guarantee her safety, not realizing it did nothing of the sort. Then Tony Stephens because he was unstable, ready to talk about the black-mailing to the police. But Charlie Keble . . . poor Charlie. Why kill him? Just a kid on the crew. My guess is, he found out about the scheme."

Sam moved his neck around, as if exercising a crick. "I'll play the game with you, pal. Just for laughs. Try this one. Maybe he was the bagman."

That made sense. Someone to pick up the payments. Someone too minor to be suspicious, whose presence around the boat scene would go unnoticed. Something must have warned Charlie that day that the scam was about to blow. But Jake had been too busy to listen.

"You never tried to kill me. Only Tom did that. A faked suicide was the logical answer. The police might even have assumed I was Elaine's partner. There's enough evidence that you could have planted to point that way. What stopped you?"

"You dumb bastard! We're pals. You think I wipe out my buddies? Anyway, I figured you were so cut up with guilt and all that about Elaine you'd keep out of the whole business. That Kim—you know, she really pulled you around. I guess Tom was right, hiring that freak to try and wipe out both of you." He shook his head in disgust. "Dropping a pile of scaffolding in the middle of Manhattan! Subtle."

He climbed to his feet and stretched his muscles. "That's a funny thing. You'd think these pro killers would be real smart. Everything planned out—smooth, professional. Bullshit! Even that French dame. I played her like a pinball machine. You know she likes to be paid off in sapphires? Friend of mine got me some Jap fakes. Can't tell 'em from the real thing. She took them without a murmur."

"Did Tom *pay* for fakes?"

"You think I'm crazy too? Maybe I didn't get the four hundred thou that Elaine swiped from me, but I've got some more stashed away."

"Money isn't a lot of use in jail."

"Who's going to jail?" He swung his arm across the chaos of boats, now limping towards Newport and shelter. "You remember Susie? My nurse? She's out there in a speedboat. Any minute now she'll pick me up and we'll be long gone before you can row to the committee there and persuade them you aren't crazy."

"I've got a gun."

"One thing I learned, Jake, is that there are people who can shoot you in cold blood and people who can't. You're not the killing type. If I were you, I'd get out of this business. Settle down and enjoy your middle age. You're a good boatman, but you don't have that edge. Fujita did. I'm sorry he had to go. He was the kind of guy I like doing business with."

"I've noticed that people who do business with you generally end up dead. Like Tom."

"I expected better of old Tom. When you stormed off to Baltimore, I would have backed him to wipe you out without working up a sweat. No way you could take him, I thought, expecially after I told him you were coming."

"So you *did* decide buddies were expendable after all."

Sam squinted at him. "You were getting too close. I never expected it. I guess you don't see how you've changed, old buddy. Not the same Jake I used to know. Killing Elaine might have been the best thing I ever did for you."

Jake started forward angrily, but as he did, Sam scrambled to the edge of the deck, peering out over the choppy water.

"I think I see my ride."

A tiny speedboat with a single occupant curved away from the gaggle of spectator boats and growled towards *Calinda*. It was the same one Jake had seen circle her that morning as they were towed out to the course.

Jake raised the gun and looked down the barrel, then let it fall. Sam was right. He wasn't the killing type.

The boat pulled alongside, and the woman in it stood up, balancing herself against the wake from the milling rescue craft. Sam scrambled to the edge of the deck and began letting himself down into the speedboat.

Something roared. A slamming explosion.

The shot lifted Sam off his feet and flung him backwards into the well.

Before Jake could raise his pistol, she had spun the little boat and disappeared among the others. Jake sprinted along the deck.

Blood was spreading from the hole in the center of Sam Lewis's chest to soak his windbreaker. It touched, surrounded, and finally obliterated the name *Calinda* sewn across the lefthand pocket. By then Sam was dead.

When she was clear of the fleet, Marie-Ange hooked a cord over the tiller and quickly unscrewed the foot-long barrel from the stock of the tiny rifle that had cost her two thousand dollars from the best underworld gunsmith in America. Both parts went over the side. So did the little box containing the soft leather squares, each the size of a postage stamp, the measured charges of black powder in their paper packets, and the tiny copper percussion caps.

They had worked well. She'd only needed one shot. The tiny projectile, tamped down into the muzzle over the black powder, went exactly where she aimed it.

That left the little box of ammunition.

She opened it and looked at the blue spheres in their black velvet cavities, as deeply evocative of her secret fears and desires as if they had been real sapphires. But they were fakes. She enjoyed the poetic justice of using one of them to execute the man who had cheated her.

As she upended the box, they slipped from their slots and plopped into the water, streaming away behind like bubbles of pure blue in the dull green, visible only for a second before they drifted down into darkness.

Unhooking the cord, she gunned the motor and sped away through the wrecked boats towards Newport.

Bestselling Books
for Today's Reader